Empire of the Undead

Ahimsa Kerp

Prologue: Allies of Hatred

Dacia: 88 CE, Spring

Thresu strode into the dusty barn, saddlebag carefully slung over his shoulder. He had let his horse run free. It was a good beast, and it deserved a chance to survive. The tall man stopped after a few steps and blinked, squinting into the darkness. Afternoon sunlight hazed through slats, lighting the rough wooden burls and knobs, but long shadows cast a dark pallor before his eyes. The smell of straw and dung filled his nostrils. The horses tied up here looked different from what he was used to, as they were smaller and shaggier. It was clear that he was no longer in Italy.

The others were there waiting for him, as he had hoped. Only two, but with them, silent and unseen, were tens of thousands. Hundreds of thousands. Whole cultures no longer had a voice, but desired vengeance all the same. They were all here, in this obscure stable in this obscure land. The men rose from their seat and each nodded. One was tall and lean, with skin as black as a starless night. He smiled but rarely. The other man was equally tall. He was thick with muscle and fat, his skin was pale, his hair black, and his eyes green. He wore many rings and armbands of silver and gold. Thresu knew not their names, but he knew their cause.

"All civilizations must come to an end," Thresu said after they had exchanged greetings. As he said it, his stomach churned and he realized he was nervous. He almost laughed at the absurdity of that. To have come so far and balk now was just unthinkable.

"We have come a long way to this place," the black man said, "and my bones know a chill they never wanted to meet."

"Aye," the big man agreed. "Why here? We are half a world away from Rome."

"Are you blind? This land is suffering from the blight that destroyed each of ours," Thresu said, taken aback. "The battle of Tapae was only the beginning of the end for the Dacians. Diurpaneus is a strong warrior, but he is no Vercingetorix, no Boudicca, no Hannibal, and certainly no Larth Tulumnes. They failed, and he too will fail."

"So your man said," the big black-haired man stated. The smell from the pig fat in his braids was dizzying. "And here we are. But it is a long way." His Latin was barbaric.

"If we start in Rome, the city will fall. If we start here, the city will fall. The difference? This way the Romans taste the fear that comes before death. It will come for them, a swarm of crawling hatred. The Romans will seek relief and all they will find is destruction. Thus, shall we have our revenge."

"I like my revenge more personal," the black man said. "I want to thrust the dagger in myself."

Thresu smiled. "Of course. We three shall not be mindless. We three shall go to Rome straightaway. They may kill us, but the wave that follows us will drown the Empire forever."

The men nodded, mollified. Thresu reached into his saddlebag. "I have a vial for each of us." His companions stared in fascination at the small vials. The substance was amber-hued, and looked like liquid honey.

The black man shook his head in disbelief. "Such a small thing, to destroy an Empire," he said in a low voice.

"A small thing, indeed," Thresu replied. "But generations of my ancestors lived and died dreaming of this. The cost could have acquired an army big enough to crush the city. But death is far too easy. This is what they deserve. Our wave begins here, and it will grow and grow until it sweeps into Italy and washes the Romans away forever. With this small thing, we will bring the Roman Empire to its knees." It had been hard paying the price—he'd spent gold that his grandfather had inherited, gold earmarked for vengeance for two hundred years. He knew though that after today, he would have no need of gold, or of anything. The die was truly cast.

"And once on its knees, we will lop its head off!" The large white man said forcefully.

Thresu nodded agreement and handed each of them a vial. His heart was beating rapidly and sweat gathered in his armpits. If he didn't drink it soon, he realized, he might lose his nerve entirely. He could feel energy coursing through his body and he suppressed the urge to laugh.

He raised the vial into the dark air of the barn. "This is for my people and my culture, usurped by blood-thirsty upstarts. This is for the greatest city that ever existed, Veii, which is now but a shadow of a memory."

His arm remained firmly raised while the dark man likewise raised his vial. His long slender fingers curled around the small vessel, hiding it. "This is for my people, and my culture, who were wiped off the face of the Earth for daring to compete against Rome. This is for my city, Carthage, the jewel of Africa, and scion of the Phoenicians."

The burly man joined them. "This is for my people, the Brigantes. Our holy men slaughtered, our histories burned, our people betrayed and enslaved. With their roads and cities, the Romans bring only evil," he said.

"Let us unleash that evil and destruction back upon them," Thresu said. His voice sounded strange in his ears. He felt that he was somehow watching himself from afar. He wondered if maybe there was some other way, but it was too late, far too late.

The men drank simultaneously. Soon it came, the blackness that soothingly obliterated consciousness. Three bodies slumped into the soft straw as the sunset lit the stable in gold and crimson. A robin trilled soothingly from its nest in the roof.

It was such a peaceful beginning to the end of the world.

PART I: ALL ROADS

CHAPTER I

Iudaea: 73 CE, Summer

It was a scorching hot afternoon and there was trouble at the docks in Joppa. The Roman Legion X Fretensis was departing after long months in the desert, and departing quickly, with more than three thousand men, siege engines, auxiliaries, pack animals, whores, and prisoners. The legions were bound for places like Iberia, Gaul, Britannia, or Dacia. Some few were even heading to the Eternal City, to Rome herself.

Only two days before, with the army inland, the port town had been a half-empty wreck that had been twice burned, and the inhabitants fled or dead. Today, however, the forces of Rome were on the march and the city was a chaotic wreck. Each unit marched with banners proudly unfurled. There were dozens displaying ships, still more decorated with bulls, and some few dared capture Neptune's attention with the visage of the Sea God.

Haphazard stalls had been set up in the ashes, amidst still smoldering ruins, to sell water, food, and wine. One sweaty, bearded man was beating the side of a marauding camel as it sipped from a broken wine amphora. The streets of Joppa had never been meant to accommodate so many, and the bay was equally stuffed with ships of all sizes.

For all the teeming humanity, the Roman army was nothing if not efficient, and they were well-practiced in dividing the spoils of war. Adult slaves were carried in cages, and those younger were chained together, or simply led onto already over-full ships. Piles of the plunder looted from the fortress of Masada were added, and then the centurions themselves began to board. Many slaves were sold outright to the slavers that accompanied every army, but the veteran men of Legion X Fretensis knew they could sell their slaves for much more once they reached Rhodes or Rome.

One skinny boy, too small for chains, was drowning in the sea of humanity. Jotham avoided the swaggering soldiers to the best of his ability, but there were too many and one stepped into him. A heavy metallic gauntlet smashed him in the side of the head. As light and pain blossomed, he stumbled blindly and collapsed onto the charred, splintered gangplank that led onto the ship. The heat sapped his strength. He could not find the strength to rise. His life, such as it had been, ended here.

A centurion stooped to grab him, but Jotham fought with unexpected strength, kicking while he clung to the ground. Before them, slaves and soldiers came to a stop. Shouted curses rose as more people found their routes blocked. Then, Larcius Lepidus himself, the legate of Legion X Fretensis and governor to the region, burst from the crowd. He shouted and the two soldiers dragged the boy onto the ship, each holding one of his tiny arms. Splinters and friction cut into Jotham's flesh, but he did not cry out. He did not make a sound at all.

Behind him, the trouble was not over. Some older boys followed his example, and a group of them in chains threw themselves down. They were considerably more difficult to move, and before the legion could restore order, they were joined by adults—the men and women too old or weak to have been caged. The boy saw nothing of this, as he sat sightlessly on his ship in a cage of his own. Nor did he see Lepidus kill two of the protesters, stabbing them in the chest and the throat.

Larcius Lepidus was wiping his sword clean, as the ship with the boy eased its way through the crowded bay and into the Mare Nostrum.

****

Jotham sat quietly as the ship tossed on the noisy sea. They were never far from one of the hundreds of islands, and always the shrieking gulls followed them. The crashing of the waves was a new sound for Jotham, and it was overwhelming. Some soldiers fed them food scraps and laughed to watch the birds fight the slaves for stale crusts of bread. The ship was low in the water being weighed down with siege equipment, spoils of war, and too many people. The adult slaves were below deck, rowing in the dark, but the children were able to breathe the fresh salty air and feel the sun on their skin.

He was caged, to be sure, but the cage was big enough to hold many more people, and there were only eight other boys with him. He didn't recognize any of them. The only boy he'd known had died the first night—one of the four skinny and scrawny skeletons for whom death had in the end, only been a technicality. A squat soldier had thrown their corpses over the side in the early dawn light. Rations on the ship, though consisting of stale bread and occasional left-over fish, were better than the boys had eaten for months, and those still living ate greedily, though most puked up their meals again later. None had their sea stomachs yet.

Jotham reached down and picked more splinters out of his leg. Some of them were too deep to grab and he bent down, snapping savagely with his teeth. The centurion who had dragged him onto to the ship saw his strange actions as he walked by.

"Those splinters are nasty. Though you deserve what you got-- you nearly started a battle," he laughed. He was not old, but his face was scarred and his nose far too big. The beginnings of a red beard curled around his sunburned chin.

The boy said nothing.

"Well, despite that, you're a lucky boy. In fact, I'll call you Felix. You're going to Rome, Felix, if you can survive this voyage."

"My name is not Felix," the boy replied softly, his voice cracking. It was the first time he had spoken for six days.

"Rome," the centurion continued. He eased closer to the boy, raising his voice to be heard over the gulls and the waves. "I've been there twice, you know. The first time, I was not much older than you. Someday, I'll bring my boy there too--"

He got no further. Snarling, the boy leaped at the soldier. Jotham scratched at his face through the bars of the cage. He screamed at the man, in passable Latin.

"My name isn't Felix. It's Jotham. And I don't want to be here!" A nearby centurion chuckled.

"You've got a wild one there, Iullianus."

The man grabbed Jotham by his hair and pulled his head back. "Calm down, Felix. We could have let you starve in the desert. Is that what you want?" The man leaned low and spoke in a low, grave tone.

"No one will buy a wild child like you. If no one buys you, they will kill you at the market, or pimp you out to some lowlife buttfucking Greek. If you want to fight back, be silent and wait for your turn to strike. You think you're the first this has happened to?" He released his grip on Jotham and walked away.

Jotham looked at the other boys, embarrassed. None met his gaze. He stared out into the sea and tried his hardest to feel sad. His anger drained, and he felt nothing, save for an overwhelming numbness. He wondered why he didn't miss his family.

The war hadn't been going well. Even Jotham had figured that out, though to the end, when they lived on a handful of grain a day, his parents had insisted they would win. "Rome is evil. You can recognize evil from the very sight of it. Good will always prevail over evil," his father had repeated many times. *You can recognize evil from the very sight of it*, the boy thought again and again, treasuring the thought like a mantra. *And good will always prevail over evil.*

"And they don't have Elazar," his mother would often add.

Jotham had met Elazar ben Simon. His voice was too unctuous, too high, and full of whining. Jotham didn't like the way Elazar had looked at his mother. He had to stop thinking about what happened next, and instead, stared at the horizon, listlessly, until the red sun collapsed exhaustedly into the wet waves. He had never seen the sun look that color before, but it did not surprise him. The whole world was now red like blood.

****

The next afternoon, they landed on an island with a magnificent city. He thought it must be Rome, but soon learned it was a place called Rhodes. Jotham had heard the soldiers mention it, and they said that it was the biggest slave market in the world. It was a gruesome place where tens of thousands of slaves a day were sold. Jotham never knew the exact numbers, but many of the rowing slaves had died. They soldiers saw their profits dwindling, and they wanted to stock up on more before they reached the markets of Rome.

A few centurions left the ship, but they returned quickly. They had more slaves in chains with them. Most were adults that disappeared below decks, but one was a tall boy with very dark skin. He was thrown into the same cage as Jotham. The boy sat there, by the bars without looking at any of his cellmates. His body began to shake and a strange sound came from him.

He was crying. Jotham moved warily to the newcomer, ready to spring back if necessary. The boy's eyes were closed and Jotham looked at him more carefully. His skin was black and he was very tall, but he didn't seem very old.

The boy's eyes snapped open. He stopped crying. "What," he demanded. "What are you looking at?"

"Why are you here?" Jotham asked. "You weren't in the, the siege."

"What siege?" the dark-skinned boy asked.

Jotham could not hide his surprise. Was he being mocked? "The fortress of Masada. With walls as high as," Jotham paused, summoning an apt comparison. "Walls as high as the clouds. Built by Herod the Great, a long time ago."

"By whom?" the boy asked wearily. His eyes were closed. He clearly was not interested in the story, but Jotham found himself talking anyway. It felt good, somewhere deep inside, to speak of it to someone.

"You are stupid, if you don't know Herod. He built the great fortress but then the Romans came and took it away. Anyway, after I was born, but before I can remember, some people called the Sicarii killed the Romans who lived there."

The boy opened his eyes and smiled. Now he was beginning to get interested. "Killing the Romans is good," he said.

"You really don't know about this?" Jotham asked, fearing that he was being made fun of. The boy glared at him. *Don't be stupid*, his eyes said.

"Well, some of us came from Jerusalem and helped in the fight against the Romans. We were trying to get them to leave us alone." They'd in truth been among the very few to escape. The Romans were capturing and crucifying Jews by the hundred, every day.

"We have been trying that too," the boy beside him said. "They don't listen."

"Where are you from?" Jotham asked, interrupting his own tale. "My name is Jotham."

"I am Sefu. I live in the great desert, and with my father and two brothers we rode across it, bringing ore and salt to trade."

"Oh yes, I know of the great desert," said Jotham, who didn't, but wanted to impress this boy. "What happened?"

"What do you think? Centurions came, many of them. We fought them, but they killed my father and my elder brother. Toqe got away, I think, though men followed. Me, they wrapped in chains and put me in a boat. I got here three days ago and now I'm in another boat." His voice was matter-of-fact, dispassionate.

"The same thing, nearly, for me. The governor, Silva, came with his legion, and for a long time they couldn't get up, because the walls were so high," Jotham said.

"As high as the clouds," Sefu said.

"That's right, but they had big machines that knocked holes in our walls. They built a big plank and came up. Knocked down our walls and took us prisoner. My mother and father, they died," Jotham ventured this information out tentatively, because saying it might make it more true. "I hate the Romans!" he said, too loudly. The Romans hadn't actually killed his family, of course, but it had been their fault.

"How many did you kill?" the tall boy asked. His teeth were very white.

"Me? None. I am only eight." He had tried at the end, though. Children even younger than Jotham had grabbed knives or rocks. Many never intended to use them on anyone but themselves, but Jotham had attacked a centurion armed with only a stick.

"I am ten, and I killed three men. With my spear," Sefu said.

Jotham looked at the boy in awe, his eyes growing big. "You are a great warrior," he said at last.

A shout brought their attention to the sea. A pod of dolphins swam with them, splashing and playing in the sea. Jotham frowned, angry that mere animals could be happy and free, when both had been denied to him. Yet, he felt encouraged. Such freedom in the world, even if for dumb animals, made his own circumstances feel tolerable. Seeing the animals jumping in the ocean surf showed him a much needed balance, and he knew it was something he would never forget.

****

He was never able to remember how many days it took from Rhodes to their final destination. He slept a lot. He was sick a lot. The open sea was frightening, but it was welcome after so much time buried in the darkness. Sometimes, he talked with Sefu, but mostly they sat and stared at the endless horizon. Another boy in the cage died, and the Romans didn't bother taking him out, even though the sea was right there. Jotham feared getting too close to the body, but Sefu had scorned them. "Fear the living, not the dead," the boy had said. It made sense, but Jotham hadn't come any closer to the body. The dead boy had died with an obscene grin, and his eyes were open, blank, and staring. His father's words echoed in his head. Was a dead body evil, he wondered?

Once he was sent down to the hold to bring up the day's water for the children. He went slowly. The war machines scared him. Like huge wooden monsters, he'd seen them toss large stones almost two furlongs. Those boulders, along with massive arrows, had nearly destroyed the ramparts on their own, without any help from the Roman army. Elazar said they would have won, if it weren't for those awful war machines. They were disassembled now, but he could sense their quiet menace. He filled up the cups quickly and hurried back to the safety of his cage.

They landed with the tide early one morning. Before them stretched a crowded, stinking city, much larger than the one on Rhodes, but even this city was not Rome, though to Jotham, it seemed at least as big as Jerusalem. The slaves were collected from various ships and loaded into carts. He did not see where Sefu had gone.

Jotham's cart was led by a smiling young man with two big oxen. It was a hot day, and the prisoners were crowded together. The boy's head was wedged beneath a man's stinking, oily armpit. The man's armpit hairs brushed his face every time the cart hit a bump. There was no room to move, and he could see nothing but flesh and the wooden planks of the cart. They arrived in Rome some hours later.

Jotham had seen many strange things in his life, but the sight of the eternal city astounded him. It was so big, bigger than Jerusalem times ten. The roads outside were crowded with messengers, travelers, and free men reveling in the autumn sunshine. *We thought we could hold off the armies forever*, Jotham thought. They could have used ten more armies to capture us. A cold depression filled him as he began to realize just how unfair the world truly was.

They hadn't yet entered the city gates when they were met by a city official. He was smiling and showed no sign of discomfort in the great heat. "Good, good," he said. "You have arrived just in time. The market is opening soon." He looked over the carts critically, and his smile died, replaced by a slight wince. "More Jews," he said reproachfully, shaking his head. "And these ones are half-starved. Oh well, someone will surely buy them."

As their litter moved into the city and towards the slave market, all of the boys stared in amazement, astounded at the sight of the city. He could see some of the seven hills it was built on. Highest was the Palatine, where the Emperor and his family lived. The other hills had grand buildings and statues on them. It was almost too much to comprehend.

He thought of the slave market, and wondered how long he would have to live in Rome before he could go home.

****

Jotham followed the large man down the unfamiliar street. He was enormously fat, with his huge belly and breasts larger than most women's were. His skin was olive-toned and he had no hair on his face.

"Come along, little Felix," Hyacinthus said, "there is always something new from Africa," he added, mostly to himself.

"It's Jotham, and I won't be a *servus* for long."

The fat man laughed. "Such fierceness. When you reach the ripe age of thirty, you can buy yourself a liberty cap, assuming your master agrees, of course. They are very stylish—red, floppy, and cone-shaped. You'll look great in them. Until then, the only escape is death."

"Thirty!" cried Jotham. "Half my life will be over."

"Being a *servus*, you have to suffer many injustices. It's a hard burden to bear," Hyacinthus intoned dramatically. "Now come, because you still have to meet your master and learn your new duties."

"Why did I sell for so little?" Jotham asked, struggling to keep up. For all his size, the big man could walk quickly. The street they were walking on was like a street anywhere in the world. Jotham was surprised how much it reminded him of Jerusalem. The same wine shops, food stalls, and old houses made up the neighborhoods, and the same cracked stone path meandered through them.

"Why?" The fat man repeated. "I paid 400 denari for you."

"Yes, why? My friend Sefu sold for much more." He had seen Sefu at the market. The gangly boy had been bought by a high-ranking noble after a heated auction. By contrast, the fat man had been Jotham's only bidder.

"He may have had some skill. You have none--too small to fight, too ugly for loving, and you can't read or write."

"I'm not ugly. My mother said—" he stopped there. He hadn't thought of her for days now, it seemed.

"My mother said I'd grow up to be King of Greece. Mothers lie, little Felix, it's what they do best, and you are ugly, too. Just as I am fat. Even when you grow, you will never be handsome. Your nose is too big and your hair too oily. And your butt is scrawny—men want something to grab onto."

"I can read and write," Jotham said. He suspected it was wiser to change the subject. "My tongue and yours."

"Latin isn't my tongue, boy," Hyacinthus said, "but this is surprising. If true, I have done well this day." He stopped walking. Next to him was a cracked wall of an abandoned building. He dug in the ground and emerged with a burnt torch. "Chalk is the pen for fools, and walls their paper. But you have much growth to reach the humble status of fool."

He handed the torch to Jotham. "Here, Felix, write something. Not your name, but something else."

Without thinking about it, he began writing something he had seen on the walls of Jerusalem and Masada. *Romani Ite Domum.* The fat Greek was laughing before he had finished.

"Romans go home. I like this. But they are already home, boy, already home."

CHAPTER II

Otia: 73 CE, Summer

He knew he was home when he could smell the stink of shit in the air. There were other smells too. Piss, sweat, blood, and the fishy ocean breeze that threatened to dominate it all. But the best scent for Gaius Sulpicius Rufus was the odor of feces, the odor of civilization. He inhaled deeply, with exaggerated relish, and long savored the scent before exhaling. "That," he said to his aide Calvinus Plautius, "is a smell I thought I'd never be treated to again. Amazing what a few years away can do to a man." The port town was bursting with activity. "I am home," he said. The three slaves behind him stood meekly, awaiting orders.

Gaius Rufus was a portly man of middling height. His features weren't sharp enough to be considered handsome, and his nose was too small truly to be called noble. His hair was curly and unkempt, which contrasted with his clothing. He wore a new toga, one of expensive cloth with exotic dyes woven into the hem. His Senator's badge was stark and distinct on the cloth. Rufus stood up straight, surveying the scene before him.

Soldiers laden with coins and loot hurried through the streets. They'd be going to the best brothels tonight, and for as long as their plunder lasted. Only when it ran out, in a week or two, would their regular whores and wives see them. Several slave ships had arrived with prisoners from Arabia, and hundreds of carts were assembled, ready to bear away the scrawny, sunburned slaves. One rolled past, close to Rufus. It splashed mud and shit onto his tunic, below his knees. Without his having to say a word, one of his slaves dropped to the ground and cleaned the excrement off.

The slave finished and Rufus breathed again, deeply, and then laughed. "I return to Italy and am covered in its shit within moments. A good sign, I think," he said. Plautius nodded, but said nothing. That was one of the things Rufus treasured most about him. Plautius knew how to remain silent.

"But let us not stop for long," Rufus said. "I can still taste the salt and the sea, and it tastes like captivity. I shall not rest until I can smell the shit of Rome herself, safely away from the sea," he said.

A litter waited for him, attached to four sickly mules. Many litters were carried by slaves, but for the fourteen mile trek into Rome, he'd need something stronger. The slaves came with the litter, one to guide the mules, and two to go before it to clear a path.

It was the first time he had set foot in Italy for far too long. He had spent the last five years on Gyaros—a dreadfully small island, and was weary of the sea, of the gulls, of the sand and shells, and emptiness everywhere. *Never again will I face that void*, he had told himself when at last he had been recalled.

Gaius Rufus had the misfortune to be exiled by Galba, during his brief reign as Emperor. Rufus' only crime had been supporting Nero, and when Nero's friend, Otho, had replaced Galba, Rufus was freed from exile. Scarcely had this news reached him, when Otho too was dead, and his exile clamped back upon him. Vespasian, a war leader, had won the war of the Four Emperors. It had taken the following four years filled with gifts, apologies, and a good deal of money, but Vespasian had removed his exile at last. Rufus was back in the land of his birth.

He was needed. The Emperor's letters had been vague, but Vespasian was confronted by many conspiracies and he needed friends. Nero had been very popular, and by recalling one known to have supported him, Vespasian was shoring up support. He knew why Vespasian wanted him. Vespasian needed a trustworthy friend of Caesar, an *amici caesaris*. Every man had skills, and Rufus knew he could organize better than any man living could. In addition to keeping him alive from conspirators, and winning his wars in foreign lands, the Emperor had started many vast building projects. Rufus settled back in his litter, restless and satisfied at the same time. Organization was his greatest strength, but he had been gone for far too long. He had no friends in court and would have to work hard to regain any power.

They traveled on the *Via Ostiensis*, the road that led directly to Rome from the port city. The countryside passed him by. He stared at the vineyards and small farms, filled with an uneasy sense of the surreal. He knew these lands well, and before him, the same stony paths winding through the same dry autumn fields. The same men, former soldiers or fifth sons, oversaw the work in the fields, and the same slaves bled and sweat as they labored. However, there were a thousand small differences, each too small to notice individually, which collectively made Rufus uneasy. He had already known that he was returning to a different world than the one he'd left, but he was beginning to understand the implications of that fact. No man ever stepped into the same river twice, as the saying went.

Beside him, Plautius was silent, staring. He'd never been to Rome, had come to Rufus' service from Iberia. His awe visibly increased as they drew closer to Rome itself. Rufus grimaced, as Plautius was embarrassing himself. The city was wicked, depraved, and ugly. It reminded Rufus of an overweight, middle-aged whore. It had been glorious in youth, there was no contesting that, but it now drooped in places it shouldn't have, and was far grander in its own estimation than any objective view would grant. For an ambitious man, however, removal from Rome was political death. Rome was where the heart of the Empire beat.

They passed into the heated, crowded city. He had forgotten the size of it. Aqueducts rose high overhead, blocking out the sun. Statues loomed everywhere, each rising higher than the last, and there were so many people. Some of them were obviously new to the city, and they were fatally slow at getting out of the way of the litters. Injuries and death were the only reward for not moving quickly enough out of the way. Many died, but there were always more people, and more of the penniless and destitute appeared every day in the city. *A great city is a great solitude,* as the proverb went.

The great fire had burned almost a decade before, but in this valley, nestled between several hills, the damage was still evident. Rufus stopped the litter and climbed out. He was staring. The colossal statue of Nero himself, which had been built after the fire, was gone, and the beautiful swimming lake was drained and slowly being filled in. Nero's Golden Palace, where Rufus had spent many a wild night, was half destroyed, by orderly crews deconstructing it floor by floor.

This isn't even strangely similar. It's just different. Entirely different. Rufus thought. That wasn't entirely true though. Though everything before his eyes was different, the smell remained the same, and that valley floor ménage of olives, garlic, piss, and vinegar.

Dozens of men were working, knocking down buildings and removing the rubble. Crews of brawny slaves hauled in huge baskets of marble, tufa, and wood. He'd known for two years that Vespasian had started construction, but the size of it astounded him. Only recently, with the final collapse of the Jewish rebellion, would Vespasian have the necessary funds to complete a project of this size.

"This amphitheater of the Flavians," he spoke slowly, "it will dwarf all others."

"It's big," Plautius, beside him, agreed, "but to what point? This is my first visit to the city, but even I know of the Circus Maximus, the Theater of Marcellus, and the Theater of Pompey. Do they not have games enough in Rome?"

"Ah, to be so naive," Rufus said. "His family is new to Imperial power, and he wants to be another Augustus. This monument will speak to his glory for all time."

And mine, he added mentally. There was no doubt that Vespasian would need him to oversee this construction. The job required a capable man, and there were none better at building than Rufus. Even better, his outsider status could aid him, as he stood outside the labyrinth of alliances affecting the Senators who had long been in the city. Rufus got back into his coach, his mind spinning at the ways he could turn this to his advantage.

****

He stared at the Emperor in shock, in disbelief at what he had just heard. A close look at the man before him revealed that Vespasian had aged, though his hawk-like features were as intense as ever. Rufus was still weary from the voyage, but the Emperor had wanted to meet with him immediately, and the former soldier was not one hung up on formality.

Rufus had quickly washed and changed. They were in a small room, with only a few servants and his son, Domitian. The younger man was wearing his consular cape. So, Rufus thought, he was one of the consuls this year, a clear sign of Vespasian's favor. His brother, Titus, and Vespasian himself had been consuls the previous year. As a second son, Domitian held several honorary titles as well as several priesthoods, though he did very little in practice.

"Have you forgotten common courtesies during your time away from court, Gaius Rufus? In Rome, we do not gape like gasping fish," the Emperor said. His eyes were nearly as sharp as his nose.

"To the war front? Past the Rhine and Main? Emperor, I must confess I was somewhat looking forward to the comforts of Rome."

"True happiness is to understand our duties toward God and man, and to enjoy the present, without anxious dependence on the future. Not to amuse ourselves with either hopes or fears, but to rest satisfied with what we have, which is abundantly sufficient," Vespasian said. He was quoting Seneca, a man Rufus had known quite well.

"I know that, of course, and I can sympathize with Seneca." Like Rufus, Seneca had been exiled for years on a small island. "But my skills would be wasted on the war front. I'm no warrior. You've heard of my island sculptures, my statues, and of course, you've seen what I have built here in Rome. I thought I might better serve the Eternal City in that capacity." This was unfortunately unsubtle, but the pace of events had shattered his normal equanimity.

"Your talents for organization are also useful in war. I've long wanted to restore order to our defenses on the Danube. It's not glamorous, but you're suited to it. You'll be far from the sea, as long as you perform ably, of course," Vespasian said. "And my son will be capable of leading the building." Rufus glanced to Domitian. The man seemed as uncomfortable as Rufus, but he said nothing.

"Gratias, Emperor," Rufus said. There was nothing else to say. He felt numb. It was exile of a different nature. This one might be dressed in prettier cloth, but the package was one he understood all too well. "I live to serve."

****

"What do you think of this place?" Rufus asked Plautius. The lanky man had accompanied the Senator to his chambers. Rufus sent away for a slave woman and turned to face his aid.

"It's large," Plautius said simply.

"Yes it is," Rufus said, laughing a bit at the other man's taciturnity. "Yes it is. It's a pity you cannot see it for long."

Plautius had not been in attendance with Vespasian, but Rufus had already told him about what had happened.

"Yes," Plautius said, "though the war presents some glory."

"No it doesn't, and make no mistake about it," Rufus said, "there is no glory in that kind of war—only endless campaigning, sleeping in mud, freezing your testes off. No, that post is not a treat. Not to mention that it's inherently unfeasible. No man alive could defend that long a border against a nomadic people. No, Plautius, this is political suicide."

"What will you do?" his aid asked.

"Do?" asked the Senator. "I'll do whatever the Emperor tells me, and I'll do it happily. It's not all gloom—I'll be far away from the sea, for one."

"You don't have a plan?" Plautius asked.

"For once, no. If I had a month or two to plan, I could perhaps exert some influence. However, whether it could reach Vespasian or not is any fool's guess, but it's a moot point—my *amicitia*, my allies, are all dead or retired. It would take time I don't have to change that."

"I see," Plautius said.

At that moment, the slave woman arrived. She was an attractive Celt, with long ringlets of hair and fine features. She smiled, somehow managing to look both vulnerable and lewd.

Rufus looked pointedly at his aid, and the lanky man took the hint. Seconds after he was gone, Rufus dropped his toga and began kissing the woman. He couldn't smell the sea anywhere. It was good to be back in Rome, no matter how shortly-lived it was to be.

****

In his dreams, he was still on the ship, still on the island, still captured by the past. Waves tossed him, whilst he was jostled by the harsh stones found on the road between Otia and Rome. Behind it all, the vast amphitheater grew until it blotted out the very sky.

He awoke with a start, still in his court clothes, and realized a servant was before him.

"You have a visitor, Senator," the servant said.

Rufus yawned largely, and stretched like a lion. The curly-haired Celtic woman slept soundly next to him. He frowned. She should have left while he slept. *Too late now.* She would have to be disciplined. "Send him in," he said. For the servant to have woken him, it would be someone important. Then again, he had an Empire of important people to speak with. He dressed quickly, knowing that he looked more disheveled than he would like.

A very tired Domitian entered. Rufus looked at him more closely. The Emperor's youngest son had become a man during his absence. He was tall, and his head reached a good hand higher than Rufus. His eyes were large and intelligent but he squinted a little in the dim light. Even at two-and-twenty, his hair was beginning to recede. Like his father, he'd be hairless before he turned thirty. Also like his father, he was very direct.

"I'm taking your place," he said, without preamble, as he sat upon a plush bench. "I'm going to the war." Domitian was blushing, but this Rufus remembered. The man's cheeks were frequently red, though no man knew why.

"That is very kind," Rufus said. He was at a loss for words. He'd been out of the game too long, and his instincts were dull. His inner voice was still drowned out by the roaring of the sea.

"It is no kindness, and you know it. I need to know the men. Father became emperor because his men knew him and loved him. Titus led the assault on Jerusalem and has many triumphs coming for subduing the Great Revolt. It is my turn. Besides, you have no place out there, and the Dacians would string you up within a week of your arrival."

"What you say is sound," Rufus said. He couldn't deny such accusations. "Yet, your father—"

"I've spoken to him already. He needs you here, and he knows it. You'd be wasted building forts and watchtowers on that muddy river."

"My skills are at the discretion of the Emperor, of course," Rufus said. This boon so after the disappointment of his meeting left him unsettled. "I spoke earlier out of surprise and fatigue."

"He knows it, and I know it. Moreover, I need to escape

Rome." Domitian said. "For many reasons. Domitia is pregnant, and gods be good, she will bear a son who has a man for a father. Though, in truth, I desire some separation from her. It is her first, and she is not dealing well with the changes."

Rufus laughed knowingly. "She who wants to remain beautiful aborts."

"Ovid, yes," Domitian agreed. "At any rate, you will enjoy this city, where I am weary of it. I yearn for the simple life of a soldier, away from bloated rumors and women."

"Well," Rufus said, "do this and I'm your man. For the long run. I have many seeds to plant here, and no amount of sleeping under the stars was going to help me."

"We are agreed," the son of the Emperor said as he clasped Rufus' hand. "This isn't about power," he said, indicating his fist. "This is about what's right. It's what Augustus would have done."

Domitian was on his way out the door when Rufus called after him. "Just one more question. You seem to have convinced him quite readily. Why was he threatening to send me in the first place?"

Domitian turned and with a slow smile he said, "Oh, he was just annoyed."

"At what?"

"At you. For supporting Nero, he would say, but his spies watched you stop at the amphitheater. He wanted to surprise you. I don't think he meant it. He would have changed his mind even if I had not talked to him. I think."

"I wonder," said Rufus slowly, but Domitian was already gone.

CHAPTER III

Palmyra: 79 CE, Summer

Life had never been so pleasant, Tettius Iullianus fuzzily decided as he drained another beer. He had never meant to stop in Palmyra, certainly not for so long, but he was free from pursuit and the oasis town was perfect. It had good food and beautiful women, and either could be had for quite an affordable price. The only thing expensive here was the wine.

That made Iullianus smile. He didn't give a fuck about wine. Most soldiers drank it daily, more than water, but most soldiers were effete Italian cowards, or worse, they wanted to be. Iullianus, despite his name and position with the Roman army, was certainly not a Roman.

He drank another beer in one long pull and eased out of the inn. A sense of urgency was building in him. The day was half gone, and he hadn't even fucked anyone yet. No beer was so good that he preferred it to a good hard skin-slapping session. His pale skin and red hair made him a novelty around here, and he was far more popular than with the women in his own lands. He sometimes fancied his cock was much bigger than they were used to, and that, or they, were better at feigning pleasure than the whores on his misty, cold isle.

Palmyra had become part of Syria and hence Rome under Tiberius. It had grown fat and happy in the intervening sixty years. Traders from Parthia, India, Rome, and even far-flung China, met here, as it was a midway point between the ports of Sidon, Tyre, Byblos, and the Euphrates. One could find everything from luxury silks to discounted camels in this cosmopolitan trading city. Palmyra's mixed nature was evident even from the people. Some wore togas, while others preferred the Parthian baggy trousers. Many women wore garments made of Indian silks. Iullianus preferred the trousers, but did not—would not—own any in silk.

He stumbled into a brothel and asked for three beers and two women. He had no permit, so the pockmarked proprietor required an entire sesterce. There were at least a dozen women to choose from, but he made his choice instantly.

Both had dark hair. One had pouting lips and large breasts, while the other was a slim Syrian with a remarkable smile. When he noticed a woman with a smile like that, he knew why Paris had jeopardized his entire city for the love of a woman.

He appreciated that they were mostly undressed. In Rome, for some bizarre reason, they dressed as men—wearing togas. They pushed through the curtain into a small room. Both tried to kiss him but he pushed their heads away and drank deeply from his beer. They kissed his chest and he downed the first beer.

"Strip," he told them. They weren't wearing much, but in the few moments it took to remove their clothing, Iullianus had finished another beer. The room spun pleasantly around him and he felt the creeping steps of slumber stalking him.

"Why don't you two kiss," he suggested. As they complied, he dropped his trousers and began to stroke his member. Despite the show before him, it wasn't hard.

"I can help with that," the Syrian said.

"As can I," the large-breasted one added.

"Fuck off," he said. "I've done this enough times. I know what I'm doing." He caught it in their eyes then—the sudden understanding that he would not fuck them. Even a whore doesn't like to feel rejection, but their feelings were not his concern. He stroked his cock with more urgency. The women showered him with soft kisses, sucked on his nipples, and stroked him all over. His cock stirred, and one of them grunted her approval. The other made to move her mouth toward him, but he waved her away. He never had sex with a proseda, and never would.

Even in a drunken haze, Iullianus was able to summon the needed fortitude. It didn't take long before he'd blasted both with his seed. He tipped each girl an extra *as* when he was done. "I must depart," he said. "I fear I can outrun all foes, save sobriety." He downed his last beer and slipped out of the curtain.

The warrior emerged into the busy streets of Palmyra. The sun hung heavily in the western sky. It was almost evening. There was no use pressing his luck—even with his head start, they would be closing in on him now. Coming to a city like this had risks, but it was worth it. He thought again of the two women and smiled. It was definitely worth it.

"Be careful," a man said, "he is dangerous, even this drunk."

Iullianus looked up in surprise. There were ten centurions before him in uniform, with swords drawn.

"By Mithras," he said, concentrating very hard not to slur his words. Like most soldiers, he often swore to the sun god, though he did not believe in him.

People on his side of the street were crossing to the other side. Behind him, the door to the tavern slammed shut. He was on his own, and he didn't even have a blade. His lead was not as great as he'd supposed. It must not have been very hard to find him. There was a downside, he mused, to being so conspicuous.

"Tettius Iullianus," said the spokesperson, "we are here to arrest you for dereliction of duty. Please come quietly." He sounded very serious. He sounded very young.

Iullianus tried to focus on the man's face. Behind him, rising high in the city was the temple of Ba'al. That temple, like so much in this area, was ancient. A thousand years old, perhaps twice that. It looked like a huge hard cock thrust into the air. Iullianus laughed.

The spokesman grimaced. "It's no laughing matter. You're not going to resist us. You can hardly stand."

"No, no," Iullianus said, holding his hands in front of him. He did want to fight, but his judgment wasn't so impaired as to make him challenge so many men. Not without a weapon anyway. "I'll come peacefully." The man stepped up nervously, sheathed his sword, and wrapped a coarse rope around Iullianus' hands. The men formed a circle around him. As they walked away, toward the agora, Iullianus started laughing again.

He'd gotten fucked twice in one day, hard and good.

There were cells and all the apparatus of justice at the agora, but to his surprise, they didn't stop there, they kept walking. All the while, the city fell behind them until only the temple could be seen, sticking up like a cock that never shrank. They walked right out of town, and into the sand and heat of the desert. Though the sun sank, it remained miserably hot. Flies buzzed and with hands bound, Iullianus had to suffer them crawling on his face, drinking his sweat.

What he really needed, he decided, was another beer. Even water would be tolerable. His request for a drink, which he'd thought quite restrained, had received him a gag—a foul cloth that smelled of sour wine and semen.

He wondered if they'd kill him. Deserters were in fact, typically crucified, or worse, but he didn't think they could prove that he deserted. Not exactly.

They stopped after two hours march, on the road north to the sea. Iullianus knew the posting inn at once. *That son of a whore*, he thought. He had been hoping that Lepidus would be too busy to spend time chasing down one lost soldier.

Lepidus came out of the inn, and smiled at the red-haired soldier.

"Remove this man's binds and gag. Hells, I said don't let him do anything dangerous, not treat him like an Etruscan." Two men behind him immediately complied. Iullianus tried not to collapse. He felt woozy and wasn't sure if he was still drunk or suffering from the heat. "Give him some water," Lepidus said.

"Fuck water," Iullianus croaked, "give me beer."

Lepidus was all smiles but Iullianus wasn't fooled. The man would have given very direct orders about his treatment. He'd probably supplied the rope and the gag. Probably the semen as well, come to think of it.

"Come inside, Iullianus. Share some wine with me," Lepidus said. His voice was soft honey. Suddenly, the red-haired man felt more afraid than when he had thought he might die.

****

"Tell me, Tettius Iullianus, what do you know about Alexander the Great?" Lepidus asked.

He was resting on the lectus, the versatile long couch used for sleeping, sitting, relaxing and eating. Inside, it was blessedly cool, and Iullianus was feeling better after quaffing three long pulls of weak Roman wine. He didn't like wine, but he wasn't foolish enough to turn it down when there was nothing else.

"Some Greek King who fucked boys and died too young," he said.

Lepidus smiled again, but Iullianus thought he could sense the frustration that lay behind it. Lepidus, though completely Roman, had been born in Corinth. "He was Macedonian, and conquered most of the world when he was still younger than you. But otherwise, that is correct."

"Do you know what the difference between the Greeks and the Romans is?" Iullianus asked.

"What?"

"Greeks invented sex, but Romans introduced it to women," Iullianus said.

"That's funny," Lepidus said, without so much as a smile.

"And, he didn't conquer the whole world, did he? He never got up to my homeland," Iullianus said eying the empty wine amphorae. Surely that wasn't all the wine they had. There had been barely enough to slake one man's thirst. He didn't even like wine, and there wasn't enough for him. That was a real problem.

"Exactly. He didn't conquer the entire world," Lepidus said. "Now, your lands were too insignificant and primitive to concern him. But in the end, he could not defeat India, not with their thousands of war elephants."

Maybe his brain had gotten soft from the sun. They needed wine and this man was talking about elephants, but he couldn't help getting drawn in.

"He had elephants too," Iullianus pointed out. He chewed on some grapes found by the empty amphorae. "Probably buggered them as well."

"If he did, Arrian was curiously silent about it," Lepidus said. "More to the point, he had a few hundred of the beasts. The Emperor of the Nanda had ten thousand, or so they say. But," he said, pausing. Iullianus knew the shift in tone well. His instinct told him he was about to get punched. "But it's an interesting point. He did have elephants, and kept a force at Babylon. The man who led them was known as the *Elephantarch*, and he had great honor."

Iullianus looked at the hairs on his arm. People talked about Alexander of Macedon far too much. He and Augustus Caesar. They had been men just like everyone else. "People used to do all kinds of strange things," he said.

"Tettius, don't play the fool," Lepidus said. His voice was disastrously earnest now. "I could have you killed. Your scouting trip began a month ago. I put it that you were on a mission, but as the weeks passed, it became more difficult. I hope you know now that I can find you anywhere."

"I am a slow learner, but even to me this is plain." Iullianus had slipped away from the army several hundred miles away.

"Not too long ago, you were a mere auxiliary. It wouldn't be hard to make you yearn for those days," Lepidus said. "There were men, counting on you, who were put into danger while you whored and drank your days away."

Very annoyingly, Iullianus felt a pang of conscience. "It won't happen again," he said.

"You put me in an awkward position. I should crucify you, but you're a valuable man. You've served me well for a long time."

"You mean since you stole me from my village?"

"Really, Tettius," Lepidus said, "these complaints were tiring years ago. Have you not enjoyed your life? You grew rich in Iudea."

"Of course I have. It's still a point worth making. I wouldn't have heard of Rome if it weren't for you."

Lepidus paused. "Indeed. And I'm still waiting for your gratitude. Make no mistake—you are valuable enough for one more chance. Not two." He paused again, letting the long silence grow past maturity and into old-age before speaking again. "Iullianus, I've named you *Elephantarch*."

That got a reaction. Iullianus leapt from the lectus.

"Juno's hairy cunt, Lepidus. I've never even seen an elephant. And no one uses them anymore—not for a hundred years, or more."

"No one uses them in the west, that's true," Lepidus said. His smile was broad and victorious. "The Parthians do. You'll find the situation out here is more fluid."

****

Fluid was a word that resonated with Iullianus over the next week, as he fed, washed, and cleaned up after a score of elephants. They had fluids aplenty. He'd always fancied himself a champion pisser, or on a good night, he could spell his name in the snow. Not even his older brother had been able to piss straighter or longer than he had. But these beasts were unparalleled. Three elephants in Rome could have smothered the Great Fire with their amber spray.

Even that was nothing, compared to the gargantuan bundles of shite they dropped. The piles were big enough that at night they used dried clumps to light a fire. It grew cold in the desert, and Iullianus was grateful for the warmth. He had not gotten used to the size of the dung, though.

Place an elephant high enough, he pondered, and its droppings would be big enough to kill a man. He had just the man in mind, too. Lepidus had been too damn clever. *Elephantarch*, indeed. How he'd kept a straight face and somber tone was beyond the red-haired man.

He had arrived, filled with dubious curiosity, seven days ago at a camp just south of Palmyra. The first man that he met was Amasis, the head trainer in charge of the camp. Amasis was the true *Elephantarch*, and he had taken an instant dislike to the man claiming his position. The big warrior had been immediately presented a shovel and sent to work, digging piss pits and shoveling dung. There were many workers present, but manual labor became Iullianus' domain. The only other person he noticed with a shovel was a toothless old man who occasionally joined him in desultory digging.

To the north, he thought of the sparkling sea. It invited escape, but he knew better than to try again. No doubt Lepidus had men watching him. Instead, he shoveled until the calluses on his hands had their own calluses. It wasn't so bad, as long as he didn't dilute his wine too much in the morning. Lately, he was scarcely adding water at all.

There were good moments. He liked the food; a spicy mix of lentils and grains called *kushari*. At night, he enjoyed staring at the dung-filled fire, watching the shapes of yellow and red dancing in the cold desert air. His shovel was of excellent quality, the same kind that the Legions used to entrench themselves while on campaign. It was made all of iron, and came up to his waist. He named it *efossion*, his little digging friend, and the old man had come out to help today. He was hardworking and silent—the perfect companion.

The tall warrior stopped and wiped the sweat from his eyes. It was early morning still, but already the air was warming. He looked critically at his trench. It wasn't very deep. "Good enough," he muttered.

"No, it's not," said a voice from behind him. Amasis stood there. The overseer wasn't a bad man, but he clearly enjoyed lording power over a bigger, stronger man. "It's not big enough to hold rat piss. It's useless."

The old man had come up beside Iullianus. His leathery face broke into a wide smile and his toothless mouth opened. "Useless," he echoed. "Useless." Iullianus was surprised. The old man spoke no tongue Iullianus knew, not even Latin. He didn't even have a name, as far as anyone knew.

"I took you on because I owed Lucius a favor," Amasis said. "But we need workers, not warriors."

Iullianus said nothing. Let this little man exult in his power. He dug into the dry earth with his spade and dug deeper. The old man joined him.

A shout at the gates sounded, and Amasis left. There were newly arrived visitors. Iullianus watched with interest as the doors opened and a team of hunters returned. They were hard men, survivors. Not disciplined enough to be soldiers, they could nonetheless march for several days and survive with no rations other than what they could hunt or scavenge.

Iullianus had been surprised at the existence of the hunting parties. But no one, apart from perhaps the distant Indian Kings, had discovered how to get the massive beasts to mate. The industry, such as it was, consisted of three teams. The first were the hunters who actually found and captured young elephants. Another group, smaller, was led by Amasis. They did the actual training of the animals. The third group was made of wives and the young children of the first two. They created the howdahs, turrets they placed on the beasts for archers to use in combat. Iullianus and the old man were not part of any of the groups. They merely dug piss trenches and shoveled the shit.

There were close to a dozen hunters, and they were leading six young elephants. The men were bandaged, scrawny, and filthy. The animals were the smaller kind, the ones found in the northern part of Africa. They were plenty big though. The men had metal spikes and hammers, of the kind used to keep the animals under control until they were tamed.

The leader of the hunters looked to be from Parthia. His skin was dark olive, and he had thick dark hair, bushy eyebrows, and a hooked nose. He was handsome, in a rugged Parthian kind of way.

Amasis met them and they spoke for long moments. Iullianus watched the new elephants for a moment, wondering if they would get along with the elephants already here. The great animals seemed to be almost like people—elephants did not always like one another. Two of the handlers appeared and led the elephants deeper into the camp. They would be sequestered at first, until they had proven adaptable. Iullianus stopped watching and started shoveling, trying to avoid pressure on his blisters and wondering if elephants had personalities evident to themselves. Were some elephants kind and caring? Were others complete arseholes?

His head rose, moments later, at the sound of shouting. The Parthian leader was screaming at Amasis. The man was shouting back, but he was much smaller and wasn't armed. Iullianus moved closer, inconspicuously, shoveling crumbling old piles of dung to the side. He could just hear the conversation.

"We bring six elephants. We are paid for six elephants," the leader of the hunters said. Some of his men stood in a line behind him, a silent promise of menace.

"That's not how it works, and you know it," Amasis said. "We pay quarter rates for female elephants. They won't fight the males."

"They fought us," the Parthian said, eyebrows glowering. "I lost Gebal and Rensi. We froze our testes off in the wet forests and we were caught by a flash flood in the plains. We were hunted by lions and tribesmen. We don't do this for fucking quarter rates."

His hand went to his sword. Amasis cried for help. The elephant trainers were out of sight--they might have heard, but Iullianus was much closer. Before he could think about it, he was running towards them, shovel in hand.

The leader didn't see him, or didn't care. One of the men behind him did notice the tall red-headed warrior running at them, and moved to block him.

The Parthian had the sword at the overseer's throat. "Blade is last thing you see. Pay now," he said harshly.

Iullianus reached them. The man who had come to meet them drew his sword, but it was a short blade, and he was much smaller than the charging warrior was. Iullianus slammed the shovel into the man's face. The sound of cartilage crumbling was very loud. The man collapsed, elephant shit smeared onto his face. The other hunters were belatedly springing into action. They drew blades, brandished spears, and one had a long coil of rope.

"What are you doing?" Amasis cried. The blade was at his throat.

"For this, you need a warrior," Iullianus said. He was alive and filled with confident energy.

"No, I will pay, I will pay!" Amasis yelped.

No one heeded his cries. Iullianus shifted his grip on the shovel, that little friend, and drove the blade into the stomach of an oncoming hunter. The man wore leather armor, and the shovel wasn't sharp, but the impact drove his breath away with a woof. The man fell to the ground.

Iullianus jumped into the air and landed on the unfortunate man's head. He felt the skull fracture beneath his heavy tread and nearly lost his balance, but stumbled forward, toward his opponents.

Amasis took advantage of the distraction; turning and fleeing back into the camp. Before he had taken two steps, the Parthian leader took a long stride and slid the sword through his back. Amasis made a strange, clucking noise, and then fell heavily. The hook-nosed leader drew another sword from his belt.

Mithras, Iullianus thought. He'd perhaps made a mistake. Then he was beset by the three swordsmen. He would not have had a chance, if they'd fought with the discipline and coordination of soldiers. He didn't have much of a chance anyway, fighting against multiple enemies armed with only a shit-stained shovel, but the men fought him individually, and there were few individuals in this land who could beat him man to man.

A sword swung through the sky. Iullianus blocked the overhand blow with the shaft of his shovel and an ugly clang, but another blade came at him, at his chest, and he had no choice but to block with his hand. His left hand flew out and he leaned back. The blade bit into his flesh.

Iullianus howled with agony as immense pain filled his body, but his hand was still there, and the sword hadn't gone deep. His blisters had saved him, he realized.

The man who had hit his hand, and the other whose blow he had parried, both slowly backed away. Everyone was backing away. Everyone, save him.

The leader of the hunters moved menacingly closer to the big warrior. His sword dipped low and he growled in anger and anticipation. Battle lust danced merrily in his eyes. Iullianus hefted the shovel in his good hand, and sighed.

An arrow flew over both of them, less than a foot from the Parthian's head. Iullianus looked behind him and saw the other three trainers, armed with bows. The old man was with them, and a few of the older children, toting rocks and sticks. They were jogging from the elephant fields.

The Parthian could think quickly. He instantly raised his off hand and swirled it in an unspoken command. His men eased back, toward the gate.

"Get back! Run, you dogs," Iullianus roared. His hand leaked blood into the earth.

The leader of the hunters glared at him with hatred, and his expression spoke clearly enough. *Another time.*

The hunters slipped out of the compound and departed into the desert.

Iullianus willed his heart to stop beating.

"What happened?" One of the trainers asked.

"Treachery," Iullianus said. Instinct told him that lies would serve better than truth. "They wanted it all." Better to keep it vague. Someone cried out as they discovered Amasis lying dead on the ground.

The others looked at him carefully. Iullianus was grateful once again for the old man's silence. He barely knew these men, so they had no reason to trust him. On the other hand, they didn't know him well enough to assume that he was lying, either.

"He never should have hired that lot," another trainer said at last. "I warned him. You can't ever trust a Parthian." They moved away, to comfort Amasis' wife and children. Others went to ensure that the gates were closed. Iullianus was alone with his pain.

Almost alone.

The old man moved closer. He had his little shovel in his hand as he stared at Iullianus, hand dripping darkly onto the earth. The old one looked at Amasis, lifeless, with a sword through his heart. He looked at the two remaining men of the hunting party, one dead, and the other blowing blood through his flattened nose. He leaned on his shovel, looked right at Iullianus.

"Useless," he said.

CHAPTER IV

Rome: 79 CE, Spring

Felix screamed with excitement. He was one of tens of thousands who had come for the grand opening of the amphitheater. The first day of games had been declared a holiday, and even the slaves had the day free. Nominally, they were able to do whatever they wished, but one would be hard-pressed to find a slave in Rome not attending the games. Felix had been in Rome for six years now, and a chance to watch the games was as good as his year could get.

Hyacinthus sat beside him. The big Greek slave was even fatter than the day they'd met, and he'd come to the games more than reluctantly. "Those are entertainments for the young and the stupid, and I've seen enough real blood not to lust after deadly entertainment," he'd complained. Felix had begged to get him to come. Despite his earlier misgivings, the Greek was shouting as loudly as anyone was. Below them, on the floor of the amphitheater, two massive bulls with deadly sharp horns were trying to kill a raging elephant.

The two of them were sitting high up, above even the highest marble seats, where wooden benches had been hastily added to accommodate the crowds. It was early, and many of the people around them were still eating their *ientaculum*. Rich and poor, the first meal for most in Rome was fresh-baked bread dipped in a mixture of wine and water. For Felix, this was enough. Hyacinthus always ate more, but today he had a few meaty handfuls of dates and olives.

It was the first morning of a hundred days of games. Each day would follow a similar pattern: the morning was filled with battles amongst the animals. The current clash involved some of the biggest and fiercest, but later days would feature lions, leopards, boars, buffalo, ostriches, camels, crocodiles, and, rumor had it, a rhinoceros. Over the hundred days of games, some five thousand animals would perish to bathe the new arena in blood. Mostly they fought each other, but some were saved for the afternoon.

It was then that the deserters, prisoners-of-war, and criminals would be killed. These executions could be so brutal that it was customary for the Emperor to leave, but Felix was eager to see them. Many of the executions would be creative and entertaining. Crucifixions were boring, but for these games they had brought back *damnatio ad bestias*.

Death by beasts. The rumored entertainments sounded wonderfully inventive. A terribly large eagle would eat the innards of a doomed patricide, cast in the role of Prometheus. A prisoner from the Celtiberians would be cast as Orpheus, playing his lute until the starving animals could no longer stand it and would rend him to pieces. A female slave convicted of stealing from her master would be Pasiphae, raped by either a bull, a man in a bull costume, or as one rumor promised, both at the same time.

Later in the day, after the executions, came the real entertainment. The gladiators, the races, and the battle recreations would be watched by tens of thousands of people. It would take place here before spreading out to other venues. A sea battle was to be fought, and that was no rumor. On the following days, the chariot races would begin at the hippodrome. If the events of this morning played out correctly, Felix hoped to have a part in later games.

Now, however, was the opening day featured fight, and it was enthralling. A Thracian black bull and a Gaulish brown one, both bigger and meaner than their domesticated cousins, were on the attack against a massive elephant. The brown bull stabbed at the elephant's side, while it was distracted by the menace of the black bull. Those sharp horns could find no purchase in the tough hide of the beast, however, and the elephant turned and charged. It was ponderously big, and it was devastatingly quick.

The brown bull was caught in its path before it had a chance even to consider moving. Tusks drove deep into flesh, and moments later, the elephant trampled the bull with heavy footfalls. The elephant's massive feet slammed into its back, splintering bone. The brown bull collapsed into a mewling heap, dying, and in hideous pain.

Felix felt some sympathy for the shattered bull, but it was removed—he desperately needed the elephant to win. One bull was down, but the boy grew alarmed. The elephant, deadly fast in a straight line, was slow in turning around. Too slow. The black bull's charge caught it in the rear leg, just above the knee. The bull had enough mass and enough momentum to impact even its mammoth opponent, and the elephant tottered.

Felix was assailed by panic and regret. "You shouldn't have bet all your coin on this one, boy," Hyacinthus said, not unkindly.

"He was so big," Felix said. "I've never seen an elephant so big."

"Bigger than African or Asian elephants," his friend said. "That one was born far away, much further south than you yourself. In Taprobane. The greatest fighting elephants in the world come from there."

"How could he then lose?" Felix asked.

"He was favored. Never bet on the favorite. Better to spend coin on long odds, else you risk losing all and stand to gain little. But watch—not yet is all hope lost."

The bull's horns were locked into the elephant's hide. The elephant turned its head and smacked at the bull with his trunk. It connected solidly, but the bull was too massive to be dislodged. The bull kept pushing, and the elephant's leg buckled.

It collapsed. Luckily, for the bull, the pachyderm fell away from it. The gargantuan beast slammed into the ground with crushing force, dust flying. The elephant trumpeted in fear and pain, and even from where Felix sat, the sound was deafening.

The black bull wrenched its horns free from its opponent's leg and shook its head. Hot steam blew from its nostrils as it backed up. Its hooves slipped a little in the dust. Felix ground his teeth in frustration. Through some bestial instinct, it knew where to strike next. The elephant's stomach was covered in the same tough hide as the rest of its body, but it could be pierced by those long, sharp horns. Behind both animals, the brown bull, still dying, cried pitifully as blood oozed from its shattered back.

The bull charged with organ-rupturing force. Then it skidded to a stop as the elephant moved its three good feet together, forming a wall in front of its vulnerable inside. The path to victory was suddenly, unexpectedly closed. The crowd cheered again and

Felix and Hyacinthus cheered with it. The bull stopped in consternation.

Behind it, the brown bull was screaming still. Its agony echoed through the vast coliseum. A force of the Praetorian Guard stood next to the vast gate, sharp blades ready to silence the poor beast, but they did not yet dare approach the titanic struggle.

In one manic lunge, the elephant jerked itself back onto its feet. The bull backed up even more, trying to create room for another charge.

The elephant charged first. It was slower now, with one foot maimed, but still far too fast. Somehow, with asymmetrical grace and head lowered, it rushed forward. It hit the black bull and lifted its powerful head. The bull, three thousand pounds of anger and muscle, was tossed ten feet into the air. Felix gasped.

The bull landed on its feet, and woozily took a step. The elephant's charge caught it again. The tusks pierced the bull's head and drove through to its brain. The great beast sagged and instantly died.

"Unbelievable," whispered Hyacinthus next to him.

The Coliseum roared its hearty approval, but what happened next was even more astounding. The weary pachyderm walked unsteadily until it was standing directly below Emperor Titus. It swayed there for a moment, then fell to its knees and knelt before the Emperor. Ten times ten thousand throats fell silent, as people stood to witness the beast's obeisance, and then the roar came back, better than ever. Rome had a new champion, and the people adored him.

Felix felt relief flow through him. He had bet all the money he could find, and had borrowed from the type of men that he really shouldn't have dealt with. If Hyacinthus had known, he would have sat on him rather than let him deal with them, but he had won, and with the day's winnings he could do something much greater— enter the games himself. "Let's go collect our winnings," he said to Hyacinthus after they had cheered themselves hoarse. The big man had bet on the elephant, the bulls together, and both bulls individually. He would lose money today, but not much. They walked out of the stands, away from the still deafening chorus of cheers.

The people of Rome needed the games like never before. Vespasian was dead. The old warrior had left Rome suddenly on urgent business and was found dead in a posting-inn. The gods themselves had grieved, and Rome suffered for their grief.

A great fire abused the city, destroying prodigious amounts of life and property. It burned for three days and for three nights, as black smoke rising so high that the very sun turned red and the afternoon light turned gray. It rained ashes for days. Agrippa's Pantheon was destroyed, as was the Temple of Jupiter and most of Pompey's theater. Fire and ash was not the worst enemy, however.

Plague came stalking through the ashes. This was worse, and not just the poor died. Disease was terribly indiscriminate, and many noblemen breathed their last. From the old and rich to the young and poor, the sickness struck all. The only ones seemingly unaffected were the Jews. The people of Rome noticed this, and lynchings became regular. Emperor Titus was forced to banish his favorite mistress, who was Jewish. Felix had stayed in his master's stables for three weeks to avoid persecution.

The gods were not satiated yet, however, and still worse was to come. The sacred Mt. Vesuvius unleashed its fiery fury, and instantly four towns had ceased to exist. The tens of thousands who lived in Pompeii, Herculaneum, Stabiae and Oplontis, died within moments, within heartbeats. This was the fractured, bleeding Empire that Titus had inherited. The people truly needed their games.

Felix and Hyacinthus collected their winnings and quickly returned to the amphitheater. Felix carefully kept his hand on his money bag. There were many thieves in the city, and most would be here today. He felt the urge to return home and stash it, but there was nowhere a slave could truly keep his possessions safe, and he did not want to miss the Emperor's speech.

Titus stood. He was a tall, handsome man. They couldn't hear the Emperor from this far away, but all knew that he was dedicating the colossal building to his father, Vespasian. Though Titus had finished the building, his father had begun the work not long after coming into power.

Hyacinthus turned to him. "Does it not bother you?"

"Doesn't what bother me?" Felix asked.

"The place," the big man said, "it took ten years for them to build, using all the treasure from the Jewish rebellion. If your people hadn't been quite so ruthlessly crushed, this place wouldn't exist."

"They're not my people," Felix said. "I am sixteen. I've lived half my life in Rome."

"As a slave," the fat man pointed out.

"They were traitors," Felix said.

"Just as mine were," the Greek said. "It seems the Romans are good at finding traitors everywhere."

"What does that mean?" Felix asked. He felt irrationally angry. "My father told me that good always triumphs over evil. He was right—he just didn't realize his side was bad. It wasn't their fault, it was Simon's."

"Calm down, Felix," Hyacinthus said with a little laugh that suggested the matter had never been a serious one. "I know you don't like talking about what happened before. Most slaves don't. I merely am curious. Please forgive me."

Behind him, cheering started. Felix looked and saw three lavishly dressed attendants appear on the marble steps below them. They carried, very slowly, a large wooden box. Two proseda, clad in very little, sauntered beside them. Hyacinthus grinned.

"What are you smiling at? You don't even like women," Felix said.

"I like what they bring," Hyacinthus said. "Watch."

The blonde woman reached into the box and pulled out a handful of wooden balls. She handed a few to her friend, and they both started flinging the spheres throughout the crowd. Large groups stood up and cheered, hoping to attract the wanton women's attention.

Felix shouted too, his voice hoarse from the earlier efforts.

"Cease. They'll not throw them up here," Hyacinthus said.

"What are they?"

"Promises. They can be exchanged for food, clothing, horses, silver, gold, even slaves," the older man said.

"I want to win one. Imagine, earning a horse in an instant. Emperor Titus is a great man."

"It's not his idea. Nero gave away golden statues, hundreds of them, but they'd never let slaves have something so valuable. They will not throw their promises into the free seats." His voice was thoughtful. "Let's go get some food. I'm hungry."

They fought their way through the crowds and left the mighty amphitheater. Directly outside, they passed the only part of Nero's Golden House still standing. Inside the palace were the new bathhouses of Titus, which had been only just been completed for today's events. Just next to them were the *thermopoli.*

These mobile carts could be moved to any street corner in the city and could be found anywhere in Rome. Felix paid the smallest coin he'd won that day and received four big dates, the likes of which he'd picked from trees as a youth, another world ago. Hyacinthus was well-known to the vendors, and he ordered hot sausages and cheese from one, bread from another, and cake and wine from a third.

They sat down on benches next to the *thermopoli.* It was between *ientaculum* and midday, so not many people were eating, but for fat men and growing boys, any time was a good time to eat. Most of the other customers who were there were slaves, enjoying their day off.

"So," Hyacinthus said, with his mouth full of bread and sausage, "you have enough money now."

"I know," he said. His excitement was hard to hide. "Two hundred sesterces," he said, resisting the urge to count them again. It was more money than he'd ever had. "I can race tomorrow." He popped a date in his mouth.

"You can," the Greek man agreed, in a tone that suggested the exact opposite. "Are you sure you want too?" Behind them, the city of Rome flowed as citizens and slaves moved into the bathhouses and the amphitheater. The roar of the crowd periodically echoed from the theater.

"Am I sure? It's what I've been practicing for, and training for. Jupiter's cock, yes, it's what I want!"

"Freedom makes for a dangerous dream. Many slaves dream of earning their freedom, boy. Some do, but not until they are old. Older than me," Hyacinthus said. "Only a few will win enough even to pay their registration fees."

"At least it pays better than your plays. All you get is a free dinner and that only when you've earned great applause," Felix snapped.

The big man's reply was stern, but not angry. "You are ten and six years now, a man grown. You must not say foolish things, or there will be trouble. Besides," he added, "I always get great applause, and you should see the size of my meals. They'd do better to pay me in sesterces."

****

Felix walked quickly, worried that he had missed most of the day's entertainment. Registering for the chariot races had, of course, been the most important thing. It had to come first, but he'd never expected it to take so long. He'd certainly missed the crucifixions. The mock battles also would be over by now. He hoped to make it back by evening, to watch the two greatest gladiators in the world, Verus and Priscus, fight against one another. That was exciting, but it paled compared to the inner energy bubbling through him as he thought about tomorrow.

He walked through *Subura*, the slum that led to the forum. Earlier today, it had made him nervous. He had walked along these narrow cobblestone streets daily, past barber shops, restaurants, and clothing stores, but never with so much money. For the first time ever, he had been a potential target, and there were enough thieves, brigands and whores that some had been bound to notice the outline of the purse. He'd made it through, and through other dangerous areas on his way to the Hippodrome.

It had taken too long, however, to complete everything. He'd had no one to vouch for him, and had to bribe the man with all his coin to complete the registration. It didn't matter. He'd earn the money back. He had to.

"Saluton, Felix," a voice said. Felix whirled around, spooked, but it was only Carpophorus. The man was a few years older than Felix was, and much taller. He was already a skilled bestiarius, and was to be part of the second half of the games, like Felix.

"Salve friend. Killed any leopards today?" That particular feat had won Carpophorus' adoration amongst the boys his age. His fame was growing throughout the city.

"Leopards are easy," he said with the confidence only an eighteen year old boy could muster. "I'm ready for the biggest. Lions, bears, tigers. I can do it."

"I will race on the morrow."

"Truly? I will watch. But you missed much excitement," the *bestiarius* said. "This afternoon's game matched three lions against a rhinoceros. A white one, with double horns. The rhino wouldn't fight the lions, and attacked a bull that was waiting on the side."

Felix laughed at the image.

"Yes, everyone cheered and laughed," Carpophorus said. "They brought out two trainers, who calmed it down. But when a company of spearmen came out, it grew enraged and gored one of the trainers right through the chest, with his horn."

Felix laughed again.

"The fury of the beast was unmatched. He had the wrath of Titans, and he attacked the bears…"

"Bears?" asked Felix.

"Bears. They came out with the spearmen. The rhino knocked one so hard and so far back that it broke on the wall," the tall boy paused. "Will you dine with me?"

"No," said Felix, tempted. Carpophorus was hugely popular and had never extended such an invitation "I go to watch the fight."

"Verus and Priscus? Their match is over."

"Jupiter!" Felix swore. "Who won?"

"Neither. They fought for a long time, and were evenly matched. Titus had both yield to him, so two men fought and two men won."

"I wish I could have been there," Felix said. "But when I see you tomorrow, I will be the only one who has won."

"You have a free day tomorrow?"

"No, but my duties will only last until midday. I shall have plenty of time."

"I should like to see that," Carpophorus said. "For now, let us eat some partridges. I know the best *thermopoli* in the *Subura*. And I'll buy."

CHAPTER V

Dacia: 83 CE, Autumn

The fire crackled and the wood smoke stretched out with greedy tendrils, smothering all in its vicinity. Zuste coughed as he inhaled the ash-filled air. It was worth it, and the warmth felt exceedingly good as it struggled against the chill of the night air. The fire was ringed by great stones, which slowly absorbed heat and melted the carpet of snow covering the ground.

They sat high in the Carpathians, some of the highest and longest mountains in the world. A day's journey up the mountain from Tapae, the mountain outpost that watched over the passes, had brought them here. The pass was one of the few entrances into their mountainous land. It was most important strategically, and should an enemy get past the defenses (of and in) the pass, it was an easy trail to Sarmizegetusa, the biggest city and political center the Dacians had.

This high up, the snowfall began early each autumn and continued to pile up through the winter. It wouldn't disappear from the alpine areas until mid-summer. Though beautiful, it was a harsh land and the forests teemed with bears, wolves, and mountain cats. It was an area that appealed to few, save bandits and hermits.

Zuste was neither bandit nor hermit, but when late summer came, he often journeyed into the mountains. Armed with little other than a bedroll and a pack full of wooden containers, he could spend weeks collecting rare plants and herbs. There were enough lakes spread throughout the mountains that he always had water, and could often catch mountain trout. Many of his fellow alchemists chose to hire woodsmen or bandits to do the actual collecting, but for Zuste, escaping to the mountains was one of best parts of being an alchemist.

He knew the area well, but he was used to hiking up here alone in the warm summer with long days and short nights. Everything was different this time. It was early autumn and far colder than he'd anticipated. He had come up here not to pick aprus or harvest seba, but for information. Though the alchemist had journeyed here alone, he now sat at the large fire surrounded by large men.

Seventeen men, in total, had secretly gathered high in the dark mountain air. There were three men of the Apuli, heavy with armbands and jewelry, who came from the center of Dacia. One wild-haired man of the Buridavenses, from the north, had made it. Three were of the Daci, who lived everywhere, and two were men of the Capri, men who lived between the mountains and the river. Two men of the Suci, including Zuste himself, were included. Three men were outsiders, Sarmatians and Goths.

That made fifteen. The last two were their leader, Diurpaneus, and his chief alchemist. Diurpaneus was tall and fearless, and he was of the Tyragetae, the clan of heroes. His hair was long and straight, his features sharp with nobility, and his eyes burned blue. He wore a wolf pendant around his neck, but no armbands.

The alchemist was called Natopurus. His sour expression was often mistaken for thought, and his long beard gave him the appearance of wisdom. Already he was matched, however, in knowledge by younger alchemists. The more Zuste and others grew in knowledge, the more Natopurus clung to tradition, and yes, even superstition.

Zuste watched as Diurpaneus stood. He meandered away from the fire, into the snow beneath the trees, and pissed.

Zuste waited a few moments and then followed him. His footsteps crunched in the snow.

Diurpaneus had tucked his member back into his leathers when he saw Zuste.

"Not now, man," Diurpaneus groaned, "I have no time for words of caution. Drink some beer. Enjoy yourself."

"This is a war council," Zuste reminded him. Clouds of warmth escaped his mouth as he spoke. He raised his hand to his mouth and chewed absently on his fingernail.

"It's a party," Diurpaneus corrected, "and I don't think I'll invite you to them anymore."

"There won't be any more, Diurpaneus!" Zuste said, frustrated. "I know that I'm not a warrior, but I have studied with the wise ones. I have seen the seven burning stars, the black flowers grow, and the entrails of the wood martens. It couldn't be clearer."

"This is not a new conversation. All the warriors agree. No one can reach us. We live in a natural fortress, surrounded by high mountains on all sides. We have raging rivers to defy even the best equipped army. We have built walls and castles to augment the natural defenses. Zuste, Natopurus, the head of your order, says as much."

"Tell that to the Belgae, who had a sea to separate them. The Roman Emperor already has created the Limes as they prepare to attack. They will come on this very road, mayhap."

"Then why? Tell me that. Why here? What draws them here?" Diurpaneus stared directly into his eyes.

"Rome is but a city, yet, the whole world feels the weight of her boot. They will come because that is what they do. They will come for our food, for our children, for our mines of silver, gold, and iron," Zuste said.

"I value your wisdom," Diurpaneus said. "Your knowledge of alchemy is well-known, and you understand many strange portents and signs, but think about it. Dacia is cold, barren. Italy is a sunny, warm, rich land. They are on the sea and can eat fish every day. Even the women there are beautiful, if you can get past their big noses. We won't see the legions here, my friend. There's nothing here for them," Diurpaneus grabbed him by the shoulder. "Come and sit by the fire. Have a drink with me. It is too cold out here."

Zuste gave up, for the moment, and followed Diurpaneus back to the fire. He realized he was far more sober than the rest of the merry, jesting men. Sitting between two of the Sarmatians, he accepted a drink and a burnt rabbit leg left too long on the fire.

Diurpaneus stood, raising his vessel to the sky. The men joined him with a lusty yell and all quaffed the sour beer. It was custom not to discuss matters of state until all participants were well into their cups. There was truth in wine, it was said. Zuste nibbled on the rabbit leg and savored the smoky flavor.

"I have gathered you, the best and greatest of the Dacians, high in the hills," Diurpaneus said, striding around the circle of men. "We are here to avoid the ears of our enemies, of whom there are many and more." There was no point mentioning them by name, and they had more enemies than just the Romans. "Zuste cautions us to be wary concerning our enemies. I trust his council…"

"You should do no such thing," yelled Polpum. He was the other Suci here, and a great warrior in his own right, though none too bright. Zuste had always disliked him, and his antipathy was more than returned. "That man is a coward and a shame to our tribe."

Diurpaneus said nothing, only looked to Zuste. The others all turned to look as well. One of the Sarmatians was so close that his breath filled Zuste's nostrils. It smelled of burnt meat. The fire crackled merrily.

Zuste stood up. "It's true that I'm not a warrior, but neither am I a coward. Is it cowardice to see the sunrise in the morning? To see the ebbs of the tide flow in and out each day?"

Natopurus rose. "Pay not attention to the young pup," he said. "His knowledge is in collecting berries, not matters of statecraft."

"Be sure that the Romans will come," Zuste said, ignoring him. His tone was not as firm as he'd hoped.

"I'd welcome them, by Zalmoxis!" Polpum said. "I could defeat a legion of them with my cock," he said, springing up and thrusting his member free from his clothes. Most of the gathered men laughed, but Zuste noticed a few who did not. He still had a chance to convince them. Some of them.

"What of the fortresses?" asked the wild-haired man of the Buridavenses. "Do they not protect our lands?" The fortresses were mighty defensive structures, and nigh indestructible, with walls that were ten meters high and four meters thick surrounding them.

"They are mighty: Sarmizegetusa Regia, Costeşti-Cetăţuie, Costeşti-Blidaru, Piatra Roşie, Băniţa, and Căpâlna," Zuste said, listing them all slowly. Many of these men would only know their surrounding area. He glanced at Diurpaneus. He hadn't meant to argue so fiercely. He'd failed to convince Diurpaneus, his friend. It did not seem likely that he could do better with the war band. "Our walls are strong. The valor of our warriors is even more fearsome, but the Romans have never lost a war, and Sarmizegetusa is a few days away, forced march. If the Romans came in enough numbers, they could overwhelm Tapae and continue to Sarmizegetusa in less than a month."

"What makes you sure that the Romans will come?" asked

Natopurus.

"It is in the snow, the flames, and the air around us. The world screams warning to us that can listen. Some wicked, deadly menace is coming." The fire crackled but did not otherwise resist, as the darkness surrounded them oppressively. He could not explain how he knew danger was imminent, other than that he did. It was an instinct, a premonition that brooked no argument. Unless he was fooling himself.

His tone, deadly earnest, seemed to have an effect on the men. Even Polpum seemed hesitant.

"This is not true," said the elder alchemist, his long beard wagging as he spoke. "I have seen nothing in the signs. Just this morning, I read the signs of the pine marten's guts and I saw nothing of import. You are surely mistaken."

"What if I'm not?" Zuste asked quietly.

"Bah. Even if they do come, we will defeat them. Long ago, the Greeks came. We did not fare so badly."

"The Romans are not the Greeks. The Greeks invented reason," Diurpaneus interjected, speaking slowly. "They were civilized."

Zuste added, "The Romans are purely unreasonable---once they start marching, there is no end to the hordes that follow. They overrun with sheer numbers and uncontrollable greed."

"Be that as it may," countered Natopurus. "The Romans came under their great war chief, Caesar, in the times of our grandfather's grandfathers. We met them at Histria and we won. Dacia is too strong for even the Romans. Their current leaders are no Caesar, despite their titles."

"Much has changed," Zuste said. "The signs have spoken. If you will not listen to the gods, I cannot aid you, but I ask that you give thought to my words. Train more warriors. Build more walls. Prepare for what is to come."

The portly alchemist heard his own words and wondered if he was mad. The signs had been so clear—yet, why had no one else seen the same? Was he deluded? Were they right to belittle his arguments? No, surely it was better, even if he was wrong, to serve as a voice of caution.

Polpum stood up. There was menace in his bearing. "I say we

prepare the Dacian way. By eliminating cowards and those who disagree with us." His head snapped, whip-like, to their leader. "Diurpaneus, why is this sniveling fool here? Let me kill him."

The leader shrugged. "I can't stop you from challenging him, but this is a festival. It would be ill to slay one of our own, for little cause."

Polpum drew his dirk. It was long and impossibly sharp and glinted shards of firelight. Zuste could not look away from it. He had carried no weapons with him, and could not use one if he had. This would be no fight at all, but a murder. He could smell his own blood in the air. Another premonition? Or just pure fear?

Zuste sat down, ignoring Polpum. "Stand up and face me, you cur." This was followed by a host of other threats. Zuste stared past him, into the fire. A few of the others were smiling. That was bad—should Polpum become an object of ridicule, he could slay Zuste outright to salvage his pride. Indeed, the big warrior was advancing upon him, glimmering threat in hand.

The portly alchemist rose and acknowledged his foe at last.

"You are a greater warrior than me. But maybe I'll get lucky." He lunged toward Polpum, dragging his right foot into his left. Falling heavily to the ground, he scraped his elbow and bruised his knee on one of the warm stones. It was a small price to pay, if it worked, and indeed, he was rewarded by laughter from all around him.

Zuste looked up, and saw Polpum sheathe his knife. The warrior leaned down on one knee, pressing his face close to Zuste's. "Your prank may have saved you," he said. "I will not kill you, fat fool, who cowers on the ground like a small child, but someday you must fight. You must learn to stand up and face your opponents. If you are correct, if the Romans are coming, we all must fight. You cannot trick fate forever."

He moved back to the fire and sat down, indicating that he was done. The Sarmatian beside him nodded begrudgingly. Zuste could sense the hostile stare of Natopurus amidst the jolly faces of the drunken warriors.

"We have heard words of wisdom tonight, truly. I am of the Tyragetae, and I say we shall be wary," Diurpaneus said. "I swear on the soul of my father, Scorilus, we shall prepare for the Romans,

but not by cringing behind walls. No, we shall take the war to them.
"

The men erupted in jubilation. Diurpaneus lifted his head to the sky and howled, long and full. The men followed him, loping like wolves and howling at the uncaring, cold night sky. Zuste's mouth was filled with ashes.

CHAPTER VI

Rome: 83 CE, Summer

The Emperor squeaked out a long fart, and though Rufus pretended not to hear it, the smell hit him almost instantly. It smelled of red wine and festering garlic. He ignored the stench as best he could while he watched Domitian lift an ornate cloth, a *mappa,* high in his hand. A vast silence of expectation encased the world.

The cloth fell. As soon as it left his hand, the great *carceres* sprung open and the charioteers sprang forward. This was a minor, early morning contest and there were but four racers, each in smaller, two-horse chariots called *bigae*. Later, in the more important races, experienced drivers would race in four-horse chariots with up to twelve teams racing at a time.

The track was in fact wide enough to hold a dozen four-horse chariots. It was split down the middle by the *spina*, a raised median decorated with statues of the gods. Domitian's deceased brother, the Divine Titus, was honored with one of the newest statues on the *spina*. There were seven large metal dolphins, and one would dip as each lap finished. On either end of the *spina* was a *meta*, an ornate column which allowed the chariots to take turns without losing speed. It was there, at the turns that the most spectacular crashes occurred.

Rufus and Domitian watched the chariot races from the Emperor's plush couch, or *pulvinar,* at the Circus Maximus, between the Aventine and the Palatine Hills. They had walked here straight from the palace through Imperial tunnels that Rufus had helped design and build. The Circus was, true to its name, a grand building. It could not hold so many people as the Flavian Amphitheater, but a hundred and fifty thousand would fit in with room to spare. For important matches, spectators would arrive the night before. The pleb seats were free, of course, but they had no shade and those in the seats risked frequent brawls and the occasional orgy. A better bet was the shaded seats for Senators. They entailed less brawling and more gambling. They were also the best place in Rome to pick up a randy aristocratic woman because the games incited their lust. Thinking of that soft flesh surrounding him, Rufus almost regretted his current position. On the other hand, his place here was a singular honor, elevating him above all other Senators in Rome.

Rufus was honored to be the only Senator in the *pulvinar*, but of course, they were not alone. His own aide, Plautius, was sitting at the back. The man was dependable and competent—a rare combination. Domitian's guards stood at the back with him; there were more at the sides of the Imperial box, and many more lined the tunnel between the palace and here. They were led by Cornelius Fuscus, prefect of the Praetorian Guards. Since his long-ago return to Rome in 71, Domitian had been close with the Praetorian Guard.

More pleasantly, there were several nude slaves, each from different parts of the Empire, who stood behind them. They were there to serve wine, food, or any other need that might arise. If he was sure it was not an insult to request their services before the Emperor himself had done so, Rufus would have tried to take them up on some of their more exotic functions.

He examined the Emperor more carefully. It had been a decade since Rufus had returned to Rome, and those ten years had not been kind to Domitian. He had gone from young man to heir to Emperor and it had cost him. Most of his hair was gone now, and his belly protruded largely from his otherwise thin frame. His eyes were bloodshot and a haunted look was etched permanently on his face. He looked twice his thirty-two years. Rufus couldn't blame him. Watching what power had done to his once friend had been frightening.

The Empire was stretched. Roman legions warred in Gaul, in Caledonia, and along the Danube. They were running out of soldiers. Last year, Domitian had been forced to create an entire new legion. While popular amongst the people and especially the army, the Senators resented Domitian and repeatedly clashed with him. In addition to political and military concerns, Domitian's only son had died two years before. Soon after the boy's death, he'd been deified. There were posters of the god-child throughout Rome—recently, coins had started to bear the boy's likeness. It must have been scarce consolation, as Domitian had lost his son and his heir. Until he had another child, the Flavian dynasty ended with him.

"I've finished your arch," Rufus said. "It will be precisely one-third the size as that we erected for your brother." Two years ago, Rufus had built a triple arch honoring Titus at the east end of the circus.

There was a long pause. He could smell the perfume of the women behind him, and the faintest remainder of Domitian's gas. Below them, the racers sped through their laps. As they completed each lap, one of the metal dolphins on the *spina* lowered. When none were left raised, the race would be over.

"That is good. My brother," Domitian said, "he knew what he wanted. It's a pity he's not here."

Rufus thought carefully about what to say next. Titus had died less than two years into his reign, just after the inaugural games had finished. Many had suspected Domitian of having played a role in his brother's demise. Rufus doubted that—Domitian seemed too regretful, too unwilling to embrace the Empire as his plaything. His first act as Emperor had been to deify his brother, but it made for uncomfortable conversation whenever Titus' name was mentioned.

"We have in addition completed the new gladiator barracks near the Flavian amphitheater, and next to the bathhouses built by your divine brother," Rufus said, wincing. Titus seemed constantly to come up. "I have diverted and built new aqueducts and there will be plenty of water for the men. The connecting tunnels are complete and one can enter the fighting grounds directly from the training grounds."

"Well done," Domitian said.

Rufus smiled to himself, hiding the bitterness he felt. The Emperor had become a tight-lipped man. He found himself missing the energetic, gangly youth who had appeared in his chambers all those years ago.

Around them, the plebs roared their approval. They were cheering not for a particular racer, but for an accident. *Furor circensis*, their mad fury was called, and it was just getting started. The stands were not even full for the early morning *ientaculum* matches. Rufus glanced to the racers below. Domitian's *pulvinar* naturally had the best view possible. It looked right over the track, though of course, both a wire screen and a canal as long as two men separated the racers from the spectators.

The front two racers, red and blue, were going around the *meta*. They all had the reins wrapped around their waist, to keep them in their baskets. The white racer leaned toward the green. Metal glinted in his hand. The racers carried curved knives called *falx*. Nominally, they were to be used to cut themselves free from their reins when they crashed. Far more often, however, they drew close enough to their opponent to slash at him. The green racer was ready for the slow slash, and his chariot swung wide.

The white racer was momentarily overextended, but he was able to right himself. He would have, rather, had that moment not been precisely when an eager fan hurled a curse tablet at him. The curse tablets were a way for the fans to get involved, and it was well known that the driver with the fewest curse tablets often won. To make sure, however, the amulets were often studded with nails or shrapnel.

The tablet hit the white driver right on the head. He wore a helmet, but the force of it, coupled with his off-balance footing, caused him to stumble and fall out the back of his chariot. Many of the crowd roared their appreciation for this move. For those close enough, the prone body of the racer made for a tempting target, and a barrage of curse tablets hit the stunned driver before he could rise. Finally, he stumbled away, hopping for a side door.

A different part of the crowd cheered as the racers entered the sixth lap, of seven. A young Blue racer was ahead, but the Red was fast. His chariot was clearly going faster than the one before him. Behind them, the Green driver was trying hard to catch up, but it did not look hopeful. With every second, the Red racer was closing in on the Blue.

"Have you placed money on this match?" Domitian asked suddenly. Rufus saw that the man's cheeks had turned red with excitement.

"No, Caesar. I only returned this morning."

"I'm told the Blue driver is the favorite."

"The red driver looks to catch up quickly," Rufus said.

"Would you care to wager on red?" Domitian asked.

"With you? Of course, and the stakes..." Rufus asked.

Domitian said nothing, only turned back to watch the final quarter lap.

It was disappointing in the end. The Blue racer took the turn very tightly and sped away, and the Red could not catch him, though he leaned so close to his horse that he seemed to disappear. The winner cruised over the finish line leisurely. Men and women wearing blue scarves were overjoyed, hugging strangers and screaming themselves hoarse. Those wearing red, green, or white, were obviously less jubilant.

That race would have enriched some of the people, Rufus thought. Slaves would buy their freedom. Men could clear long-owed debts. Conversely, some would have been broken by that result. One race could lead to a lifetime of servitude. Rufus tried to imagine the level of desperation necessary to risk it all. Had he been that desperate during his exile? He imagined not.

"You have won, Caesar. The blue racer was as good as you said," Rufus stated.

"He will lose at the Greek Kalends! Never! He wasn't threatened by these children. Though blue is not a noble color. I should like to see new colors. Purple perhaps. Or Gold. Those would make for finer colors, don't you think?"

"I suppose so," Rufus answered.

"As to our wager," the Emperor said, leaving the sentence unfinished.

"I am, as always, your servant. I can gift you one of my wines. Perhaps a Falnerian."

"Exile," Domitian said.

Rufus felt his heart cease beating. Realization dawned belatedly. He'd displeased the Emperor, and this race was the way for him to show his disapproval.

Domitian watched his reaction carefully. "You've turned white. Was exile so bad?" he asked.

"It was not unbearable, though I confess I am not eager to revisit it," Rufus said. "If I have displeased—"

"I am exiling Domitia," the Emperor said. "You have lost our wager, and I want to send her to Gyaros. You did much to increase its beauty, and it will comfort her."

Rufus was shocked. When their son had been deified, Domitia

had been honored with the title Augusta. She should have been above reproach.

"Caesar," he said, his throat feeling dry. Something unpleasant had just occurred to him. "I have of course left stewards to maintain the property. It looks the same as ever, I have no doubt, but it's no place for the Augusta. It's a simple, humble place." In truth, it was a horrible barren place devoid of humanity. "Send her to Kythnos instead. It is nearby, but not as dire a home."

A silence longer than any stretched before them. Rufus followed the Emperor's glance down as the next race set up. Teams of two would race with *quadrigae*, or four horse chariots. The setup bored him. From the corner of his eye, he could see a slave woman's naked breasts. They were overly big, with small pink nipples.

"That is exactly what the Augusta needs," Domitian said. "I have struggled with this idea for a long time. It is the right thing to do. It is what ... my father would have done."

"There will be talk," Rufus said. "I am loathe to broach such unpleasant slanders, but ... there are rumors...concerning Julia Flavia."

"Julia?" Domitian asked. "My niece. What do the rumors speak of?"

"They say, I think I've heard them say ... that," Rufus stammered. His normal bluntness was not appropriate here.

"That I'm fucking my niece? I do have an informant network, Rufus. I know what they say."

"I thought as much," Rufus said, regaining some composure. It felt like he was talking to his old friend again. "With ears as big as yours, I'd hope you could hear rumors that oft-repeated."

Domitian stared at him. Rufus regretted his quip, but the Emperor started laughing.

"Gratias, Rufus," the Emperor said.

"Why?"

"You have no idea how refreshing it is to speak to someone who's not constantly trying to curry favor. Now, try to remember everything you can about exile. I want you to talk to Domitia into leaving. As soon as possible." He rose, and Rufus followed suit.

On their way back to the palace, Rufus realized Domitian had never answered the question about his niece.

CHAPTER VII

Dacia: 83 CE, Autumn

"Go," she said, kissing him on the lips, "go and kill them all." Her voice sounded flat to her, as though the vast roiling emotions in her were too profound to be expressed by something as mundane as her voice.

He winked at her, gratitude lifting the corners of his lips into a smile. "They'll never even catch us," he said, "those clumsy turtle-fuckers. By Zalmoxis, we will kill so many of them that they will never come back." His voice was solid, dependable, a platform of bravery she could cling to, and yet she could not drown her fear.

Somehow sensing her worry, he had grasped her hand then, his fingers warm and reassuring. "Rowanna, I'll come back for you, and for Dapyx."

Her lips moved together in an attempt at a smile. "I know you will."

He was three steps out the door when she saw it.

"Brasus," she called after him. Plucking the great hard-wood shaft from the wall, she chased after him.

"My spear," he said, smiling in admonishment of his own forgetfulness, "what would my father have said?"

"He would have cuffed you on the head for trying to fight the Romans without the spear of *his* father, and his father before him," Rowanna said. The weapon was as much heirloom as tool of war, and it had a lineage greater than either of them.

"I have to go," Brasus said, hefting the spear in gratitude. "Give my love to the boy."

Rowanna watched him go, watched the space he had been in long after he'd departed. Most of the village was leaving. Leaving to face another Roman excursion into their land. Roman fools. They would die as their forefathers had died. The wolf people knew no masters, gave no quarter. This she knew, with all of her being. And yet. And yet, she feared.

It was bright outside, but she sat in the cool darkness of her home. She drifted to a place between wakefulness and sleep, and only when Dapyx appeared to clutch at her knees with grubby hands did she emerge from her reverie.

"Where have you been?" she asked. "And where are the apples?"

"I was playing," Dapyx said. "And I think I lost them." She knew where the scamp had lost them. His knees were dirty and his arms scratched and bloody. It was impossible to keep the boy from climbing trees.

"Brasus is gone," she told him, "he went to fight the Romans."

"Oh," Dapyx said, "well, you'd better make me a spear. I need to go too."

"Not yet," she said, hugging him close to her. His blue eyes burned into her. "But not long from now, either. When you're ten, you can learn the spear and the sword. Now tell me, what's new in Sarmizegetusa?" She had explicitly told him not to go to the nearby capital.

"There's a storyteller from Gaul who--" Dapyx stopped in sudden alarm as he realized the trap.

"I thought so," she said, swatting him on the backside.

"I am sorry," he said. "But my friends wanted to go, and I couldn't let them down. Everyone goes to Sarmizegetusa."

She stared at him.

"Everyone," he repeated uncomfortably. "I want to go back today and hear the end of the story."

"Forget it," she said. "You do not get to go back today, but if you go get the apples, maybe tomorrow I'll bring you there to hear the rest of the story."

Her son scampered off as the sun set. Where was Brasus now? Would they march in the dark, or set up camps in the forests? She would miss his warm body against hers. Rowanna sighed, wishing that she, too, could have fought for her land and her child.

****

"Hannibal," the storyteller intoned dramatically, "crossed the Alps with thirty-seven war elephants. He fought the Romans again and again, killing them at every battle. By the end, he was an old man, with only one eye. His men were old too, or dead, or they betrayed him for Roman riches." The dark-haired man paused for emphasis. "Many years had passed and almost everyone who had crossed the mountains with him was dead. Can anyone guess how many elephants he had at the end?"

Dapyx looked to her in askance. She had heard of Hannibal before, but never in such detail. The Gaulish storyteller was clever, telling of Roman defeats at a time like this.

"I don't know," she whispered. A few people, not all children, shouted out guesses. The storyteller held his hand up for silence.

"One," the storyteller said. "A single beast, a mean old Syrian named Saurus from the deserts. He was an ornery bastard, and had only one tusk. The other was lost in battle, and some say it broke off in the walls of Rome itself, one misty morning."

Despite herself, Rowanna felt captivated by the story. She could see the fog and walls looming up behind them. Before them, angry elephants snorted and tossed their heads impatiently. The dark warriors of Hannibal waited for their chance to remove the Romans from the world. If only they'd succeeded!

"Saurus wore a red cloth and carried a red shield, because all who saw him knew that he was Hannibal's own mount. He lasted longer than his master, old Saurus did. In fact," the storyteller's voice lowered until he was speaking in a stage-whisper, "some say he's still out there, looking for Romans to kill."

Someone blew a trumpet loudly from behind them. Dapyx jumped, which was fortunate since he didn't notice that his mother was equally startled.

"Can we go see the elephants?" her son asked, when the laughter had died down and the storyteller's assistant was passing through the crowd looking for tips. Rowanna had a coin in her hand and laughter on her lips when she saw them.

The horn had been blown not as part of the story, but by a returning war band. It was unusual for them to be back so soon. Had something gone wrong? Rowanna rushed to them, and screamed.

Brasus had returned. What was left of him, anyway. One of his hands and both his feet were gone, and he was burned across his body. He lay on a wicker stretcher, carried by two of her neighbors. They were on the street, some distance away from the crowd gathered around the storyteller.

"Come to me," she said to Dapyx. "Come and see what they have done to us."

As her son walked to her, she became convinced this was a dream. She turned to her husband. Though he could barely breathe, he gripped her hand with his one remaining limb. There was no strength left in his body. His mouth moved, forming words, but there was no air to aid him. Within moments, his body fell still forever. Beside him lay the spear of his father. "He wanted you to have it," the man next to her said as he saw her looking at it.

"What happened?" she said. Dapyx was beside her, staring in shock at the corpse of his father. Behind her, the people were laughing at more of the storyteller's antics.

"The damn legion surprised us. They got past the forts and ambushed us. We should have had more men in the passes. We had not even set up camp when we ran into them. They rolled burning balls of fire through the forest, right into our ranks. Brasus was near the front, as always. He never even saw it coming."

"You live." It was not quite an accusation.

"We killed them, killed them all, but we lost some good men. Brasus meant a lot to us all, that's why Diurpaneus let us bring him back. He's chasing them out of the country already. He wasn't ready for them, but we know the sly dog. He'll get them." He trailed off as the look on Rowanna's face struck him. "We'll kill them all. We'll get vengeance on them for you."

She wasn't listening. She grabbed Dapyx's hand so hard that he squealed in pain, and pulled him to see the remnants of his father. She did not know what her son would do, but his little face set into a hard expression. "Let me go with them," he said, "let me avenge my father."

"Not yet," Rowanna said, "the time is coming, but you are not ready yet."

"When will I be?" he asked.

"When you no longer have to ask your mother for permission first."

The trumpet behind them blew once more, and Rowanna found herself wondering how a Roman legion would fare against elephants. What she wouldn't give to find old Saurus and ride him into battle like the mighty Hannibal himself. For now, though, she had her son to think about. He did not know it yet, but his childhood had ended today.

CHAPTER VIII

Rome: 83 CE, Autumn

The official didn't even look at Felix as he took his equipment, carefully ticking each item as he received it. Two Red faction guards loomed behind him, and slaves were closely watched to ensure they did not steal anything. Felix handed the items over, one piece after the other: helmet, shin guards, leather breastplate, a sweaty red jersey, a whip, and his *falx*. He was left only with his sweaty, dusty toga.

Felix scowled as the crowd roared above. This far below the Circus, it was muted but clear, like distant thunder. He rubbed his body down with oil, removing most of the stench, and entered the large door that led into the Red Faction's quarters. They could do near-everything in these quarters; train, eat, sleep, bathe, fuck, piss, and shit. When the next races began, the chambers would rumble and vibrate as the chariots passed overhead. It had been a distracting sound at first, but he was growing to like it. It reassured him.

Several Red faction *aurigae* were preparing for later matches. They were all young, for two reasons. *Aurigae* needed to be tall, but light. Teens fit that profile perfectly. Secondly, chariot racing was a dangerous sport. Very few survived it for more than a year or two.

As he entered, his friend Italicus was waiting for him. Italicus was of a similar age to Felix, and one of the only young racers who consistently beat him. His own race would be later that day, amongst stronger competition.

"Great race, Felix," Italicus said. "This is your best finish yet in the Circus, before the Emperor."

"Second place be damned in a pool of four racers, only three of whom finished. Twenty sesterces. Bah," Felix said. It was an amount that would have boggled his mind only a few years ago. "I will get little of the purse, regardless, but to have had Caesar himself witness my victory? It was an ill day."

"At least you finished the race, amicus. I saw what happened to the white driver. He was lucky to survive, and will owe his master a new chariot, and remember—it was Pharnaces who beat you. I have not bested him yet myself."

Pharnaces, like all chariot racers, was *infames*, a slave of low cast, but he grew more famous with each passing day. Already, there were billboards throughout the city with his face. His horses were always of the highest pedigree, with champions on both sides of the family. He was seen about town with women far above his station.

"Pharnaces is a fraud," Felix said. "He risks much with his tight turns, and those will come back to haunt him, and his advantages. With steeds such as his, I could win all matches…"

"He has earned those horses, friend. He was like me, like you, not long ago. There is much to learn from a man like Pharnaces," Italicus said. "I used to race with him, you know."

"Bah," Felix waved him away. Italicus was right, but was in no mood to hear it. It was time for a soak, he decided, brushing the sweaty hair from his face. Like many *aurigae*, he had adopted the Greek style of long hair. Hyacinthus thought it was a sign of Greek superiority, but then Hyacinthus thought everything was a sign of Greek superiority. Felix had asked him to watch the matches today, but he suspected the large man had not made it. Not only did the Greek not enjoy the Circus, he was busy working on one of his experiments. Of late, he would talk of nothing else but his inventions. He aimed to be another Archimedes.

In truth, he did not see much of the Greek man anymore. Since Felix had won his first competition at the inaugural games of the Flavian amphitheatre three years ago, he had done little other than race. He'd been sold twice. His current owner owned many *aurigae*, and it was rumored he owned slaves in all four factions. Felix had met the man two or three times, but like his compatriots, he lived at the training grounds not far from the Circus.

Felix stretched and headed towards the baths, which were located closer to the entrance. He passed the stable-master, who was eating his midday meal from a couch on the edge of the room. He caught Felix's eye and waved him over. Across from him sat an old man. Felix scowled as he noted the man's presence.

Felix walked toward the stable-master and his dining

companion. "Salve, *equos nutriebat*." He glared at the old man. "And you, magician. I paid you many sesterces, near half my winnings, and yet, there was no curse cast on Pharnaces!"

"I did curse him, his horses, his chariot, and the ground beneath him," the old man said mildly. "He was protected. The blue magician is powerful."

Felix was too angry to speak. The old man was good for nothing, but he would still gladly collect money from all the *aurigae* of the red Faction. The man was, or claimed to be, a Druid from Britannia. That was old magic, strong magic. "His horses were too fast. Did you not poison them, you fraud?" Felix asked.

The old man looked to the *equos nutriebat*. "Must I go through this every time a brazen youth loses?"

The stable-master nodded. "Felix, you did well. No one has come so close to beating Pharnaces, but insulting your team negates that credit."

Felix sighed. He always tried to stay in control but of late, he increasingly found himself growing angry.

He took three deep breaths. "My apologies, druid, *equos nutriebat*. I spoke from emotion and disappointment. War brings out my emotions."

"Good," said the stable master, "but you are wrong. It is not permitted to blunder twice in war. Tonight, we can discuss the four mistakes you made. Pharnaces only made two of them, which is why he won."

****

Felix leaned back and scrubbed his back without thought. He was racing in his mind, taking the corners tighter and driving more aggressively. He wished he'd gotten close enough to use his *falx*. Without realizing it, he sighed heavily.

"Cheer up," Italicus said. He had joined Felix in the baths soon after the boy's arrival. They'd left the compound which had its own small but simple bathhouse and sat in a large public bath. There were several other men in the baths, but they were older men of no faction. "There's plenty going on in the world apart from your race, you know," he said.

"I'm in the mood for good news. Tell me."

"The Senate has added an African Senator. The first black

politician ever to serve. We live in a modern time, amicus."

"This is supposed to cheer me?" He scrubbed at his back, frowning at the unexpected effort.

"You are from Africa. Do you not feel some emotion toward that kindred spirit?" Italicus was laughing.

"Not much. Here, all are Roman," Felix said. The bath had done little to cleanse his foul mood. "Still, you implied tidings of more import."

"Idle gossip is now of no interest to you? That race must have affected you more than I thought. The real news is guaranteed to improve your mood."

"Has Pharnaces caught syphilis?" Felix asked.

Italicus smiled. "Not that I know of. But this is almost as good. You remember what happened to Afer?"

Felix shuddered, and glanced reflectively down at his penis. *Still there*. He'd seen Afer two days after it had happened. They had gotten drunk together, until Felix had enough courage to ask.

"It was horrible," Afer had said, drinking deeply from his wine. "The worst thing that has ever happened to me. And I was born a slave—I didn't have the golden free years that you did."

"My early years were spent starving in the desert, surrounded by maniacs. Slaves are spoiled compared to that," Felix had complained. "But," he had lowered his voice, "did it really happen?"

"It really did," Afer had said, drinking more wine. "He crushed my balls with his big pink fingers. So hard I thought they might pop. Fuck it hurt!"

He had another drink. Then another and he had continued. "He had an old knife. Old but sharp as Cicero. Only a little bit rusty. With my balls scrunched up, he just chopped them right off. Didn't even let me get drunk first."

Felix could feel his own jewels clenching in sympathy.

"It could have been worse," Afer said. "Afterward, they told me sometimes they take a slave, cut off the balls and then his cock too. The next day, they make him drink water."

"Drink water?" Felix repeated, slow to reach comprehension. "Why?"

"So much water that he bursts and pees a new hole. That or he dies," Afer said. "At least I've still got my cock."

Someday, you'll be fucked by half the noble women in Rome, Felix thought. A handsome, sterile slave was in high demand. Still, he did not begrudge his friend the slightest. The image of that blackened and bloody member was never going to leave him.

"Yes, I remember. I never should have asked him to show me." Felix said to Italicus, unconsciously shaking his head in rejection of the memory. "It was horrible."

"I saw it too. He's still lucky to have his shaft. The good news is that we won't ever have to worry about that. The Emperor has banned castration for slaves."

"Truly? Why have I not heard?"

"It was only announced this morning," Italicus said.

"Caesar is a great man, the greatest Emperor since Augustus." A thought struck Felix. "But who will the matrons use to please them?"

"Maybe they'll need some handsome, famous *aurigae* to sate their lust."

"Maybe. Pity they will end up with you instead," Felix said.

Felix grabbed his testes and whooped. Italicus joined him. The old men in the bathhouse stared at them with mild disapproval, but the two cheered even louder.

Their laughter died as the famous Pharnaces entered the bathhouse. He had a faction-mate on either side of him—both competent racers in their own right but clearly hanger-ons. He glanced at the two charioteers in the bath and stiffened. A smile slowly spread across his face.

He undressed and splashed into the pool, right next to Italicus and Felix.

"Did I hear you talking about castration?" he said. "Fitting conversation topic for men with no cocks." His friends slid in beside him.

Felix felt he had no patience for this. His anger, so strong earlier, had faded, sunk away to the deeps of the pool. "You raced well today, Pharnaces."

The older boy laughed in shock, trading unbelieving glances with his friends. "Of course I did. I don't need second-rate amateurs to comment on my ability."

"Gods, Pharnaces," Italicus said. "Three years ago you weren't such a prick. Does it only take a little Roman cunny to change you?"

"I don't know. I've never only gotten a little Roman cunny." His friends laughed. His face did not so much as crack a smile. "Why don't you leave now? I don't want my water dirtied by red factioners."

"We were just leaving," Felix said. He still felt no anger. Or rather, any anger he felt was buried beneath a weary sadness. There was no need for this aggression, not now. The very idea of factions suddenly seemed divisive and unnecessary to him. What would it take for humans to join together?

"Oh no," Italicus said. Felix felt suddenly like he was looking into a mirror. "Am I not good enough to be your friend anymore? Is Felix here not good enough either? You act like you're high and mighty, but I remember when you wet yourself before your first battle. Ever tell any of your new friends about that?"

He stood, fists clenched. "I think you were right, Felix. Apologies. Italicus is a miserable bastard."

At that, all three of the others stood up.

"Mithras," Felix hissed. He glanced to the other men bathing, but seeing the violence unfold they had quickly departed. They had, wisely, probably anticipated a turn of events when rival factions had shown up in the same place. He did not feel Italicus' burning anger, but he did not want to lose to Pharnaces again.

"You are a failure," Pharnaces said. "A waste of life, a slave and a dog. Get them."

At his words, his companions advanced. The struggle was as brief as it was one-sided. Pharnaces and his faction mates were older, bigger, and stronger. Soon Italicus and Felix were restrained. Pharnaces watched, and then impassively said, "Dunk them."

Both went under beneath strong hands. Italicus struggled and thrashed but Felix merely held his breath. It was not so hard. Still, moment after moment fled and his head began to ache. His lungs compressed, eagerly hoping for air and getting nothing.

At some unheard instruction, the red faction mates were dragged up. Then, a brief hoarded breath later, dunked again. This continued to happen, and Felix lost all track of consciousness, until at last they were brought up for good. Italicus looked awful—red faced, eyes lolling, and water dribbling from his mouth. Felix suspected he didn't look much better himself.

"...not ever want to see you in here again," Pharnaces was saying. It was difficult to hear. "Not here, not anywhere where I, or your betters are. Understand?"

All he could do was nod. Felix did so, miserably. Beside him, Italicus vomited into the pool.

They stumbled out of the baths, arm in arm. All Felix could think about was what a waste it had all been. Why couldn't they all just have been friends?

PART II: THE DEAD WALK

CHAPTER IX

Dacia: 88 CE, Autumn

 Rowanna's buttocks had grown numb and cold. She had been sitting in the massive apple tree for the best part of a day, and no amount of shifting could now prevent her arse from aching. Her eyes ached with weariness, but the woman hadn't dared sleep for more than a handful of moments. Sleeping was too risky--to sleep was to fall, and to fall was to meet death—and worse.

The forest was silent as she listened. No birds sang or trilled. No squirrels played in the branches or buried food. All had fled from the lifeless menace. Rowanna said a prayer of thanks to Zalmoxis, grateful once more that *they* could not climb. She pressed her back into the comforting safety of the trunk behind her, and then glanced down to the base of the tree.

Those unliving demons were below her, at the base of the trunk. Waiting. As she watched them, one raised its ruined face to her, staring with blank white eyes. Its face, smeared with coagulated blood, sickened her. Her stomach was a broiling pit of fear and revulsion.

Three days ago, no one had ever heard of these monsters, and then, as if by magic, they had appeared. A crawling, dreadful, menace lurking in their midst. The news of two destroyed villages had reached them yesterday, while the morning mists still hung on the mountains. She had still lived with her son just outside Sarmizegetusa, in one of several makeshift villages on the edge of the large city. Men from her village had joined a larger contingent of warriors from the city. Her son Dapyx had been chosen to join them; his first such honor. He was the only child of four that had survived his first year. He had been a beautiful boy and had grown to be a tall fifteen year-old man. It hadn't occurred to anyone that this wasn't some new perversion from the Romans. The memory of the legions burning towns and villages was less than a year old.

She shook as she recalled how brightly he had smiled that morning, only a day ago, only a lifetime ago. His pride had been a glowing nimbus suffusing his body with light and honor, but it was no match for hers, little though had he known it. They were the wolf-people; warriors and hunters without peer. As her son grasped his spear tightly, she felt a sense of fulfillment stronger than any she'd ever had before. She saw in him his father, who had died years earlier fighting the Romans.

The men marched away, singing and laughing. The day dragged for those left behind, as they waited for tidings. By the time the war party returned, the sun was sinking behind the mountains and the air had grown chill. Rowanna hurried with several others to the edge of the village to await them, but as the men came into sight, the women stopped short.

Warriors had left in the sunshine, and in the gathering gloom, a nightmare had returned. Bloody, twitching corpses of men, some they knew and some strangers, shambled menacingly into the village. They moved disjointedly, emitting low moans as they shuffled closer. Dogs throughout the village barked in alarm. The woman next to Rowanna gasped.

"Their eyes. What's wrong with their eyes?" she asked.

Rowanna had heard her, but she wasn't listening. She stared in horror, unable to accept the creeping truth. Dapyx had come home. Rowanna had screamed when she saw, in the torchlight, his vapid bloody face. His eyes were completely devoid of pupils, were just white beacons of forlorn hunger. She had screamed his name, as all of the women were screaming.

Men too old or frail to have been on the raid appeared suddenly at their side. They were armed with axes, spears, and swords. Even this far from the border, years of the warring had taught them to be ready for a fight at any time. They stepped forward uncertain, but defiant. If these creatures who had been friends and family meant them harm, they too would find what it meant to confront the wolf people.

Rowanna had little time to feel relief. The men quickly discovered that their weapons did not hurt their foe. The village cooper was overwhelmed by the lifeless creatures and they dragged him to the ground. They began to eat him as he screamed in anger and fear. Rowanna looked on in horror as Dapyx drew closer to her. Terror rooted her to the ground.

Dapyx was coming for her and her alone. Whatever had happened to him, he still recognized her. He moved slowly and she realized that part of his foot was gone. Flesh and bone poked out of a ruined boot that was roughly hewn, as though it had been chewed off. She had cried then as the blacksmith leapt before her. He had a long spear in his hand.

"Run!" he cried to the motionless women. He stabbed powerfully with his spear into Dapyx's heart.

"No!" she screamed, and she wasn't sure who she was speaking to. The other women were running away, but she remained transfixed on the scene before her.

Her son walked through the spear, the point bursting through his back. He then proceeded to grab the man who had stabbed him and take a large bite of his face. With a roar, the blacksmith had pushed the spear deeper into the boy and flung him away. Then he'd fallen, moaning, to the ground. His hands were clasped to his head.

She leaped to the blacksmith. The bite had been impossibly deep and she could see grey pulpy bits of brain leaking through his fingers and out on the earth. Her son was several feet away, still on the ground but struggling to rise. More of the shambling wretches drew closer.

"Gratias," she whispered to the blacksmith. She then drew his knife. She stood with it held before her, challenging the monsters. She meant to fight them with it, and die gloriously. Then a better idea struck her. She cut the smith's throat, ending his agony. With that, her courage deserted her and she ran.

Without thought or reason, she ran from that which should not exist. There were more shambling creatures coming from Sarmizegetusa and she realized that anywhere with people was a danger. There was only one place she could think of, and she ran, as behind her, blood spilled and the dark of night settled upon the land.

****

Rowanna shuddered against the great trunk of the apple tree. She had always thought herself brave. But yesterday she had learned otherwise. When confronted by those abominations, she had run away, away from the song of death and violence. She had returned home to reclaim the one thing of value she owned, and then carrying the spear that had belonged to her husband, Brasus, she fled. Stumbling and tripping, she buried herself deep in the forests at the slope of the mountains. At last she had come across this ancient apple tree that she knew well. Her family had enjoyed many fruits from these branches over the years. When she was younger, she had slept on the grass beneath the tree and it felt safe. The lowest branches were higher than a grown man's length, but she had always been a good climber.

Rowanna had been exhausted by the time she had found the tree, but some instinct had told her to get off the ground. Placing the spear against the trunk, she jumped to the bottom branch and pulled herself up. She had fallen asleep, wearier than she could ever recall, with her head resting on a branch and her body pressed between two branches. The ground was littered with fallen fruit and the smell of apples was around her as she dreamed.

The aching woman awoke in the morning and barely stifled a scream. The creatures had followed her, slowly, menacingly, impeccably. As the sun rose, she caught sight of some that had stumbled into the clearing below her. She didn't know if they could smell, but they had a hunger so intense it could devour the world. It was only a little surprising when the monster that had been Dapyx, limped after her in the wan morning light. His chest had a hole so large she could see where his ribs had been snapped backwards.

Trapped. She had climbed higher up the tree. The leaves were changing, on the verge of dropping, but for now, it was still hard to see through them. When she peered through them, her heart beat faster. There were at least a dozen of the dead down there, milling about. Some scratched at the tree trunk, and one tried to bite it, but it was made of an armor they could not pierce with teeth and nail. So, they waited, waited for her with the patience of the dead.

The pale thing that had been her son was still staring at her.

She rubbed at her sore buttocks, thankful she didn't have any splinters. Picking an apple, she threw it down at the creature watching her. It hit it in the head and bounced off. The thing didn't even notice. Rowanna sighed.

Whatever happened, she wasn't going to give them the chance to kill her. She certainly wasn't going to become one of them. She stabbed the knife deep into the tree. It was no good against the monsters, but might be useful still if she could escape them. Her eyes closed wearily as she brooded.

Some time later, her eyes opened. A need even more immediate than survival had awoken her, and was pressing at her bladder even as she crawled out on the branch. Several of the walking dead were below her. Rowanna squatted carefully, balancing, hanging onto a branch above her, and emptied her bladder. The amber fluid hit one directly and splashed two others, but they paid it no more attention than they had the apple core, but the one with piss in its eyes stumbled, and fell. She felt somewhat better, discovering this small way to fight back. She was of the wolf people.

Then, unhurt, the creature slowly rose and moaned softly. The others started moaning too, in a nightmarish chorus. Dapyx's voice was unrecognizable, but she knew he was part of the eerie ensemble. Fear assaulted her deep in her body. Rowanna crept up carefully and moved back towards the trunk. She leaned against the sturdy base and ate an apple. Then she ate two more. Her stomach growled at her. She would need some real food soon.

The creature that had been her child stood there, mouth gaping stupidly, chest gaping stupidly. She laughed aloud as she watched the ridiculous creature that had, ages ago, been her son. Her laughter rang through the forest. She grabbed onto the branch above her and braced herself as she kept laughing. Her feet dangled below her and she swung them back and forth. The creatures were all watching her, alert to her sound, but they could do nothing but stare.

"Stop looking at me!" she screamed. Bloody faces and vacant stares. She realized that she'd go mad if she stayed up here for much longer. Perhaps madness was a blessing. Perhaps it had already happened.

Something was moving on the tree. Rowanna flinched, fearful that a creature had somehow climbed up. The yellow leaves rustled and she relaxed. A squirrel climbed along a branch and moved toward her. She relaxed for a moment and then sat straight up.

Something was wrong.

The squirrel was missing a piece of its back, and the hole was surrounded by blood soaked fur. Its little rodent eyes were completely white. Rowanna screamed and swung her foot up and around the branch, booting the animal off onto the ground below. It landed with a thump and skittered away. Rowanna's heart beat quickly as she watched it disappear. Things were worse than she had thought. Whatever this curse was, it affected animals too.

****

The moon was high and night air freezing when she awoke. Rowanna's bladder was full again. It seemed that apples were better at quenching her thirst than satiating her hunger. She crawled carefully in the blackness along the branch. Her hands found the branch above her head and she clung as she carefully adjusted her clothing.

She sighed as the liquid flowed down onto the ground. It was too dark to see if she was hitting one of the lifeless or the ground. As the pressure on her bladder ceased, she shifted to be sure she didn't splash on her foot. Her left foot slipped and her balance was lost. Her hands tightened on the branch above her as her foot swung out over open air. She pushed herself backwards, trying to get back onto the branch.

Crack.

She fell backward, into the darkness. Her hands held onto the branch, but it no longer held onto the tree. She fell through branches and leaves and landed awkwardly. Her ankle landed on a round apple and cracked with the impact. Pain seared brightly through her body. She couldn't afford to think about injuries though, as low moaning alerted her to the presence of the lifeless.

Below the tree, away from the leaves, enough star and moonlight filtered down that she could make out the dark shapes. One form was in front of the others. It reached out with shadow hands, its white eyes reflecting white moonbeams.

Rowanna swung the branch in her hand with all her force. It slammed into the side of the undead creature's head with a sickening crunch. The thing collapsed onto the ground but almost instantly started crawling towards her.

There were groans coming from behind her. Suppressing her fear, she snarled and spun around on her good foot.

The creature that had been creeping behind her was too close for her to swing the impromptu spear again, so she jabbed fiercely toward its face. The broken, jagged branch end jammed into the creature's eye. It kept walking, hands full of need as it reached for her. As its fingers brushed her, she pushed the branch further into its eye. Its white eyes dimmed and the thing collapsed heavily, wrenching the wooden weapon from Rowanna. Through her fear, she felt an unbearable sense of loss and sadness.

Fingers grabbed at her foot as the crawling thing reached her. Other creatures loomed closer, moaning forlornly. She wished for her knife, but it was high away, sitting uselessly in the tree, and there was no way she had the time to extract her spear. Her only hope was to get back to her tree. She leaned down and scooped up a rotting apple.

Ignoring the pain splintering her ankle, she leaped through two of the shambling creatures. She slammed the apple into the one on the right's forehead. The flesh of the juice and fruit streamed into its eyes and it stupidly swung its arms through the air, temporarily blinded.

The other could see perfectly well, however. A cold hand grasped her hair, holding her in place. Its other hand reached for her face. The creatures, all of them, were coming for her. Rowanna was not going to be a meal for these blighted monsters. With a wrench, she tore away from the hold. She cried out in pain as she left a handful of hair in the thing's grip, but she had made it.

The Dacian woman leaped as high as she could from her good foot. Her scrambling fingers found purchase and she pulled herself up, panting from exertion.

Behind her, the white-eyed abominations reached the tree trunk and clumsily reached for her. Rowanna snarled at them in defiance. She stared in surprise at the sight before her. Her body was scratched and bruised, her ankle aching, a patch of her scalp bleeding, but her eyes shone with feverish joy in the moonlight air. The creature she had stabbed in the eye was still down. It was dead, it seemed, for good. For the first time since it had begun, she had a purpose. She had a knowledge that must be passed on, and she had learned how to kill that which was already dead.

There was only one thing bothering her, scurrying at the back of her skull, but she would have to wait until morning even to consider that. She leaned back against the trunk and fell asleep almost instantly.

****

The next day arrived, wrapped in mists and drizzling moisture. Rowanna shivered from the cold, but the leaves above her kept her mostly dry when it did rain. She couldn't see much of anything in the grey fog, but perhaps that was for the best. She could still hear the creatures below her as they moaned softly.

She leaned back into the tree and examined her ankle. It hurt with stiff pain and the skin had turned a deep purple. She didn't think it was broken, as the bones felt attached still. Her stomach growled and she sighed in frustration. She had to get out of this tree. She understood how to kill these monsters now, but could barely walk. She was unsure she could kill them quickly enough, to keep them all away. She climbed up the tree, slowly, keeping the weight off her injured ankle, and found the knife she had taken from the blacksmith. She needed to get Brasus' spear, but did not dare venture back to the ground.

As the day brightened and warmed, the niggling concern that had occurred to her the night before returned. She moved on her stomach down the branch, holding tight to her support.

It didn't take long. She had to hack off some of the leaves below her, but she got a pretty clear picture. The lifeless creature she had stabbed in the eye was still lying in the cold earth. His back was still torn open from the wound the blacksmith had given him. Dapyx. She screamed with anger, rage, pain, and sadness.

She didn't know how long she sat there, staring at the ground until everything blurred and lost focus. The emotions ran wild, like horses breaking free, and they were so powerful that she could not put a name on it.

When she looked up, moments or hours later, she heard a great crashing through the forest. Someone was shouting, too, but they were too far away for her to hear the words. She hadn't heard any of the lifeless speak. She leaned and glanced into the forest, looking for signs of another survivor.

She slowly turned around and crawled back up the branch. Only then did she decide to yell back.

It didn't take long. Only moments after she shouted, a portly, bearded man ran into the clearing. She peered intently at his face. He had pupils. She was nearly certain that he had pupils. He stopped short as the lifeless beneath her tree registered his presence. The creatures shambled into motion, came towards him.

"Help," he cried, "where are you?"

"I'm up here," Rowanna shouted. The man was lumbering slowly. His hands were bundled with packages.

There were too many of the lifeless between the man and the apple tree. One was still crawling from the attack the night before. "They're behind me too," he called helplessly.

Without thinking, Rowanna swung down from the tree. She was only ten feet off the ground and she landed on her uninjured ankle, but it hurt badly. She found the spear and instantly stuck it through the back of a shambler. It collapsed jerkily.

"Come on," she yelled. "Climb the tree." Dapyx's body lay behind her, filling her mind.

"My hands are full," the man complained. "Help me."

She drove her spear through the mouth of an oncoming monster, pushing down on the haft and driving the point up until the light dimmed in its eyes.

"Drop it," she yelled.

"I can't," he responded, breathlessly, "these are too important."

She jabbed at heads and swung into their faces. They were slow and clumsy enough for even an immobile woman to kill them. Three, four, five and more undead fell to the ground. But more came, from other parts of the forest.

Rowanna used her weapon as a crutch, driving the point into the earth. She pushed back toward the tree and leaped onto the bottom branch, leaving her weapon behind. The portly man followed her, but did not climb up. His hands remained full, with what appeared to be a large leather case.

"Drop your things," she yelled. "Climb up."

"I cannot. Take them. Take them now," he said, reaching the case toward her. The creatures were closing in on him. Rowanna leaned down to grab at it, but he was nowhere close enough.

"If it's not worth your life, give it up," she told him. How had this foolish man survived this long?

The man looked nervously over his shoulder and dropped his things. He scrambled clumsily up the tree. One of the lifeless reached for his foot, but the man pulled himself up the tree in time. He was covered in sweat and breathing hard.

"My elixirs are gone. They had better stay safe down there."

"It doesn't matter. I can kill them," she said, her voice breaking rocks.

"I think … I think I can cure them," he said.

She stared at him, tough exterior crumbling. "There's…there's a cure?"

He nodded proudly. "I think so."

Rowanna didn't cry. There were no tears left. Her eyes closed and she shook, as images of Dapyx flooded through her head and the boy sucking at her breast, taking his first steps, growing into a young warrior.

Her eyes snapped open. The bearded man was staring at the creatures at the base of the tree.

"How can this be possible?" she asked.

"Just look," he said softly.

Below them, one of the lifeless was ransacking the man's case. It pulled out a small vial filled with blue liquid. It dropped it into its mouth and bit down on the glass. Even from their high seats, they could hear glass crunching.

"Ouch," Rowanna said.

"Don't worry. I don't think it can't feel anything. But look," the man said.

A heartbeat passed, then two. The creature, one of the warriors of Sarmizegetusa, dropped to the ground and began writhing. Its skin slowly darkened, and its eyes—shiny and white—suddenly had brown pupils again.

"By Zalmoxis!" Rowanna said.

"Friend, come to the tree if you want to live," the bearded man called to the prone man below them.

The man stared up in confusion. "What?" he asked. Blood leaked out of his mouth.

The other lifeless had noticed something unusual however. There were only four left, after so many had been killed, but all four were heading to the prone man.

"Hurry," called the bearded man, "they're coming."

The man stared stupidly at them. He shook his head, driving away dark dreams, and began to rise.

The first of the lifeless reached him.

"Oh no!" Rowanna whispered in horror. She reached for her knife and cursed as she realized she couldn't reach them in time.

The lifeless grasped the man's head with each hand and lowered its mouth onto the man's skull. He began to scream, but the others reached him. One ate his arm, while two more went for his stomach and tore through flesh to reach organs. His screams did not last long. Rowanna and the man watched the scene in grim silence, both aware that no words were appropriate for the moment. When it was done, and the lifeless had shambled away, the man spoke.

"I am Zuste, an alchemist from Sarmizegetusa. Apologies for the belated greeting."

"I am Rowanna, also from Sarmizegetusa—well, from Cotiso, just outside."

Zuste nodded. "I know it well, or I did. There's not much left of it now."

"What about Sarmizegetusa?" she asked.

He shook his head. "There were some people in there. But there were a lot of … those as well."

"How did you end up here?"

He stared into the distance, chewing on his fingernail.

"I am making for Tapae," he said at last. "It's a few days' march, so maybe they haven't reached it yet, and it should be well defended, regardless. With luck, Diurpaneus will be there. If anyone can fight these menaces, it will be him."

"Do you have more potions in there?"

"I believe so. If they haven't broken."

"You can cure them, and I can kill them. We shall make for Tapae."

The decision came easily to them and they set off a few hours later, laden with apples and the intact vials. Rowanna was hobbling on her good ankle. Around them, the forest crawled with lifeless, and behind them, beneath the apple tree, lay Dapyx, his dead body moldering into the earth.

CHAPTER X

Rome: 88 CE, Summer

When Calvinus Plautius rushed into his room, Rufus was in bed with three Iberian women. None of them were wearing clothing and the Senator, at least, was badly hung-over.

Plautius stopped awkwardly. "Apologies, Senator. But we must talk."

With great effort, Rufus opened one eye. "Cocks and cunts, man. Unless Vesuvius has blown again, I think it can wait." His hands sought out a woman's breast—in the tangle of bodies, it was hard to tell which woman it belonged to.

Plautius cleared his throat but did not leave.

"Is it a fucking volcano, Plautius?" Gaius Rufus asked. As he did, a dark-haired woman slipped under the blankets. The blanket near Rufus' groin started rising up and down with the movements of her head. Rufus moaned hoarsely.

"No, Senator. It's not a volcano. It's just that Proculus has left the city. Hours ago. I only just learned."

"Proculus?" said the blonde woman. "That old ass? My friends and I are much more

fun."

Rufus looked at her. "You know who Proculus is?"

She giggled. "Everyone in Rome has heard of him. Even those who just arrived."

"Bugger that old warmonger! Of all mornings, he picks this one?" Rufus sighed and begrudgingly moved the woman's mouth off his cock, and disentangled from the other two. He raised, nude, into the antechamber and forgoing his toga, instead, dressed in an airy tunica. It was the sort favored by proletarians, shopkeepers, and slaves. He handed another to Plautius.

"Get changed." Rufus tied his shirt up with a simple belt.

The aide looked at the simple tunic with dismay. "I'll look like a poor equite."

"That's the idea," Rufus said. "No hint of our status must be shown." Turning back to the women, he said, "Stay here a while. We'll have fun when I come back."

After they had moved out of his rooms, Rufus summoned his guards. "Those women inside, they're not to leave my chambers alive. Don't fuck them first either. There can be no chance of them talking."

The soldier nodded grimly and moved to the door. Plautius said nothing, but his face showed disapproval. "You presume much," Rufus said. "The gods have pierced my head with a thousand spears, my balls turn blue from lack of finish, and you come bursting in with a name that cannot be said. There are consequences to actions." He strode to the door with a determined stride.

As the two men moved into the city, Plautius caught Rufus up on the situation. A litter would be too conspicuous, so they requested two horses from stables just outside the city. Within an hour of Plautius' interruption, they were galloping north.

Gaius Cilnius Proculus had risen greatly in favor in Rome during the last year. He had spent years in Britannia, of all places, then returned to Rome to ever-increasing favor. He had even reached the consulship last year. Rufus now understood the indignation he'd been confronted with when he'd been the outsider welcomed into the inner circle, but, he told himself, it wasn't jealousy or spite that guided his actions today. It was hope.

The slaves were busy harvesting in the golden autumn air. Most of them grew grapes, as wine was far more valuable than food, but they passed farms of wheat, willow plantations, olive orchards, beehives and acorn woodlands. Rufus himself owned a few snail farms that made him a good deal of money, but they were much further north of the city. He realized he hadn't even seen them and decided to visit them when he had a chance.

They stopped at an inn for midday meal, where they ate shoulder of hare and drank two flagons of wine. Not long after, the pair exchanged their mounts at the attached stable and rode on. Two hours after lunch, at a crossroads, they turned east. The farms grew larger, more removed from the road. The few slaves they saw were exotic. Thracian, Egyptian, and Parthians worked these fields.

These lands, further from Rome, were owned by ex-soldiers rather than Senators, and stocked with slaves they'd won in far-away wars.

The late afternoon had fully arrived when Rufus slowed his horse and turned to Plautius. "It would be a hell of a ride if we didn't catch him," he shouted over the hooves beating on the granite roads.

"We'll catch him. He's riding in a litter, and shouldn't be expecting trouble."

"He's a Senator and a consul. He wouldn't be alive if he wasn't always expecting trouble."

"He'll have guards," Plautius said.

"Indeed. Four of them. Two are mine. One will be delaying them throughout the day, and the other will remember my posting inn when it grows dark. They will, naturally, be an asset when it comes to later events."

Plautius nodded thoughtfully. The two men continued to ride.

They arrived at the posting-inn in the waning hours of daylight. Long ago, it had been a popular place to stop. Then Vespasian had stopped there and suddenly died. It had fallen into disuse, but not disrepair. It still had every appearance of an operating inn, though it smelled of dust and sour wine. Rufus had purchased it through enough intermediaries that it couldn't be traced back to him.

There was another inn further up the road to Ravenna, which was six or seven hours away. Rufus wondered how his agent would direct Proculus here. "Tie the horses up," he told Plautius. "And remain out here with them. Do not be seen."

Rufus entered the inn and lit the sconces. In the center of the room sat a dusty table. Stacked on the back of the table were several stacked piles of wood. Next to it were two amphorae of olive oil. Rufus sat down at the dusty table, chin resting on his hands. His thoughts had been digesting during the ride, and he thought he had a good idea now.

Gaius Proculus had left the city early in the morning. He no doubt assumed that no one had seen him. That meant only one thing—Domitian had summoned him to the warfront, to Dacia.

Proculus would set sail from the harbor at Classe, just outside Ravenna.

The situation in Dacia was dire, to be sure. That war had gone poorly. Last year, the Roman forces had been ambushed by screaming Dacian warriors. It had been a massacre. They'd lost their war machines, their flags, and their general was captured and killed. It was the least successful venture by the Roman legions in living memory. Worse, taxes at home had increased and both Domitian and the Senators faced increasingly unhappy plebs.

Rufus had been against the war. They didn't need anything from Dacia. He had particularly been against appointing that Praetorian buffoon, Cornelius Fuscus as commander of the legions. Logically, when both had gone poorly, he should have received thanks, but logic was becoming an increasingly scant commodity for the Emperor. Gaius Proculus was a war monger and had risen high through his bellicose counsels. Domitian valued his consul with increasing consistency. That had to be stopped.

Killing Proculus was highly risky. If Rufus was even suspected, he'd be killed, slowly and horribly, but if he could achieve it, he would stifle a dangerous influence to the Emperor, help to end the war, and regain his own position with Domitian. It was a gamble he had to take.

The sound of hooves alerted him to his mission. The horse was galloping quickly. He remained with his back to the door, but slid his blade out and held it in his lap.

It took only a few moments. The door cracked open and shut as footsteps behind him sounded. He recognized the voice at once.

"I saw your horses and had to stop. I bear grave warning--" he stopped as Rufus turned around.

"Gaius Sulpicius Rufus," he stammered. The shock on his face couldn't have been more satisfying.

"Surprise," Rufus said. He stood, and let the sword swing before him.

"Listen to me," Proculus said, his voice shaking. Rufus realized that the old man was terrified. "We must put aside our quarrel."

"That would be convenient for you, wouldn't it," Rufus asked. He stepped closer to the man. "I have a better idea."

He raised the blade.

"You don't know what you're doing. They must be warned!" the man screamed. He turned to the door, but as he opened it, Rufus ran him through the back with his blade. After the body dropped, Rufus turned him over. Blood was leaking everywhere.

"It's not actually personal," Rufus said, lowering his head close to the ground. "This is for the good of Rome."

Proculus punched him in the jaw.

"You shit!" Rufus yelled. His sword hand reached down and he cut the man's throat. He watched as life fled from the man, then he pulled the body away from the door. He cleaned his blade on the man's toga before sheathing it. Building a small pyre took almost no time at all. He doused the body and much of the building with oil and pulled out his flint fire starter. It only needed a little tinder for the flames to leap out.

Rufus stepped from the inn into the cool night air. Plautius was waiting by the horses. Proculus' lathered horse was tethered next to the other two. Steam rose from the beast, rising into the night air.

"I thought he left in a litter," Rufus said.

"He did," Plautius said, "this morning. He arrived only on this beast."

"Alone?" Rufus asked. Plautius nodded. "Where have my guards gone?"

"He arrived alone. Do you think they suspected the plot?" Plautius asked.

"Perhaps. Yet he was quite surprised to see me. I believe he did not suspect." They never do, he thought, thinking regretfully of the energetic women he'd left in his chambers. And of faithful Plautius, hadn't the man realized how the events of this night must end?

A groan sounded behind them. Proculus was dead and burning, and the sound wasn't from the inn. It was from the road.

Something was wrong. Three men were coming over the road. They were perhaps Proculus' delayed guards, or maybe even travelers, but Rufus didn't think so. There was something wrong with how they moved. They walked not, but instead, shambled with a disjointed grace, as if puppets held by ungainly children.

"Light a torch, Plautius."

The man turned to his saddlebags and within seconds, smoky torchlight lit up the night.

The three continued to come closer. A night breeze blew, carrying dread and horror. The horses whinnied nervously.

One was tall, dark, and lean. His face was scarred and he had a sword hilt protruding from his heart. The second was even taller, light-skinned and bulky. Half of his left arm was missing, and his chest was punctured with spear wounds. The third looked Roman, with cruel, patrician features. He did not have any noticeable wounds. His mouth opened and he groaned again.

None of them had pupils in their eyes. "They're dead," Plautius whispered, beside him.

Rufus shuddered. "And yet not. Something terrible is before us."

The three creatures crossed the road in eerie unison. They moved with a deadly purpose that was incongruous with their jerky movements. One of the horses whinnied with fright.

Rufus still had his bloody sword in his hand. "Give me the torch, and draw your blade."

The creatures were only moments away. The broad one, with rings and jewels on its pale shoulders and arms, reached out for him.

Rufus struck out with his blade. It sliced into the outstretched hand, between the thumb and the nearest finger. The thing seemed not even to notice, and Rufus had to leap back to pull his sword free.

The lifeless creatures advanced. The Senator thrust out with the torch. The fire flickered around the thing's hand, but it wasn't hot enough to damage it.

Rufus backed up slowly, flame and blade held before him as a shield. This was a hopeless fight, but behind him were only untamed fields and a burning building.

Plautius screamed. Two of the monsters, the black one and the noble-looking one, had advanced on him. He struck out with his sword repeatedly, but could not fend off both of the things.

"Help," he cried, "for the love of Jupiter help me." Rufus stepped once toward him, but it was already too late. The dark creature grabbed his sword arm and bit deeply into the man's flesh.

The blade fell from Plautius' numb fingers. The other was beside him, reaching with fetid breath for the man's neck. It bit down hard and Plautius sagged, held up only by the two creatures feasting upon his flesh.

The roof of the inn collapsed suddenly as the fire grew. Bits of burning debris littered the surrounding radius. Rufus could feel the heat from where he stood, and then he knew what to do. He ran around the lifeless thing—they seemed blessedly slow—toward the inn. He tried not to listen to the sounds of Plautius being eaten, but the ripping and tearing sounds were impossible to ignore.

He reached the posting-inn. The building was burning intensely. Oppressive heat assailed him as smoke sailed high into the sky. He sheathed his sword and picked up a burning board. Two of the white-eyed monsters advanced upon him. The third, the dark one, was snapping apart the bones from Plautius' exposed ribcage, and searching for his heart.

The lifeless slowed as they grew closer to the heat. It was growing uncomfortably hot and he moved sideways, trying to keep the firebrand between himself and the creatures. Having two of them here was good, but the one eating his former aide was too close to the horses. Those beasts were the key to escape.

Rufus laid his burning board on the ground. He had to entice the third monster toward him. The other two immediately shambled toward him, as the third was gnawing on something bloody in its hands. It had discovered Plautius' heart, it appeared.

Rufus leaped back to the board and lifted it. Gods-be-damned, this was the worst plan for survival he had ever had. He swung around the two lifeless and ran, hoping they could not catch him from behind. He sprinted as fast as he ever had. The cruel-featured creature gnawing on Plautius' intestines did not look up until the Senator was three steps away. With both hands and all his strength, Rufus swung the board into the thing's head. He couldn't hurt it, but he hoped to knock it down.

He was aiming for the forehead, but the thing started to rise. It connected with the lower jaw, tearing it away. Flames licked at the things face. The force threw it sideways into the dirt. Rufus stopped, drew his sword, and looked at the wreck of Plautius' body. He paused briefly.

"You deserved better," he said, before lopping the head off. The neck was half-severed already, and it took no great force. The jawless creature was awkwardly rising, and the other two were catching up. Rufus leaped onto the back of his horse, cutting the reins connecting it to the hitching post with his sword. He held Plautius' head by the hair in his left hand.

He turned his horse away and galloped west, into the night. It did not even surprise him a half-hour later, when he passed four dead men and an abandoned litter on the road. He stopped here, and it didn't take long to cut off their heads, either. Those he left there, lying on the dusty road.

He rode on into the night, nodding in his sleep and mind blank, for once, of ambition and schemes. When the sun had risen and he was almost within sight of Rome, he flung the head of Plautius away. It landed in a stream and floated gently away.

CHAPTER XI

Dacia: 88 CE, Autumn

Rowanna crouched next to Zuste and held her breath. They were wrapped in fog, and hidden behind brown-green bushes as dozens of men thundered past them, up the muddy goat track that led into the mountains and ultimately to Tapae. From where she knelt, she could only see their legs as they marched past.

The two Dacians had heard them and hid moments before the centurions came into view. Tucked behind knee-high bushes, and nestled in the wet, dew-covered grasses, they were well-hidden from Roman eyes. Still, with so many soldiers, they both knelt nervously.

There was a panicked movement to the men running up the hill. Very little of the famous order and discipline of the Roman legions was on show. It took a few moments for Rowanna to realize: these men were running for their lives.

Rowanna leaned in as close as she could to the alchemist. "What are they running from?" she whispered. She had a pretty good idea, but seeing an entire army routed put the menace on an entirely different scale.

He turned his head and leaned in just as close. "I think we both know the only thing that can break a Roman legion." This wasn't true, entirely, as both of course knew of the Dacian victory over the Romans that had happened only a year ago. The Romans had fled from that battle with similar speed, but the only army now on the valley floor was made of lifeless monsters, not Dacian warriors. "Now, hush and be quiet," he whispered. There weren't many soldiers now, but the slow and the straggling auxiliaries were slowly following their fleeter compatriots.

It was the third day since they'd left the apple tree. As they climbed out of the valley and into the mountains, it grew colder but they hadn't dared build a fire. The lifeless were everywhere and seemed intelligent enough to track them down by scent, even without lighting signal fires. They'd left behind the beeches, hornbeams, oaks, lindens, and maples, and had climbed into forests of pine and silver fir. It was slow going. Rowanna's ankle had gotten worse and their progress was continually slowing. Zuste said he knew half a dozen herbs that would help, but as winter drew closer it was more difficult to find them, and he didn't want to go too far from Rowanna's protection.

The lifeless were everywhere. The pair had to travel carefully, sticking to game trails in the forest when they could. Every night, her eyes watering from the pain in her swollen ankle, Rowanna stood watch, holding her spear with grim force. Every day, she killed half a dozen more lifeless that wandered too close to them.

Three hundred or more men had passed them by the time it grew quiet. By mutual assent, Rowanna and the alchemist both rose and quietly slipped back onto the path.

"There might be more," he whispered. She was limping badly. She carried a spear as a crutch, and the rest she had made were strapped to her back. They'd made a strap for his leather case, and he carried it slung to his back.

"There might be," she agreed. "We can't hide forever. I don't even know who our enemies are anymore."

"Don't say that," Zuste said. "Romans will always be our enemies. They are opposed to the existence of the entire world, unless and until they can control it."

"Perhaps," Rowanna said. "Perhaps they were. No longer. The Romans killed my husband, and I will never forget that, or him, but they aren't our true enemies. Not anymore."

Zuste said nothing. They moved up the trail as quickly as possible. It had been churned by the pounding feet of the centurions, and before long, both were ankle-deep in the brown earthy mud. The pine forest was silent as they walked up the steep trail. Rowanna was alarmed at the lack of wildlife. Even in the wet mist, there should have been birds singing or insects chirping. The silence was eerie.

Rowanna noticed Zuste looking at her with concern. She wished he wouldn't. She tried not to grimace too much, but it was impossible to hide her pain completely. She did not complain, and Zuste wouldn't get too far ahead of her. When they did see lifeless, it was still up to her to kill them. Zuste had one more vial of the elixir that seemed to return life to the monsters, but he had not wanted to waste it. The ingredients were forbiddingly expensive, as well as difficult to find. In addition, they ran into many lone monsters each day—simply changing one more creature into a human would not help them in the long run. So it was up to her and her spear. She aimed for their eyes, now, and could kill them without much difficulty.

The sky above them rumbled opened and a massive deluge of rain fell. It was miserably cold and the mud trail beneath them began to run with water. They walked to the side of the trail, but often sunk into mud. It was bad enough for Zuste, but when Rowanna's sprained ankle was caught in the earth, blinding pain wracked her body. Both of them shivered from the cold.

After two hours, the Dacian woman had to stop. They hadn't caught up with the Romans, and hadn't seen a sign of them since they'd crawled from the bushes. Zuste was rewrapping the bandage around her ankle when she spied them.

"Zuste," she hissed, "look."

Below them, meandering through the mists, were dozens of lifeless. Some were crawling, others shambling, but all crept through the rain, slowly shuffling up the mountainside.

"Zalmoxis' balls," Zuste said, "they're everywhere. I didn't realize they were so close."

The decision came to Rowanna instantly. "We need to catch up to the Romans." She stood stiffly and began to hobble away. Her bandage was still half-wrapped, and it trailed behind her into the mud.

"Out of the question," said Zuste, catching up with her. "We need to avoid all perils, be it the monsters behind us or the monsters ahead of us."

"The worse thing the Romans will do to us is take us prisoner. A week ago, I would have died before I allowed that, and I would have killed as many of them as I could. Now, it sounds much better than the alternatives."

"Well," said Zuste, hard rain dripping into his face, "we can decide that later. For now, let's just get up this trail as fast as we can."

"You can decide. I already have. I can't make it to Tapae now, not without rest. I will tell the Romans how to kill these monsters and perhaps they will help me get to Tapae," Rowanna said firmly. She did not like having to turn to the Romans to protect her, but she liked far less the niggling doubts that they might not be able to.

"I'll stick with you," Zuste said. "I have my misgivings, but if I can leave you safely with the Romans, I can perhaps make it to Tapae myself and get help."

Rowanna grunted assent but said nothing. The spears on her back felt heavier than ever as she labored up the mountain. She lost track of all thoughts save for a consciousness of effort.

"Tell me," she said at last, "did you lose anyone? When our city was destroyed?"

"Friends aplenty," he answered, pausing for breath. "That is not what you are asking though. No, I am unmarried or married to my craft, mayhaps."

She remained silent, her lips pressed together.

"And you?"

"I am not married either. Not for many years."

"Did you lose anyone?" he asked. His voice shook a little.

"Brasus, my husband, died fighting the Romans long ago. I did not realize then what a gift he received—to have died before this insanity! I lost my son, Dapyx. He was all that I had."

She stopped, sure that she was about to confess to his death. Strangely, no tears hung in her eyes. Zuste had a strange look in his eyes as he reached into a deep trouser pocket. When his hand emerged, it held a bulging bag of coins in his hand.

"Where did you get that?" asked Rowanna.

The bearded man seemed taken aback. "I'm an alchemist. We don't come cheap."

She nodded. No one in her town had been that rich. It took some getting used to.

The alchemist hurled the full purse deep into the woods.

"What are you doing?" she cried.

"Do you really think there is anyone left alive who will take our money?" he asked. "All that bag is to me is weight and noise—and I am plenty enough heavy and loud on my own."

The rain continued to pour from the sky, gradually growing harder until it turned to hail. Those stinging ice balls hurt like hornets but the pair did not dare stop to find cover. The lifeless were no longer visible, but both Dacians knew they were closing in on them through the mist. The pair draped their cloaks over their heads and walked, slowly, grimly, and forcefully up the mountain. In time, just as the mountain flattened out and they found themselves no longer climbing, the hail subsided and left only more of the cold rain.

As soon as they reached flat ground, evidence of the Romans was manifest. The first thing they saw was spikes. Behind them lay a massive camp where they could see watchtowers soaring into the clouds. Initially, it was the spikes that drew their notice. Long wooden shafts stretched at thirty degree angles in all directions. Behind the wooden spears was an earthen rampart and beneath it was a large ditch. Guards armed with spears patrolled the perimeter in great numbers. It would be horribly difficult for the lifeless to enter the camp.

"Every Roman camp is built the same way, Diurpaneus once told me. It's the law of their Caesar. Makes it easier to raid them, he said." Zuste told Rowanna. "But this one is the largest I have ever heard of."

There was a gate before them. It was a rough wooden swinging barrier still under construction. A sodden centurion met them, blade in hand. "Faces up," he commanded. The two Dacians raised their faces into the rain.

"Names?" the man asked. The pair told him, and the man was visibly relieved. "You can talk, and you have pupils. I think you're still human, and you're in luck—our commander has ordered us to protect all the natives that we can. Head in to the *praetorium*, it's at the center of the camp. Try to find some dry clothes, and don't get in the way of the soldiers."

The pair exchanged a disbelieving glance as they entered the colossal camp. Even in the rain, there were thousands of Romans. They all moved in such orderly groups. Many were digging trenches, latrines, and deep pits. Others were cutting spiked poles as long as two men. It looked like the army was planning on staying here permanently.

"It's nearly as big as Sarmizegetusa," Rowanna said. It wasn't as large and it certainly didn't have the amenities—the Dacian city was modern and comfortable. It had workshops, storage buildings, agricultural processing areas, even ceramic pipes that filtered in fresh drinking water. This place was certainly bigger and more orderly than either of them had ever seen in a temporary camp.

They stopped a tribune and asked where they could find the commander. He pointed away, back into the camp. "He's is deeper in the camp, that way. Between the isolation hospital and the center camp cook fires. You'll also see the tents of the *contubernia*. Follow this road."

In the heavy rain, few bothered them. All of the troops wore hauberks and sandals, though many had covered up with cloaks. The men were orderly and efficient, but there was an underlying panic that permeated the camp. Much of the camp appeared hastily constructed or half-built. The Roman tents, made of treated leather, were surprisingly waterproof even in this damp mountain storm.

"They're afraid," she said softly to Zuste.

"Of course they are," the man said. "We all are."

"But they are Romans. They are strong. It's an unusual sight."

"I've been getting used to unusual sights for some time now," Zuste said, somewhat stiffly.

The rain softened as they walked deeper into the camp. They were already as wet as they could possibly be. Rowanna's hair was dripping wet and hanging in her face. Her sodden clothes couldn't have held any more moisture and her very bones felt wet and cold. Zuste was, of course, just as wet beside her.

They smelled the cook fires before they saw them. Huge pots filled with soup boiled away, and even in the rain the Romans were roasting meat on the open fire. The good smell assaulted them and Rowanna realized she was starving.

"Can we get food?" she asked.

Zuste frowned. "We'll need a chit or a token of some sort, I suspect. Let's talk to the commander first."

They could see the isolation hospital. Between it and the campfires were a handful of tents. One of them was larger than the others were, but not by a large amount.

"Is this it?" Rowanna asked. "It's where they said it would be."

"No," said Zuste, who spoke as though he had some experience in these matters. "The commander's tent is always bigger by ten than the commoner's tent. He must have moved." The portly alchemist looked around. "It could take hours to find it in this weather."

"I'm going to ask," Rowanna said. She walked up to the tent.

A big man wearing armor sat at the back of the tent. His long red hair was damp from the rain. He held a large drinking vessel in one hand and stared at a table before him.

"Pardon, centurion," Rowanna said. She felt Zuste reach her side as she spoke. "We have just arrived at camp and we are looking for the commander."

"We bear vital information for the Roman commander," the bearded man said. "I am Zuste the alchemist, late of Sarmizegetusa. She is Rowanna, from the same place. We come peacefully, fleeing the lifeless monsters." Zuste said.

The big man rose and stretched. He stared at the two with piercing eyes. Rowanna realized he was quite handsome, and surprised herself with that thought. It was true though. He didn't look like any Romans she'd ever seen before. His green eyes and sharp features could almost make him a Dacian, though the red hair was quite unusual.

"I am Tettius Iullianus, the legate and closest thing to a commander you'll find in these parts. Now," he said, drinking deeply, "who the fuck are you and what do you have to say that is so important?" His Latin was superb, but slightly accented. Rowanna had learned Latin from her father, who had been a trader. She could converse in it, but Zuste spoke it near as well as his native tongue.

Rowanna and Zuste looked at each other, unsure where to begin. The big man spoke into the silence.

"You two are wet and probably hungry. Go get dry clothes, have some food, and then come back and we can talk. Unless, what you have to say is so important that it can't wait?" His tone was vaguely amused, as if he was talking to children.

"It can wait. Gratias, Legatus. Your generosity does your kind a credit," Zuste said.

****

Dry clothes and warm food restored a forgotten humanity. Rowanna couldn't eat much, her stomach had been empty for too long, but the big alchemist had three bowls of soup and half of Rowanna's roasted rabbit. They had acquired dry clothes and gotten new bandages from the hospital. Rowanna had even been issued a simple crutch, of sorts. It was a wooden pole with a sharp end on one side and a padded top she could rest her weight on.

The late afternoon sky was dry when they returned to the tent of Tettius Iullianus. They explained their ordeal to the commander, telling him in some detail what they knew of the lifeless and how they could be killed.

"You need to kill their brains," he said flatly. "This isn't exactly news—you think I didn't learn that the first fucking time I fought them?" He was sitting across from them at the back of his tent.

Rowanna slumped. "It was … hard-fought knowledge for me," she said quietly.

Iullianus looked at her in surprise, as though he had forgotten that she was there. "It sounds like you've survived an experience that not many trained soldiers could have. I am not belittling that. But the lifeless, they destroyed an entire legion in the last week. You saw some of the few survivors escape and join us. They will be integrated into our forces, though few enough officers escaped. Those men already knew how to kill them, and an entire Roman legion was armored with that knowledge. And yet."

Rowanna looked at Zuste. The bearded man said nothing, but Iullianus caught the look.

"There is more?" he asked.

Silence.

The big man stood and strode aggressively to the bearded alchemist. "Listen, I am being more frank with you than I could. Most commanders in my place would not have allowed you into the camp, let alone clothed and fed you. I need you to act in kind."

Zuste sighed. "I understand. It may be difficult to comprehend."

"The dead are walking. My comprehension is better than it used to be," Tettius Iullianus said with a gleam in his eye.

"I am an alchemist. I know how to create more than a hundred potions, and an elixir to stop your heart, make your beloved fall in love with you, or to heal the itching sickness."

He looked at Iullianus, and his brown eyes stared steadily into the other man's green orbs. "I may have a cure for the lifeless."

Iullianus frowned. "A cure? You were not exaggerating. What do you mean?"

"I can create an elixir vitae, one that restores life to those who have lost it," Zuste said.

"By Mithras! Such a cure would be help beyond hope, but your words indicate that you two did not have such an elixir on your journey. What is it you need?"

"Herbs that are hard to find in the autumn. Most importantly, I need chaga, but it can be hard to find. Fire, some time, of course, and an ambix and a cucurbit--"

"I've got an army here. They can help collect what you need. Go back to the hospital and see what kind of equipment you can use."

A trumpeting roar sounded from outside. It was louder than anything they'd ever heard before, and Rowanna had to fight the impulse to block her ears.

"What in the hell was that?" Zuste asked.

"Don't panic," Iullianus said. "Those are some friends of mine. I brought them from the Syrian desert." He hesitated. "I was planning on visiting them this evening. It would please me if you'd come."

Rowanna and Zuste nodded.

"Follow me," the large red-haired man said. The two Dacians followed him out of the tent and through the camp. A few centurions looked strangely at the trio—the commander of the army flanked by a portly barbarian and a limping middle-aged woman.

As they drew closer, a strange smell assaulted Rowanna's nostrils. It smelled something like a barn, but far stronger. At the far west side of the camp, the Romans had built twenty-feet high fences. The ground rumbled as they approached. There was one massive gate, big enough for a Titan. By the look of it, it was strong enough to keep a Titan out as well. How—and more importantly—why had the Romans assembled such a massive construction out here? What were they protecting? Or were they protecting themselves?

Zuste hesitated. "Is it safe?"

The red-headed man laughed. "No, not entirely. But if you listen to me, no harm will come to you." He walked into the enclosure and the Dacians hurried to follow him.

Rowanna's eyes grew large as she beheld the beasts before her. Massive creatures with long trunks paraded in their large enclosure. They were massive, grey, and noble.

"Twenty war elephants," Iullianus said. "I personally trained many of them. They did so well in skirmishes in Syria that I was picked to lead the replacement legion after Cornelius Fuscus got himself killed last year."

He leaned in conspiratorially. "Of course, originally, these animals were meant to fight the natives, those who live in these wild and barbaric lands. Hardly fair, I know. But having them against the undead menace that threatens our world is a great consolation for me." He turned to Zuste. "If you can live up to your promise, we just might have a chance against these things."

Rowanna stared at the elephants in awe. They were such noble creatures, but frighteningly big. She could not imagine Dapyx trying to fight against Roman legions augmented by such as those.

"These animals made that sound we heard?" she asked.

"Aye, but that's nothing," Iullianus said. "You should see them piss." He laughed and then drew closer to the pair. "I have something else to share with you two as well. Come with me."

They left the elephant enclosure and walked through the camp. Many of the soldiers were erecting tents and digging more ditches. "Apologies. I arrived only two days ago, and you know what we're up against. After I saw what happened at Tapae, I put out the word that all survivors were to be allowed in without questions."

Rowanna looked at Zuste with growing dread.

"After what happened at Tapae?" She asked, her voice sounding shaky even to her.

Iullianus looked at her. "I hadn't realized you didn't know."

"Didn't know what?" Zuste asked. Rowanna noticed his voice sounded strained as well.

"It's gone. Destroyed."

"What about Diurpaneus?" Zuste asked.

"Diurpaneus?" the Roman asked.

"Our King," Rowanna said.

"The one who destroyed the Roman legions last year," Zuste added.

"I see. You must mean the one we call Decabalus. He's a wily one, but if even if he's still alive, he doesn't have much land to rule."

Zuste frowned but said nothing. Considering his feelings about the Romans, Rowanna thought he was quite restrained.

They were just left of the center of the camp. "Now we have a *carcer* here, a small prison. I meant for it to serve as quarters for any who needed, except that we have a prisoner now. I will send him to Rome tonight and it can be yours."

"Are you sure the lifeless cannot reach us in here?" Zuste asked. He still saw shambling shadows lurching for him every time he closed his eyes.

"Relax. Did anyone ever tell you that you worry too much?" Iullianus said.

He called something, not in Latin, and two tribunes appeared. Both had dark red hair and green eyes. They were so young, Rowanna thought, not even as old as Dapyx had been. She turned away from the two, surprising herself by finding it difficult to see other boys. She could only see herself jabbing the spear into her son's brain.

Iullianus spoke to them quietly and they both entered the *carcer*. He turned to them with a naughty grin and said, "They are not your typical tribunes, but the lads are apolitical and know how to fight. Here they come."

The pair of tribunes came out of the building. They had a prisoner held carefully between them. The prisoner's hands were clasped behind his back and his head was slouched down in defeat.

As they reached the trio, the prisoner had lifted his head and revealed his bloody face and white eyes. Rowanna screamed.

Zuste took two rapid steps back, causing Iullianus to laugh loudly. "He's restrained. I captured him earlier this morning, on the road back to Tapae." He nodded to the duo and they led the lifeless prisoner away.

"That handsome fellow is going to be my present to the city of Rome. Give them some idea of what they can expect out here. And now, your home awaits."

The two were warm, dry, and safe for the first time in as long as they could remember and both were sleeping soundly before Iullianus had made his way back to his tent. Outside, the darkening sky was heavy with gray clouds as an army of lifeless crept closer to the camp.

CHAPTER XII

Rome: 88 CE, Winter

Rufus sent the last of the lickspittles that had come to beg favor away just an hour short of midday. He had gone overlong with them, and still many had left unsatisfied. It was the price of power, and ten years ago, he had a fraction of the clients that plagued him today. Was the price of power ever worth it? He was exhausted and yet had more to do.

It was the Kalends, the first day of month, and that meant another Senate meeting. He groaned in disbelief at the prospect. "Imagine the things the fucking Roman Empire could achieve if we didn't waste so much time listening to old men fart and complain," he said to Fulvius. His new aide was a stuffy Greek who occasionally flirted with competence but had no genuine acquaintance with her. Plautius' presence was missed.

"You must go," Fulvius pointed out dourly. "It is your duty, master."

"I can do as I want," Rufus said, but it was petty. As always, he thought about skipping the gathering, and, as always, he didn't want to pay the fine. The fines for voluntarily missing a Senate meeting were prohibitive, even for the wealthy. There was no escape, not unless he was out of town or into his sixth decade— Senators over sixty years were free to do fuck all, should they desire. That age was, unfortunately, still a few years away.

It was a moot point. This day, however, he grumbled, he needed to speak to the Senate. What a bothersome task. Addressing the Senate had a special place on his list of least-favorite actions. Perhaps he would wait until the next meeting. No. He'd been putting it off, but did not dare wait any longer. He called for his slaves, who dressed him formally, and waited for a litter.

The trip to the Curia Hostilia, situated in the Roman Forum, was not a long one. Other than litters, of course, there were no wagons or carts allowed in the city during the day. Even foot traffic lessened as they drew closer to the Forum. The place was politically sacred. It had been an instrument of the Roman government since the time of the Republic.

Rufus paused by the outer western wall. It was decorated with the Tabula Valeria, a painting illustrating the Roman victory over the Carthaginians. More interesting, the ground below him was slippery with slow-drying blood. Earlier that morning, a magistrate had killed a lamb and read the auspices. They'd obviously been positive this morning, as they always were unless someone powerful did not wish so. If the reading had been admonitory, the meeting would have been postponed. In the time of Augustus, each Senator would have brought offerings of frankincense and wine to offer the Gods, but that expensive custom, thankfully, had fallen into disuse over the last twenty years. He was relieved not to have lived in the Republic, which had been borderline barbaric at times.

Rufus entered and took his place, noting the amount of new faces. The makeup of the Senate had changed since his return to Rome a decade ago. Under Vespasian and Titus, the Senate, along with many other posts, had been filled almost entirely with Flavian flunkeys. Domitian, for all his faults, rarely favored his own family members. He admitted many provincials into the Senate, and allowed many below the Senator class to run the imperial bureaucracy. It was controversial, but the candidates who made it through were annoyingly competent. Rufus wished he could take some credit for the move, but Domitian had thought of it and fought for it himself.

The Emperor himself was not yet there, as per his typical predilection. Domitian held most of the important offices in the Senate, and was acting Consul. The session couldn't start without him. He normally took his place between the two Consuls, but Catalus had been missing for three months now, and he was presumed dead. Not a person had connected Rufus with Catalus disappearance, and he had begun to hope that he was safe. Domitian had not replaced him, and he might not until the next year began. The other consul, a severe man named Sextus Iulius Sparsus, was there, as always. He'd probably arrived early, Rufus thought with disgust. Sparsus was cut from the cloth of a Cato. A stern man who disapproved of everything, including disapproval.

The Senators sat in straight, parallel lines. Behind them, any member of the public was welcome to come listen to the debate. Today, there were not many, other than the usual town criers and semi-important equites who were as rich as Senators were, but of common ancestry and who had not yet been elected into office. Other than times of war or danger, there typically weren't many who came to watch. Rufus couldn't imagine coming here voluntarily, and some people had too much time on their hands.

Muttered conversations filled the emptiness caused by Domitian's absence. Time passed, until he belatedly appeared at last, nearly an hour late. That wasn't unusual; nor, unfortunately, was his attire. The Emperor was dressed grandiosely in the uniform of a triumphal general. Around his head was a golden laurel wreath with dangling gold ribbons. He wore a tunic that had been embroidered with palm leaves, and his toga was purple with an embroidered golden border. There was an ivory baton in his left hand and a golden gladius in the other. Rufus hid all signs of disdain but he was embarrassed for his old friend. Germanicus himself would have looked pretentious in all that gilt and gold.

As Domitian strode to his place, the other Senators rose. What did the other Senators think? Were some of the more simple-minded taken in by this simple pageantry? Domitian was beginning to claim every border skirmish in the Empire as a major victory. At the same time, in Rome, he was ordering more of his opponents killed, including his own cousin, Flavius Clemens. His megalomania was swelling to dangerous heights, and he had taken to being addressed as *Dominus et Dues*, Master and God.

None of the Senators dared laugh or even smile openly, but Rufus could smell the current of mockery that flowed through the building. It made for an inauspicious beginning. Worst of all, Rufus realized, was that it was midday. The emperor was always erratic and nervous at midday. Some foolish astrologer had predicted that he would die at noon, and Domitian was even more paranoid at that time than others.

The next few hours passed slowly. The consuls were the first to voice their opinion, followed by praetors, tribunes, and finally, other Senators. They spoke of fines, taxes, fees, and other petty grievances. It would be hours before he could broach his subject.

Boredom and apprehension warred in the pit of his stomach. Domitian himself appeared to have fallen asleep more than once.

At last, his chance came. Rufus stood, and ignored the eyes of his fellow Senators. His antipathy toward the proceedings was well known.

"Salve, *patres conscripti*," he said, addressing the house. "If all rumors that reached the Senate's ears were but a drop of water, we would all drown in the never-ceasing deluge." There was a small, polite laugh at that from his peers. "However, there are ominous reports I know we have all heard recently. Savage, flesh-eating barbarians are terrorizing the corners of the Empire. They say you can't bribe them, can't give them lands."

"Ha," Sparsus snorted, rising. "As Caesar said, men gladly believe that which they wish for. They've said that of every group of twenty or more barbarians who saddled a horse and burnt an inn. Let them quaff a Falernian or fuck a fat farmer's wife and they'll be Romanized within a year. You speak of absurdity!"

Rufus maintained his neutral expression, but inwardly he swore. As Consul, Sparsus was a man that not many would wish to cross. He realized that he should have approached this more subtly. Rumors, bribes, and innuendos could have established his case better. Still, Rufus felt he could convince most anyone of anything, given enough time. Unwanted, the vision of shambling shadows backlit by flame and ash appeared in his mind. He couldn't give up.

"I believe it because it is absurd," Rufus said. "I speak not of raising new Legions or increasing taxes. As our good Consul says, there are endless waves of barbarians that threaten to ravage Rome. I simply propose we appoint a committee to investigate this new menace."

"Committees," Sparsus said with disdain. "Paying men to sit on their arses, it's expensive and wasteful. Without raising taxes, the Emperor would have to pay for it himself."

Domitian, who had only been paying half-attention, looked up in alarm. He stood and crossed to the center of the chamber. "I don't have any money," Domitian said. "I'm still rebuilding from the great fire, the civil war, and the fires of Titus. It's non-ending. I've added a fourth level to our Flavian amphitheatre and have built fifty new buildings, including a new Temple of Jupiter, the Arch of

Titus, the Odeon, and a new palace on the Palatine Hill. I've implemented the Capitoline Games, which in addition to the chariot races and gladiator matches have oratory, music, and acting. And I've created new *ludi*, with new warriors."

Domitian's speech sounded rehearsed to Rufus, and he realized his agenda had become subservient to the Emperor's platform. The ludi he spoke of, the gladiator schools, were filled with dwarves and women. Such were Domitian's ideas of "new warriors."

"And that is merely here in Rome!" Domitian thundered. "It was always me who funded the Limes Germanicus, even when my father and brother was Emperor."

"I understand, Caesar," Rufus said, hiding his anger beneath an unctuous smile. He did not dare broach the man's wrath.

"I can fund the committee myself," he offered. "Along with anyone who—"

"This then has become a private venture, Senator, and not one you should trouble us with," Sparsus snapped. He muttered something to his friends about "the old days" and Rufus was forced to take a seat. Nothing he could think of would convince the rest of the Senate to oppose both the Emperor and the Consul. He did not hear another word that was spoken.

By the time Rufus escaped the Senate, the day was waning. It had been a complete waste of time. There was only one other course of action he could think of taking. It would be difficult to find the appropriate people, but he knew exactly where to start.

The Games. It had to be there. It had been some time since he had been to them, and he would have a busy few weeks ahead of him. Sparsus had probably been correct about the inefficiency of a committee. They would tell him what they thought he wanted to hear. No, this was a problem of action and would require men of action. He prayed, rather more fervently than his usual want that he would have enough time.

CHAPTER XIII

Dacia: 88 CE, Winter

Zuste and Rowanna had been in the Roman camp for a week when the Consul arrived. Zuste had spoken of leaving, of searching for Decabalus, but each day had seen greater attacks from the lifeless. So far, the efficiency of the Romans was enough to counter the undead menace. So far. It was strange for both of them, and their new appreciation and dependency on those who had done such harm to them. They hadn't seen much of Iullianus the last few days. The Roman commander had duties aplenty, but he allowed them free reign of the camp. Zuste spent his time eating and drinking with the soldiers at the cook fires. He made lists of ingredients and heavily armed soldiers went out in careful groups. A blacksmith worked on making the equipment that he would need. He had everything he needed save for the elusive chaga, a fungus that grew on dying trees.

The Dacians shared meals, but Rowanna otherwise spent long hours of each day in the elephant enclosure. The great beasts were growing used to her presence and would let her walk up to them and scratch their foreheads or their sides. Her ankle was healing and she only slightly limped when she walked without the crutch.

They had just finished their midday meal when they saw the Consul. He was an aged man, haughty, face filled with an expression that Zuste took an instant dislike to. The man reminded him of the cocky soldiers that had plagued his home for so long.

The Consul had not been in the commander's tent for long when shouting sounded. Zuste looked at Rowanna pointedly.

"Iullianus is not a man to suffer fools," he said with satisfaction.

She said nothing, but her expression showed concern. Zuste realized that she was worried.

"You think this man's arrival could be bad?" he asked, idly chewing on his thumbnail.

"I don't know," she said softly, "but I can't see that it will make things any better for us."

"You may be right," Zuste said. "Did Iullianus not say he had orders to attack Dacia? A messenger from Rome could be bad indeed."

"We should leave, and leave now," Rowanna said.

"Outside the camp, we are dead," Zuste reminded her. "Here, we have a chance of survival. And I am close to having the necessary equipment to making more elixir."

"You are the one who hates the Romans," she said.

Before he could answer, a centurion marched up to them, as rigid and formal as could be.

"You are summoned to speak before the Legatus," the Roman said.

Both the Dacians rose, but the Roman snapped, "Not you. Him." He didn't even look at Rowanna. His gaze remained straight ahead. She sat back down in surprise.

"I shall get some answers, at least," Zuste said to the still-frowning woman. "Stay here and I'll return shortly."

Zuste followed the man into Iullianus' tent. The Consul was standing, his white hair still wet from the ride. He glared in the direction of the Dacian man but did not stop talking to Iullianus, who was seated with an infuriatingly mild look on his face.

"You cannot do such a thing. Your whim is subject to Caesar," the Consul said.

Iullianus remained calm. "Caesar is not here. He knows not what we face. Were he, he would march his Imperial arse right back to Rome, same as I."

The Consul narrowed his eyes. "You are refusing a direct order."

"Consent makes the law," Iullianus said.

"I can imprison you. You could be killed. You should be killed."

"I met Domitian once, before he was Emperor. He seemed a reasonable man. I think he'll appreciate me returning a full legion to him. Maybe he'll make me rich. Maybe he'll name me his heir."

"This is outrageous. I repeat, you are ordered to advance further into Dacia."

"I will not."

"You are not a real legate. You're not even a Senator!"

"I am a warrior."

"You are a coward!"

Iullianus looked to the alchemist. "Zuste, let me introduce you to Sextus Iulius Sparsus, Consul of Rome. The sole surviving Consul, it appears. Consul, this is Zuste of Dacia."

The man barely deigned to notice Zuste.

"Zuste, he wants me to invade Dacia. Please tell him why that is not a good idea."

The Dacian man bit his lip. He had no wish to be dragged into this debate, but he spoke. "It's not safe, not for a man, not for an army of men. The lifeless are everywhere."

Sparsus sneered. "Why do you confront me with this barbarian's opinion as if it were something that mattered? I never thought I'd live to see the Legion X Fretensis refuse to face danger. I shall return to Rome and report your cowardice. You never should have been named commander, anyway. Without your friend, Lepidus, pulling strings, you'd have been killed long ago. He is lucky that he died, rather than live to see the mockery you've made of his legion."

Iullianus stood. He seemed to tower over the Roman man. "I did not ask Lepidus for command of his army. I was as surprised as you no doubt were, but I am doing everything I can not to lose it. I am no Fuscus, and my legion will survive or I will die seeing it so."

Sparsus sneered. "What threat is there to excuse such cowardice?"

"Have you seen one?" Iullianus asked. His voice was dangerously soft.

The Consul blinked. "What?"

"Have you seen one? One of these shambling creatures, have you seen one?"

"I've ridden past many of them. They are far too slow to offer menace to a man on horseback. And that's hardly the point—"

"That's exactly the point, Consul Sparsus," Iullianus said. "I propose to you that we go hunt one. You and I. You can take a good look at one, and afterwards, if you still feel the same you can lead my legion."

The Consul narrowed his eyes suspiciously. "It would be better for you to do as you're told. The orders are of the Emperor Domitian," Sparsus reminded.

Zuste heard a distant noise, but it was gone before he could place it.

"Then I order you to observe one of these creatures. On foot. Then you can judge the wisdom of my decision."

Sparsus nearly spluttered with outrage. "You've been too long away from Rome. You can't order me to do anything, Tettius Iullianus."

"I've got an army that says otherwise. Wouldn't you agree, alchemist?"

Zuste said nothing. He could hear, from afar, shouting. Then, deafeningly closer, came the roaring of the elephants. Seconds later, the blasting of trumpets sounded. It was strange for him to hear the trumpets and not feel fear; this was the sound of an ally

"What is happening? Why are your men sounding the alarm?" Sparsus asked.

Iullianus smiled wickedly. "You don't have to go very far at all to fight one of these monsters after all. Grab your sword and come with me!"

The big red-haired man sprinted from his tent. Zuste did not even look to see if the Consul was following before he ran out to Rowanna.

She was alone at the cook fire, and the legionaries had answered the alarm call. The large spear she always carried was in her hand. "What happened?" she asked as Zuste reached her. The big man was out of breath and he took a few moments to answer.

"Iullianus told the man they would fight the lifeless. Then they attacked. That Consul is a real bastard."

"Zuste, there's something wrong," Rowanna said. Her eyes were pleading with him. "This isn't just another attack."

"The lifeless attack several times a day. They haven't even reached the camp yet."

"I know. I know. I'm being irrational, but the elephants were spooked today, and they screamed just now. You must have heard it. They haven't been alarmed like that before."

Her voice was strangely tight and Zuste realized that she was trying to keep the fear from conquering her. That made his blood run cold. Rowanna was far braver than he was, and she had been his protector on their journey here.

"Let's go see those loud, stinking beasts then. No, not the Romans—the elephants," he said to her, the joke weak even to his ears. She smiled absently as they left.

The camp was eerily empty. The sounds of war cries and the screams of the injured could be heard from everywhere around them, but they saw no other living souls as they made their way to the elephant enclosure. Even the large watchtower at the center of camp, usually manned by several men at all hours, was curiously empty.

"You were correct. The watchmen should still be there," Zuste said. "There's something strange going on. This is no common attack."

Rowanna nodded wordlessly.

They reached the enclosure and nodded at the handlers. The great beasts were nervous—some paced with thunderous steps, others swayed to unheard music. There was no sign of the lifeless.

"Can they swim?" Rowanna asked, eying the stream that provided drinking water.

"The elephants?"

"The lifeless."

"I don't think so," Zuste said. "Fresh, running water is bane to evil creatures of all sorts. That is a fact of science, and I don't think that water is deep enough for swimming."

Rowanna sighed. "I have the oddest feeling. Let's return to the main camp."

They had reached the gate again when Iullianus rushed in. His hair was wild and his left shoulder leaked a dull-brown blood.

When he registered them, he smiled broadly. "I think we might all have a rather big problem on our hands," he said cheerfully. "It's probably best if you stay in here—the camp has been overrun."

"The lifeless," Zuste said, "did they get you?"

Iullianus laughed. "No, this was a present from a certain Consul who objected when I ran my sword into his stomach. That ancient bugger was faster than I expected."

He scratched at his wet hair. "Please stay out of the way. If this doesn't work, run away, into the mountains or into the forests, as far as you can."

"If what doesn't work?" Rowanna asked.

The red-haired Roman was already on the move. He climbed up an elephant, looking as agile as a monkey, where he yelled and several of his soldiers followed suite. Iullianus waved to Zuste and Rowanna, who had moved back well away from the gate, and then his elephant plodded forward.

"It's good," he yelled, "to be the *Elephantarch.*"

Within moments, a score of war elephants were charging after him.

"That," said Zuste, his voice slightly awe-stricken, "that is not the least impressive thing I have ever seen." The enclosure was resoundingly empty—except for the Dacians, all others had left.

"We need to see the battle," Rowanna said. "If the Romans are overrun, we need to know."

Zuste nodded. "A sound idea. We can climb the watchtower back toward camp, but be careful. I don't want to have to save you if we see any of those monsters."

Rowanna laughed. "Believe me, alchemist, I don't want you to have to save me either. Come on, let's go."

Zuste hefted his spear in a parody of the Romans. "It's heavier than I thought," he said, as they passed through the gates.

"It's not heavy," Rowanna said. "You're just fat and out of shape." Her voice trailed off as they came into view of the camp. Ash-grey smoke billowed into the wet sky before them. The roaring of elephants, the shouting of men, the groaning of the undead, these sounds assailed them all at once. Without speaking, they both began running.

The sentry tower remained deserted. Rowanna reached the ladder first and had climbed all the way up before Zuste reached the tower. By the time he had laboriously clambered up the ladder, Rowanna was smiling.

"All is well," she whispered. "I think all is well." Zuste looked east, toward the main part of the camp.

It took Zuste a few moments to realize what he was seeing. The camp perimeter had been overrun. So many of the lifeless had been impaled on the spikes that, eventually, others of them had climbed over their bodies. Now there was a horde of lifeless in the camp. Many were—or had been—Roman, their uniforms hanging in tatters, but most were wearing the furs and leathers of Dacians. So many of us lost, Zuste thought.

The living Romans had formed ranks with large gaps between them. It was through these gaps that the elephants charged. The mighty beasts were charging now, running at a speed that seemed impossible for creatures so big.

"You could learn something from them," Rowanna said, smiling.

"Let me catch my breath from that sprint, and I'll thrash you," Zuste said.

The elephants hit the line of lifeless and the monsters died in droves. Most were stamped into jelly beneath their heavy feet. Others were lanced by tusks, stabbed by the elephant riders or shot with arrows from the waiting Roman soldiers.

Rowanna began laughing with relief and Zuste chuckled beside her. "Almost feel sorry for the poor wretches. They don't have a chance." Rowanna was laughing harder now. Zuste glanced at her with curiosity. She was laughing still, perhaps, but tears ran down her face.

"You are well?" he asked.

She nodded, incapable of speech. A handful of moments passed, and the woman spoke slowly, "I needed this. Needed to see the lifeless lose, to see a victory of life over death."

"Then look again," Zuste said, "the elephants are turning around."

The edge of the camp was still held by many long spikes, with a deep pit before it. Even animals as mighty as the elephants could not charge through that without harm. The elephants turned with complete synchronicity, all wheeling to their left to prepare for another charge. As they turned, they slowed, and as they slowed, the lifeless began to press in on them, and as the lifeless pressed in on them, the elephants stumbled.

One rider was low enough for several lifeless to reach. They tugged onto his foot and the man toppled into the ravenous arms of the monsters.

"Oh gods no," breathed Rowanna, "no, no, no."

The beasts were being boxed in. A man stood high on his mount—from here he was a small shadow, but Zuste felt sure that the man was Iullianus. The elephants started moving again. Slowly at first, but gathering momentum, the elephants regained speed. The beasts could not attack the lifeless beside them or behind them, but they trampled another wide swath of walking corpses before them. The lifeless did not flee or panic. They remained in place and accepted their destruction.

The elephants charged through the channels between the Roman forces. Here they could turn at their ease. A centurion climbed the riderless elephant, and quickly, men grabbed more arrows and spears.

"Those animals are amazing. So intelligent and yet," Rowanna said, smiling like a little girl, "I did not realize they could be that destructive."

"They brought them to fight us," Zuste reminded her. "It would have been nigh as bad as the lifeless."

Rowanna said nothing as more smoke billowed up. Roman archers were lighting their arrows and sending them into the horde before them. It was a sound tactic—fire burned through the lifeless as though they were dry papyrus, but the damp rain mitigated much of the damage it could do.

"We need a better weapon," Rowanna fretted. "Even the elephants have to turn around, and they're vulnerable. When can your elixirs be ready?"

Zuste looked a long time at the battle before answering. "I don't have the necessary ingredients, nor the equipment to create them. Another couple days and I could have begun in earnest. Now it may be moot—the Romans are as good as defending their camp as they are at finding aprus or seba."

"You often speak ill of those risking their lives to save yours," Rowanna observed.

"They care not for my life," Zuste answered. "And but for a stroke of luck—otherwise ill I'd grant you—those men would be raping you and slitting my throat. Maybe even the other way around, from what one hears about these men."

The Dacian woman snorted but said nothing. Before them, at the edge of sight, the elephants charged once more. Once again, they crushed the hapless walking corpses before them, churning them into muddy pulp. This time, the elephants turned sooner and much wider. This kept them going, but still they slowed down a bit. The lead elephant charged into a large group of lifeless.

It gored and stomped the advancing monsters, but there were so many that the impossible happened. More and more of the undead flowed from the dark forest. One after another flung itself onto the beast, climbing over each other until the creature was obscured by rot. The rider, his telltale red hair visible, rose and stabbed at them with his long spear and short sword.

His beast stumbled and the man lurched. Though he was three meters high, he leaped to the ground, where he was instantly surrounded by waves of the creatures.

Zuste looked to Rowanna. The look on her face matched the feeling in his gut; neither had any words to offer. They could just see the events unfold.

Iullianus struck one lifeless through the neck, swept low and grabbed a fallen soldier's sword, and still in the same motion, drove a blade into each of the oncoming lifeless' eyes.

He leapt back, withdrawing both blades. He snarled, his hands full of death. Seconds later, he was enveloped by the undead and was no longer visible in the seething mass of purification.

Even without their leader, the Roman army did not break. Three more elephants and riders had been similarly taken down, but the rest had returned from their loop. With careful precision, the archers shot into the seething mass of horror again and again. Before them, those with shields braced for another impact.

"We should go help them," Rowanna said.

Zuste glared at her in annoyance. "You are good with a spear, but they won't welcome us. No, I think maybe you were right earlier. I think we should leave. Now."

Rowanna nodded. They had each climbed down the tower and were walking quickly toward the south gate when Rowanna stopped Zuste.

"I was just thinking. Iullianus will turn into one of those."

"Probably, unless they eat him entirely," he said.

"We could ... We could save him. You still have one more elixir."

"By Zalmoxis, woman! There is one cure left in the world, and you want me to waste it on a Roman?"

"That Roman helped us. He saved our lives," she said. The battle behind them roared as the undead warriors engaged the Romans.

"He came to kill us. Just as he and his kind always have."

"Maybe he did, at first, but in the end, he saved us, protected us. What about

forgiveness, alchemist?"

"What about saving the elixir in case one of us gets bit out there?" Zuste hissed. "Even with your spear, we don't have much a chance against this many lifeless. We need it."

"Iullianus could protect us," Rowanna said softly, "and he could help guide us back somewhere safe."

"Somewhere safe? Like Rome? You're quite taken with this fellow, aren't you? Your own kind isn't good enough for you anymore?"

"Gods damn it, Zuste, you know that isn't how I mean it. You're right that we can't survive out there. We need him."

Zuste sighed. "Even if I agreed, which I don't, we'd never find him amidst all those shamblers."

Rowanna smiled. "We can try," she said. They both knew then that she had him.

CHAPTER XIV

ROME: 88 CE – Winter

Felix had time to take one deep breath and then the *mappa* fell. The gates flung open and he surged forward. He stood, legs apart, in a *quadrigae*, a large chariot led by four horses. They were a mismatched quartet of beasts clothed in the same scarlet colors that he himself wore.

His eyes flicked to the track ahead of them. In the first place, the closest to the *spina*, was Pharnaces. The man had not failed to win for months now. He was the pride of the White team, and had been so since being bought from the Blues some time ago. Today was meant to be another victory for him. Pharnaces had been a rising star when Felix had first lost to him. He was now as successful as any slave in Rome, save perhaps for some of the elder gladiators. His horses were magnificent white stallions from Thrace and there were rumors that he had dined with the Emperor. The two other White racers, a savage Syrian and a long-haired Greek, excelled at creating dissension and carnage amongst their rivals. Neither ever tried to win; they simply destroyed the other racers.

Felix understood their role all too well. He himself had no chance at winning. He was one of two Reds racing today to ensure that Italicus had a chance at defeating Pharnaces. The Green and the Blue factions had three racers as well, but Italicus was understood to be the greatest threat to Pharnaces.

On this, the first part of the first lap, all twelve of the *aurigae* were close together. It would take some time—or an accident—before any of the riders could create separation. Felix checked his reins, making sure they were tied tightly around his waist. They were fastened tightly enough to make breathing more difficult. There was some risk if he fell, being attached to the reins could lead to serious injury or death, but with that risk came the reward: he could control the horses with all of his body weight. That made no small difference on tight turns.

Italicus caught Felix's eye and grinned. Felix smiled back, suppressing his jealousy. He had been racing for eight years and accrued an improbable amount of success, but the *equos nutriebat* still would not let him challenge Italicus for the red team supremacy. The other Red *aurigae* was a German boy of fifteen, all arms and elbows whose raw talent had elevated him over more experienced racers today.

The twelve men and almost fifty horses raced along the *spina* and quickly reached the *meta*, the turning point in the Hippodrome. Felix cracked his whip and leaned into the turn, his horses mere spaces away from the blue racer's own. Sand flew up as his wheels skidded through the turn. A scream drew his attention. There was trouble in the chariot beside him.

One of the Green *aurigae* had tried to take the turn too quickly, and both of his wheels were in trouble. Felix knew of him—he had been a champion at Joppa who had recently arrived in Rome. The first wheel snapped in half and the second, torqued with tension through the turn, quickly followed. The Green racer's body tumbled heavily to the earth, bouncing with bone-wrenching force. It was called a *naufragia,* or a shipwreck, and this one was magnificent. The crowd of a hundred thousand people roared their approval at his fall. It didn't seem that he would have long to enjoy the comforts of Rome.

Within seconds, slaves appeared. They carried a litter, but he could not tell if the man was still alive. All this he assessed in a fraction of a second as he whipped his horses into faster speeds. There was no time for further thought. There was a gap now, and instantly, Felix leaned his horses into it.

The other Green *aurigae* was trying the same thing, and he was less than a heartbeat behind. Felix did not hesitate. His hand lashed out and his horses surged forward. The Green man, a swarthy Egyptian, cursed as he aborted his move, but Felix was already looking at the racers ahead of him.

Italicus and Pharnaces were next to each other, just beginning to emerge from the rest of the racers. This being a shorter, five lap race, Pharnaces would not hold back as he was accustomed to. Felix looked to his left and saw the long-haired White rider. The man grinned at him with an evil confidence.

Felix was ready for whatever he tried. He hadn't survived these long years without learning enough to defend himself when necessary. The man reached beneath his white tunic and Felix could see something shiny out of the corner of his eye.

He held a slim blade, much smaller than a *falx*. Just as Felix could see what was happening, the man flung the blade at him. It pierced his red jersey but not his leather jerkin beneath it. That was odd. The man would have known that he wore light armor, as did most racers. Felix glanced at him to see another maliciously confident smile, and then the next turn was on them.

There was more room, so Felix leaned in even harder. His chariot scraped against the marble *spina* as his horses turned. He leaned into the turn, crouching to better center his weight. His whip slid into his hand and he cracked it over his horses, spurring them into a faster gait.

Above them, he knew, one of the five dolphins had lowered. There were four laps to go. The racers were spreading out now. Felix was in the middle of the pack, between a Green racer and the White knife-thrower.

A pulsing in his gut alerted him to the knife. He angrily yanked it out and let it drop at the bottom of his chariot. He'd like to throw it back, but his aim was poor. Even standing still, throwing at a stationary target, he usually missed. Throwing at a moving target while he himself was moving was utterly useless. His gut twinged again, and it felt like something was clawing at him. But there was no time to think about it. He glanced behind and saw the German boy was falling behind while battling a Blue and a Green *aurigae*.

Another glance ahead of him revealed that Italicus was still matching Pharnaces step for step. He was apparently feeling confident, but Italicus used his whip on the side of Pharnaces' horses. Felix winced. It was a bold tactic, one that could gain him valuable time if the horses shied away from the blow, but it surely would warrant retaliation from the older man. Even as Felix watched, Pharnaces slowed his horses. Italicus missed his next whip stroke and leaned, just barely off balance.

"Little red bitch," a voice yelled to him. It was the Greek *aurigae*. "I'd like my knife back. You won't need it, not where you're going." The man smiled at him again. He was neck-and-neck with Felix as they approached the next turn.

"Why, does your mother need it to shave her beard?" Felix

called back.

The man's smile did not disappear, but it certainly lessened.

Some instinct warned Felix that someone was on his right, on the outside of the track, and he glanced to see the Syrian there. His baldhead gleamed in the sunlight as the crowd roared their approval at the White team's tactics. It was unusual for the second or third rider to have horses that were so fast, but Syrians were well known for their excellent steeds.

Felix was boxed in. He could slow his chariot, but that would leave three White riders to confront Italicus. He could not even turn, other than in the area that his foes would allow him.

Neither of them was turning. The bloodstained wall loomed ahead of them. It suddenly made sense to Felix. The two men would crash him into the wall. Then they could turn and deal with the third red rider as he caught up. They must trust that Pharnaces could deal with Italicus himself. Or they would let the Red *aurigae* lap them and deal with him then.

The crowd was really roaring now. Felix slowed his horses as the wall loomed imminently close but the men surrounding him whipped at his horses and they sped up. The beasts would shy away from the wall, of course, but his chariot would not fare as well. He might not die, but at this speed that was not certain. His gut ached as he stood on the front edge of his chariot, precariously balanced. His long hair, still worn in the Greek style, streamed behind him. He grasped his *falx* and cut all four of the reins entirely from his body. Then he slid the blade into a small scabbard under his tunic and took a deep breath.

The world slowed down, just a little.

He saw the sneering Greek man to the left of him, and the deadly serious Syrian to the right. His horses, sweat lathering on their heated skin, charging forward. The wall of the hippodrome was ten meters high and stained with the blood of other racers. He could hear nothing but the beating of his heart.

Felix jumped.

He had been hoping to hit the Greek driver, perhaps knock him out of the chariot. But he'd misjudged their speed. He just grabbed the back of the chariot. His body was suspended, but his legs and feet dragged painfully in the sand. Something sharp—a rock or rusted blade—cut deeply into his leg.

Then the speed of the world was back to normal. He felt his body bouncing painfully as the chariot sped on. The spectators had hushed as all watched this unexpected confrontation take place.

The Greek driver glanced back and grinned. He seemed to be genuinely amused. "We weren't going to kill you," he said, "or maybe just a little bit kill you." He gripped his *falx* menacingly.

Felix grabbed at the back of the chariot with his right hand and slowly pulled himself up. The chariot began to turn to the left. They would only just avoid the wall. The Syrian was trapped between the wall and Felix's chariot. He would be fine, but would fall behind the other racers. The Greek, however, would have only missed a few beats. His chariot was already heading back into the turn.

Felix grabbed at the other side of the chariot with his other hand. The muscles in his arms screamed. He could scarcely see in the dust, and his battered body was threatening to give up. The blade sheathed on his body bruised into his skin. The Greek was busy whipping his horses back into top speed, but he kicked back at the edge of the chariot. His foot narrowly missed Felix's left hand. He lashed his whip out, driving the horses into a greater frenzy.

The man laughed. "You are a worthy foe, Red. It is rare to meet one who can see the unexpected." He spoke without looking back, as he whipped his horses into a frenzy. They were well past the *spinae* now. Two Green racers had passed them, but they were still ahead of the pack.

The whip lashed again. Felix was shocked to feel it hit his hand, and he instinctively let go. It was, of course, the worst possible thing he could have done. His body fell back to the ground. Only his right hand kept him attached to the chariot. There were too many racers behind them, and if he let go, it was not at all sure that he could get off the course before they caught up with him. From far away, he heard the sound of a massive impact, and moments later, screaming.

He could taste the grit of the track in his mouth, could feel it in his eyes. His leg felt sticky with the blood that coursed down it. He wanted to close his eyes and sleep or die. Instead, he pulled himself up again. This time he got his left foot onto the chariot. He had mere seconds, and tied the snapped off reins together around the back of the chariot. The White racer, still amused, glanced back at him. "Such an enterprising little fuck," he said, and then swung his foot savagely at Felix's head.

He missed. This time, the battered and bloody lad was ready for it. He leaned as far back as he could and let go of the chariot entirely. He grabbed the smiling man's sandaled foot. "What are you doing?" the Greek cried. "We'll both die."

"So be it," Felix spat out, mouth too dusty to say more. Both of his feet were on the edge of the chariot now, and he could use all of his weight to pull. He was not sure if the hastily tied knot around the post could hold his weight and there was no time to check. He yanked the man's foot with as much force as he could. The Greek lurched forward, stumbling to the edge of his chariot.

His opponent smiled grimly. "You made a mistake," he said. He raised the blade in his hand and struck at Felix.

This, too, Felix had anticipated. Striking more quickly than the eye could follow, he let go of the man's foot and grabbed his knife hand by the wrist. Felix just had time to see the surprise in the man's eyes before he was flung from the back of his own cart.

The Greek screamed as his body bounced, caught on his own reins as he was dragged down the track. Felix fell, too, of course. He hit the ground on his back with an explosive oomph and lost all the air in his body, but he hadn't fallen as far, and was attached to a much closer area.

The knot around the chariot strained, but held. Felix grabbed the knots with both hands and slowly, excruciatingly, pulled himself back onto the chariot. There was scattered applause from the crowd, but most were too stunned by the maneuver. Nothing like that had ever happened, not in Felix's memory.

He was still tied to the back post and there was no blade in the chariot. He could not control the horses either. They were at least running in the right direction, but he could not compete without taking control. Though his side would long be bruised, he was glad of the blade. Within seconds, he was free from his reins and the Greek driver was cut from his. His unconscious body tumbled far down the track, into oncoming drivers.

Felix scooped the cut reins in his hand and turned the horses. It took an effort that his aching body was not happy to give, but they were well-trained animals and he cut the corner tightly. The dolphin had already dipped down to signify the end of the second lap. He was behind all the racers save the Syrian, who was turning his horses the long way around to get back onto the track.

There were several *aurigae* missing. Two Greens, a Blue, and the German boy were down. That could mean that the Green team was entirely out, no large surprise, as they were consistently the worst team of late. Their faction had dwindled to the smallest of sizes. At any rate, they were all on the other side of the wall, so he did not know if they had all come together in one large shipwreck or if they had crashed in individual skirmishes. He found that he didn't care if the German teen lived. He had some talent, but knew nothing about Rome and her customs. He was proud of his ignorance, even. Felix had no time for those type of people.But there was no more time to dwell on such matters. He had reached the *spina* and was catching up with the four racers ahead of him. The remaining blue racers were together, their chariots rushing forward together in roaring unison. They were not far behind Pharnaces, who was himself a few lengths behind Italicus.

Felix blinked and looked again. It seemed Italicus could win the race today. That was unthinkable. Pharnaces lost matches but seldom, and he had not ever lost to the Red faction. Fifth place was not glorious, but the fact that he still breathed was no small consolation. It could be a great day for the Red faction.

He took the turn tight and hard. The new chariot was slightly bigger than he was used to, but it handled well. He held the reins in his hand but felt vulnerable without them around his waist. His left leg ached and his stomach pulsed with renewed pain. He felt his consciousness was on the verge of fleeing and prayed to Jupiter to allow time enough to finish the race.

He called out Jupiter's name again, seconds later. Belatedly, he remembered the sound of the crash and screaming and now he understood why. There was a pile up of broken chariots, broken horses, and broken people. It was strange. Though racing was a dangerous sport, today was unusually bloody. Felix resolved to sacrifice more to the Gods, if he survived.

The gangly German boy had not. His first high-stakes race would be his last. Felix could see his body being dragged off, head bobbing at an impossible angle. A team of medical slaves stood on the sides, waiting to help with injuries to the Blue, Green, and White Racer.

Another darting glance showed him that Italicus was taking no chances. He was taking the turn as tightly as possible, not willing to risk Pharnaces out-daring him. He could not see, of course, but the Red champion had no such ideas. He was, in fact, taking the turn at a negligently wide angle. That was unusual. He was not the type to give up easily.

There were more immediate concerns, however. Both of the blue racers were skirting around the jumbled shipwreck. Without thinking, Felix lashed out at his horses and drove them toward the wall. There was not enough room for a full cart to get through, but if he didn't try he would already lose. Pieces of broken chariot stuck out haphazardly and a great black horse whinnied in agony, its reins caught in the wreck of wood and metal.

The horse closest to the wreck stumbled, and Felix shouted at it while he whipped it. He thought about slowing them down and going around it, but there might just be enough room. His own chariot, had he still been in it, could have almost certainly have made it. This larger one, however, was not as sure a thing. Felix dropped to a crouch, his white-knuckled grip grasping the front of the chariot. His knees tensed painfully as he sought balance.

Part of a shattered wheel. That was the only thought he had as the object in question flew over his head. It had come from the stand, and he had only just ducked it. It landed in the back of the chariot, a heavy wooden bludgeon that had just missed. Not content with curse tablets, someone had thrown race debris. There was no end to the escalation of violence this day, it seemed. It only took a few moments for his thought to become prophecy.

There was another loud sound ahead, and he could hear horses screaming. Felix shut out the outside world and concentrated on fitting through the narrow gap. On the wide side, the cold stone wall, several meters high. On the other, a jumbled mess of wreckage. He realized he was holding his breath. This was foolish—there was no way his chariot could fit through there, but there was no turning back now.

He shut his eyes and the horses moved in, so close they were all touching. Sparks flew from the back of the chariot and the right-hand wheel jumped as it ran over … something. The chariot caught for a heart-wrenching moment. Felix could see the crowd above him. A few hurtled curse tablets, wine bottles, or bricks at him, but none had good enough aim to hit.

Then the horses were through. His chariot lurched forward and he rocked back on his heels. He was just able to hang on. He was closing in on the blue, but both of them were just turning around the median.

He could see the Blue *aurigae*, surprise dawning upon his face. The crowd was really roaring now, and, moments later, someone screamed. There was another gathering of medical slaves, and they looked stupefied.

He did not understand what was happening, but he eased the horses away from the wall. He would have liked to take the turn more tightly, but his uneasy instinct took control and he made the turn sliding away from the wall. As he rose from his crouching position, he watched another tableau of destruction before him.

****

It would take some time to understand what he saw. Not until he talked with the stable-master would he learn all that had happened. After Felix had escaped from the Syrian's trap, the man had ridden his chariot directly to the blind spot behind the turn. In an act of reckless daring, he had then climbed out of his chariot and left it there. It had evidently been pre-arranged, for Pharnaces had known to take a wide turn without communicating with the man.

At the great speed he was going, Italicus had not had time to react. He had been thrown forward from his chariot, into his horses, which had trampled him unknowingly. Four of his ribs were smashed and his head had caved in two places. Italicus was another Red racer who had not survived the day's race.

Pharnaces had swung by gracefully, and with a wave of his hand, he acknowledged his faction mate. The Syrian had not lived long to celebrate, however. The Blue racers were close behind, and the inside driver had ridden his horses right over the man. The racer would later claim it was an accident, but all knew what he had done and most approved it.

All of this was yet to be discovered. Felix saw a blur of bodies and raced on. Only one Blue rider and Pharnaces were left. He whipped his horses with reckless frenzy. He didn't know that Italicus no longer lived, but he no longer raced, and that was enough. Enough to spur him on.

The rest of the race would always be a blur to him. He remembered passing the Blue racer, remembered the man's startled eyes as Felix's great horses moved him past. He remembered the penultimate dolphin dipping down, signifying the last lap. He remembered chasing after Pharnaces, seeing the man slowly growing larger as Felix's horses galloped with relentless power. The wrecks were still there, on each side of the track, but Felix weaved around them without a conscious thought. He remembered drawing even with Pharnaces, and the utter dismay that flooded his features. The two had raced, matching stride for stride, through the turn and into the final stretch. By the end, Felix had pulled away just enough. He had won.

He slowed his horses. Perhaps the people were cheering, perhaps the hippodrome was booming with their boisterous applause, perhaps trumpets blasted out triumphant fanfare, but Felix heard none of it. The Emperor was not presiding over this race, but the magistrate stood graciously. He held a palm branch in his right hand and clenched a victory wreath in his left. There would be money, much for the Reds and less for Felix himself, but that would happen later. The magistrate draped the wreath around his neck and handed the palm branch to the battered man. Felix took the palm branch and absently raised it to the heavens. The roars of approval somehow increased in volume, but he still heard nothing save for his own thoughts. Italicus was dead. Pharnaces was defeated. Only he remained. He was Felix, the lucky, and the greatest living *aurigae* in Rome.

CHAPTER XV

Dacia: 88 CE, Winter

Men screamed, elephants died, and the walking dead swarmed as ceaselessly as an army of ants. The battle had turned, and bereft of their leader, even the hardened Roman legion was breaking from the ceaseless tide of death that assailed them. Some of the auxiliaries had already, fled into the dark forest. Others understood that no salvation laid that way and continued to fight on.

The Dacians crept through the battlefield, avoiding the lifeless as they searched for Iullianus' body. They somewhat knew where he had fallen. Even amidst the chaos, the dead elephant he lay next to was a beacon on the battlefield. The lifeless were thick in this area, but Rowanna went after them with methodical brutality, stabbing them in their eyes or up their groaning mouths until their twitching bodies fell to the cold ground. Even Zuste fended off a few of the more aggressive ones, his arms filled with a strength fueled by fear.

They reached the fallen war elephant, but could not find the red-haired man anywhere. Behind them, the masses of the creatures flowed into the remaining Roman forces. The entire camp was, in fact, quickly becoming a large group of the lifeless monsters.

Rowanna stabbed at a lifeless menace who, until recently, appeared to have been a centurion. The creature had no pupils, but otherwise did not have the corpse-like appearance of the other lifeless. It reached for her throat hungrily and she stabbed it in the hand. It grabbed at her with its other hand, and she pulled her spear out and jabbed it at his chest. The thing still wore armor, and the point bounced off.

It had its hand around her throat, and all around more of the creatures shambled toward her. Rowanna felt a thrill of panic flutter down her back and into her stomach. Her hand reached down to grab her knife and she stabbed at the thing. Her blade sunk deep into its cheek, but it did not stop the thing. Its grip strengthened around her windpipe. The raspy, anguished sound of groaning filled her ears.

"Zuste!" she cried in garbled alarm. The word hadn't left her lips when the head in front of her split open. The blade was pulled back and the fat alchemist was before her, sweating even in the cold. "There's too many of them," he panted. "We've got to go."

She didn't say anything. She was busy staring behind him.

Zuste shook his head. "Listen to me, woman. Time is running out." He grabbed her by the shoulder. "We must leave."

"Zuste," she said, "look."

Zuste whirled in irritation. "Zalmoxis' balls, will you—"

He fell silent as the creature behind him came into focus. That great height and red hair could only belong to one person, or in this case, one ex-person. The thing that had been Tettius Iullianus moved with a jerky, spasmodic motion toward them. His mouth dripped blood as he noisily chewed on a mouthful of meat. His eyes were ivory windows reflecting hate and hunger.

"I hate this," Rowanna said in a small voice. Zuste was digging in his bag, brushing away the reaching hands of other lifeless. "Hey," Rowanna said, "follow me." She danced on the edge of the storm away from them.

Zuste followed her heavily, his hand tucked into his cloak around the precious vial. They moved back into the camp, away from the mass of lifeless. Several of the creatures twitchily followed. When they had gotten well into the camp, Rowanna stabbed the lifeless that had followed them. The end of her spear was blunted and it was clear from her shaky arms that she was growing tired, but one after another, the lifeless dropped.

Until there was only one.

"Do it!" Rowanna called. "We don't have long." A great tumult went up as the Roman army, matched by a menace even more impeccable than itself, finally broke. "We really don't have long." Men everywhere were fleeing, and those lucky enough still to be on elephants rode in all directions—some into the forest, others back through the camp. There was no refuge here anymore.

"Hold this," Zuste said, thrusting the vial into her hands. He charged forward and leaped into the air, straight into a lifeless Iullianus. The big undead man fell to ground with the alchemist on his chest. "Now, Rowanna, now. Pour it in his mouth!"

Zuste tried to pin his opponent, but the other was strong. Iullianus clawed at the bearded man's face and snarled savagely.

He heard her grunt behind him and something heavy fell to the ground. He couldn't even look, as just then the big Roman's fingers found his eyes and began to press.

"You lifeless Roman pissbag!" Zuste yelled, pulling the hands away with all his strength and only half-succeeding. Then he rocked back as the creature beneath him began to rise.

"I'm here," a voice said beside him. "Make him open his mouth."

Zuste did not think. He head butted the thing as hard as he could, forehead to forehead.

Crimson pain blossomed in the garden of his mind, and Zuste went reeling, falling off Iullianus completely.

"What are you doing?" Rowanna asked, panicked. Zuste heard her but could not answer. His body was still buried under the petals of pain.

He shook his head and rose, staggering. "That was a bad idea."

"So is this." Rowanna said. Iullianus had risen and was before her. She looked so small compared to the big man before her. She still had her spear in her left hand, but the tip was pointed down. She shoved her right hand, the one with the vial, toward the big thing's mouth.

His jaws clamped down with ferocity, but her hand was even quicker. It pulled back, and the lifeless thing bit only glass and elixir. It chewed on them, still advancing on Rowanna.

"Hey, *caput capitis*!" Zuste called, using the first bit of Latin he'd ever learned. He threw a fallen helmet and hit the thing squarely in the back. It turned and growled at him. Rowanna continued to back away. Iullianus turned and took another step toward her.

Then he fell to the ground. He collapsed as quickly and awkwardly as a marionette with its strings cut.

Zuste walked to Rowanna, who was panting from the effort. He suddenly wondered what it would be like to make her pant from a different kind of excitement. He shook his head, trying to dismiss such thoughts.

"Zuste," Rowanna said. There was something he didn't like about her tone. Women were very good at reading those kind of thoughts.

"I'm still here. I'm not too hurt yet, either." He smiled at her, making sure to look her in the eyes.

"I've been wondering. I know you're an excellent alchemist, but how did you come to have the cure for this?"

He smiled nervously. "I didn't, really. It's just a potion to cure warts. When they busted into my shop, I threw everything I had at them, more out of defiance really. That was the only thing that worked."

Rowanna frowned, but said nothing more.

"Look," said Zuste, pointing to the big man on the ground. His head still ached but rational thought was returning.

Iullianus was moving again. The Roman rose slowly, as though he had been sleeping for many years. His joints creaked and his neck was stretched at an awkward angle. He coughed once, harshly, and then gagged as he spat a mouthful of raw meat and broken glass to the ground.

"The strangest thing," he said. "Am I drunk? I feel so disoriented. Like a dream—no, it's gone." He spat another mouthful of stringy flesh to the ground. A look of great consternation passed over his face.

"Apologies," he gasped, before squatting down and voiding his bowels. Chunky feces exploded from his anus. "I've never felt a pressure like that before," he said with an embarrassed smile as he gazed up at them.

Zuste could not look away from the chunks of undigested flesh that fled from the big man's nether regions. They were bits of his own men, and quite easily could have included bits of the Dacians as well. Did the big man have no memory of it whatsoever?

More lifeless were coming, from everywhere now. Many had until recently been Roman warriors, and still more were coming from the forest. Their rotting flesh, their pupiless eyes, and their shambling gait made Zuste feel ill. Worst were the Romans—they were monsters encased in armor. "You need to finish," Zuste said.

"Easy for you to say," Iullianus said. "You don't have half a dozen weasels fighting from your stomach to your bowels." He glanced behind him, and saw the tide of danger flowing toward them. He was standing up a heartbeat later, pulling up his trousers. "It's a good thing I just shat myself, or I might have just shat myself. Let's go."

They moved quickly. With the commander back on his feet, so to speak, a handful of Roman warriors made their way to the little group. There were fallen dead everywhere, and it was easy to scavenge enough spears, blades and shields for everyone. Iullianus returned to his tent and emerged with a battered shovel. "My sword has broken. This is *efossion*, my little friend. It will not break."

They formed a ring, one that was continually spinning whilst moving back into the camp. When one of the lifeless reached them, it was stabbed or clubbed by one of them. For now, the humans were moving faster than the bulk of their enemy.

"Back!" Iullianus said. "We must fall back." The lifeless were all around them. "To the watchtower."

They made their way to the tower with methodically grim precision. More survivors joined them, and they numbered close to two dozen. Iullianus stopped them with a gesture.

"We are too many, now for the tower. Wait here." He leaped to the ladder and scaled up it. Halfway up, he lost his grip momentarily before he grabbed the ladder again. He said, audible to those below him, but apparently to himself. "My body doesn't feel right. What happened?"

Zuste moved to Rowanna. "He doesn't know?" she asked.

"He appears not to. I wonder if it would be better to leave him in the dark. Those memories would be a burden for any man."

"Perhaps," said Rowanna. "Though if ever a man could bear the burden of every truth, it would be that one."

"At any rate, we don't need to distract him now," Zuste said. "If we survive this, we can decide what to do later."

Rowanna nodded her agreement as Iullianus climbed back down.

"It's grim," he said. "Our chances are the same as pulling wool from an ass, but we'll take as many of those bastards with us as we can."

"Commander," one of his troops barked, "we saw you fall. How did you survive?"

131

"I blacked out. They must have thought I was already dead, until these two found me. Now, there will be time for catch up later, but until then, the best place is the elephant pens. They might be gone, but it's got high walls and flowing water. We might hold out there for some time."

Again, they formed the circle, and again they made their way through the camp. The lifeless were growing denser, and the light was fading. The sound of moaning filled their ears, though it was difficult to tell if it came from wounded men or hungry lifeless. Probably both, Zuste thought. He was not the warrior any of them were, but with a sharp enough spear, he could fend off single attackers. The lifeless were numerous, bloodthirsty and vicious, and it was only their slowness that gave the remaining humans a chance at survival.

They reached the elephant camp and closed the great gates. Two riders had managed to return, so they had two of the great grey beasts. They were clearly agitated, stomping, and trumpeting. One was bleeding from his flanks and it snorted with pain.

Iullianus immediately sent men to the top of the walls. They scaled up like monkeys, climbing with purpose and agility. Others he sent to the river to collect stones—they had many bows but fewer arrows. Stones made for primitive, last resort missile weapons. He sent more to wash the elephants and remove their war gear.

It was only then that he turned to the Dacians, who were standing behind him. "What a smell," he said. Even amidst the smoke, blood, and death of the day, the stink of the elephants was palpable. It was a strong smell, but not unpleasant. It smelled earthier than human feces, Zuste thought. "The things are like great cows," Iullianus apologized. "Their stink can become overwhelming."

"Now, we should be safe, however much that word means now," the Roman commander told them. "I am going to have a short sleep. I don't mean to sleep the entire night, but I am so tired."

"Are you sure we can sleep?" Zuste asked. "Shouldn't we work on an escape plan?"

"Look around, friend. Mountains at our back, eyeless bastards at our front. I picked this area because it could contain elephants." The big man yawned broadly. "I am sorry, but I just can't keep my eyes open anymore."

He lay down in the mud and was almost instantly asleep.

"I shall join him," Rowanna said, lying down on some relatively dry grass. "Wake me up if we are about to die."

"How can you sleep at a time like this?" Zuste asked. "We should plan. We are not safe here."

"Soon, soon," Rowanna said, her eyes already closed. Zuste looked around him, but the other Romans were all busy with their tasks. He was quite hungry, he realized. He wondered if he could make anything appetizing out of elephant food.

Soon, a small fire was crackling and Zuste roasted some nuts he had found. It wasn't much, but it helped settle his stomach. He was so nervous that even his appetite was hampered. From outside, he could hear the groans and clanging of the lifeless. There seemed to be more every moment. The great gate seemed too massive for them to tear down, but he wouldn't dismiss the idea for certain. They really didn't know anything about the lifeless and what they could or couldn't do. More problematically, it would be equally difficult for the living to get out.

He popped a chestnut into his mouth and chewed slowly. Without thinking about it, he looked over to Rowanna and she was sleeping. Her breasts rose and fell with deep breaths and her mouth hung open. She was really out, sleeping as though she hadn't a care in the world. He wondered how he felt about her. At first, she had been someone who could keep him alive, but who had also needed his help. She didn't need his help anymore, but his feelings were changing. He was nearly as worried for her as he was for himself, and that was saying something.

He munched on another nut and wondered how they would be able to get away. For the first time, he wondered if there could ever be an end to this scourge. If so, how would the world be different? These thoughts fragmented into a thousand others, and he never even noticed that his eyes were closing.

****

The cold woke him up in the night. His little fire had gone out and someone had covered him with an itchy, thin blanket that reeked of animal. Blearily-eyed, the alchemist looked around in the gloom. There was enough torchlight coming from the top of the walls to see most of the camp.

Rowanna still slept. She, too, was wrapped in a few blankets. Beside her, he noted, were several Roman soldiers he did not know. Zuste fought a surge of jealousy, as he realized that Rowanna was perhaps the only living woman for a good many days. Iullianus was easy to spot, as the big red haired Roman was close by, talking to two of his men. They, too, had large blankets draped over their shoulders. Their breath steamed into the dark mountain air.

He noticed the alchemist's glance at once and smiled at him. "Zuste. Pray, join us. We are discussing survival, bedding women, and other likely futile subjects."

The bearded man made his way over to them. His blanket trailed in the earth behind him. The cold night settled assertively in his bones and he shivered. "*Amicus*," Iullianus said, "when the two of you arrived, I assumed you were a couple. Since then, however, I have noted that your interactions lack a certain kind of intimacy."

"We are not married," Zuste instantly realized it would have been better to lie, but it was too late. "But we have been through a lot together, these last couple days."

The Legatus nodded sagely. "Indeed, you have." His voice was all understanding, but his eyes sparkled at Zuste, belying his tone.

"Couple or not," one of the other men said, "she might be the last piece of flesh most of us get to experience." He was tall with sandy blond hair and looked to be a Gaul or Northern Italian.

The other soldier scoffed. "Typical. It's the end of the world and all you can think about is getting your dick wet."

"We are not going to gang rape anyone," Iullianus said. "Least of all, an ally and a friend."

The sandy haired man did not give up. "You can do what you want, when those things get through. Just don't try to stop me from mine."

"When those things get through?" Zuste asked. "Will the gate not hold?"

There was an awkward silence. "I mean, this not as an insult, friend," Iullianus said, "but I fear you may be too big to climb up and see for yourself what we three have seen."

"What? What have you seen?"

"Outside the gate are more of the lifeless than we have ever seen—maybe four or five times more than the horde that smashed our army yesterday," Iullianus said. His tone said he wasn't finished, that the worst was yet to come. Zuste could not imagine anything that would feel him with more fear. Then the red-haired man said, "We lost many elephants out there today. Now we have seen the cost of that lost. We are faced with lifeless war elephants, rampaging against us with a power we cannot contest. No, our gate won't hold for long."

CHAPTER XVI

Rome: 88 CE, Winter

Rufus sat in the *peristylum*, the shady open courtyard beyond the atrium. Floral notes wafted from his garden, and from his stool he could admire his garden. It was one of the best in Rome, but this morning it did not please him. Another morning was passing outside around him as petty men whined for his favor. It was almost, he thought, almost enough to make him miss exile, though he still savored the lack of salt and fish in the air. The only good news was that Sparsus had left the city. For now, Rufus had as much power over the Emperor as anyone, though that meant little these days.

"Senator?"

"It cannot be done," he told the freeman cringing before him. "Though I can claim him as a friend, Caesar invites whom he wants to his parties. And I truly don't believe he cares how beautiful your daughter is."

It's remarkable, he thought. *Give anyone a bit more money or power, and next thing they want is to cozy up to the Emperor.* That man's father had been a slave.

The man nodded, obviously displeased, but he knew better than to press his case too far. "Gratias, Senator," he said, backing out of the room. He was met by Fulvius, who sternly led him away through the atrium.

Rufus rose from his stool and filled his glass with water from a large pipe. He had just installed new lead pipes and they were massive. This was good for bathing, drinking, and gardening, but the Emperor taxed heavily on pipe size and Rufus rued more of his money going to Domitian. It seemed you just couldn't get rich enough—there were always more people who wanted some of his money.

Rufus looked up suddenly. There was shouting coming from outside. An abruptly muffled scream half-rang out. Rufus took three long steps toward the atrium before the sudden disbelief flooded through him.

Three dirty and rough men sauntered into the *peristylum*. They'd obviously forced their way past Fulvius. One was eating an apple, snapping into it with juicy bites.

"Salve, Senator Gaius Sulpicius Rufus," said the tallest of the men, "we are here to give you a message."

"Who sent you? Is this another of Cornellius' pranks? What are you about?" Rufus asked, bristling at the use of his cognomen by a mere *servus*.

"No prank, Senator, no prank. We are deadly men, and dangerous." His hand fell to the blade at his hip.

"We are sent to tell you," said the man beside him, " that my master knows about the land you've bought. He knows about the slaves you've taken. He's not happy, and he wants you to stop. Your rank won't save you if you continue."

The first man reached into his clothes and emerged with his penis in his hand. "Consider yourself warned," he said. He began pissing on the marble floor, and the scent of acrid urine hit Rufus almost immediately.

A few of Rufus' household slaves moved forward but he stopped them. His slaves were not armed and he had no doubt the men before him were indeed deadly. Even more, he wanted to see this message delivered to its fullest. He could be sure to respond in kind.

"Who is your master?" he called out to the trio. The pissing man was just beginning to run dry.

Harsh laughter greeted his words. "We surely don't have to tell you that, Senator," the second man said. "Just hope you never have to meet him. Next time, he might not be accommodating."

The man wheeled around, followed closely by the apple-eater and the pisser, who had hurriedly tucked his member away.

Rufus summoned his slaves to clean the mess and canceled the rest of his appointments. It was mere moments later that a scream alerted him to the full extent of the message. Foreboding filled him as he strode into the atrium. It was, as he had to admit, exactly what he'd expected, and it was also exactly what he would have done. He sighed deeply and stared at the scene before him.

Fulvius lay dead on the ground, his throat slit deeply and savagely. An apple core lay on his chest.

****

The moon was high in the night sky by the time Rufus left his home. It had taken time, but his home was full of armed men—some conspicuously so, others hidden throughout the household. Pairs of ex-gladiators guarded the entrances to his home, and his litter was surrounded by a dozen of trustworthy ex-soldiers. All this preparation had come too late, but better to stop that particular attack before anticipating future ones.

It had been expensive, however, especially on such short notice. Rufus was not used to having problems with money. With his recent purchases, he had spent much of his savings and even had many of his properties outside Rome sold off. Though he tried to keep it quiet, rumors were coming back to him. Maybe he should not have added those new pipes after all, he thought with a rueful smile.

He wished again that he'd been able to add the new quarters to his home. This would have meant guards at only one place, and less vulnerable travel time between the two places. However, there was no room, and his neighbors were as wealthy and inquisitive as he was. His new training quarters would not be far away, but they would be essentially invisible from everyone who mattered. They were located in the heart of Subura, the most dangerous slum in Rome.

Rufus reached the first of his training centers without incident. "Two guards come with me," he said. "The others stay here by my litter. This won't take long."

There were guards here already, eyeing all who approached what had until recently, been the ground floor *tabernae*. It was a big building, and the inside looked like the interior of a ludus, where gladiators trained. Strong men from all over the Empire, men that he owned, practiced their sword play and developed battle tactics. It's no wonder that the owners of other gladiator schools felt threatened. He really should have seen that coming. He realized it could look like a threat to the Emperor as well, and decided to tell Domitian of his actions before the ruler could grow alarmed. A sudden idea bloomed from that thought. If he did not have to be circumspect, he could have the best men in the city.

"Senator," the guards greeted him with aloof reverence. There was no mistaking the conditioning of former gladiators, and no other slave had been broken as thoroughly, as exceptionally.

He was met by Buikhu, the Egyptian *servus* who would be administering Rufus' growing army. His tunic was rumpled and appeared to have been hastily thrown on. His forehead glistened with small beads of sweat, and his black hair was tousled messily. Though Rufus had not met him until recently, the *servus* came highly recommended by a friend of his in the Senate.

"Senator, I was not expecting you this evening. Please forgive my appearance. Can I serve you wine or some food?"

Rufus waved his hand negligently. "It is of no concern, and I won't be here for long." He sat down on the lectus wearily. "I've made a mistake. I've looked so far that I missed the threat before me. There may be, I don't know, warnings, attacks, or other unpleasantries coming your way. I want you to be ready to repulse them. Without losses, but without showing our strength either. Do you understand?"

The dark-haired man nodded. "Indeed I do, Senator. You want me to perform the impossible," he said, without a trace of humor.

"You understand perfectly. That is good," Rufus said, equally dryly. "One more thing. I am going to be buying more slaves soon, perhaps as early as tomorrow. Make sure you are ready for them, and their needs may be exotic. And what of your connection?"

Buikhu blinked at the sudden conversation shift. "Senator, my cousin is a liar and cheater, but he says he can get us into the Hippodrome. I am inclined to believe him."

"Good," Rufus said again. "On second thought, I will have some wine."

****

The crowd roared their approval for him. Men chanted his name, women flashed their tits, and all worshipped at his feet. Felix stood before them all for a brief second, letting them see him in his glory before he disappeared into the tunnel leading back down to his team.

He was the star of the gold faction, a group created by the Emperor himself. He had just won his fourth consecutive race. More impressively, at the age of twenty-four, he was amongst the oldest *aurigae* still alive. There were a few legends in their thirties and forties, but none had started at such a young age. It took great skill, and perhaps more importantly, great luck.

He greeted some of the younger racers, children who weren't much older than he had been when he'd started. Racing worked up a large appetite for him, but first, he had to meet with his *equos nutriebat*.

The man was young, just into his thirties, and if he had ever raced, no living man in Rome had witnessed it. He had clearly been given the post as a favorite of the Emperor. He was, for all that, fair and even-handed, and Felix almost liked him.

"You raced well today, Felix, and you earned more coin. If you stay alive, you may actually be free in another ten years."

"Oh, I will be alive," Felix said, "and I will do it in less time than you think."

The stable-master laughed. "Such confidence. If every grown man had the immortality you lads think you've got, the world would be a different place."

"I'm too important to die," Felix said, laughing, though he did not jest. "You heard them up there."

"If every man they loved was too important to die, there would be too many charioteers for the all the grain of Egypt to feed." The man's face grew serious. "Have you done anything unusual recently?"

Felix thought for a moment. "No, not that I can think of. Why?"

"After you bathe, there is someone who wants to meet you."

"Who is it? Can it wait until after I eat—winning gives me such an appetite?"

"He's the kind of man you don't keep waiting."

That only meant one thing to Felix. "He represents a new owner? Blood and piss, how many times must I be bought and sold?"

There was a brief silence. "He doesn't represent your new owner, boy. He is your new owner."

"An equestrian? In the bowels of the city?" Felix asked.

The other man spoke softly. "He's not an equestrian, Felix. He's a Senator."

Felix ran to the meeting, forgetting both bath and meal.

****

The man before him was a personification of a Roman. His graying hair was still thick, but he was balding at the top. His patrician nose was sharp and disproving.

"They tell me you are a Jew. Do you follow that religion's precepts?"

"My parents were Jewish, Senator, and they were traitors. I am a Roman," Felix told him stoutly.

"Good. In your races, you've caused the deaths of many of your competitors, but face-to-face is different. Could you kill a man while staring him in the eyes?"

"I believe I could, depending on how much harm that man meant me."

"Excellent. It is known throughout Rome that you are fearless. I wonder though. Privately, is there anything you fear? Many otherwise stout men fear fire or the night, for instance."

Felix paused. "There is only one thing."

"Don't worry. I'm too old to get angered by anything you say. Go ahead, tell me," Rufus said.

"The only thing I fear, Senator, is obscurity."

Rufus laughed. "Oh yes. Slave or free, all young men dream of greatness. I fear your duties with me will earn you no songs, no kisses from pretty women."

"Senator, why toy with me? You own me, and I shall do as you say."

"You misunderstand. I own you, but I want you to embrace the role I have for you. You may even enjoy it. I also have a large, Greek flower at my home. Very large indeed, if you take my meaning."

A breath passed and then another before realization dawned. "I have known such a flower, but it is lost to me. If you have found it, I am greatly pleased."

"It is indeed true. Why would I lie to a slave," the Senator said. "Come."

Felix followed the Senator out of the building, scarcely remembering to wave farewell to his former faction-mates.

CHAPTER XVII

Dacia: 88 CE, Winter

There was no transition from sleeping to wakefulness. Rowanna's eyes snapped open and she was immediately awake. The night had grown colder and darker and someone had thrown blankets over her. They reeked, emanating a base animal smell that was almost too intense to bear. Much worse was the low moaning, audible even from here that came from the other side of the gate. She wondered if the unearthly sound was what had woken her up.

It had stopped raining, and the only remaining clouds were wispy things that did nothing to shade the starlight. The moon was half-full. Most of the Romans gathered around a small fire, dicing. The three elephants loomed as dark shadows against the night sky. She had seen them sleeping standing up and wondered if they were now resting. There was no sign of Iullianus. Zuste was over by the stream, head down in thought.

She made her way over to him. His eyes were dark, and he did not even attempt to smile.

"What is wrong?" she asked.

He shook his head. "Ask Iullianus," he mumbled.

"Zuste. Are you angry with me?" she asked.

"What does that matter?" he asked. "We have hours at best to live. Why worry about something like that now?"

"Hours?" Rowanna asked. "The gate will hold longer than that."

"Maybe," Zuste said doubtfully, "but look up there."

He pointed up to the top of the gate. There was a pair of men up there, balanced on the top of the wall. Even in the dark, one was obviously Iullianus. "He thinks and plans…but they have seen more lifeless. Many, many more. And, Rowanna, there are now undead elephants."

His words sunk into her brain, instantly drowning her hope and cheer. "Those noble creatures, it doesn't seem right," she said.

"Not right?" he said angrily. "What's not right is that they will break through those doors and we will all be dead. Or worse—we will become like those things." He paused, breathed deeply. "Maybe it's not so bad. Maybe they were the smart ones all along."

Without thinking, she slapped him. Not as hard as she could, but as though he were her misbehaving son. The bearded alchemist stared at her in shock, rubbing his cheek.

"We could have given up by the apple tree, or on the way up here, but we've survived too much for such talk!" She was yelling, and a few of the Roman soldiers looked at her, but she didn't stop. "We're healthy, we have food, weapons, and we have strong warriors with us. I can kill them, you can cure them. We can't die. We won't die."

Zuste said nothing, just turned and stared at the river. Eventually, he spoke again. "They can come in through here, you know. Eventually, they'll figure it out."

Rowanna looked to where the cliff ended and the river began. The wall ended halfway through the river. It was far too small for an elephant to escape, but certainly big enough for men to come through.

"When did you see this?" she asked, panicked. It suddenly seemed as though every shadow, every splash, was a lifeless intruder.

"Just a small time ago," he said.

"Why haven't you told Iullianus?" she asked, getting angry. "We can't give up."

He held up his hands defensively. "I haven't given up, not really. I think I have a plan. I have been running it over in my head and it might work. It might get us all killed, but that's beginning to look inevitable now." His eyes lifted to the sky. It appeared as dark as ever, but he said, "Dawn is not far off now. Let us speak with the Romans."

****

"By Mithras, I've heard better plans," the Legatus had said when they had spoken to him. He leaned wearily upon the handle of his shovel, as it looked to be the only thing holding him up. "In fact, if I've heard of a worse plan, it escapes me."

"May my gods and yours strike me down if it fails," Zuste said. "It's better than waiting for the inevitable."

"Peace, friend," the tall man had said with a smile, "but what do you say to the idea that we slip out through the hole?"

The Roman tried not to smile as both Dacians gaped at him. The idea of flight had not yet occurred to them. Perhaps it would not have ever occurred. A smile small did emerge on his face, but it was one of fondness. They were so like his own people, these Dacians.

"Trust a Roman rat to run when he can fight," the alchemist said. "Why not stand here, against them, and at the worst, kill more of them than they can convert of us?"

Iullianus wondered at the man's sense of obligation. He wasn't craven, but nor did he habitually spoil for a fight. There was something deeply hidden—Zuste's secret, or one of Rowanna's that he was protecting.

"It so happens that I agree. However, I will present my men a choice. They may take their chances with the stream, or stay here with us."

Thirty men— almost half of their forces—slipped out the river way in the next hour. "I hope they freeze to death," the Dacian alchemist said. Iullianus said nothing, though he too was disappointed. What was the Roman Empire coming to? They'd been much more motivated when they had conquered other lands. His home, for instance.

"Promise me one thing," Iullianus had said to the collected men, "if I am bit or wounded, kill me immediately. I would not want to live as one of those creatures."

The Dacians looked at each other very pointedly. There was definitely something secretive going on. He would have to ferret it out from them later. If there was a later.

The next two hours had been busy, and they'd collected all the elephant dung they could find and built it into a horseshoe shape surrounding the gates. When they'd finished, the wall of dried feces was nearly a meter high all around. More importantly, it was nearly two meters long. They added all the dry grass, papyrus, and cloth sacks they could find. Before the wall, they'd dug a pit that was over a meter deep. It wouldn't stop the lifeless, but it would slow them down.

"If this works, alchemist," Iullianus said to Zuste as they leaned on their shovels in the pre-dawn light, "I don't know if I'll be more surprised or grateful. Probably equal measures of both." He motioned to the two men who were perched on the gates.

"If this works," the bearded man replied, "even I will want to kiss myself." The thumping at the gate was heavy now, a slow insistent pounding that shook the foundation and cracked the wood. The men on the gates held on and signaled their readiness.

"I won't," Iullianus said, "not with the role you assigned me." With that, he sprang forward, towards the gate. The others formed a line. Rowanna had tried on some spare armor, but it was too heavy for her. Nothing the Romans had would fit Zuste, but everyone else was as covered as they could be. All had spears and swords, but behind them were dozens of stakes and sharpened wooden poles. This was one modification that Iullianus had suggested. Behind them all, between the battle line and the stream, were the three elephants. They were the auxiliaries and shock troops all in one.

The Roman commander reached the gate. "Brace yourselves," he called. "Unless the gods favor the insane, we won't live long today. If things get bad, head to the stream." He looked up at the two men perched on the top of the gate. "Except for you two. Just hold on and pray Jupiter is feeling kind." They laughed.

He turned and moved the great wooden bar from its posts, and turning, sprinted back. He was followed by a lurching, shambling tide of rotten death as the creatures massed forward. Before, they been as numerous as stars in the sky, but now, they were as many as grains of sand on the shore. Iullianus could see the lifeless elephants lumbering amongst the others. Lured by the scent of blood, they had trampled the human lifeless and had been throwing themselves against the barrier between them and their meal with agonizing force.

"Now!" Iullianus called. A volley of four arrows sprang into the air, followed moments later by another. None hit the elephants in the eye, as they were supposed to.

"Damn," he said. He motioned to the men on the wall. "Now! Now!" he said, whirling his hand in the pre-arranged signal.

The two men had barely clung to the gates when they had swung open. Now they reached into their bags and dropped lanterns filled with lamp oil. Each had three, and when all of them had been dropped, they threw emptied drinking bladders that had also been filled with oil. They coated many of the lifeless that inevitably surged forward, though the majority were not touched—had not yet reached the gate.

Iullianus stopped before the pit and laughed as the lifeless reached him. His soldiers and Rowanna were there, ready to fight this menace. He hefted his heavy shovel and battered the heads of the ones that drew too close to him. They did not rise. Many of these were half-naked walking corpses. But there were some—former Dacian warriors or centurions—who wore armor. These centurion lifeless were a new danger. They were protected by armor, and so newly dead that they were hard to kill. The centurions had few weak points—their armor covered them from their ankles to their necks. Some even still had shields strapped to them, though they did not hold them in a useful way.

There were three centurions advancing on the Legatus now. He surged forward, and pushed heavily on one. It fell down, and quickly, the other two were knocked over as well. Before they could rise again, they were trampled by their own kind. He laughed victoriously, but something about the monsters bothered him—as though he had a forgotten but vivid nightmare about them.

Iullianus retreated back to the others. Beside him, Rowanna held her spear with both hands. She had no skill in the technical sense, but her enthusiasm made up for it and no lifeless was safe near her. She fought with a passion the Romans had never known. She was nearly as fierce as the women of his own tribe, who had exemplified warrior women for him. Iullianus had never before thought of her as attractive, but now, in the middle of battle, he wondered what it would be like to challenge that passion with his own weapons.

He killed reflexively as he imagined the Dacian woman completely nude, growling at him. He realized he had grown quite hard. Shaking his head to clear the images, he stabbed another lifeless.

Finally, too many had reached the gap. "Fall back," he called, though he did not move. He stabbed, swung, and pushed against the swarming lifeless. After the others had made it back, Iullianus sprang back over it, onto the dung hill, and then back to the reassembling line of warriors.

"Trying to be impressive?" asked Rowanna. He shrugged with a guilty smile. They turned to watch as the first line of lifeless dropped suddenly. The pit was not deep, but it slowed them enough for the creatures behind them to crush them. The elephants were too big to bother with the pit, but they were even more uncoordinated and ungainly than the human lifeless.

"Oh, look at them," Rowanna said.

Iullianus glanced and felt a stab of fear. Seeing the war elephants' white, soulless eyes, just above their massive tusks, was a chilling sight.

"We still have some of our own," he said, but his reassurance sounded hollow even to himself. "Though even my mighty *efossion* is outmatched against that foe."

As lifeless of all kinds reached the mound of dung, Zuste appeared with a lit torch in each hand. A dozen men reached into their belts and lit their torches as well.

Zuste looked in askance to Iullianus. The nearest lifeless were only a meter away, but too many of them were not on the dung pile yet. Another flight of arrows came, and one hit an elephant in the eye. Iullianus did not see who had shot it, but he made a note to discover the man who had made the shot and promote him. The undead animal did not seem to feel pain, but with its vision restricted it stumbled and fell, crushing many of the lifeless beneath it.

There were still too many not on the pile, but the forefront were coming too close. The tide of undead swelled behind them, and Iullianus knew he could wait no longer. "Now!" he cried. Instantly, the burning brands were flung into the giant dung horseshoe. Both the lifeless and the dung pile had been soaked in oil, and the resulting heat was immediate and intense. The fire roared and crackled, burning through the oil-soaked monsters like dry kindling. The humans moved back as the heat grew more intense.

Iullianus was worried. The fire was burning too hot, too quickly. There were still hundreds or thousands of lifeless pressing forward and it did not look like the fire would last long enough to incinerate them. "It's not going to last," he yelled in warning.

Suddenly, Zuste was beside him. He seemed to guess from the Roman's expression what the man was thinking, for he smiled and said, "Did anyone ever tell you that you worry too much?"

The portly man reached his hand into his tunic and it emerged with three glass vials. Without a noted lack of ceremony, the alchemist threw the first one in. The fire flared up, larger than ever.

More of the lifeless were coming though, and Zuste hurriedly threw the other two vials. Iullianus guessed that they had already killed a thousand in these few moments, but there were several thousand more to come. He had counted five lifeless war elephants, though he had never been certain there weren't more. From here, he could see three in various states of burning. None, at least, appeared immediately ready to attack.

The alchemic fires were burning as fiercely as ever. Very few lifeless emerged, and those who did, were quickly dispatched by the nearest soldier. Nevertheless, Iullianus doubted whether they would be able to hold out against odds such as these. Each defender would have to kill hundreds of attackers.

Iullianus called two men to him. To the first he said, "Grab the supplies we prepared. Make sure they are watertight." To the second he said, "The thing we discussed. Do it." The man had a very sharp, very long spike at his side. Iullianus knew that he himself should have done this duty, but it was too hard. He'd been through too much with the noble beasts, and he couldn't kill them himself. But even worse was to leave them here alive to be devoured by the lifeless and possibly face their corpses again.

"Fall back," he said. "Prepare to get wet."

He heard splashing, much more than one man could possibly make. He whirled, braced to see lifeless emerging from the frozen stream. Then he stopped, suddenly uncertain. There were many figures climbing from the water, it was true. They were dressed in rags and looked wild, as though they'd been sleeping in trees or caves, but they moved with grace and precision, and he could hear them talking. The man he'd sent to check on the supplies had been overwhelmed and had a knife at his throat. A tall man emerged, and the others seemed to defer to him.

Iullianus strode up to him. They were nearly the same height—it had been a while since he'd talked to anyone his own size. "I am the Legate Tettius Iullianus. Release my man at once," he said, "and explain what you are doing here."

"We came," said the other man. He had sharp features and blue eyes, and a large wolf pendant hung around his neck. "To kill some of the baleful." His Latin had the same accent as Zuste. The Dacian man waved to his men and they released their Roman prisoner.

"Then we will have time enough for talking later," Iullianus said. He yelled to the man who had reached the elephants and motioned for him to stop. It was surprising at how much relief he felt.

More and more men emerged from the river. They looked cold, but they had skins covered in animal fat that seemed to help. Within moments, there were two hundred Dacians behind them. By Iullianus' estimation, they were all warriors, though they had the lean look of men who had been skipping meals for too long.

The Dacians had bows with them, and they quickly strung them. At the same time, men with axes, swords, and spears, ran to the line of fire and reinforced the handful of Romans who fought there. When the fires began to die down again, Zuste ran up and down the line, throwing vials that exploded with intense heat. He had seen the man playing with potions for the last several days, but hadn't any idea just how useful an alchemist could be.

Iullianus waved to his men on the gates. He could not hear them over the battle, but they gestured to him. They seemed to be pleased, or at least less dour than they'd been since climbing up there.

"It's a clever thing, these fires," said a voice beside him. The tall Dacian was suddenly next to him. The man looked familiar and his bearing was unmistakably noble. He held an old sword that looked to have already seen some use that day.

"One of your kind thought of it," Iullianus admitted, stabbing the face of a lifeless soldier whose armor had burned into its skin.

"I had heard there were Dacians here, from those who escaped in the dawn. It was they who alerted me. I admire a commander that values humanity and life over obedience."

"I admire anyone who risks their life to save mine. If you brought beer, we can be best friends," the red-haired man replied. Just then, a horde of burning corpses emerged from the fires and there was no longer any time for talking.

Iullianus realized how much the rules had changed. An army of men would not charge into a raging fire, and when they lost half their forces, they would break. Many armies, in fact, would break from far fewer losses. These things would fight until the last of them was killed. He wondered if there was a way to use their single-mindedness against them.

The fires roared again, surging forward and there was time to breathe. Many of his soldiers had fallen, along with several of the Dacian warriors. He realized suddenly the terrible menace that was represented. There was no time to check for life. A wound in this battle was a death sentence. He called some men to him and soon, they were beheading their own dead.

"What are you doing?" The Dacian leader asked, suddenly beside him.

"They will rise again," Iullianus said, swinging a borrowed sword down on a groaning Dacian. It didn't cut through the neck entirely and he raised it again. "You must know that."

"I do," the man said, "but such a solution had not occurred to me."

"If you have a better idea," Iullianus said, "I'm willing to hear it." The blade came down and the wounded man's head rolled away.

"It is difficult for me to see Romans butchering my men, whatever their reasons. Let me take care of them."

Iullianus gestured to the battlefield. "Have at it." He turned to confront the last of the wounded soldiers. It was the man he had sent to the water, bleeding from a dozen small wounds.

"Please," the man said. Iullianus drove his blade into the man's throat, filled with anger. How dare that man plead? He knew the circumstances, knew that there could be no chances. He was furious that he felt his eyes moisten. Anger was a short-lived madness, but he needed to stoke it, to embrace it. He needed anger to survive the world.

It was then that the monstrous elephant lumbered through. It was coated in flames. Quicker than a heartbeat, it snatched up a Dacian spearman with its trunk. The man's body crumpled in that strong mouth and he disappeared down the thing's throat.

It was nearly too much. Dacian and Roman warrior alike backed away from the terrible burning beast. Undead humans were frightening enough, but these men did not know how to fight the burning beast before them. Iullianus glanced at the three elephants that were still alive, but they would be no help. They were afraid of flames and if one fell, it would be on the wrong side of the fires when it came back.

Suddenly, the Dacian leader was before the beast, a long spear in his hand. The elephant lowered its head and stabbed with its tusks. The man leaped away, dropping his spear. The beast was a bit slower and stupider than when it had been alive. It scanned the area ponderously with gleaming white eyes.

The tall Dacian man regained his feet almost instantly. He went from run to crouch to run so quickly it was almost impossible to see the spear he had reclaimed. He was far too close when the elephant saw him and with a leap, he drove the point deep into the thing's eye.

Nothing happened. The elephant-thing didn't seem to notice. Its trunk grabbed at the tall man and once again he dropped to the ground, just avoiding the grasping limb. The elephant charged forward but the man rolled away and sprang up. He either had a flair for the dramatic, or was very lucky.

"Archers, fire!" Iullianus called.

Several bowmen aimed shots at it, but the arrows burned, bounced off, or went unnoticed.

"Lead it back to the fire," Iullianus called to the Dacian leader, hoping it was a good idea. At any rate, he didn't want that thing anywhere near the remaining elephants. They were nervous enough as it was. The man made no sign that he had heard. Indeed, he began dancing back toward the stream. He kept himself in the beast's sight the entire time.

Groaning alerted him to more lifeless emerging through the fires. Some were not burning much at all. Where was Zuste? Iullianus killed three of them in thrice that many seconds and glanced back. The Dacian man pulled his spear from the elephant's right eye and plunged it into the left. It was blinded, but still moved with lumbering power.

Iullianus felt his mind shatter, just a little, as he contemplated the enormity of the task. Beheading worked well for human lifeless, but there was no blade in the world sharp enough to cut through an elephant. A hundred men wouldn't be strong enough to strike, even if such a blade existed.

He left the line and found Zuste, collapsed on the cold earth.

"Are you hurt," he asked the alchemist.

"Exhausted. Not wounded," he said, his face coated in smoke and grime, "but I have no more elixirs. The fire is on its own." Iullianus found it hard to listen to him. Something about Zuste and his potions jogged his memories.

"There's no time to rest. Grab a sword and kill them that way," he said, but it was only half-hearted.

The elephant had stumbled into the line of warriors at the fire and knocked them aside.

Immediately, undead monsters stumbled through the dying fire. Iullianus sprang away, his blade whirling in his hand. He motioned toward the elephants and the man immediately set about untying them. It didn't take long, mere moments, but for Iullianus and the others battling the deathless creatures, it took a lifetime.

****

It was over. Hours had passed and day was reigning. The sun shone somewhere behind the clouds. The lifeless were dead. The undead elephant had crashed back into the flames and melted into bones and flesh. The last three living elephants were no more, two had been chewed to death by lifeless, and the third had panicked and charged away, into the camp, but the lifeless were no more. Thousands of them had burned, and the others had been stabbed, hacked, or speared to death. Only twenty of Iullianus' men remained alive, including the two who had climbed the gates.

Seven more had survived the battle, but they had been injured and subsequently beheaded. It had been hard for the men who were only slightly wounded, but this was a matter that could not be taken seriously enough. The Dacians had lost more men—just shy of a hundred of them would not rise again, in life or unlife. It was sometimes hard to tell which had died as men, and which had died as monsters, but the lifeless were no more.

Zuste was exhausted. Though he had done little fighting, his elixirs had kept the fire burning hot and bright for most of the battle. He'd hardly slept and had done more sprinting today than perhaps the rest of his life put together. His stomach alerted him to the fact that he was starving, but there was little food to be had.

Rowanna limped to Zuste and hugged him with exuberance. "Your plan," she said, "your plan and your fire, it gave us a chance." She was half-covered in blood, had deep bruises along her wrists and arms, and bits of brain clung to her disheveled hair. She had never looked more beautiful.

"I was lucky to have made so many, though I would have given much for more. Even yesterday, I thought I had a supply that would last long. I never would have thought so much fire could be needed."

"It was," Rowanna said, "and I thank the gods that you were here."

That one hurt him, deep in his gut. He was saved as Iullianus approached. Though he was streaked with smoke and gore, he appeared to be largely unhurt. Of course, that was the point, and any who had been wounded in the slightest were no longer alive. The red-haired Roman treated them to a great conspiratorial grin. "That was a good trick, alchemist. It wouldn't have mattered were I not such a fell warrior, but it was good nonetheless."

"Neither of our efforts would have mattered had not a small army shown up," Zuste pointed out.

"Indeed," Iullianus said, "the enemy of my enemy, as you know."

"What now?" Rowanna asked.

"Not what." Iullianus said. "Where, and where else but Rome?"

CHAPTER XVIII

Rome: 88 CE, Winter

The Senator and his newly purchased *servus* arrived at the training quarters in the Subura some time later. It was not far from the center of town, but even the short ride had caused Felix to sit in the litter uncomfortably. He shook his head, slightly rueful. The man who was so comfortable racing chariots was almost comically leery of the luxury and conspicuousness offered by a Senator's litter.

"Go forth," the Senator urged, "I will speak with you when after you have seen it all."

Felix climbed out of the litter and stared at the building before him. It was old, perhaps pre-dating the building reforms of Augustus, but it was big and it was sturdy. The building had already survived earthquakes, fires, and civil wars, and it looked capable of surviving many more.

They walked into the building, past two bulky guards in the former tavernae. The big man was waiting for him there, trying to suppress a huge grin and failing.

"Hyacinthus, old friend," Felix said, "I doubted that I would ever see you again. Why did you not come to my games?"

"Felix," he cried, enclosing the boy in a mammoth hug. Felix realized how long it had been since he had seen his friend as he tightly hugged back. The man's hair was sparse and gray, new lines clung to his face, and he was fatter than ever. It was a mild shock to think that Felix now was almost the age that Hyacinthus had been when they had first met. "Look at you. From skinny *servus* to champion *aurigae,* with all of Rome singing your praises. Though, such games are not for me, they are too dramatic, too full of bloodshed for this learned man."

The two men caught up as Hyacinthus showed Felix around the complex. Everywhere were caches of weapons, men training, and ever vigilant guards. Finally, with evident excitement, Hyacinthus brought him into a large room toward the back of the building.

The room was full of vials and bubbling liquids. Felix had seen such places indicated in plays and understood where he was at once. "This is a place of science," he said. "Your dream has come true."

The boy glanced behind him, making sure they were alone. "Tell me, what is this all for?"

Hyacinthus shook his head slowly, admonishingly. "I haven't asked, and I won't, but it's not hard for an intelligent man to guess. It shouldn't be difficult for a brash boy like yourself too either," he added.

Felix smiled reflexively, but his mind was distracted by the thought that he was owned by a Senator who clearly aimed to be the next Emperor.

They sat and talked. Hyacinthus had gone to a few competitions, back when Felix was still with the Red faction. He also admired Felix's hair, which was still worn in the long Greek style. Felix told him of his first major victory, and of how hard it had been to leave the Red faction.

"In the end, I was the only good racer left alive. I had to leave if I wanted to make something out of my career," he explained.

"Seen everything?" Rufus interrupted from behind them. "Good. We have some research to do. Let's go."

****

"Attend with me," the Senator says, "we will watch from my box." Felix looked in surprise to Hyacinthus, who did his best with a shift of his eyes to imply that this was unusual to him as well. They were at the Flavian amphitheater, where a match unlike any other had been promised.

Felix, along with most of Rome, had heard rumors of trouble toward the eastern fringes of the Empire. Everyone in the city knew that an entire legion had been lost last year, but now, there were stories of something stranger, something darker in the forest of Dacia. Felix chalked it up to the usual nonsense, but it was true that the stories were more persistent than usual.

"What I have heard," Hyacinthus had told him, "is that the Emperor Domitian has captured some sort of monster they found there. One of the creatures that has been making so much trouble. It is supposed to be massive, heavily muscled, with sharp teeth and keen eyesight. A monster straight out of Virgil."

Now they stood behind the Senator in a luxury neither had ever suspected existed. They could actually see the Emperor, and the great man sat on the Imperial platform only a few hundred feet away. There was food, including expensive delicacies like roasted snails and truffle stuffed quail that he had never even tried. The wine was three times as good, stronger than anything Felix had ever tasted. He had to add extra water to make it more palatable. When they had arrived, there had been a host of servants in attendance, but Senator Rufus had banished them all with a gesture.

"Imagine," the Senator said, "that you are going to war, and you need the strongest, bravest men in the world. Who would you add?"

"You already know my first choice," Hyacinthus said. "I imagine there are men of the legion who would fit this description. I know the famous ones, the soldiers Rome sings of, but the Senator would know better than I."

"Let's speak of men not in the army," the Senator said. "Who else?"

"There is a warrior I met when I was a boy," Felix said, "from Africa. He became a great gladiator. I saw him from time to time but he left Rome some years ago, and I do not know if he still survives."

Hyacinthus made a few notes in Greek, it appeared. "What was his name?"

"I do not remember," Felix said. "In truth, it was a long time ago."

Hyacinthus narrowed his eyes. "This will go better if you think before you talk, boy."

"Who else?" said the Senator.

"Carpophorus would have been the best," Felix said. "He was the best *bestiarius* this city has seen. He died a youth, however, before he was twenty. Killed by a fucking rabid dog in Ostia."

"There's Pharnaces," Felix continued, "but he is old, almost thirty, and he has not won a major race in years." Felix realized suddenly that most of the people he had ever known were already dead. That was a strange and discomforting thought. Were his days likewise numbered?

A roar from the crowd brought their attention to the gates. Torquatus and Sophus strode in. They were two of the most popular and successful gladiators in Rome. Torquatus was a Thracian, and Sophus was a Gaul. The two had fought once, in an Emperor's exhibition and Sophus had won—but it had been a close thing, and a legendary fight. Domitian had spared Torquatus' life and the two had become fast friends.

Felix nodded appreciatively. Either of the two men constituted a formidable foe—together, they represented a challenge that few could survive. Though, who could say what was needed to confront a mighty monster?

The opposing gate rose. Felix, like many at the amphitheatre, stood to get a better view. He squinted, trying to make sure that his eyes did not lie. Hyacinthus beside him hadn't bothered rising. "Your eyesight is far keener than mine. What do you see?"

Felix frowned. "A man, just a man. I think he's drunk."

He couldn't believe it, but it was true. The man was so inebriated that he could barely walk. Instead, he shambled forward jerkily, with a lurching gait. There was a slim blade strapped to his waist. Torquatus and Sophus exchanged looks with one another.

"A drunken man," Hyacinthus repeated with surprise, "what jest is this?"

"Watch carefully. You'll find it is no trick." Rufus said from behind them.

"It must be," Felix said, "or someone who wandered in by mistake," he added, though he knew how improbable that was. "I expect the real creature to appear any time." Something odd about the drunken man caught Felix's attention.

"His eyes," he said, "they're all white, with no pupils."

Hyacinthus looked slightly interested, as if someone had told him the rain that day had been purple. Felix had a caught a glimpse of Rufus' expression as he too looked down at the drunk man. Felix could discern an emotion in an instant—he knew when rival charioteers would break before they themselves did. Felix knew that, for just a moment, the Senator had been deathly afraid.

Torquatus and Sophus began sparring with each other. "What are they doing?" Felix wondered aloud. Even as he said it, he guessed. "They fight for the chance to avoid killing the man."

"Indeed," said Hyacinthus, "they must have insulted someone powerful. The first blooded will have the ignominy of killing his drunken opponent. There is no glory here, only mocking revenge."

"Don't be so sure," the Senator said. "Withhold your opinion until the fight is finished."

"How can there be any doubt?" Felix asked, but the Senator said nothing.

The stumbling man slowly advanced on the gladiators. He had been dressed in armor and had a sword at his hip that he did not draw. The two gladiators were evenly matched, and neither drew blood. The drunken man was only a few feet away when Sophus finally cut the arm of Torquatus. It was a shallow cut, but it meant that Torquatus had lost to him again.

He turned to face the drunken man, who still had not touched his blade.

Torquatus turned to the condemned man and raised his sword high, saluting him. A drop of blood fell from the cut he had received. The shambling man acted with ungainly speed, reaching for the raised arm with both his hands. Before anyone could react, the drunken man had pulled the gladiator's arm to his mouth. He immediately began chewing on it. Torquatus' sword fell to the ground.

"Is he trying to eat him?" Felix asked.

"I've seen many of disturbing sights in my time," Hyacinthus said, shaking his head, "but that's a new one."

"It's slightly disturbing," Felix agreed, "but is he here because he is a cannibal? Or are we still waiting for the real monster?"

With his free hand, Torquatus slammed his fist into the other man's forehead. It didn't seem to affect him. The gladiator was panicking a bit now, and he slammed his fist into the drunken man's head a dozen times, with little to show for his efforts.

The crowd was as quiet as Felix could ever remember hearing it. Everyone was standing, staring at this new kind of entertainment. The drunken man continued to chew on the bloody mangled arm. Quite a lot of blood was falling now, coating the drunken man's face and chest. Sophus could be heard laughing at his rival's misfortune. Torquatus' hand slipped to a dagger at his side. Quick as a cat, he plunged the dagger into the man's colorless eye.

The man didn't fall. He chewed, swallowed, and chewed away at the flesh on Torquatus' arm. The panicked gladiator leaped into the man before him. They came crashing down to the ground and Torquatus was on his feet. He scooped up his sword with his left hand—his right arm was a mangled mess. The man was still on the ground, protected by armor. There was a gap, though, between his stomach and his waist. Torquatus screamed triumphantly as he plunged the blade into the man beneath him. The sharp blade sunk to its hilt, point emerging wetly through the man's stomach.

Torquatus turned and screamed a primal victory scream to the audience. Loud, belated cheers resounded throughout the amphitheatre. Sophus was suddenly beside him, borrowing some glory as he too preened before the crowd.

"That was unexpectedly interesting. Yet, I don't know that I have learned the lesson you wished to teach," Hyacinthus said to the Senator.

"Continue to watch," Rufus said, his voice was tight, "this is not yet finished."

Felix scanned the amphitheatre grounds. The drunken man was squirming. He rose with awkward slowness to his feet. The dagger remained in his eye, and the sword still poked through his stomach. Nothing poured from either of his wounds, though his face was a scarlet sunset of smeared blood.

Something about the sight was utterly wrong. Felix felt something shift inside him and he felt as though he was going to be sick. Bile filled his mouth.

"I don't like this anymore," he said quietly.

"Good. That means you are learning," said Rufus. "Continue to watch. Pay attention. For now, the real show begins."

The thing—for Felix could not think of it as a man any longer—stumbled into Sophus. It grabbed onto his shoulders and its mouth sank into the back of the man's neck. The two collapsed to the ground, their armor clanking heavily. The thing bit savagely at the man beneath him. With three great rending chomps, it swallowed mouthfuls of flesh and muscle. After the second bite, the man beneath him stopped struggling.

Torquatus had no sword. With seconds, however, he had whirled behind the monster and pulled out its small blade. The creature was so intensely devouring the man beneath him that it didn't seem to notice. The roars of the crowd had dwindled to a murmur, as all watched in fascination.

The sword rose into the air. Felix watched with fascination and dread as it seemed to hover in the air for eternity. Then, with a whoosh, it swung down and separated the thing's head from its body. The head tumbled away in the dust, and its body instantly collapsed, twitching, onto the corpse that until recently had been a gladiator.

There was scattered cheering, but it was decidedly understated. Guards ran in to drag away the bodies, and Torquatus wearily stumbled back to the gate. The medical slaves were already coming to meet him, stretcher at the ready.

The Senator's box was quiet for a few moments. Then Rufus spoke. His voice was somber, grave. "That thing. There are many more like it. Thousands, maybe, or more, and I want you both, and all of my guards, to learn to kill them."

Felix looked to Hyacinthus with alarm. For the first time in a long time, he felt like he wasn't living up to his name.

It was then that the messenger from the Emperor arrived.

CHAPTER XIX

Dacia: 88 CE, Winter

Rowanna slipped back into the camp, seemingly unnoticed in the waning evening light. Her hair and clothes were still wet but she didn't care what they thought. It had been entirely too long since she'd bathed in the river and nothing—not ice, not her people, and not the lifeless—was going to stop her. The battle that morning had left her covered in blood, sweat, ash, but the worst were the bits of brain and organs that had leaked onto her. The others were men, and hadn't seemed to care, but she was entirely willing to risk her life in order to bathe in a freezing stream, despite orders not to leave camp.

The water was melted snow, grabbing her with frozen fingertips. Rowanna had slipped into the stream with her clothes still on—they needed a wash nearly as much as she did. The cold was shocking, and the fingers on her right hand instantly turned white. Her body was instantly shaking. She had left her spear on the bank, just in case, but had not needed it.

It was a relatively safe time to be on her own. There had been no sign of the lifeless all afternoon. They hadn't seen any since killing the hordes of them that morning. After the battle, the survivors had opened the gates and walked with the Dacians for hours. They'd joined a camp filled with other Dacians. Rowanna hadn't known any of them. Zuste had, and she had left him chatting with some important looking warriors.

The camp could not have been more different from the Roman one. There was no dyke, no fence, and few guards. There were dogs, pigs, women, and children, scattered amongst the men. There was not even a latrine, people just squatted where and when they needed to relieve themselves. Rowanna was amazed at how quickly the Roman way had become the norm for her. It made sense—seeing how organized the Romans were, she could see how they continued to win battles against the Dacians.

She smiled at a few people and received a handful of half-smiles back. It was good to hear Dacian spoken again—her Latin was not bad, but it was a language that lacked music. These people did not know what to make of her, and none of them were from her village. Her stomach growled as wood smoke drifted through the camp. It was past time for a meal—a proper, hot meal.

It took longer than it should have, and the brief winter evening had come and gone, but eventually, Rowanna found the campfire with her friends. Sparks jumped and cracked into the still night air. Something was cooking—it smelled like roast rabbit. There were three men around the fire, but she did not know one of them.

She instantly knew something was wrong. Her king—Decabalus—stood there with a face as hard as misery. There was a man beside him, a man with a furiously bushy beard and robes similar to Zuste's, who was seething with fury. Iullianus looked like he had eaten something he did not like, something that was still wriggling down his throat.

"Rowanna," Iullianus said, "where have you been? We looked for you."

"I went for a swim," she said. There was no use trying to hide it. "I would have left word had I thought it important."

Iullianus grunted. His expression was still sour. Her King spoke next.

"Outside the camp? You were forbidden to do so."

"It was not important," Iullianus said. "You missed the departure of your friend."

"What do you mean? Zuste? Where is he?" she asked.

Iullianus looked at her. There was something strange in his eyes. Did he pity her? "He's gone, Rowanna. Gone. We'll not see him again."

"What? After what he did? He saved us!" She looked to Decabalus, her eyes pleading.

"After what he did," Iullianus repeated sadly, "I was able to save his life. He is on his own now."

"Why?" Her voice was a fluttering spirit, sinking beneath the waves

"That man," snapped the man in the alchemist robes and long beard, "he is to blame for everything. I still think we should have killed him."

"We already have," Iullianus agreed. "He will never survive out there, not on his own."

Rowanna stared at the two in shock. "I'm going after him," she said, turning on her heel.

"Do not go, woman," said the King.

"Wait," Iullianus added, "he will not want to see you." She stopped and turned back to them.

"Will someone," Rowanna asked, "please tell me what's going on."

All three of them shared a long look. She could not imagine what they had to tell her.

"Sit down," said Decabalus. When she had done so, he offered her a spit of roast rabbit. "Have something to eat."

"I'm not hungry."

"As you will. Listen, Zuste has been a friend of mine for a long time. He always gave good advice, and helped our country against the Romans," he said. "No offense, friend," he added with a smile at Iullianus.

"No argument here," the big man agreed, "the Romans are vicious bastards."

"Have you met Natopurus? He is—or was, when I still had a kingdom—my chief alchemist. He helped Zuste, and others, learn much."

The bearded man nodded at her curtly, but he spoke to Decabalus. "Just tell her. I don't understand the point in dicing words around this woman."

"This woman is stronger than you know," Iullianus said.

"This woman has a mouth, and ears. Two of them," she said, losing her carefully cultivated calm.

"What do alchemists do?" Decabalus asked.

"They make potions," she said. "I don't see--"

"They make potions," Decabalus repeated. "Some to heal, some to hurt. Some create fire, others create more terrible things."

Rowanna stared at each of the three men. In the firelight, their faces looked hardly human. "What are you saying?"

"Rowanna," Iullianus said, "Zuste created the baleful. All of this, it's because of him."

"That's impossible."

"Nothing is impossible with alchemy," said Natopurus.

"I don't know about that," added Decabalus, "but I do know that Natoporus was approached by a strange man last year. He was willing to pay more money than anyone should ever be able to pay. We're talking the kind of wealth that Caesar or Crassus would envy. Natopurus knew the man could want nothing good, but it was a great deal of money. In the end, he came to me. I decided to kill the man and take his money, but by then, someone else had sold the elixir to him."

"What makes you think it was Zuste? There are many alchemists in Dacia, and countless others in the world."

"Rowanna," Iullianus said in a strained voice, "he has the cure. You two told me you used it."

"Not even I could have created a cure that quickly," said Natopurus. "Not unless I had created the potion first."

"That's not proof," she insisted. It was growing harder to see. She angrily blinked away the tears, surprised and embarrassed at her reaction.

"Not overwhelmingly, no," Decabalus admitted. "However, when we approached him, he admitted to it."

"There is blood on his hands," growled Natopurus. "Enough blood to choke a sea."

"He left us, immediately and willingly. I will miss him, but we won't see him again," Iullianus finished.

Something occurred to her. "You just said it yourselves, we can't lose Zuste, he has the cure."

Natopurus laughed harshly. "This is what comes of having a woman tell you your business. He gave me the formula before he left, of course. It was created not without some intelligence, but some of the ingredients are so rare as to be impossible," he added. "And it's a small amendment: *he is the cause of all this misery.*"

"To be precise," Iullianus said, trying to lighten the mood, "the Romans would have killed and enslaved you all if the lifeless hadn't come along."

Natopurus snarled and Decabalus said something, but she wasn't listening. Unbidden, she thought of Dapyx smiling in the sunshine with the other warriors. His smile had outshone the sun.

Something splashed on her face. She was shaking with fury. Without realizing it, tears were leaping from her eyes. She suddenly remembered the fat man had thrown away a purse of gold into the woods. It had not made sense at the time, but now it all fit together.

It was true. Zuste had created the lifeless. Rowanna leaned her head back and screamed.

****

They awoke the next morning and found their camp covered by a slight blanket of snow. Rowanna thought of the alchemist and wondered how he was surviving in the cold. She did not like thinking of him, but half of her wanted to protect him and the other half wanted to kill him. It would be best if he died, she decided. He could lie down and rest, and his body could be covered with snow so that the lifeless could not trouble his corpse. A better end than he deserved, and, yet, she realized some part of her hoped he would live.

She shivered in the frigid morning air, wondering if that fate would be shared by all before much longer had passed. Her feet were going numb—she wore a pair of small sandals the Romans had given her, but they did not provide much warmth in the snow. Most people were still abed, though it was still the half-light of early dawn. Only the children were awake--laughing, throwing balls of snow at each other and at trees.

She was watching them, trying to stay attached to the present, when she almost walked into the man before her. She had apologized before she realized who it was. Natopurus.

"They make too much noise," he said, having followed her gaze to the children.

"Without their laughter, what good is anything we do?" she asked him.

The man stared at her incredulously. "Women. Always good for a meaningless platitude," he said at last. "They want to see you over by the fire," he added, before walking away. His steps sounded heavy in the snow.

She watched him walk away for a handful of moments. Some of his surly manner she had found in Zuste, but the fat man, if pushed, would respond to his inner humanity. This man lacked that spark. He lacked, it seemed, any semblance of humanity at all.

She walked over to the fire and found Iullianus and Decabalus, feeling the cold settle in her bones. She was getting old. No, she'd been old, but had forgotten. Now she was remembering. Only her bones had never forgotten.

The two men nodded at her, but did not stop their conversation.

"If you go to Rome, then Caesar will kill you," the Dacian King said. "Do not throw your life away."

"I wouldn't expect you to understand, but I will take the survivors back to Rome."

"What survivors? Twenty men? From a legion? I am not Domitian, but even I would kill the general who bore those tidings to me." Decabalus laughed, a little scornfully.

"Perhaps that is my fate. As long as I can die with a beer in my hand, no man will say it was a bad death."

Decabalus smiled at that. "I never thought I'd agree with a Roman, but those words ring true."

"I am not a Roman," Iullianus said quietly. "And what of your people?"

"Leaving them here is as good as killing them. I cannot allow that to happen."

Another long stretch of silence followed. Iullianus idly picked up a stick and traced shapes in the snow. Rowanna marveled at how these men used silence—it was for them another language.

"My duty is with my people, but I have a mind to send ten warriors with you. They will take your orders, but I need them to come back to me after you reach Rome," Decabalus said.

"What of me?" Rowanna asked.

"You may do as you please, though I had thought you would come with us," Decabalus said. "We are not Romans, like our tall friend here. Our people are free to venture where they wish. I am king of no one who does not wish me to be."

"I am no Roman," repeated Iullianus.

"Truly?" asked Decabalus, with a wolfish glint in his eye. "You have a Roman name. You dress like a Roman. You lead

Roman armies into battle, conquering territory to expand Roman borders. Where you were born means nothing, Roman."

Rowanna thought that the red-haired man might hit Decabalus then. Instead, he paused for a moment, head cocked thoughtfully. Another silence that said more than words ever could.

"I see your point," he conceded at last, "though it is hard to accept. They certainly don't accept me as a Roman. When I was a boy, I killed Romans by the score. A man never knows where the road will take him."

"If I am to have a choice," said Rowanna, filling up the silence, "I should like to know more. What will you do?" she asked Decabalus.

"Survivors have reached me from Berzobis. It was a Roman fort, but they are gone and it is yet untouched by the baleful. It has walls high enough to keep them away. I will gather my people and take refuge from this storm there."

"A dangerous plan," Iullianus said. "A safe haven yesterday is not a safe haven today. You could arrive to find the place crawling with lifeless. Or wake up a month hence to find yourselves besieged by them."

Decabalus gave him a helpless look. "I am the King. I have to protect my people, and we have a better chance surviving behind walls than we do out here."

"Perhaps. Staying in this infested land is courting death, if you ask me," Iullianus said.

"I did not. But reporting to your king an entire legion massacred seems just as dangerous."

"More. I am braver than you, though," Iullianus grinned, "and Romans don't have kings."

"Certainly not," agreed Decabalus. "One man who rules half the world, with wealth enough to buy armies and navies, who can conquer a nation with a word—he is certainly no king."

"Exactly," said Iullianus. "The Romans are masters of saying one thing and meaning another. I accepted your aid with gratitude, and I welcome the men you send with me as well. But the man I need to bring is the alchemist."

"He's long gone, dead, or worse," Decabalus said, lowering his voice and glancing to Rowanna a little too late.

"Not him. The goat-looking one, who constantly looks as though he's sitting upon a hornet's nest," Iullianus said, drawing a smile from Rowanna. "He said it himself. He knows the cure."

"Which my people will need."

"So too the world."

Decabalus was silent as he thought. "No, I cannot chance it. You might not make it to Rome. The Caesar may not believe you, or understand the necessity. You likely will be thrown into chains and sold into slavery without even getting a chance to tell them. I can have him write it down."

"Not good enough," Iullianus said quietly. "If we are bit on the way, we will need him. We will need the cure."

"I cannot help the Romans. Do not think I forget why you came here. I am a reasonable man, but do not presume to dictate my course," Decabalus said, his voice boiling with rage. "I lost many men saving you, you who came to kill and enslave my people. I did not do so in order for you to command me."

"I guess this is me warning you," Iullianus said. His smile was a bare blade.

"I'm afraid my decision is final."

Iullianus moved so quickly that Rowanna didn't have time to cry out. Decabalus was fast though. He had half-risen, his hand on the hilt of his sword, when the red-haired man's blade pierced his chest.

He eyes fell upon the weapon. Iullianus grabbed the hilt with both hands and twisted.

"Ah, it is regrettably true that man is a wolf to man," he said softly. "But you cannot put your needs above the worlds."

As Decabalus' body slid into the snow, spurting crimson, Rowanna glanced at the camp with panic. So far, no one had noticed. Most were still asleep, and it was considered improper to approach the leaders with matters less than urgent.

She didn't even realize that she was in danger until she heard the footsteps. The big man was before her. His blade drip, drip, dripped steaming blood into the snow.

"Do not scream," he said.

She found herself strangely ready. So many had died already, and this could be a clean death. An end to pain, fear, and cold. She could find some solace in that. "Do it," she said, bowing her head before him. Her hands reached up and moved the hair from the back of the neck. "Make it quick," she said. Head down, she only saw the white snow, but she could hear the blood falling into it.

"Hera's swollen nipples woman, have you got a pair," Iullianus said. "You heard what he said. He gave me a choice of killing him or letting the world die. I don't have to kill you. Unless you scream, but I would truly prefer not to kill another today."

"I would truly prefer not to die today," she answered, wondering if she was telling the truth. Wondering if she knew what truth was anymore. The cold peace of death had seemed utterly comforting. "But how will you get the alchemist now?"

Iullianus looked in surprise at the dead king's body below him and at the bloody sword in his hand. "You know, I hadn't really given it any thought yet."

CHAPTER XX

Rome: 88 CE, Winter

Rufus sat down warily in the Emperor's study. He had been waiting for far too long and it was already late afternoon by the time he came in. Apart from the Emperor's Praetorian Guards and a half-dozen servants, he was alone with Domitian. This was unusual, and it left him feeling unsettled and edgy.

"Salve, Rufus," Domitian said perfunctorily. Rufus responded in kind and looked closer at the man across from him.

The Emperor was ill. He had dark circles under his eyes and he was growing a beard. He had gained weight noticeably since the last time Rufus had seen him, and his head was nearly bald. Only some long, wispy hairs on the sides of his head attested to the Emperor having ever had hair. The study was clean, but there were flies everywhere, crawling on the Emperor's clothes and bare skin. Domitian seemed not to notice.

The Emperor looked straight at Rufus, his cheeks blushing with excitement.

"I know what you are doing," he said. "Did you really think you could hide it from me?"

He knew. It was never a good time to cross the Emperor, but now was particularly bad. Just last month, a man named Mettius Pompusianus had been put to death for the crimes of having a map of the world painted on his wall and reading the speeches of kings in Livy. Rufus knew Pompusianus, and the man probably had been conspiring against the Emperor, but he had to admit that his own guilt seemed much more evident. He had not updated his will in months.

None of that stress showed. His face did not as much as twitch. "I hide nothing from you, Caesar. I am your servant."

Domitian laughed. "Yes, my loyal servant. If half my court were as loyal as you, I would have no cares. I would be the greatest Emperor that Rome had ever seen. Oh, what I could do if all had such loyalty as you, Rufus."

"Just so, Caesar," said Rufus, ignoring the obvious sarcasm. He brushed a fly from his arm. It sailed onto the ground and slowly flew back into the air.

"I know you are building an army, Rufus," the Emperor said.

"It's not an army, Augustus. I merely worry—"

Domitian laughed again, a high nervous laugh. "You expect my guard to slit your throat right here, I suspect. I know why you have acquired men of valor and fame." He lowered his voice and leaned in closer to Rufus, though they were alone. "It's to kill *them*, isn't it? You see, I remember. You warned the Senate, fools that they were, and they did not listen."

Rufus remembered very well who had not listened that day, but it was folly to point that out. "I have learned it is better to take a false threat seriously, than to ignore a credible menace, Caesar. But I did not know the full danger that the creatures represent, of course."

Domitian was silent for no short amount of time. He looked everywhere in the room, save for at Rufus. At last he said, quietly: "The gladiator Torquatus died soon after his fight. He is no longer dead. He is no longer Torquatus."

Rufus stared in surprise. There were several flies on Domitian's arm now, but he did not seem to notice them.

"Caesar, I did not know," he said.

"No one knows. I have kept this knowledge from all but my most trusted slaves," Domitian said. "But you know what it means."

Rufus thought of several things, but was not sure what Domitian meant.

"*Mortui non mordent*. As Theodotus said to the Egyptians, the dead do not bite. But the world has changed. The dead can return to life," the Emperor said. "Believe me. When that savage Celt in Dacia sent me the prisoner, it was with dire warnings. I had the creature in here, where you are sitting now. I have it in prison now, in a cell with that philandering actor, Paris. He has been making eyes at my niece, Julia. If Jupiter is good, it will kill him, or at least gnaw off his cock. But this is no joke. What I saw in the amphitheater only confirmed what I had already learned."

"Ah, how can I help you, Caesar? My men are more than willing to aid, of course."

Domitian motioned and a *servus* brought him his wine. It was kept in a chest packed with snow transported daily from the Alps, so that it would always be chilled. That, Rufus mused, was the difference between even the richest, most powerful Senator, and the Emperor.

"My dreams have been troubling of late, Rufus. I dreamt I was in a forest, alone, and then the trees died and shriveled away and there was nothing. And then I saw light, and from that light came Minerva, and she threw away her sword and spear and shield, into the darkness, into non-existence. Her clothes followed, and I was staring at her nipples. They were entirely white, even whiter than her heavy pale breasts, and I couldn't look away from them. She saw my attention, frowned at me. I think her breasts frowned at me, or at least, I understood they did not appreciate my staring. Suddenly, she was rising, mounted upon a chariot drawn by white horses, and together they turned and plunged into the abyss."

Rufus had not realized that the Emperor was declining into insanity so quickly. There were flies crawling over him and he still did not notice. "White nipples, Caesar?" he asked.

"The dead are coming back to life. What man does not have secrets? What man does not wish the dead to stay buried?" Domitian said.

"Wise words," said Rufus.

"Can you picture a small posting station, just north of here? An important man died there, one of the best that Rome has ever seen," Domitian said. His voice was sad.

Rufus breathed deeply and willed his heart to stop beating so quickly. *He knew this too?* It was impossible, but somehow the Emperor knew. All this then had been a game.

"Caesar," he said, fighting the urge to run, "I can explain."

"I killed him," Domitian said, not listening. "I plotted against him and when he fell ill, at the very same location our father died. How fitting. I poisoned him! How could I not? The gods could not have spoken to me more clearly. Now, Minerva has fallen to the abyss. She who is divine has left the world we've created. What power has the gods when the dead roam the earth? I know he is out there. I know that Titus is coming for me."

Rufus' felt relief, but it was short-lived. Hearing a confession such as this was tantamount to a death sentence in its own right. He was also surprised, too surprised to hide it. Another fly landed on Rufus' arm. He tried to brush it off, but the creature did not move. He flicked it, and his finger connected solidly—the insect went flying away.

"Vile rumors, Caesar. I knew you both and this does not—"

Once again, Domitian interrupted him.

"The sea hare. I have to take action, Rufus. Titus is coming for me. I can't even guess who else. Our father? Nero, whom we dethroned? Augustus Caesar himself? The dead rise and all of them will come for me. If they still exist, the gods must be laughing now—to be Emperor now, when the world is ending."

"Take action, then," Rufus urged. "I will head north, with my men, and kill any lifeless we see. They need never reach Rome." Rufus was fairly certain that Proculus was really dead, but it would not hurt to be prudent. He had a niggling feeling that even if alive, Proculus was not a problem worth considering. If he met with Titus, he could make sure the emperor's walking corpse stayed dead as well.

"North," Domitian said. "That's a start. I still have intelligence, you know. There are still some loyal to the throne, even if the gods themselves have abandoned us. I sent out spies after you warned us. At first, I heard nothing. Just another system of rumors that fed upon themselves. Recently, the reports have multiplied. The creatures have moved from Dacia, into both Moesias. Soon they will be in Italy herself. Ever do they draw closer. Ever does he draw closer."

"What can I do?" Rufus asked. Three flies were on his arm now. They were sluggish and uncoordinated. He suddenly realized what that meant and forgot to breathe.

"Emperor," he said, his voice rushed and urgent, "you said you had the creature in here? I think these flies must have something of the curse. They must have sucked from his sweat or his blood. If they could bite, we would both be dead. Or worse."

Rufus slapped at the one on him, squishing them and smearing their guts against his arms and legs. They smelled awful, like rotting guts and feces. Domitian reached into a sheaf of papyrus on his desk and his hand emerged with a stylus. He stabbed the creatures. They offered no resistance and many fell to his blade.

Two guards were beside the Emperor immediately, but he shook them off with a smirk. For the first time in ages, Domitian actually looked happy. He had stabbed a dozen of more flies and for now, the room was empty of them. Rufus called for a *servus* to wash the guts from his arm.

"Decisive action," Domitian said. "I need more of that. Every great emperor took decisive action when the time came, and every failed Emperor did not." He spoke slower now, the manic cadence of his speech fading away. "This then is my Actium. I am raising five new legions. The port cities will be closed—Ostia, Brundisium, Ravenna, Pisa and Misenum. And send the Legio II Adiutrix to Tuscany. I want them to build a wall so big that it stops anyone—anything—from invading. A wall that stretches from sea to sea."

"You want to close down Italy?"

"That is what I said. It's the only way to be safe."

"Dominus, I assure you—we need the ports. Food, slaves, wine, everything comes from overseas. The people will starve."

"Oh, let them starve," Domitian agreed cheerfully. "Enough circuses and even the bread doesn't matter."

Rufus tried once more. "Our grain grows overseas. Our fleets buy fish from overseas. Our beer and wine come from overseas. Without our ports, Rome is nothing. Money will be meaningless and chaos will spread. The empire will crumble."

Domitian's face didn't change in the slightest. He gave no indication that he had even heard the Senator. "He won't get me. I won't let him. I killed him once and I'll do it again, if need be." He stabbed the stylus into the wood before him. The thin blade quivered once, twice, and then fell over onto the desk with a muffled clang.

CHAPTER XXI

Rome: 88 CE, Winter

If Hyacinthus thought their owner's abrupt departure was odd, he said nothing of it. Felix said nothing either. Though he was a man grown for a long time now, he still felt half-a-child around the big Greek. It was good seeing him again, but it felt odd. They had not yet developed a relationship based on the men they had become.

They stood outside their master's litter. He had been summoned by the Emperor, and then disappeared. That had been increasingly long ago, and Felix was bored. There was nothing to do this close to the palace, and the only people to pass them were guards, Senators, or slaves. They were all coming or going, and none of these doors were guarded. They were too far into the inner-sanctum for that. Even the slaves who had carried the litter had left, awaiting their summons in their dark rooms. Standing there made Felix anxious. He didn't belong here, so far from the hippodrome, and he suspected that everyone knew it.

"When I brought you to our first master, you promised to buy your freedom by thirty," Hyacinthus said suddenly. "Do you remember?"

"I do not remember," Felix said with a small laugh. "But I had many follies as a child."

"So you have not saved enough money?"

Felix laughed. "I have enough money, thrice over. And I will have that much again, by the time I am old enough to become free. Should I live that long," he added. He stretched his arms into the dusty air and yawned elaborately. "But the cap is for fools. There are more starving freedman in the city than even you can count, and yet every *servus* gets meals and shelter."

"You are growing wiser," Hyacinthus conceded. "Yet, there is something you are missing."

He ended his sentence abruptly as a man stumbled from the door before them. Felix knew him almost instantly, it was the actor Paris. He was infamous throughout the city. Like his namesake, he habitually stole women from men of higher rank than him. It had taken, rumor had it, a patron placed very highly indeed to keep him alive.

"What is he doing here?" he asked.

Hyacinthus shushed him. "Look," he hissed.

It only took half a second for Felix to realize that the man was not drunk. He was not, in fact, a man any longer. His white eyes, lacking pupils, swept the street before him. His neck had been bitten savagely, as a clotted mess of blood attested to. He walked with the same shuffling gate that the monster in the amphitheatre had.

Felix instinctively grabbed for his *falx, but* when his hand closed on air, he felt conspicuously unarmed. His stomach leaped into his mouth and he suppressed the urge to vomit. It had been disturbing to see the thing from afar. This close, however, the wrongness of it shouted at him, blinded him, and nauseated him. The smell of carnage and rotting death assailed his nostrils, and the sound of its shuffling feet made the hairs on the back of his neck rise.

His real father's words suddenly came back to him, for the first time in a decade. *You can recognize evil from the very sight of it.* The thing that had been Paris was not far from them, but they were on the other side of the litter from it. It would stumble past and not see them.

"We must kill it," Felix whispered. "It is evil. We must kill it."

"Evil perhaps, but it is dangerous," said the Greek man. "How can we stop it? You saw what the other one did to the two gladiators."

"I do not know," said Felix, "but it must die."

"Wait. We can call the guards," he said.

It was too late. Felix was running directly at the thing that had been Paris. "Follow me!" he shouted as he rushed the monster. Paris was just reacting to the new presence, confronting the man, when it was punched in the head. Felix wasn't strong in the way that some gladiators and praetorians were strong. His muscles did not ripple, but he had a wiry strength born from restraining a thousand horses through a thousand tight turns.

Paris' head jerked back from the force of the blow. Its arms flew up as one foot swung clumsily behind. Felix hooked his foot behind Paris' and pushed the thing down to the ground.

"Now!" he yelled to Hyacinthus. "Sit on this thing." The lifeless was on its back but it was already struggling to rise. The young man placed both his hands on the creature's chest.

"That is foolish," Hyacinthus said, taking a step back. "I don't want to turn into one."

"They only attack through biting," Felix said. That seemed to be true from the earlier fight, but there was no way to be certain.

The creature flung Felix's arms off and began to rise. Felix punched it in the nose, three times in quick succession, and then put his hands back on its chest.

"We don't know that, Felix. And I'm not willing to take the chance."

"Hyacinthus!" Felix thundered. "Sit on this creature right now!"

His tone brooked no disapproval. The big Greek man moved over and hefted his bulk over the struggling creature.

He sat down with oomph, as his large arse pinned the lifeless creature's torso to the ground. Felix held its arms together above its head. It gnashed teeth at them, groaning miserably, but it could do nothing.

Felix laughed. "It worked. It actually worked."

The Greek man glowered at him, "You didn't think it would?"

"I was not entirely sure. I had a hope." He smiled at his friend, and it was the smile that had won him friends and maidens, but it was not effective now.

"You had a hope? If I turn into one of these drooling creatures, the first thing I will do is come for you and kill you," Hyacinthus said.

"You'll have to catch me first. You might be the first lifeless that is too slow to catch its own food."

Hyacinthus grunted. "That might be true. Which is all the more reason for me not to get bitten."

Felix was still smiling until he looked at the thing below them. "Its eyes … what's wrong with its eyes?"

"How can it see?" Hyacinthus asked. "Moreover, how can it live? There is much to study here."

Another voice interrupted them. "What are you two doing?" Rufus asked, as he walked from Emperor's chambers. He was accompanied by two Praetorians.

Felix and Hyacinthus looked quickly at one another and then back to their master. "Already we excel at the mission you have set before us, master," the Greek man quickly said. "We have captured a lifeless creature for you."

"Here? This close to the palace?" Rufus moved closer, peering at the pinned creature who struggled helplessly against the weight of the big man. "He looks familiar."

"It's Paris, Senator," Felix said, "the actor."

"The actor," Rufus said, his voice flat. He stopped still for a moment, and then motioned to the Praetorians. They stepped up, drawing their short swords in unison. "Kill it," he said. "Aim for the head."

They stabbed it through the head without hesitation. "Senator," Hyacinthus protested, "there is much to learn from these creatures."

Rufus barked out a single laugh. "Ever the man of learning. Not to worry, there will be more inside."

"How do you know?" Hyacinthus asked.

"This one was meant to be in a cell. If it escaped, the other did as well. And any who got in their way. It's time to go hunting."

****

"There were many," Felix said defensively. "Perhaps I killed them all."

The stern captain beside him said nothing. He was flanked by a score of men, all of whom had leaped to attention when Felix and Hyacinthus had burst into their room. Since then, they had followed the littered trail of corpses back, but had not seen any of them still capable of movement.

He had killed six of them on the journey there, and there did not seem to be more, but it was nearly impossible to be certain. It didn't take much skill to kill them, which was indeed fortunate. Felix had borrowed a sword from one of the Praetorians, and he was able to use it to good effect, but there were already too many of the creatures. It was stunning to think what one creature could do.

Four of the lifeless had been prisoners, but two had been guards. The Praetorian Captain was a seasoned veteran, but Felix knew that the tales he'd been told were wildly difficult to believe. Once dead, there was little clue that they had even been monsters. If he could not show them a marauding lifeless, or the Senator, soon, he could be in trouble.

They found Senator Rufus and both Praetorians standing out in the cool evening air. Rufus sent the Praetorian Captain to look after the Emperor and then returned to the others. He had a look of disgust on his face. "I can't stand the way they smell," he said. "Did you see many?"

"The lad killed half a dozen," Hyacinthus answered. "But we have not seen any for some time."

The Senator nodded. "We found only three, including the gladiator. They will not walk again, but I mistrust this city—there are too many people, living too closely to one another. We will leave tonight."

"So soon?" Felix blurted out. "What about our training?"

The Senator laughed his single syllable laugh again. "You will have training enough before long, young man. More than enough."

CHAPTER XXII

Dacia: 88 CE, Winter

High in the mountains there was a cave. The alchemist had slept in it several times over the years, when he was collecting roots and herbs in the late summer or early autumn. It was not well-hidden and there were always signs of others--charred remnants of fires and small animal bones deep in the cave. He had always had it to himself, though, and so he did again.

Though it kept the worst of the wind and snow from him, it was cold and miserably wet. The rocky walls of the cave were constantly damp and dripping. The ground was the worst, however; uneven, rocky, and always numbingly frigid. Zuste tried not to complain. He was lucky to be out of the winter weather. It rained often, but it snowed just as much. Finding the cave had been a stroke of luck. Even luckier, he had not seen any lifeless this high up in the mountains.

When he'd left the Dacians' camp, he hadn't even said farewell to Rowanna. He had wanted nothing more than see her again, but he couldn't face her. It was he who had killed her son, along with so many others. She could never have forgiven him. He didn't know that he could face her hatred, knowing all the while that he had earned it. Without Rowanna there, he hated himself enough for the both of them, enough for the world.

He knew that they had meant for him to die. Because he was fat, because he wasn't a warrior, they had forgotten that he was a woodsman. None, not even Natopurus, knew better than he did, what herbs and roots one could survive by. He had as much knowledge of the area as any man, even when it was swathed in mist and snow. Giving little thought to survival at first, he'd remained alive more from habit than desire. These mountains normally had shepherds, some even in the winter, but they were free of men now. Living men, at least. There had been few lifeless—most had been killed in the battle, and a single man drew far less attention than a camp of hundreds. Twice he'd killed one in a panic—clubbing their heads with a great branch he'd dragged halfway up the mountain.

The cloak of solitude was not new to him, but after the companionship of the Roman camp, he wore it heavily. He surprised himself several times by finding tears slipping down his cheeks. Ever and always, he considered death, but the urge to live, even this miserably, was too strong.

He wasn't eating much, but he had enough herb lore to get by, even in the winter. His clothing felt looser on him and he was losing a great amount of weight. He didn't even have to shit much anymore, which was kind of a relief. A man was never as vulnerable as when he was squatting over a small hole in the ground, and with the lifeless around, it was a real danger. His beard, which had always been full, kept growing. There were streaks of grey in the coarse black hair. He was getting old. He began mumbling to himself and occasionally realized that lucidity was perhaps slipping away from him.

There was no room for sanity left in the world now, and that was entirely his fault. If only he had known. He couldn't even remember the man's name. Something foreign, though he'd looked like a Roman. He had said he hated the Romans too, more even than Zuste. The joke was that he had not even hinted that it would hurt anyone other than the Romans. Still, the alchemist should have known. He had been blinded by the lure of the money, and the man had paid him several fortunes.

The alchemist laughed at that. Silence fled timidly as the cave filled with the sudden sound. All the gold that was buried under his home in Sarmizegetusa. It was sure to have been burned down now, the money discovered and taken. He hoped so. Even if he could make it back, he wouldn't ever be able to spend that money. That blood money. Not that, he suspected, he would he be willing to give it up if given a choice.

The wind howled, wolf-like, and even in his furs, Zuste shivered. He could picture the man who'd paid him as clearly as if he were sitting in the cave next to him. He'd been so focused, and he had not been wrong, the alchemist realized. The Romans had killed his people, killed all peoples. The lifeless killed because it was their nature. The Romans killed because they were greedy, cruel, and savage. They were the threat. He'd almost forgotten that. He would have to take care not to do so again.

"The empty headed traveler will sing in the presence of a robber," he muttered, his voice hoarse from disuse. The cave swallowed his words as though they'd never been spoken at all. A chill ran down his neck, and without knowing why, he looked up.

At the mouth of the cave, three pairs of yellow eyes stared at him.

"Zalmoxis," he whispered. He had not built his fire yet this night, and though he had a large stick, it was not sharpened. It was a club suitable for killing lifeless, the baneful, but he'd never intended on using it against wolves.

Nonetheless, he knew a show of strength was his only hope. As the creatures drew cautiously further into his cave, he leaped to his feet. He grabbed his club and brandished it, banging it on the walls and floor. "Come on in! You want to eat old Zuste? Well, just try it, you furry fucks!" He shouted this and other inanities at them, barely conscious of anything other than the need to make noise.

One of the wolves growled. None of them retreated. Zuste swallowed his bitter fear as his mind spun in panic. Wolves were not natural predators of men, but they were strong and quick enough to kill a man. It was only their temperaments that kept their jaws from the throats of vulnerable people. With the lifeless prowling their haunts, it would be enough to make them aggressive, to forget their timidity, and to ensure their rampant bestiality.

The wolves moved deeper into the cave. He wasn't sure if there were more behind the three or the late evening light was playing tricks on his eyes. Regardless, he had to act now.

Zuste charged. He raised the branch above his head and brought it down in the middle of the wolves.

They scattered and his branch missed them entirely, hitting the floor. The force of the attack broke the stick in half and he cursed. There was at least one wolf behind him now, as well, and he whirled. The broken, pointy stick felt like a sword in his hand, and he waved it ferociously.

The wolves were all deeper in the cave than him now. They drew together and one of them whined. There was something so plaintive about that sound that he lowered his stick. "What is wrong?" he asked.

Claws on stone drew his attention back to the front of the cave. More wolves stood there. Many more. Their eyes did not shine with any color at all. They were, in fact, white. Pupiless.

The alchemist wasted no time. He charged the lifeless wolves, his stick raised once more. Like their human counterparts, the animals were listless, slow. His first hit cracked down solidly on the shambling wolf, but it did not seem to notice. Trying to picture what Iullianus would do, Zuste spun into action like a warrior-god.

His left foot caught his right as he spun, and he toppled into a heap. His weapon skittered off across the cave floor. It felt right, to have his world end in an isolated cave, and his death was in the form of a weapon of his own making. The justice of it relaxed him as the undead wolves surrounded him.

He could not close his eyes, however. That final surrender was not available to him, justice or not. He could smell rotting meat on the teeth of the nearest wolf. Zuste leaned his head back, offering his throat and hoping for a quick death.

Then the wolf was gone. Beside him, yipping and snarling, were the three wolves that had first entered his cave. Zuste rose, bewildered, but joined in the fight. Lacking his branch, he clasped his fists together and brought them down on the undead beasts' heads. When that didn't work, he jabbed his fingers into their eyes. That slowed them down and the other wolves ripped them apart.

One of the living wolves was split open and the remaining two were hobbling. Zuste, feeling ridiculous, offered them shelter with words and gestures. They slinked out. He worked for some time in the darkness, removing the bloated bodies of the lifeless wolves. The floor would have to wait until the morning, when he could bring up some water from the river, but his home felt like his again. The moon was high in the sky at this point. It was later than he'd stayed up for some time.

He felt giddy. Not only had he survived, but he had also come to a decision. He wanted to live. He needed to live, and to stay here was tantamount to suicide. Eventually, he would not survive the marauding lifeless. When the weather grew better, he'd return to

Sarmizegetusa. Though he risked death, it was better than this limbo in which he now dwelled.

****

The next week was a busy one. He collected fibers, bark and other ingredients. Though his hands froze to blue, and he wasted long hours sifting through the snow to find nothing beneath, at last he had enough material to make a net.

He had found other useful plants as well. The roots of the plant the Romans called Amoracia, which could cure coughs and infections alike. The main root he kept, but the branching ones he planted back in the ground, so that the plants would continue to grow. Even if humanity failed, it was his duty to keep nature's state as perfect as he could. He found several spindly willow trees and carefully removed several long strips of bark. Properly prepared, they could reduce fever and ease pains.

Some would make their ropes and nets out of catgut or sinew, but plant fibers were not only more abundant and easier to create, but they could stand getting wet as well. It took some time, as he had to extract and prepare. He had collected what he needed and had a collection of elm, flax, white oak, and willow. From there, he slowly twined the cords together. It took two weeks, but at the end of it, he had a net and several long lengths of very basic rope.

The first thing he did was tie a low piece of rope so that it hung at the entrance of the cave. His worry was that a group of lifeless would enter and trap him. The rope might trip the clumsy bastards, or at least give him some warning. So far, he hadn't seen any lifeless on his excursions, but he still whirled at the smallest sound. The snow continued to pile and Zuste worked slowly and meticulously as it grew colder and whiter.

CHAPTER XXIII

Brundisium: 88 CE, Winter

It had not been easy to convince the Dacians that their leader had changed into a monster, but Iullianus had managed it. "He must," Iullianus had said, "have taken a wound in the battle and not told anyone. Only his great strength kept him alive as long as it did." The stunned Dacians had banded together under Diegis—a sturdy bear of a man, who promised to lead them to safety.

There were not any warriors to spare, but Iullianus had convinced Natopurus to come with them. Rowanna came as well— the idea of being a childless mother, surrounded by others' children, made her feel too sad and too old. They came down the Carpathian Mountains and a week later, crossed the Donaris river, traveling south into Moesia. It was a strange land, full of Thracians, Dacians, and others that spoke a language that none could identify. It had been recently reorganized by the Romans. The roads were good, there were soldiers everywhere, and forts they could sleep at every night.

With Iullianus' help, they'd entered the tiny town of Salmydessos, and within a few days, found a ship willing to take them across the Adriatic. Neither of the Dacians had been on a ship of any size before. At first, it had been a marvel. The sea had been a shade of blue that Rowanna had never seen before—like the sky on the clearest of summer days, but richer and more vibrant. The waters turned rough the first night and she was violently sick for the remainder of the journey.

They had landed in a busy port city called Brundisium late in the evening two days later. It was huge—far bigger than Sarmizegetusa, though vastly more dirty and more violent as well. Danger lurked palpably on the streets. There were more people living in the town than perhaps all of Dacia, Rowanna suspected. It was full of travelers who were on their way to or from Greece and further east. They had found a room at a cheap tavern, and Rowanna had fallen asleep immediately, before dinner. She had barely managed to sleep on the ship, and welcomed the bliss of dry, steady land. The other two had come to the room after she had fallen asleep and had shared the other bed.

When they awoke the next day, the city gates were closed. A Roman army had crept up in the night and besieged them, and none were allowed to enter or leave the city. Rowanna had laughed when she heard. Natopurus had been furious, as had Iullianus, who had that morning immediately gone to the Forum and presented himself to the Senate.

He met Rowanna and Natopurus on the city walls later that afternoon. From their high vantage point, they could see the army camped out on the frozen ground before them. Behind the besieging legion was the Via Appia, which led straight to Rome.

Rowanna wrapped her arms around her knees. The wind had a chill to it and at their height, it blew more steadily. A movement caught her eye, as Iullianus was climbing up the stairs to the wall. As he approached them, his sad smile and slight head shake told them everything.

"They wouldn't listen to you?" Rowanna asked.

His slight head shake and frown answered the question for them.

"They told me no, by Mithras. Can hardly blame them, cockless old bastards though they were. I don't look like your average Roman."

"Not to mention," added Natopurus, "that a commander with no army is no commander at all."

"There is that, too," Iullianus conceded. "I doubt much that my appearance or lack of army mattered. The decree has come directly from the Emperor. I inferred we are not in the only city that has been closed."

"What will we do?" Rowanna asked. It seemed ludicrous to have come so far only to fail now.

"After the Senate, I reconnoitered the city's gates, thinking we could bribe or kill our way out."

"And?" Natopurus asked.

"No chance. There are far too many soldiers posted at each."

"Well," said Natopurus, stroking his long beard, "the solution is clear. We cannot leave on the ground, so we shall leave by air. I'll go make a potion."

"What?" Rowanna said.

"That is a fantastic idea," Iullianus said. The other two looked at him.

"I mean the part about not leaving on the ground, not the flying bit. Even Zuste could not have done that."

"Zalmoxis' cock. I'm the best alchemist there is, far better than that herb-collector, but I cannot do the impossible."

"When the dead walk," Rowanna said, "impossible is not a word with much meaning."

"It is true that we cannot fly. Nor can we walk," Iullianus said.

"So what will we do?" Natopurus asked.

"The docks," Rowanna said, though the idea of getting back on a boat to her was about as loathsome as she could imagine.

"Clever girl. We have to get out of this city, and there just may be a pirate who will take us."

"I want to go," said Rowanna.

"Me too," Natopurus growled.

"Impossible. I am conspicuous enough as it is. Escorting a walking beard and a fair-haired foreigner—it's asking to be noticed. Meet me back at the tavern tonight." He stood, his lean body already moving into action.

The Dacians descended the steep steps more slowly, and behind and beyond them, the Roman army waited with the patience of a corpse.

****

When Iullianus entered the tavern that night, he was beaming. He found the Dacians sitting at a table covered with plates of bread and fish. They ate in the Roman style, with their hands. The part of table not covered with food was instead devoted to beer and wine. The two had, it was apparent, been drinking for no small time. The tavern was filling up slowly as night settled over the city.

"Well," Rowanna asked, "what happened?"

"I'll answer your question with one of mine. Who is the greatest man to have ever lived?"

"Ever?" Rowanna asked. "Probably Spargapeithes, the greatest King the Dacians have ever known."

"Hmm," Iullianus said. "Could he have secured a boat out of a city closed by the Emperor himself?"

"No," put in Natopurus. "He probably would have just killed everyone who got in his way, the legion included."

Iullianus scowled at the two of them. "Perhaps I'm not as great as your greatest King. When it comes down to it, I'm no Nechtan the Great either, but I did find us a ship."

"Amazing," Natopurus said. "You are a hero of the ages."

"When do we leave?" Rowanna asked.

"Early tomorrow morning, on the first tide."

"It's evening now," Natopurus observed, "what shall we do until then?"

"You can do as you like," replied Iullianus. "As for me, my plans should soon be evident. *Corripe Cervisiam!*" he added, illustrating his words by seizing a beer from the table and downing it in moments.

"You don't drink like a Roman," Natopurus said.

Iullianus put his beer down to the table slowly. "I may grow tired of saying this someday: I am no Roman. My people live as far away from Rome as you, and maybe further even, because you cannot reach us by land. We have our own battles with the Romans."

"Then why would you ever serve them," cried Natopurus exasperatedly. "If you're one of us, you don't act like it."

"I was taken at a young age," Iullianus said with a shrug. "I can scarce remember my parents or village."

"We can teach you some of our customs," Rowanna said. "For instance, Dacians have the best drinking games."

"Who needs a game when you've got a beer?" he asked.

"This might not be the right time, Rowanna," Natopurus added.

She wanted to see this through. She raised her drink into the air with her right hand, and at Natopurus with her left. "Three, two one," she called. By habit, she spoke in Dacian.

"Let's speak in Latin for the benefit of our pupil," Natopurus chided.

"Tres, duo, unos," she said with exaggerated pronunciation, again pointing at the alchemist. Natopurus chanted quickly and pointed to Iullianus.

"Three, two, one," he said, "what?" he asked, as both smirked at him.

"Drink!" they exclaimed. "You didn't point."

"I don't think I have the best teachers," he said, drinking deeply from his beer.

As loser, Iullianus had to pick the next game. He chose one that involved flipping his dagger into the air and catching it. The Dacians chose to drink rather than to attempt such a maneuver.

Others in the bar quickly joined them. It did not take long for Rowanna's head to spin, but Natopurus earned the most drinks. It seemed he was as unlikable to Romans as he was to his own people. Many hours later, the alchemist stumbled up and fled out the door.

Knowing laughter followed him out. Rowanna sidled up to Iullianus. "I need to sleep," she told him.

He slowly focused on her. "I will take you. You don't know what dangers might be lurking."

"Gratias," she said, sipping from the bottle of fieldberry wine in her hand. She offered some to Iullianus, who poured a large amount down his throat.

"For something that isn't beer, it tastes pretty damned good," he said.

He led her back to her room, his arm wrapped around her waist. Her body tingled at his touch. They entered the shared room and both paused, awkwardly.

"We had better leave the door open," Iullianus said. "Natopurus will be back soon and we wouldn't want to make him think…"

Rowanna dropped her clothes to the ground. "Make him think what?" she asked, stepping into his embrace.

Iullianus leaned down and kissed her. Without looking, he pushed the door shut with one hand. She heard the bolt drop, securing them away from the world. His other wrapped around her waist and pulled her closer. They kissed with fevered intensity for a few moments. She could feel her excitement deep within her stomach. He then leaned down and took her nipples in his mouth. Her breasts were not as high as they had once been and her nipples were quite small compared to most women, but his tongue and lips made her feel incredibly turned on. As his tongue moved from one breast to the other, the big man slipped out from under his clothing to stand before her.

She had never seen a cock like his. It strained and leapt into the air with the energy of an unbroken colt. It excited and terrified her at the same time.

She didn't remember lying on the bed, only remembered the feeling as he first slid into her. They both cried out, as he slid deep into her wet hole. There was no time for niceties. Instead he pulled her legs up, so that one rested on each of his shoulders, and fucked her as hard as he could.

A loud banging noise was coming from somewhere, and the small sober part of her still cognizant of the world, knew they were both screaming, moaning like the undead, but she didn't care. She loved how she felt, wanted it never to end. Iullianus was pumping her more rhythmically now, pulling out quickly and then slowly thrusting in.

A loud knocking sounded again at the door. She realized it was the banging she had been hearing.

"Let me in!" Natopurus yelled from outside.

Iullianus froze, his turgid cock poised at the edge of her spread lips.

"Don't stop," Rowanna begged him. "Please don't stop."

He nodded to her. "Apage! Go away!" he called out. "Come back later." He thrust hard, sliding as deep as he could into her. Suffering from pleasure, she cried out hoarsely.

"Let me in!" Natopurus cried out. "It's my room too."

Iullianus paused for a moment, and then his big hands reached down and turned her around. She was facing away from him, looking toward the wall. She felt each of his hands grab her waist and then he slid into her, even deeper than before. Her head was spinning, and she didn't have long. She pushed back as hard as she could, clamping down on his cock every time it entered her.

His breathing changed and he started fucking her both faster and harder than he had before. One of his hands slipped down and fondled her breast, grasping her nipple roughly. It was too much, and suddenly Rowanna was screaming with pleasure as the orgasm punched through her. Seconds later, waves of pleasure still rippling through her, Iullianus growled and spurted his seed deep into her. "Yes, yes, yes, yes," she crooned, knowing only that this was the only thing in the world that mattered.

They fell down together. Within seconds, both of them had passed out.

****

Rowanna awoke the next morning to the sound of rain. She rose gingerly from the bed and looked out the small window to see that a dreary grey mist had swallowed the city, though it was not raining hard. It was quiet and there were very few people yet awake.

She examined herself carefully. She was still naked, and felt very sticky. Her legs had finger-sized bruises where the big man had gripped her. Her breasts hurt from being tugged and her cunny was immensely sore. Iullianus had been more animal than man.

She looked to him. Iullianus still slept, stretched out in the bed like a sleeping cat. She smiled, slowly remembering the events of the previous night.

And then her heart started racing as she remembered Natopurus. "Oh no," she whispered. She went to the door, still nude, and unlocked it. She opened it slowly. There was no one there.

"What are you doing?" Iullianus asked from behind her. His voice was foggy with sleep.

She quickly closed the door. "Natopurus. He never. We did not open the door."

The red-haired man laughed. "That's right. I had nearly forgotten. I wonder what happened to him."

"Aren't you concerned?" she asked.

"Not really," Iullianus said, rising from bed with the bottle of fieldberry wine in his hand. He drank deeply from it and winced. "Beer makes for a better morning after drink," he said with a sigh. "Natopurus is a man of the world, he understands."

"He's not in the hallway."

"Hopefully, he found a woman who was willing to let him come between her sheets. Some women would really like that beard of his. She could wrap it around her tits."

Rowanna laughed despite herself.

"We'd better go find our ship," Iullianus said. "Some haste may be in order." Not long after, the two were in the common room. Natopurus lay sleeping on a table. Even in sleep, his face looked angry and his beard was matted with chunks of vomit.

Wan light streamed in through the front door. Iullianus shook the alchemist awake.

"There's no time to lose," the Roman said.

"Cocks and cunts, you Roman scum. Wait a moment. Not all of us tasted a woman's flower last night." He looked at Rowanna with an ambiguous stare that she found unnerving.

He sat up slowly, his back creaking audibly. "Never do that again," he said. "I came with you of my free will and I do not appreciate being excluded." He reached carefully for a flagon of water.

"Not to worry," said Iullianus. "We will get our own room next time."

Rowanna was about to protest this presumption, but the look he gave her made her laugh again instead.

"It's like that, is it?" said Natopurus darkly. "Well, let us go." The Dacian man sighed and stood up. "I would like to eat, but I suppose I'd lose any food on the ship anyway." He brushed the flecks of vomit from his beard and washed his face.

"Maybe the sicknesses of sea and drink will negate each other," Rowanna suggested.

Each of them moving with more deliberate care than usual, they moved out the door into the rainy morning.

The docks were not far. Following Iullianus, they slipped through a few alleys, avoiding the guards posted at the harbor entrance. The tide was well on its way out, but a few ships bobbed at their berths.

"That's it," Iullianus said, pointing to a far ship. It was an older vessel with only one sail. "That is our escape."

No people were visible on the ship at all, nor any sounds of preparation. The gangplank of the ship was down but there was no one on it.

"I don't feel good about this," Rowanna said, clutching at Iullianus' arm. They were looking at the ship from a dilapidated wooden building. The Roman guards were far enough away that they would not be able to hear them.

"Indeed. There is something sinister about that silent ship," Iullianus said. "Stay here, and be careful. Don't let the guards see you."

The ship creaked loudly.

As Iullianus stepped forward, Natopurus added, "Step carefully. There's a smell in the air that I dislike."

The red-haired man turned and shrugged helplessly. "One should be born either king or fool. And I, well, I am no king."

He slipped across the street, footsteps improbably silent. The guards were facing the other way, toward the city, and would have only had a few seconds to see him. He sprang lightly onto the boarding plank and within a few steps was on the ship.

"Jupiter, help me now," he said softly, though his voice carried across the water. He drew his sword and started swinging. Rowanna leaped away, springing into the street. But Natopurus caught her arm and pulled her back into the doorway.

"Look," he said. She followed his gaze. The legionaries on guard were trotting over to the ship. A severed head tumbled down the gangplank. It was pale, disheveled, and bloody. The eyes that stared out from the head were completely white.

Rowanna started shaking. "Not here, not now," she said.

The Romans had drawn their blades and had their shields cautiously extended. They went up the plank two by two, as alert as for any battle.

The skies around them darkened with the suddenness of a candle being snuffed out. She'd seen such transformation in the mountains, but never like this. The rain poured down, a heavy curtain of a deluge.

"We must return to the tavern," Natopurus said. "We will die out here."

She shook her head, already soaked from the torrential downpour. "We must help him." She could barely hear her own voice.

"Do as you please," Natopurus shouted. "Fair you well."

He turned and slipped around the building into the alley. She ran across the dock, onto the plank. There were too many lifeless, she could tell already. Iullianus was surrounded by them. The Roman soldiers were slashing at them, but the ship was crawling with corpses. Three of the soldiers were already down. A lifeless was chewing on one dead soldier's foot, sandal and all.

Rowanna moved quickly through the rain. Her spear was on her back and reached awkwardly to heft it in her hands. The lifeless turned its head to her and she stabbed it in the eye. With a bloody gurgle of surprise, the thing fell to the ground.

Iullianus had a short blade in each hand. He pivoted, striking at creatures coming at him from all directions. When he saw Rowanna, he cried, "Get out of here. I'll meet you at the tavern when I'm done getting my exercise."

He sliced a creature's head in two with one blade, while the other weapon lashed out and stabbed another shambler in the chest. His hand was extended for only a moment, but it was long enough for a longhaired creature to latch onto it and bite deeply.

"Fuck!" Iullianus yelled. With his other hand, he withdrew his sword from the creature's head and stabbed viciously. He hit the thing on his arm directly in the nose. His blade came out through the other side of its soggy skull.

Then a lifeless latched onto his back. It chomped at his neck.

"No!" Rowanna screamed and she sprang forward. She stabbed at as many lifeless as she could, aiming for their eyes. Even with her spear's reach, she could not get to Iullianus before she, too, was surrounded.

She was aware of the Roman soldiers breaking and running as she stabbed at the dead dirty hands that grabbed for her. It was time to flee the arena of the ship, but she was trapped by the flesh-eaters, they were everywhere. A sea of teeth, groans, nails, and hunger.

Suddenly, there were hands on her waist. Warm, human hands. She turned to see Iullianus. She sighed in relief, but something was wrong. His skin was pale, his pupils shrinking before her. There were lifeless gnawing at his legs and at his arms.

"Feel so strange," he said weakly. "Never should have played Dacian drinking games." He took three steps, hefted her into the air, and threw her off the ship.

****

Rowanna climbed from the harbor some time later, coughing dirty water from her soaked lungs. She'd just managed to keep hold of her spear, but there was no one to use it on. The plague had not spread from the ship, not yet. Iullianus, his red hair visible even in the rain, was squatting over a Roman corpse, shoveling brains into his mouth from the dead man's broken skull. He did not see her. She found her way to the tavern, numb, exhausted, and immensely sad.

The tavern was full of travelers taking shelter from the storm. They stared at her with wide-eyed wonder, but she paid them no heed.

She marched down the hall and burst into the room, leaving her spear against the door. Natopurus sat on the floor, vials and potions spread out before him. He had changed into dry clothing. A small dagger lay on the table beside him.

"You're still alive," the alchemist said, his tone neutral. "Do be careful, as this is a delicate process."

She marched up to him, clothes dripping and hair clinging wetly to her face. "They got Iullianus. We haven't got much time."

He laughed. "That's good. Remember, we want the Romans to die."

"He's not like the others."

"They're all like the others."

"Natopurus," she said slowly, "I want a potion to cure him. I know you have one."

"Yes, I do have one. I certainly don't intend to waste it on a Roman, no matter how taken you are with him." He picked up a vial filled with grey powder.

"That has nothing to do with it! He led us here, and where will we go without him?"

"As to that," Natopurus said, pouring the powder into a wooden bowl filled with a blue liquid. "I'd rather lead myself than trust that man."

She had to do something. "I'm sure there must be some way I can convince you," she said. Her voice was lowered seductively. She hated herself for resorting to this, but time was slipping away. She leaned down, brushing her breasts across his shoulder. Her clothing was sodden and she dripped onto him and into his bowl.

"By Zalmoxis, woman. I warned you to be careful. And, no. I don't know what that Roman saw in you, but I like my flowers a little fresher."

She stared at him, her mouth hanging open as she blinked in surprise. She wondered what Iullianus would do? She'd tried pleading, had tried sex. What was left, save violence?

There was a scream from the rain-soaked streets. Rowanna was instantly up and peering out the window. It took a few moments, in the gloomy grey, to see what she feared. There were three of them, shambling through the streets. Lifeless.

"What is it?" Natopurus asked, his back to her as he added a sprinkle of red powder.

"Lifeless," she said dully. "There is nothing in this city that can stop them."

"Apart from the army outside."

"They've torn apart other armies. It only takes one creature, and no city is safe."

He grunted but said nothing. He was still concentrating heavily on the process before him. "What are you making?" she asked, watching the lifeless stumble ever closer.

"Something to clarify my mind. Alchemists take such things often."

"I never saw Zuste do anything like that."

"I tell you," he said bitterly, "that man was scarce an alchemist. He was more interested in sleeping under the stars than selling potions. And I needn't remind you that this world we live in is because of him."

That was all it took. Before she knew what she was doing, she had his dagger in her hand and had the blade pressed into the back of Natopurus' neck. She crouched behind him, squatting on her heels.

"Give me the cure," she said, her voice reverberating with command.

He raised his hands slowly. There was a long pause before he spoke. "No. You will have to kill me, and you do not know where the potion is. Without my knowledge, you won't find it. Forget the Roman, Rowanna. He is already gone." His voice was as smooth and calm.

She grabbed his hair with her other hand. Pulling his head back, she whipped the knife out across the front of his throat. She could see the startled fear in his eyes as she stared back at him coldly.

"Last chance, alchemist. Give it to me."

"You're crazy. Do you love a Roman so much you'd kill a countryman? Remember, even a god finds it hard to love and be wise at the same time."

"Love has nothing to do with it. I think he can keep me safe." Her voice was ice as she pressed the dagger tip into his throat and fresh blood blossomed onto the blade. She wondered at his question: did she love the big man? It had been the disparaging of Zuste that had enraged her.

Even with the knife at his throat, the man laughed. "He's doing well so far." The alchemist reached into the bag at his side and withdrew a small vial.

"Here," he said. "You have convinced me of your duty. Take it. I will make another."

Rowanna released his hair and pulled the dagger back from his throat. She took the invaluable glass container and examined it. It was filled with a blue liquid that seemed to sparkle even in the dull light. Acting on a hunch, she threw it to the ground with as much force as she could. It hit the floor and shattered, glass shards cascading away as the precious liquid leaked into the wooden floorboards.

"What are you doing?" Natopurus cried. He sounded more upset than she had ever heard him.

"I know what the cure looks like," she said, hoping her voice sounded confident. "Zuste had them too. Do not try to fool me."

He laughed at that, too, but did not fully hide his fear. "You are not as stupid as I would have thought," he admitted. "Though the elixir you destroyed was worth more than your life, and all in it."

There was more screaming and the sound of heavy footsteps from outside. Rowanna could feel time slipping away. She glanced to the door, and was stunned when a fist hit her squarely on her jaw.

She remained on her feet, and reflexively got her hands up in time to block the next blow. Natopurus scrambled to his feet. She rose too, the knife held before her.

The alchemist snarled at her. She stepped into him and slid her dagger into his stomach. The blade passed through the lowest part of his beard and sunk into his soft flesh.

The alchemist didn't say anything, only glared at her with a look of impotent sadness, of betrayal and suffering. He sank to the floor without making another sound. Blood spilled from his guts.

She grabbed his bag. Inside were three vials, a trio of opaque bottles indistinguishable from one another. Not wanting to take any chances, she quickly searched his body and the room. There was nothing else.

She cleaned the blade on his cloak and walked from the room into the now empty common room. Patrons and owners alike had fled before the advent of the lifeless. She realized that these people hadn't seen the undead monsters before, maybe had not even heard of them yet. She was only beginning to comprehend their ravenous menace, and how much worse for those who were only now learning of their existence?

She held her spear firmly and the wooden shaft felt good in her hand. Wooden shaft. She giggled a little at the second meaning of that, and then abruptly stopped. Was she going mad? Was there even any point in such a thing as going mad when the world had already beaten you to it?

Rowanna stepped into the drizzling rain. There were lifeless everywhere. They were not in large crowds, not yet, but they were all around her. Most were coming from the harbor, and looked like they had been sailors or soldiers. She slipped into the side streets and avoided most, running around the few that did see her. It felt wonderful to have her ankle healed.

Only once did one get close enough that she had to stab it. The creature surprised her and her spear was of no use. She used the still bloody dagger and jabbed it into the pale white eye. Her blade did not sink deep enough, however, and it grabbed her head with grey hands. She twisted the blade and drove it deeper, until blood and ocular juices spurted across her. The monster dropped down, dead for the final time.

The city smelled of blood and smoke. She walked aimlessly, looking for Iullianus and seeing how much of the city was still human. It seemed most people were locked in their houses, but she warned a few off the streets. There was no sign of the big Roman, however. She returned to the harbor, but the ships were empty. The monsters were spreading out, looking for food.

Some time had passed and a wintery sun had burnt off the morning clouds. The city was eerily silent, save for the occasional screaming. It was growing apparent that the city was too vast to explore. She headed for the city walls and climbed up. There appeared to be no lifeless here—no people either, for that matter. The view from the walls was stupefying. Wind blowing her hair back, she realized that the army outside had drawn much closer. The centurions had formed up into what looked like battle ranks. They knew, then, what awaited them in the city. That much was a relief.

She walked along the walls, circumnavigating the city. Every hundred paces the walkway crawled down, halfway to the street. There were guard towers there, and below them small gates to the outer city. There were no guards there today, however. It was on the fourth such platform that she found him.

His hair and size gave him away. Iullianus saw her the same moment she had seen him. He stared at her with blank white eyes. She felt a flood of emotions so strong that she couldn't identify any of them, but she had to put her hand on the wall to steady herself.

Slowly, deliberately, the thing that had been Iullianus slipped his hand down to his waist. Seconds later, it emerged with his cock. He tugged at it slowly, still staring at her with his pale dead eyes.

His hand moved in a well-practiced motion. *Jerk ... jerk... jerk.* She could not see if he was growing hard or not. Did blood flow in the undead?

This had to stop.

She ran down the stairs, hand grabbing a vial in the dead man's bag. The red-haired monster continued to jerk its member at her. With a scream, she flung the first vial at it. It burst on its face, leaking green liquid. Rowanna moved closer, hand grasping the next vial. She slammed her shoulder into its gut, driving the big thing to the ground. She had the awful feeling that it was still masturbating. Its arm moved and all that she could hear was *jerk* ... *jerk... jerk*

She punched it in the stomach. The creature struggled against her as an angry, disturbed moan split its mouth. That was all the chance she needed. Her knees pressed on its chest, and she emptied both containers into its mouth.

The sound of moaning alerted to her to more lifeless coming. She glanced up, and back, and there were two coming, but they were not close. Not yet.

The elixirs mixed into a brown color and were rapidly running down his throat. She leaped to her feet and spun around. The lifeless were closer, stumbling in their haste to reach her. One had, until recently, been a corpulent man and the other was a topless whore—also recently dead. Iullianus groaned as his skin began to stretch.

"You poor bastards," the woman muttered. She wanted the safety of the stairs, but couldn't leave a just-changed Iullianus here alone. She remembered all too well what had happened to the man below her tree, seemingly so long ago.

She knew what Iullianus would do, and wondered if using his actions to guide her own would ever end with a good result. She stepped away from him, toward the lifeless. Like Iullianus, their flesh hardly looked dead.

She went after the woman first, fearing that she might be quicker. Her spear ripped through the woman's face and the topless creature fell to the ground. Rowanna smiled and turned, but the fat lifeless was much closer than she had realized.

It reached out with massive fists and claimed her right hand in a clammy grip. It was so strong that her spear fell from her fingers, clattering onto the ground. Its other massive hand reached for her head and she only just pulled back away from it. Snarling and pulling her closer, the lifeless grabbed at her waist with its free hand.

She was pressed up against it, her nose befouled with the stench of death and blood. Its mouth opened and chunks of unchewed flesh were stuck in its teeth. It pulled her closer and chomped at her neck.

Another fist hit Rowanna in the cheek. Her head flew back. Her ears were ringing, but she had avoided its plague bite. Three mighty punches landed on the fat man's face. Rowanna was dropped to the ground, rolling.

Iullianus was there. He slammed his fists into the thing's head, again and again. With crushing force, he knocked the fat man to the ground. Rowanna found her spear and stood again.

Then he, Iullianus, promptly squatted to the ground too.

The look on his face was indescribable. Panic and alarm, underscored by surprise, was only the roughest approximation.

"What are you doing?" Rowanna cried, scrambling for her blade. The fat zombie was already stumbling back to its feet.

"By Mithras do I have to shit!" Iullianus said, loudly squirting out soggy chunks of undigested meat.

The big lifeless stood. It lurched toward the prone man, but Rowanna was quicker. Her spear launched forward and this time the fat man did not get a chance to grab her. The creature fell to the ground with a heavy thud.

Just a few moments later, Iullianus finished.

"I don't know where I am," he said, looking around. "The last thing I remember is fighting on the ships. Did I do anything strange?"

The Dacian woman stared at him, at an utter loss.

He smiled reassuringly. "My grandfather had a touch of the battle madness. I must get it from him. The world goes black and red—and when you wake up all your enemies are dead." "Battle madness," Rowanna repeated slowly.

"Aye, I think I had it back in the camp where I met you and Zuste. It's a bother—being heroic and not even remembering it. He never told us it gave him the shits, though."

She almost told him the truth then, but he seemed so happy. There were enough burdens in the world without her adding another one to someone she cared about. Instead, she ran to him and wrapped her arms around him.

"A man could get used to this," he said. "Where's Natopurus."

"Dead," she said shortly.

Iullianus stared at her, breaking the embrace with a step back. "He's the only chance we had at ending this menace."

She hadn't really thought about that. "I took his potions," she said weakly.

"That's something. Where are they?"

She hesitated. What could she tell him?

"Well, where are they?" he asked again.

She looked around helplessly. "Gone. I broke them in the fight with the lifeless."

"*Foci il leat*!" he cried, not in Latin. "Humanity is doomed."

Now, for the first time today, she could feel tears welling in her eyes. Everything was going wrong.

Before she could reply, the gate slid open. A cohort of soldiers burst in. The leader, a tall blond man, looked at them. "Eyes. Show me your eyes," he commanded. The two hastily complied. "They're human." He motioned toward the dead lifeless. "You two do this yourselves?" he asked, his voice more impressed.

"She did most of it," Iullianus said, "I was too busy taking a shite."

The fair-haired man's laugh boomed through the empty city. He motioned for them to come closer. "Listen, this is a dead city. No one will survive. If the shamblers don't get them, we will. In return for your help, I'll help you. Slip out these doors, and tell them Adalbern sent you. You'll be on your own, but it's a good deal better than the alternative."

Iullianus saluted him sloppily. "Gratias, soldier." He took Rowanna's hand and pulled her through the door. They did not stop for a long time, not until the afternoon sun had disappeared and the chill of evening was all around them.

When they finally looked back at the doomed city, pillars of smoke were hovering over a hazy orange glow. Brundisium was a city of fire and death.

CHAPTER XXIV

Italy: 88 CE, Winter

They departed Rome late in the night, cloaked by a mantle of darkness as they crept out of the Eternal City. Three hundred deadly men—gladiators, soldiers, Praetorians, and mercenary warriors—carefully snaked along the Via Appia Antica. It was the first time Felix had left the city since he arrived, a lifetime ago. He was excited, if apprehensive of the danger that lay ahead of them.

The men escorted fourteen wagons. Seven were full of food for men and horses, and three of them contained extra weapons and armor. Of the three largest, however, each had six chariots stacked carefully inside. It was not a large number, but well-trained *aurigae* and their chariots were expensive, and more to the point, rarely for sale. Even a man of Rufus' position had been hard-pressed to obtain the eighteen charioteers that accompanied them.

These thirteen wagons were linked to each other as they slowly rumbled down the cobblestone roads. There was a ring of men surrounding them, preventing any curious drunkards from coming too close. A force of one hundred men went before them, clearing the Via Appia Antica of all traffic until they had passed. In truth, their presence was unnecessary—few living walked these roads, save for themselves.

Another hundred men marched behind the wagons, and with them came Senator Gaius Rufus. He rode a black horse and was in constant communication with the men in the front. The sixteen *aurigae*, including Felix, rode with him as well.

Behind them all, far behind, rumbled the fourteenth wagon. It was led by two of the surest-footed horses in the Senator's stables. Only one man rode with it, and Felix wondered how his big friend was holding up.

He'd seen Hyacinthus personally packing the wagons. Felix did not know what had gone in them, not exactly, but whatever it was had been packed with enough straw to feed a hundred horses. He had offered to ride with the Greek, but both Hyacinthus and the

Senator had been adamant. Whatever was in the big man's wagons was utterly secret.

Some time later, when they could no longer see the city behind them and the morning sun had burnt away the last of the dew, an idea struck him. Did Hyacinthus have some of the lifeless in his wagon? Perhaps he was experimenting on them. Felix looked to Rufus as his suspicion deepened, but the Senator was sleeping in his saddle.

Felix looked back at the trailing wagon. He could just see it, looming at the edge of the horizon. Hyacinthus, or his outline, was scarcely visible. Felix turned back, and looked at the road ahead. Something bothered him, vaguely.

They were outside the city now, and the lack of people was surreal. The Emperor had cleared the roads and there was little of the usual traffic that would typically clog the streets this close to Rome. All of the land had been cultivated and they had ridden past grapes and olives for hours.

Nothing was obviously amiss, but the feeling of wrongness was too deeply entrenched to ignore. He looked back again. The last wagon was not moving. Hyacinthus was waving wildly.

Dark shapes had emerged from the tangled fields of vines.

Without thought, Felix turned his horse and rode as quickly as he could back toward the last wagon. He was dimly aware of shouting behind him, others following, but he focused only the scene before him. His thighs clenched around the animal's broad flanks as he drew his falx.

There were only three shambling lifeless. He could not see Hyacinthus. One of the horses neighed as the creatures drew closer.

Felix felt the cold handle of his knife in his hand as he drew closer. He held on as tightly as he could, wishing he could ride better. Though he knew horses well, they were typically pulling rather than bearing him. Felix looked ahead.

The big man emerged from his wagon. He held a container in his hand, cradled like a baby. Hyacinthus was, if not running, shuffling quickly toward the lifeless. As one, they turned and moved toward him. He turned and moved away, off the road, and away from the wagon.

He seemed to notice Felix, and a look of alarm crossed his face. He shouted something, but Felix could not hear him. Not over the beating of the horses' hooves, the beating of his own heart.

Hyacinthus lumbered into a thicket that grew between a farm and the road. He was still shouting, but Felix was not close enough to hear. The charioteer slowed his horse, watching in horror as the three creatures closed in on his friend.

Hyacinthus screamed and the tail end of his statement reached Felix's ears. "—come any closer!"

Felix pursed his lips in puzzlement. The big man took several steps back away from the ravenous creatures and flung the item in his hands at the ground before them.

A crack of thunder roared. His horse reared and he fell to the ground. Long habit caused him to twist and lean forward to minimize the damage from the fall. He wasn't quick enough, though, and he hit the cobblestones hard enough to scrape flesh from his knees and elbows.

There was no sound at all, for a few long moments. Felix rolled over so that he faced the sky and gasped for air. He still could hear nothing, save for the fevered beating of his heart.

A massive plume of smoke drifted pleasantly into his vision. He rose slowly, painfully, and with some effort, managed to stand. His ribs ached and he still felt as though he could scarcely breathe. Some hearing was returning to him, coming back from a far-off land. His eyes found Hyacinthus and his own condition became suddenly less important.

The smoke that rose into the air came from the spot where the lifeless had been. A fire raged there and the heat was intensely foreboding. Hyacinthus stood several paces back; his face was sooty with ashes and dirt.

"What happened?" Felix asked. "Where are the lifeless?"

The fat man pointed wordlessly to the fire. Felix could see nothing recognizable as

human, or even formerly human. All that he could see was charred and blackened beyond identification.

"How?" he asked.

"I cannot tell you," Hyacinthus said. "It is my secret. The reason that the Senator bought me. Ultimately, the reason he bought you too, I suppose."

Felix looked offended. "You can tell me now, I think. That ship has sailed."

"It's not that I don't trust you, I do, as much as anyone in the world," he said, "but this is a danger that could ruin the world."

"Ha. That seems a moot point, now," Felix said.

"Perhaps it is," Hyacinthus said. "Even in light of walking dead, the less my substance is known, the better."

"Tell him," said a voice. The Senator had arrived, and he joined them with his hand on his sword hilt. His hard expression did not change as he examined the burning slag of bodies. "It's better if he knows, and for me to know as well. Should anything happen to you, it would be best for the knowledge to survive."

Several dozen men had arrived with the Senator, but they had stopped at the edge of the road. Rufus waived to them and they turned and marched back down the road.

Hyacinthus looked at the Senator for a long moment, as if he was about to challenge him. "Very well," he said at last. "Though I warn you: without long years of study, recreating it will be impossible." Sweat was sliding down the man's round face.

"I understand. You are proud of your creation, and rightfully so," Rufus said. He moved away from the fire, and the other two followed him. They walked back to the last wagon. The horses were panicked and Felix went to reassure them. "Now, tell me," the Senator said. "Tell me everything."

Hyacinthus walked toward the Senator. He held the bottom of his toga in his hand and twirled it nervously. "As you know, this wagon is filled with containers. They are quite fragile."

"Yes. I am quite aware of their nature," Rufus said.

"There are three separated chambers in each pot. The bottom contains water. Plain, harmless water. You could drink it, were you able to reach it. The middle layer is a mixture of my own: mostly quicklime and *thion*. It smells like Hades, but nothing else works nearly so well."

He was silent for too long.

"And the third layer?" Rufus asked.

"Naptha," the fat man said. Felix had never heard of it.

"I thought as much. What else could you have needed so much denari for?" Rufus said.

Hyacinthus nodded. "I understand it is a difficult process to collect it from the sea. Unfortunately, it's the only thing that works."

"How did you devise it?" Rufus asked.

"I have spent long years studying the process. It's a delicate one, and a false step can result in a quick death. I have been intrigued since I encountered a reference in Thucydides. The Athenians used something like this during the Siege of Delium. Of course, they had an elaborate mechanism to dispense their solution. I have only these." He gestured to the cart beside him.

"The amphorae?" Felix asked.

"They are not Roman. Call them *tzykalia*, or *kytrai* if you must. But never amphorae."

"What's the difference?"

"Little, perhaps," Hyacinthus said, "but it behooves us to call things by their real names."

"And it can obliterate life to nothing, in seconds?" Felix asked, pointing the billowing smoke and roaring fire. "That damage was from one of them? How many do you have?"

"Ninety-seven, now," Hyacinthus said. "We left with ninety-eight, of course. I wanted to make a hundred, but I ran out of naphtha at the end."

"Nearly a hundred!" Felix said. "I thought you were taking too much care of this wagon. You are taking too little!"

"I know," Rufus said grimly. "I had not thought to see the creatures this close to the city. We were fortunate there were not more of them, and that Hyacinthus acted as quickly as he did."

"I'll have more guards ride with you," the Senator said. "The future of the Empire outweighs all of our lives." With that, he rode away, back up the road to the assembled guards.

The sound of fire crackling and popping filled Felix's ears. The worry in his big friend's eyes was visible, and Felix gave him a reassuring smile.

"So, what do you call it?" Felix asked.

"I was thinking of calling it," Hyacinthus said, "War fire."

PART III: WOE TO THE CONQUERED

CHAPTER XXV

Dacia: 89 CE, Spring

He wasn't ever hungry anymore. His shrunken stomach had given up that fight, but it was glad of the pine needles, grubs, and coarse meal he occasionally ground. Only in his dreams did he remember the food he had loved so much.

Everything he ate was cold. The alchemist could probably have started a fire if he'd desired, but he did not want to alert others to his presence. As winter gave way to spring, each day without signs of the lifeless was putting off the inevitable. He had sharpened seven long spears and had them next to him at all times. His basic rope at the floor of the cave was now four feet high. It still wouldn't stop the lifeless, but if they came while he slept, the delay could save his life.

Spring came to the mountains late, but now even here there were blossoms and wildflowers above the tree line. In late afternoon, the streams were swollen with melting snow. It was then that he decided to go fishing. In his dreams, he had seen the fish frying on a fire that warmed his hands and feet. He woke and could not take his mind from the mountain trout.

He traveled far from his cave that afternoon, farther than he yet had during the long, cold months of winter. It was nice to feel free, to feel safe. He had not seen—living or not—wolves again. The sunlight made him feel a new man, and he danced a little as he walked through the green grass.

There was a clear stream that until recently had been frozen over. Now it was rushing, filled with snow melt, and it took some time to find a calm area. He lay on his stomach, head peeking into the stream. Chuckling with pleasure, he at last used the net that had taken so many hours of winter to create. It was hard, and he felt like an ass at a lyre, but he caught on and had three fish in the first hour. They flopped their life away on the bank next to him. His stomach rumbled and the idea of making a fire was ever more enticing.

He was happier than he'd been for months. "I'm going to eat you little fishes," he sang to them. "I'm going to put you in my stomach and you're going to taste so good." He grabbed one of the fish and held it before him. He realized he had chewed his fingernails to nubs.

"Please eat me," he said, in a high, fishy voice. "We will be so tasty."

"Yes, little fishy, I think I'll do just that."

The only warning he had was a low moan behind him, a sound from his nightmares. He sat there for precious moments, mind not comprehending.

Then he rolled away, onto his back, and leapt up. There was a lifeless before him, only meters away. It had once been a woman, but she had been dead for months now. Her jawbone was gone and much of her skin was blackened by frostbite.

She moaned hunger at him again. He surprised himself by not being scared. One lifeless was not a threat, and this creature was slower and more shambling than most.

He only needed a weapon of some sort and the thing could be destroyed. He looked past her, into the forest for a large branch or walking stick.

"Oh bad," he said. "Oh bad bad bad bad bad bad bad." His voice was hoarse with disuse. There were four more lifeless that he could see. All had the pale, ice-burnt look of the first. He whirled around. There were more on the other side of the river.

Zuste wondered if they'd been frozen in the snow and released by the spring thaw, but he didn't have much time for idle thought. There were more monsters than he could count, now, creeping through the forest. They advanced toward him with the ponderous inevitability of time. There was nowhere to go. He took a regretful look at his fish, lying there uneaten on the shore, and then he moved.

Zuste leapt into the icy stream. He was not a strong swimmer, but he could stay afloat indefinitely. But that was in summer, in a lake. The chill of the water assaulted him, blasted him, turned him upside down, and shook him with its frigid intensity. The force of the current carried him away quickly, but he was rapidly growing numb.

The cold presented as great a threat as the lifeless, if he stayed in it for too long. Turning his head back, he saw the silhouette of several creatures at the river shore. They were stooped over something. He realized in horror that they were eating his fish! For a brief, irrational moment, he hated the lifeless for that more than anything else.

The strong current fought him, and it took no little while to climb out of the water. By the time he did, he was shivering uncontrollably. It was growing dark and he could not make it back to his cave tonight. Not with the lifeless out there, ready to seize him in the dark. He thought of Rowanna and knew what he must do, though his buttocks clenched at the thought of it.

First, he stripped off his frozen, sodden clothing, and hung it on a tree to dry. It was strange to be standing naked, shivering, and alone in the forest. He felt so exposed without the cave walls around him. There was no question now that a fire was a bad idea. Instead, he gathered leaves, moss, and grass into a large ball, all the while keeping a careful eye out for any moving creatures. He didn't think they had followed him, but the forest could be crawling with the ravenous monsters. Still carefully watching, he rubbed himself vigorously with the assembled foliage. He didn't feel entirely warm, but he stopped shivering.

His gaze fell upon his own naked body. No man would call him thin, but he was not the corpulent man he'd been. He wondered if the changes in his body could come close to the changes he'd gone through mentally, and started laughing at the absurdity of such questions. He stopped immediately. Ovid had advised laughter to the wise, but silence was needed now. He forced himself to focus. He needed shelter.

There were no apple trees this time, so he climbed a white birch tree that was the tallest around. Three branches forked together at the bottom, making it easy to ascend. From there, he very carefully slid up the tree, his soft naked skin scraping against the tree bark. He was almost ten meters up when his hand brushed something hard, something dark.

Zuste hissed in excitement. It seemed too good to be true. Chaga. It looked like ashes that had coalesced into a hard disc. It was a parasitic fungus that grew on some mountain trees. It was among the rarest of alchemical ingredients and it was the most important item he needed to re-create his elixir vitae.

He climbed up further and saw that the tree was covered with chaga. It meant the tree was doomed, of course, but he could not stop laughing. He didn't care if it doomed him. There was enough chaga here to allow for a hundred elixirs, a thousand. At last, he had a weapon with which to fight the horde.

****

He somehow slept through the night, his body wedged between two branches. Most of his weight rested on his posterior, which was scraped and sore. He woke up in the pre-dawn light, shivering in the eerie cold. He still had mud on his body from the river. His hand flicked it off his leg. It didn't move. He realized with heart-seizing panic what that meant.

Leeches.

With ill-thought panic, he reached down to rip it off. As he did, he realized there were more. On his arms, chest, and legs, and on something worse.

"Zalmoxis, no," he whispered, seeing the leech clinging to his cock. He didn't know what happened next, but as he pulled and tugged at the swollen thing, rising to give himself better leverage, he slipped from the tree.

He hit the ground with a solid thud. His nose hit hard and he could taste blood. All the air was driven from his body with a painful whoomph, and he gasped for breath.

Scrambling up, the alchemist ripped the bloody leech from his member and flung it as far as he could. Blood leaked from his smashed nose into his mouth as he tore away another dozen of the fat clinging things. With a grunt of triumph, he flung the last one away as far as he could.

His body was a seething mass of bloody sores. Though none of the wounds hurt, they gushed with a surprising amount of blood. He moved gingerly, still feeling sore from the fall, and collected his clothing, checking it carefully for any of the bloodsuckers.

Only once his clothing was on, did he start shaking. Blood loss combined with delayed energies rushing through his body was almost overwhelming, and he sat shaking on the river bank, hands clasped around his knees, for a long time.

It was only later, after the morning mists had burnt away from the mountain tops that he thought the leeches might have been something else, something worse. Could the leeches have killed him, caused him to become lifeless? But he had not changed yet. He wondered about that.

Would he know if he had changed? He knew of several mushrooms that, when ingested, gave visions seen only by those who had partaken in them. Was that what being a lifeless creature was? Or did they operate on an animal level, as removed from thought as from poetry or sculpture?

It was interesting. Iullianus, that great oaf, had not even seemed to notice changing. *Some of us have farther to fall*, he thought glibly. He wondered if the Roman and Rowanna had made it to Rome. If they had even tried.

He realized he was smiling. *I need to find them. I need to bring them the cure.* He did not know how to get to Rome. There had been a map once, a rough thing sketched by a Gaul, but he could not remember much of it now. The roads would take him there, after all, all roads led to the Rome.

Zuste sighed. The Romans were such a young Empire. They caused untold destruction out of ignorance. Greece, Egypt, and Carthage, all had been upstarts. It took an ancient culture like the Celts, like the Dacians, to realize the futility of world conquest. He sighed again, feeling far too old for his years. Even without the lifeless, it seemed there was little hope for the world.

It was, however, far too nice a spring morning for brooding. The sun was bright now, and he felt recovered enough to stand. His nose had stopped bleeding and although sorely bruised, he was not otherwise injured from his fall. It took a few hours to scale the trees and collect all the chaga that he could. In the end, he had a pile that was far too big for him to carry. He would need to grind it to a fine powder anyway, but without any of his tools, this presented a challenge. When he had made the initial elixirs, he'd been able to use rotted chaga, which was the most effective. For this, however, he would need concentrated wine and water. It would take time, and he could not do it all in the cave. Every man, he realized, reached a time when he had to leave his cave and emerge into the greater world, and his time had come.

****

It was many days or weeks later when he emerged from Sarmizegetusa. He'd climbed down from the mountains, finding that spring had bloomed in the valley. The flowers buzzed with insect life and the verdant shoots that clad the forest were fragrantly vibrant.

There were almost no lifeless. Even the city of Sarmizegetusa itself was mostly free of them, though it was full of bloated, dead, rotting corpses. The stench was nigh unbearable, but the alchemist had been able to cleanse his shop with a powerful fragrant elixir. He had washed the blood from the floor, threw out the two corpses, and then boarded the door and windows. His place had been rummaged—his gold was gone. However, there was good luck, for his alchemical instruments were mostly still there. The water was still flowing and he didn't require much food. A small amount of foraging every few days provided him with enough sustenance.

He had felt safe, and had known how dangerous that was. He had seen a few lifeless from afar, and he occasionally heard them at night, but it seemed that without prey to feed on, the creatures dispersed. Though, there seemed to be more in the city than when he'd arrived. Perhaps they were able to track humans, as the frozen creatures had found in the mountains. It had become clear that it was time for him to go. He had worked with little sleep for ten days until he felt ready, however belatedly, for the apocalypse that he had created.

In his pack was enough dried food to last him a few weeks, if he was careful. Within the bags, padded with black wool, were seven *loculi*, leather satchels he had found on dead centurions. Each *loculus* had ten vials of elixir vitae. The bag itself was stuffed with more wool. He could drop the entire bag three meters onto hard rocks, and the vials would not break. He had an additional two vials in the pockets of his trousers.

His hands clasped a tall *pilum*, the Roman spear. Different from Rowanna's, it consisted of an iron shank ending in a pyramidal head, which was attached to a long wooden shaft. Zuste kept the spear point sticking up and used it as a walking stick. In addition, he strapped a short sword to each side of his waist. He had a smaller knife strapped to his ankle, and several more in his pack. Also in his pack were enough dried powders, herbs, and ingredients to make that many more, though he could not find room for his equipment. He supposed he ought to feel ridiculous, but instead, he felt like an avatar of Mars himself. He couldn't wait to see the look on Rowanna's face when he found them. He did ever doubt that he would find them, however improbable reunion seemed.

****

It took him long days of walking before he encountered any real danger. The broad cobblestone road was ringed by fragrant pines, and it had been easy to find a tree to sleep in during the night. To his great pleasure, he had thus far avoided both leeches and falling from the tree, as well. But he grew less cautious and by the third afternoon, he had let his guard down. Rounding a broad bend in the road, he nearly stumbled across three lifeless ripping apart a corpse.

With blood-smeared faces and hands, they rose slowly. Former centurions, they were big men with armor and helmets. Their eyes gleamed with pale light. They reeked of carnage, of danger. Two of them lurched around him while the third came straight for him. The alchemist tried to suppress his panic as he realized what was happening. They were flanking him!

Zuste did not much feel like Mars anymore. He took several steps back, breathing deeply, and switched the *pilum* in his hand so that the sharp end faced his foes. It was meant to be thrown, but he liked the length of it. He wouldn't have to get too close.

He was aware of the two stumbling through the edge of pine forest, trying to get around to him, but the threat directly before him was more immediate.

The alchemist screamed and ran at the thing, holding the *pilum* with both hands as he charged. He aimed the spear at the bloody-handed monster's neck, just above the cuirass.

He didn't miss by much, but he struck it in the armor. The impact knocked the lifeless back a few steps, but it bent the soft iron tip as well. His weapon was useless.

The two lifeless from his side were coming at him now, slowly shambling at him from his left and his right. Zuste screamed at them wordlessly. His left hand dropped into his trouser pockets and his right hand whipped out the gladius from his side.

Spinning, not sure where to attack first, he withdrew the vial and held the blade before him.

Inspiration struck, but it was too late. The creatures reached him, bloody hands extended. Zuste whipped his blade across, slicing at their hands. The blade struck bone and stopped. The hilt was pulled from his hand as the monster wrenched away. The first of the lifeless reached him as well, mouth open and hands grasping with hunger. Zuste was surrounded, and he could feel them tearing at his head, at his shoulders, at his waist. One still had his sword lodged in its arm, but that didn't seem to bother it.

Zuste punched one in the nose with all the force he could muster. It didn't notice—merely opened its mouth with a hungry moan. There was too much weight pulling at him, and he found himself on the ground. On his side, awkwardly, as he had twisted to avoid landing fully on his pack. His left hand still clenched the vial, but curing one of these monsters would not save him from the other two.

There was a mouth in his face. It was coated in congealing blood and the teeth were dotted with rotting chunks of flesh. Even through his panic and fear, Zuste's eyes watered from the stench.

One of the things bit into his arm, and the pain of the dull teeth was immensely unbearable. He screamed and could feel another grasping his skull. He realized that he might be making the last decision of his life.

The lifeless on his shoulder bit again, hot blood spurting across its face. With his rapidly numbing hand, Zuste uncorked his elixir vitae and swallowed it. *If this works, I'm the greatest genius of my time*, he thought wryly. He felt an energy flow through him and a font of health seemed to fill him.

With sudden strength, he tore away from the bloody things, stood up, and faced them. He drew his second blade as they stumbled up after him, and acting on the impulse that had come to him too late, removed the other elixir and coated his blade in it.

The lifeless were before him, vexed still to be fighting when they'd rather be eating. The former soldiers were too well protected by their armor for him to think of another strike at their chest or heads.

Instead, he dropped low, slashing at their legs, at their fleshy calves. He sliced shallowly, trying to avoid bone. His blade hit and the flesh sizzled. The big lifeless he'd hit stared stupidly, more stupidly than usual perhaps, and collapsed.

The other two were trying to flank him again, but this time the alchemist was too fast. He coated his blade twice more, and twice more it flew out, stabbing until the creatures fell.

He chuckled deeply. *Were I not here to see this*, he thought, *I would be highly dubious of it have ever happened.*

Zuste sat down at the side of the road and checked his vials. That took some time. Two of them had burst, and one was showing cracks, but the rest were safe. That was a relief beyond all reliefs. Only after he had carefully placed them all in his pack again, with the wool surrounding it, did he look to his shoulder.

The wound was revolting. The drying blood mixed with the dust of the road. He cleansed it with some of his elixir vitae, and then with some fortified wine. Then he tore a long piece from his shirt and tied it around his shoulder, as tight as he could. It took some time to do, as it was an awkward angle.

A shadow suddenly blocked the sun. He looked up to see a centurion looming over him. His heart raced as he realized his blade was not at hand.

"Saluton, friend. Could you tell us what has happened?" the lead soldier asked uncertainly. Behind him, the other two were squatting in the grass, their bowels evacuating. "We have lost the events of days." Zuste looked up at him, his breath catching. He had pupils. They were men again!

"It's simple," the alchemist said. "I am enough of a genius to cure you, and enough of a fool to try to save Rome."

"Rome," the centurion echoed uncertainly.

CHAPTER XXVI

Italy: 89 CE, Spring

"I cannot do it," Felix said dully. He stared vacantly at the broad road, surrounded by burnt fields and hard earth. They had left Rome three weeks ago and already forty men who had left the city with them breathed no more. It was still too muddy to use the chariots, but the *aurigae* were growing better at riding horses.

Winter had ended and the year of the Consulship of Augustus and Nerva had begun. The *Libereralia* was over, but it had been a cruel jest this year. A holiday meant to celebrate freedom from evil, burdens, and care, was sadly difficult to honor, and not that they would have had much time to celebrate.

"Kill her," Rufus commanded again. The blonde girl stared up at them with wide-eyed fear. She could have been no older than six.

"Senator, she is alive," Felix said. He could not keep the shock from his voice.

"Her parents are dead. She will be one of *them* before the morrow."

"Yet, she still lives," Felix said. His hand moved away from his sword. Bodies were scattered around them—some had been human, but most had been lifeless. All were bloody messes.

"For now. Would you rather wait until she became one of them?" The girl was ever so slightly, backing away down the road.

"Yes, I would. I am not in the habit of killing children."

"You are in the habit of doing what I say. I am your *dominus*."

Felix stepped toward the girl, trying to hide his reluctance.

"What you do is a technicality. She'll be meat for the monsters tonight."

"We can bring her with us." He drew his blade, knowing the futility of his argument. They were a small, quick-moving military force, and there was no role for children. The Senator was right.

The girl screamed at the sight of the blade and turned to run. Felix caught her within three steps, plunging his sword through her back and into her heart. Her small body fell quivering to the cracked ground. "It's all right," Felix said to the gasping girl as he withdrew his blade. "It's all right. Nothing can hurt you now."

She coughed, and blood bubbled from her mouth. The light in her eyes slowly died. Felix slowly wiped his sword on her body, feeling a sadness he had not known he was capable of. Hers was just another body among so many others.

"If I ever," Felix snarled, storming past the Senator. "If I ever find out that this was created, as the Emperor suspects, woe to the men involved. I will kill them all."

The Senator lifted an eyebrow. "There is no room for children in this world."

Felix marched back to the horses, only belatedly realizing that the Senator's words had been aimed at him. He clenched his fists and sighed, and then looked to his mounts. These, at least, he understood. The horses were noble beasts that seemed to stay above the sordid world humans constantly slogged through. Felix felt himself shaking, though he knew not if from anger or shame.

Hyacinthus stepped carefully toward Felix, who continued to comb his horses. For all his usefulness, the man could not abide the sight of blood and he always hung back during battles. He had used the war fire three more times, but as of yet, they'd only met small groups of the lifeless.

"I saw what happened," he said. "Felix, war isn't easy. Life isn't easy. But you—"

"What do you know?" Felix snapped. "It wasn't you out there. It's never you out there." He stopped, realizing he was not being reasonable. "Apologies. This adversity grows beyond my ability to cope."

Hyacinthus nodded slowly. "I suspect it's only going to get worse."

"Worse? I don't see how that's possible."

"He's right," said the Senator, approaching both of them from behind. A horse whinnied at him in recognition.

"He's right," he said again, more softly this time, "it will be much worse."

Felix looked to the two men. His hands stopped moving on the horse. "What do you mean? What are you talking about?"

"Felix, we've been fighting these monsters for three weeks now," Rufus said. "We have barely managed to move a day's ride outside Rome. Take a look around," he instructed. "We've burnt the crops, destroyed the homes of people, and yet, we lose men we cannot spare."

"There are more arriving," Felix said.

"Yes, the Praetorian Guard should arrive here soon. If Domitian keeps his word—which is no sure thing. His paranoia knows no bounds, but should they arrive, they are no long term solution. In time, they too will die. There are too many lifeless, and every day they grow. They grow while we lessen."

"There is a logical solution," Hyacinthus put in, "but it is too dreadful to be of any practical use."

"What?" cried Felix. He thought he knew what was coming, now. Perhaps he had known all along, but he still needed to hear it said.

"'The lifeless prey on the living," Rufus said. "As long as there are people who are alive and cannot defend themselves, we cannot defeat them."

"No," Felix said. He didn't want to hear it said after all.

"We will have to kill all the people who are still alive. Once they are dead, we can finish killing the lifeless," the Senator said. "That's why the Praetorians are coming. They will aid us."

"Why not evacuate them? Move them to someplace safe?" Felix asked.

"Where? Nowhere is safe," the Senator said. "Nowhere. It just takes one of those creatures and an entire city is lost."

"Rome hasn't been lost yet."

"Felix," Hyacinthus said admonishingly, "Domitian burnt half the city and has the other constantly on patrol."

"You know that to be true," added Rufus. "The races have been cancelled. The gladiatorial games too. Even the Emperor is not feasting as he once did. Rome relies on the grain of Egypt. With the ports closed, food grows scarce."

"Why do you make me lead," Felix asked suddenly. "The other men are veterans, and they know I am ill-equipped for the task. They don't respect me, and rightfully so. I'm not a warrior, nor have I led men, Senator."

"You're a killer, and that's close enough," Gaius Rufus replied. He must have seen the look on Felix's face, for he added: "Do you know why I have you lead? Because I trust you. You belong to me, and you have a habit of making good decisions. Most importantly, we need a little luck on our side, Felix."

Felix stared out to the horizon, doubting the truth of his own luck. There were thousands of people out there. People who dared not leave their homes for fear of the lifeless, and now something worse was coming. A legion of humanity. A legion of death.

****

The days grew warmer and longer as spring began to bloom, but no blossoms budded—no trees sprang forward with green leaves. It was a time of blood, smoke, and death. The numbers of lifeless grew ever more, despite the vast quantities that had already been killed and burnt. Domitian's Praetorians arrived—big burly Celts and Germans, with great two-handed swords.

They had taken to burning alive most of whom they found. At first, Felix had been adamant to kill the living as humanely as possible, but there wasn't time. Their horses were constantly lathered from rough riding, and the tide of walking dead pushed ever more adamantly toward Rome. That could not happen, because that city was too vulnerable, had too many people to allow even one of the walking dead into the city.

So, they butchered men, women, and children—burning them alive or riding them down. After a while, Felix stopped paying attention to whether or not they were lifeless. He told himself that all were enemies of Rome, witting or no. Gritting his teeth, he killed everyone. He was far from the best fighter in the forces, but the other *aurigae* looked up to him, and he found himself gaining a mantle of leadership.

Spring rains had caused great amounts of mud, which mixed from the ashes of the burnt crops and towns. The already-exhausted horses really struggled, and Felix's chariot was strapped to a wagon. Overhead, the grey sky gleamed damply.

Felix found Hyacinthus at the campfire. The big man smiled at him sadly. "It's very fitting that we are so close to Tarentum," he said.

"Why?" asked Felix. He sat down next to his friend and grabbed some roasted rabbit. There was no food but what they could catch.

"You've not read your Dionysius of Halicarnassus then?" Hyacinthus asked.

"Not for some time."

"Not since I insisted upon it, when you were but a boy. You are not alone. Few people have time to read anymore. Not with so many other things to distract them."

"What happened?" Felix asked.

"This was many years ago, three hundred years or more. After Rome was founded, but before she had really become herself."

Several of the other men at the cook fire took notice of the Greek's speech.

"Tarentum then was a Greek colony, and the Greeks were the power of the day. A proper civilization, mind you. Not this copy you see here."

"You Greeks always remind us of that," one of Praetorians interjected. "I guess we need to remind you that we won."

"You Latins always need reminding. The world is always changing," Hyacinthus said. "Anyway, Rome had just destroyed the Samnites, and was in the process of defeating the last great power—the Etruscans. Tarentum knew that they were doomed, unless they did something."

Hyacinthus paused, taking a great bit of the meat before him and chewing slowly. It began to drizzle, and the fire smoked angrily in protest. He continued, his mouth enunciating around the food.

"But the Greeks were a culture of wisdom, of learning. They knew little of fighting, and did not wish to drag themselves a fight that was not theirs. So they did the intelligent thing."

"They negotiated?" Felix asked. If he'd heard this story before, it was lost in the recesses of his mind.

"Even better," the Greek said, "they hired someone to do their fighting for them."

"Ah," said a swarthy Praetorian, "King Pyrrhus."

"Indeed," Hyacinthus said. "Pyrrhus was king of the strongest of the Greek colonies at that time—Epirus."

"I've never heard of it," a German soldier said.

"Of course not," Hyacinthus said. "This was three-hundred years ago. The world changes! Think you that Rome will still be here in three centuries?"

"Rome is eternal," Felix said, a little shocked. The rain was coming down harder now, and some of the soldiers were erecting a cover to shield them from the worst of the downpour.

"Then what are we doing out here? And even if the Empire survives the lifeless, it won't last forever," Hyacinthus said. "But that's not immediate." They moved under the cover as the rain started falling in cold hard balls of ice. The weather seemed an appropriate accompaniment to Hyacinthus' regretful tone.

"The Romans sent their legions against the Greek phalanx. It was, by all accounts, a very close thing. The legions were strong, though they could not break the phalanx, but for all its strength, the phalanx was used for defense and could not overrun the opposing army. They might have battled for days, but Pyrrhus had another weapon. It was late in the day when he sent his war elephants into the fray. None of the Romans had ever seen such a thing, and they were routed."

Hyacinthus was silent for several long moments. "Accounts differ about how many died on each side. Rome lost the battle, but Epirus had fewer men and had suffered grave losses. Suffice to say, Pyrrhus was recorded by Livy as saying, 'If we are victorious in one more battle with the Romans, we shall be utterly ruined.'"

The big man rose and walked away into the rain. He disappeared almost immediately into the gathering darkness.

"Well, bugger that. Greeks just don't like to admit when they've lost," said the swarthy Praetorian, and the soldiers began to laugh. A German produced some dice and the gambling commenced. Felix did not join them—he never won at dice. His name did not, it seemed, apply to games of chance.

Felix sat beside them, not at all listening to their banter. Hyacinthus was right, as always. These victories were ruining them, ruining him. What good was saving Rome if it came at the cost of slaughtered children? There had to be another way. That or perhaps the Eternal City deserved to die.

A trumpet sounded an alarm. The sentries were banging their swords on their shields.

Felix leapt to his feet, thoughts replaced with instinctive action. Someone was attacking the camp.

CHAPTER XXVII

Italy: 89 CE, Early Spring

"If I ever," grumbled Iullianus, "get out of this alive, I will live somewhere with no mud. Be it the hottest desert or the bottom of the ocean, I will make my way there and call it home." His feet and legs were caked with dark wet earth. That wasn't so bad. Each night they had to sleep on the least muddy patch of ground and he woke in the mornings to find mud in his mouth and ears. He was surprised each morning when he took his morning piss and no mud came from his cock. Each day he thought he was as filthy as possible, and each successive day proved him wrong.

"I'd happily live in mud, if it had neither the lifeless nor any Romans," Rowanna answered. They had waded through waist-deep mud in some parts, as the rains continued ceaselessly throughout the miserable spring. Iullianus scowled in concentration as he scraped more of the caked earth from his boots. It was a futile gesture, but it made him feel better to be doing something. He did this every night, to Rowanna's amusement. She more readily accepted her current state.

The mud had slowed them down, but it was the Romans that had sent them into hiding. They had found their first patrol several days ago, and had approached them carefully. The centurions had attacked them without questions, despite their protestations of life.

Iullianus had killed three of them before he and Rowanna had managed to escape. Since then, they had done everything they could to avoid the patrols. It was growing harder. They were everywhere, and they were not looking for survivors. Not only were crops being burnt, but so too were entire forests. The villages they had marched into were deserted or burnt out. They avoided even other living villagers, as they were just bait waiting for whichever type of doom would be the first to find them.

"It makes sense," Iullianus said, only half-aware that he spoke out loud.

"Moving somewhere with no mud?" asked Rowanna, her eyes closed. "I thought you said you didn't enjoy living in desert." She was thoroughly soaked and shaking from the cold. Her hair plastered against her face reminded him of the first time he had seen her.

"I didn't, but I meant the Romans. They're killing everyone."

"That's what they do," she said quietly.

Iullianus laughed a little. "Yes, who better suited for this catastrophe but the most heartless Empire that ever existed? Still, it's rather inconvenient for us. They've given up on killing the lifeless, or only killing the lifeless. They've gone for their enemies supply lines. The living."

"You mean they're not just heartless bastards, they're heartless bastards who are also quite ruthless?" Rowanna asked.

"Indeed. It is what I would do," Iullianus said. "I wonder who is commanding them. At any rate, it does us few favors. We stay near the roads, and the Romans get us. We head into the countryside, and the mud slows us long enough for the lifeless to find us. We'll never reach Rome."

"Without the cure, we have no role to play there," she said.

"It's a pity we came to Italy at all. It would be nice to let the Romans and lifeless slaughter each other without us getting caught in the middle. At this rate, I worry more about their patrols than I do the walking dead. Though, it is odd. I cannot find which legion it is. I had thought I might perhaps know the commander."

"They are smarter, and quicker," she said. "It is hard for Dacians to understand how ruthless they are." She lay down on the wet ground and withdrew a large cloak they had confiscated from a dead farmer. It smelled of the grave and had bloodstains that no amount of washing would remove, but it was large and was the best blanket they had found. "I suppose you can't find an Empire by accident."

"This I understand all too well," Iullianus said. "The only thing that has saved my people is how far away we are from Rome. They have to cross Gaul, sail across the sea, and march up Britannia just to engage us. And they've still managed to enslave half my country."

He normally didn't discuss his past, but Rowanna was easy to talk to. Furthermore, they both knew that either of them could be dead or worse by tomorrow. It was not freezing, not like it would be in either of their countries this early in the spring. Nevertheless, it was cold enough and wet enough that they relied on each other's body heat every night. They occasionally had sex, but often were too exhausted from the day's efforts of survival to summon the requisite energy.

"Your people," Rowanna murmured. She leaned into the big man and wrapped her arm around his chest. "I think they are not unlike mine."

He felt like there must be some fundamental difference, but he could not articulate why. "I suppose we are. We have no cities or forts such as you. I suppose we are less civilized."

"If Rome represents civilization, then that can only be a good thing."

"Rome represents one kind of civilization. The Greeks, the Egyptians, the Brigantes, these were all very different. Though, it is not lost on me that all, ultimately fell before the Romans. It is ironic, however, that the qualities that make the Romans real buggers help them to save the world from the lifeless menace."

Rowanna said nothing. She was asleep already. He envied her that ability—it was not easy for him to sleep, and then it was only a half-sleep at best. He was too cautious, too wary of menaces that could approach in the night. Dark dreams plagued him and visions of bloody flesh filled his sleeping mind.

She had suggested sleeping in trees, but there were few remaining since the Romans had burned the world. The copse they currently rested under had only slim corkwood trees. These provided some protection from the rain, but a child would be too heavy to climb them.

He lay there, eyes closed for several moments until he was sure that she was asleep. Then he rose and moved away from her. Squatting on his heels, he stared out into the night. The stars were hiding behind the clouds, of course, but he could see a glowing hint of the moon. He had tried to honor his promise to Lepidus, but this was beyond foolish. Only luck had kept them alive for this long. They needed to get out of Italy. Even captured by slavers or pirates would be better than this.

He listened carefully. It was quiet. The lifeless could not move without groaning and moaning, and the Romans and their horses were even louder. He was horrified by the thought of waking up, surrounded by enemies, and each night it didn't happen, made him think that it was only that more likely the next time.

They had to make for the sea. Tarentum was not far—even at their crawling pace they could be there before the end of the month. From there, anything could happen—they could perhaps sail to Egypt or Iberia. It was the right decision. He sighed as tension that he hadn't realized existed, fled away into the dark night sky.

He rejoined Rowanna, and pulled her warm body tightly next to his. In the cold spring rain, on the cold spring ground, surrounded by cold enemies, he slept.

He opened his eyes and found the world had withered away. Rowanna was nowhere to be seen, and broken, cracked earth stretched before him as far as the eye could see. He took an unsteady step forward, but his body ached with a heavy inertia and it was only with great effort that he moved at all. A distant but insistent hunger reached for him and filled him with uneasy dread.

In the distance something green shone. Not a tree, though he could not be sure what it was. The green shone with a vitality that caused him to cry out. He had to see what lay there. Some of the earth chasms were so deep that he could see the fires of Hades burning below. Taking care not to cross these, he shambled forward as quickly as he could.

With infinite patience, he crossed the barren landscape. The muscles in his legs ached with fierce intensity and his back felt as though the bones were in the wrong places. Grey and yellow gasses sifted across the land on a listless wind, and the putrid stench gagged him.

At last he drew near. Planted in the earth was the largest shovel he'd ever seen. The blade was buried in swollen earth, but the handle rose far above him. Green blossoms of life sprouted from the shaft, defying the desolation with their very existence. The big man reached out to grab it, to touch it, to embrace it, and then he stopped.

He screamed, though the sound was swallowed by the wretched land. His hand was no longer his, but a monstrosity of rotting, decayed flesh. As he looked, the skin around his small finger bubbled and dripped off, leaving a jagged white bone. He reached for the shovel anyway, but it drew away from his tainted grasp and when he clenched it, the green leaves instantly withered and died.

****

They awoke before dawn, shivering in the early morning cold. This was the best time they'd found to move. The lifeless were sluggish from the chill, and the Roman patrols did not start until after the sun came up. It was hard to rise, however. Together, their clothes had mostly dried and Rowanna's breasts were pressed comfortingly up against his own chest. The joy he'd felt the previous night was subdued but still present.

They rose and hid the signs of their presence as best they could. The lifeless were mindless, but they seemed to sense humans from afar and there was no reason to help them. And as for the Romans—if they weren't employing trackers, they soon would be. Iullianus had little woodcraft, and Rowanna only slightly more.

They had few possessions: the weapons they carried, their cloaks, the extra cloak, and a small handful of food. Perhaps the most valuable tool they owned was his shovel, which in addition to killing the lifeless, dug privy pits, made for a walking stick, and made for a seat when the ground was too muddy. With trade blocked and fields burnt, there was little to subsist on. It was yet another reason they had to leave the peninsula, Iullianus mused. They walked along a deer trail that climbed up and down small hills as the sky slowly lit up behind the clouds. The rain continued intermittently, but it was a light spring shower that might have almost been pleasant in other circumstances.

He called a halt when they reached a small shack at the base of a bare hill. It had been modest even in its prime, and now was dilapidated from years of bad weather and neglect, but it still stood, and the roof had more wood than holes.

"Why would you build at the bottom of a hill?" Rowanna asked. "Surely you'd suffer from floods and poor lighting."

"I know not why, but the Romans haven't found it yet," Iullianus said. "There may be food." They cautiously entered the building. It was clear. They found soggy cucumbers, grapes sour with age, and ground almonds. It did not taste good, but they feasted on it, saving only some limp vegetables for later.

"We must go," Iullianus said. Bits of almond hung in his teeth.

"Now?" she asked. "I have not yet begun to get dry."

"Nor shall you. It's a forced march today. We'll let our feet follow the way." He marched out of the shack.

Rowanna followed him out in the foggy morning.

"You've a sense of purpose today," she said.

"We're heading south, to the sea," he said. "I decided last night. You were right—we never should have come here. We can surely find a ship there and journey to somewhere without lifeless, Romans, or mud."

She stared at him for a moment. He knew her well enough to realize that she was not happy. "We have no money. The ports are closed, regardless. It seems like a great deal of trouble, with little chance of success," she said.

"The large ports will be closed, undoubtedly, but there will be hundreds of bays and harbors too small to patrol. We don't need a large craft, not with summer coming," he answered. "And we have no choice. If we don't escape this, we will both die. Sooner, probably, rather than later."

"I'd almost rather die than get back on a ship," she said.

Iullianus laughed, louder than he wanted to. She smiled at him, a little reluctantly. "I mean it," she said. "I'd perhaps rather stay here than board another mobile *vomitorium*."

"At least this time you won't have any food to vomit up."

"That's a depressingly optimistic way to look at things."

"It's what I do best." His smile was meant to be charming but it faded almost instantly.

"Did you hear that?" Rowanna asked. Her hands were already reaching for the *pilum* strapped to her back.

"Silence," he answered, crouching slightly. He swiveled his head and listened intently.

A low groan reached them.

"By Mithras," he hissed. Slowly, with deliberate care, he drew his blades. *Efossion* stayed clasped on his back. Rowanna had the spear before her and she twisted to face the direction they'd come. Good instincts, he thought. He had not taught her that.

Both of them froze, hoping not to attract the notice of the lifeless, but more groaning sounded.

"They're all around us," Rowanna whispered.

Iullianus scanned the land. It was bleak and dark, covered in grey clouds. He could not see a thing. The sounds were strangely muffled in the eerie fog. They sounded from all directions.

"Maybe we should go back inside," Rowanna said.

"No, we need to see what's coming." An idea struck him. "I need the high ground. Stay here, and yell when they arrive." The red-haired man looked carefully at the building.

"It will not hold my weight," he said. "Perhaps you will have more success."

She smiled dubiously but approached him, placing her spear down carefully next to him. He clasped his hands together and boosted her up. Her fingertips just caught the edge of the roof and she grunted as she pulled herself up.

She was silent for a long time.

"Well?" Iullianus asked at last. "What do you see?"

"Zalmoxis!" Rowanna said.

"What?"

"Look to the hill."

Iullianus swiveled his head. There were dozens of lifeless shambling unsteadily toward them. It was difficult to see through the fog, but they looked long dead—there were more bones than flesh, and their clothes were moldering and tattered.

"Get down," he said, "we must flee."

"I was wrong about one thing, at least," Rowanna said as she sat on the edge of the roof. The big man moved to help her, but she jumped down before he could reach her. She leaned down and clasped the shaft of her weapon.

"Yes?" Iullianus asked. The fastest of the undead were closing in on them.

"I would rather fight the Romans after all," she said. She rose and hefted her spear. The heavy point drove into the face of a twitching lifeless a meter away. Her expression did not change as she stabbed at another, scraping flesh away from bone.

He grabbed the Dacian woman by her elbow. "We can't win this fight. Nor hold out for long. We must flee."

She snarled and jabbed her hardwood spear in the gut of an advancing lifeless. With a wrenching twist, she tore away its stomach and intestines plopped out. The monster did not stop, rather, it jerked forward as more long tubes of intestine spilled out.

"Let's go. Now," he said.

There were too many coming from the hill to the south, so they turned the way they had come. Once running, none of the lifeless could catch them, and the few that were in their way were felled by fists to the head, or simply knocked over by the advancing humans.

They hadn't run for long, however, when Iullianus felt a powerful pain in his side. He tried to keep going despite it, but it was too acute to ignore. Rowanna ran awkwardly, her *pilum* held with both of her hands.

"Apologies," he panted, "I cannot go on."

"We can't stop," she said. "Keep going."

"I cannot," he said, breathing deeply. "Grant me a moment."

"I have you seen you run for hours and not tire," she said.

"This soldier needs more food than he's been getting," Iullianus said. He had always been healthy, able to out drink and outfight men a dozen years his junior. Now, some part of his body felt useless, atrophied.

She said nothing, but was looking past him.

"Look behind you," she said.

He turned, and for a moment he was back in the forested mountains of Dacia. There was a horde, nay an army, of shambling monsters coming for them. There were more together than they had seen since leaving Dacia.

"There's no inspiration," said Iullianus. "Like that of a thousand undead corpses running at you. I will run again."

"Do not call them inspiration," Rowanna said, "for they are the opposite—they are death, decay, and the end of dreams."

He turned and Rowanna shrugged and followed his loping, lupine run. They sprinted away, legs churning across the barren land. If the jagged stitch in his side did not lessen, neither did it worsen. He supposed that was no small favor. After struggling for too long, Iullianus slowed to a steady jog, and then finally to a gasping halt. Rowanna had slowed with him and she looked at him in askance. Iullianus looked carefully behind them, but the mists obscured their undead pursuers. "Let us make for the road," Iullianus said. "A Roman patrol would perhaps distract them."

"Is   anything   wrong?"
"My body feels strange. It's never struggled like this. I may be ill, but that's of no worry to you."

Rowanna nodded at this and together they headed back toward the road. When they had left the road, they'd moved half a day away from it. Here, further south, it must have swung toward them, for they found it not long after.

"Which way?" Rowanna asked.

"South," Iullianus answered immediately. "We need to reach the sea. Now more than ever."

It was raining again, as heavy sheets were cascading relentlessly upon them. The foreboding sky was pregnant with dark thunder. They both knew there were lifeless behind them, but it was too wet and too misty to see far at all.

The mud worsened as it grasped at their feet with a relentless clutching. For the first time in his life, Iullianus understood surrender. The endless struggle of survival was beginning to overwhelm him. He needed to stop, to rest. He turned to Rowanna to suggest a break, but the grim look of determination on her face shamed him and he said nothing. He concentrated on walking and not thinking of how cold he was.

As they walked, the rains eased up. It was still cloudy, mostly, but the sun shone over the soaked earth. The sunlight was a ray of warmth and life, and Iullianus felt his spirits warm along with his body. The road cut into a canyon, with high rocky walls on either side. The sun was high enough that it sparkled upon them even with the cliff walls straddling them.

"Be careful," Iullianus said after they had been in the canyon for some time. He had seen something moving. His eyes were unused to the light and he scanned the road ahead, one hand on his brow to block the sun.

There were more lifeless on the road ahead of them. They seemed to be looking for something.

Rowanna flicked her eyes at him and then back to the road. "I see them," she said. "We have to run once more."

So saying, the two of them jogged once more. The creatures were too slow and it was no hard matter to run around them. Iullianus whooped with pleasure as he knocked one down with his shoulder.

"You're feeling better," Rowanna said, as they emerged from the canyon at last.

"I am. Do you see this road?" he pointed to the long stretch of cobblestone. "All we have to do is follow it, and we will walk directly to the sea."

"What about the Romans?"

"I doubt they have come this far south. They must protect the city itself, and can only journey so far."

Rowanna nodded. "And how long must we travel down this road before we reach the sea?"

"Truly? I do not know. I think less than a week."

The sun was shining, they were making good on their escape, and they had a plan. Iullianus was so happy that he began whistling a jaunty camp tune. They strode through the afternoon, more light-hearted than he could remember. He was still whistling when they stumbled into the Roman camp.

CHAPTER XXVIII

Italy: 89 CE, Early Spring

The sound of Roman trumpets blasting was familiar to Rowanna, and until recently, it had always been the sound of the enemy. Even her time at the camp in Dacia had not taught her to think of it as anything but threatening. Here, she could see the trumpeters standing high in a watchtower. It was a sparse camp, unlike the one she had taken refuge in before. There was no trench, no palisade of sharpened wood. No defenses at all, though the layout of the camp was otherwise the same. They stood in the middle, near the commander's tent.

Within heartbeats, soldiers poured out, surrounding them. They held blades toward the pair, but as of yet had not attacked. Rowanna knew it was merely a matter of time, and she hefted her spear, ready to take as many with her as she could. Iullianus had opted for the opposite tactic. He had laid his swords on the ground and held his arms open widely.

"Salve," he said, "I am Legatus Tettius Iullianus of the Legio XIII Gemina. We are not enemies. There is no reason for bloodshed."

The men surrounding them separated looking to a medium sized, swarthy man who could have been no more than twenty. He stepped forward, the tension on his face visible. "Salve, Tettius Iullianus. I wish I could greet you as a friend, I truly do, but we are of the Legion Mortis. None meet us without tasting death as a result."

Rowanna could tell posturing when she saw it, and knew a fight was coming. Were they Dacians, they already would be throwing punches. What did civilization do to men that made them act less like humans? She took a deep breath, wondering which would be her first target. It would be difficult. These men all wore armor, and most of them were big Germanic warriors. She wondered if she would even be able to kill one of them before they got to her.

Iullianus took a halting step toward the spokesman. "I know, and I commend you for your strategy. However, we have come rushing from the wilds of Dacia with news about a cure."

This had a visible effect on the man. He muttered something in Greek and moments later, the fattest man she had ever seen appeared. He could eat Zuste twice and not notice. The two conferred in low, hushed voices, and then the first man left, disappearing into the ranks.

"Felix has told me you speak of a cure." the fat man said skeptically.

"It's true. I have seen it," Iullianus said. "So too has this woman, Rowanna of the Dacians. Our companion was an alchemist, and he could reverse the curse."

"This is not something easily believed," the fat man said. "I know of what I speak, and I have studied the works of Hippocrates of Thessaly. Long days have I spent toiling in search of a cure, but my vain efforts are fruitless and unworthy." The ring of men tightened up around the two. Rowanna felt the shaft of her spear growing sweaty in her grip and she considered striking now, before it was too late. The fat man looked directly at her. "Where is this alchemist? Where is this cure?"

"That is something I can discuss with you later," Iullianus said. "For now, there are more lifeless around here than I've seen in months, and they are coming this way. You can decide to kill us after, but for now, you need all the help you can get."

"That seems reasonable," the fat man said. "I— "

"What's this?" The original spokesman had returned, but he had not come alone. The man with him was a Roman Senator, and he looked every bit as haughty and regal as he should. Rowanna hated him upon sight. She gripped her spear even tighter as she noted his lack of armor. When the fighting started, she knew where her spear would be aimed.

The fat man quickly explained to the Senator what had been discussed. As he did, the Senator regarded the pair before him with intense scrutiny. His face did not change, but Rowanna became aware of how grimy they must appear. Weeks of camping in the rain had left them entirely disheveled and dirty.

"You claim to have the cure with you?" he remarked when the fat man had caught him up.

"As good as," Iullianus said.

"You speak Latin well, though I can hear a hint a barbarism in your accent," the Senator said. "But we both know that 'as good as' means no."

"That is true," Iullianus was forced to admit. The Senator turned to the fat man.

"They don't have it because it doesn't exist. Really, Hyacinthus, you should know better." Then the Senator said, "Kill them."

"Wait," called Iullianus. The legionaries drew their blades.

Rowanna did not hesitate. She sprang forward and jabbed her spear point into the nearest man's face, just below his helmet. Blood spurted from the wound as she savagely jerked her spear back. Iullianus stepped forward and punched a tall Celt in the face. The force of the blow wrenched his head back. The big red-haired man drew the other's gladius as he fell to the ground.

"Heed my words, for this fight is not wished by me," Iullianus called to the Senator. "There is an army of lifeless coming the likes of which you cannot imagine. We don't have to spill each other's blood."

Rowanna glanced down at the man she'd stabbed. Blood leaked from his face into the wet ground. He laid still and unmoving. *It's too late for words*, she thought.

"We cannot take any chances," the Senator said. His tone was heavy with finality. As he turned away, Rowanna whipped herself around and jabbed at a man who was easing toward her. She caught him in the arm, and one of the few places with no armor. He screamed his pain, and his weapon fell to the ground.

"Donar's cock," swore one of the Praetorians, "this woman is lethal."

Trumpets sounded again from the makeshift towers. Rowanna could not see beyond the ring of men around her, but everyone was looking toward the road.

The Senator had stopped mere steps from his tent. "What is it now?"

The young man at his side was scanning the road. "It's more lifeless," he said. He sounded confused. "But they seem to follow a leader."

"Kill these two and go kill them, Felix," the Senator snapped. "I shouldn't have to tell you that."

"Yes, Senator," Felix said. He sighed and drew his weapon. The other Romans were mumbling. "I don't like this," muttered one of the soldiers closest to Rowanna.

The Senator looked at the road behind them, his mouth opened in shock. He closed it quickly, but even from where she stood, his face visibly paled. She swung her head around and saw a muddy battalion of lifeless advancing upon them. At their head was a large black corpse. It had a whole in its chest and was missing its lower jaw, but it moved with more speed and grace than any lifeless she had seen before.

He paused, face stricken. Several heartbeats passed. Everyone seemed frozen, save for the advancing lifeless.

"I have changed my mind," he said in a soft voice. "Adriax, summon your guard to me. Felix, lead the men—two formations, you understand. And Hyacinthus, prepare for the worst."

His gaze fell upon Rowanna and Iullianus. "You two, you may join our fight, should you wish."

"Senator," said the injured Praetorian, "she killed Marcus, and the bone is sticking out of my arm."

"You shouldn't have let her stab you," the Senator snapped. "And Marcus was a daydreaming fool."

The injured Praetorian dropped his shield and reached for his blade with his good hand.

"Bugger all that," he said. "He owed me money." His sword was in his hand and he stepped toward the Dacian woman.

Rowanna readied her spear, wishing she was fighting a lifeless. How could she strike against so much armor? Before either of them had moved another step, Iullianus was behind the man. The red-haired man grabbed the other man's helmet and exposed the Praetorian's throat, resting the edge of his sword against the bulge in the man's throat. He leaned in so close that his mouth nearly touched the man's ear.

"This is the part where I should threaten you. Tell you that if you bother her again, you will die. You'd understand, begrudgingly, but you'd do it. In time, we'd grow to be friends."

With a flash, he thrust his sword into the man's throat. The sharp smell of blood filled Rowanna's nostrils, and she watched dispassionately as the dying man slumped to the ground. She wondered if she should feel something—she reached for sadness, for regret, but she found only emptiness.

As a man, the other Romans drew their blades. Rowanna exhaled, and then breathed in deeply.

"Hold," the Senator commanded. He strode toward them all, glowing with authority.

Rowanna turned to the Senator. His eyes had gone cold, but he said, "Gratias, Legatus, for removing that insolent man. No one will avenge him—he has paid the price for his insubordination. Now kill these creatures or it will matter not what we think of each other."

Iullianus slid over to the young man. Rowanna followed him. "Listen," he said, "there's no fighting these things. It might be better to regroup, let them come to us. I could build walls, funnel them toward us."

"You don't understand," Felix said. "This is what we've been waiting for. Instead of killing them in scattered bunches, we finally have them gathered together. It will make it so much easier for us." He looked at the ground wistfully. "If only it were dry," he said.

"How many have you fought, at one time?" Iullianus asked.

"Some. Two or three dozen, at least. Why?"

"There are thousands of them out there. Last time I saw this many, they destroyed my legion."

"That legion didn't know what we know. Besides, Senator Rufus is the commander. I only lead the war efforts."

"What wars have you fought in?"

The lad was silent for a few moments. "The Hippodrome is like a war—life and death are on the line."

Rowanna resisted the urge to grab and shake the lad. Iullianus must have felt the same way, for he said, "So too are such things at risk in childbirth, but I wouldn't want my mother leading an army."

Helpless frustration warred with anger as the boy considered those words. *That look.* Rowanna felt an icy fist clench around her heart and her legs shook. Though he was too short and too dark of hair, the lad had for an instant worn one of Dapyx's expressions.

Iullianus was addressing the soldiers. He sounded, she realized, exactly like a Roman general. Which was no surprise—that is what he was. It was strange though, to have the man she had traveled with and gotten to know so well show another side of himself, a side that she had forgotten existed.

"There is a canyon not far behind us," he was saying. "Drive them back to there or we can hold them off in shifts." He stopped, and the cadence of his voice changed. "We must push them back, or else they will swallow us in a sea of menace." He pulled the shovel from his back to go with the bloody blade in his hand. "Aim for their heads!" he cried. "*Malum delenda est*!"

Rowanna knew enough Latin to translate: "Evil must be destroyed." She did not know if she was welcome, but she charged forward with the others, a dead man's blood still warm on the point of her spear.

CHAPTER XXIX

Italy: 89 CE, Early Spring

The arrival of the two in camp had been strange, to say the least, but both had quickly proven their worth. The big Celt, for surely he was one, despite his accent, fought fearlessly. He leaped into battle like an avatar of Mars, but the woman, that plain, brooding, middle-aged woman, she was something else. Felix had occasionally raced against highly-skilled female charioteers, but never had he seen a woman move with such deadly purpose. He was relieved not to have to face either of them.

The line of Romans had hit the lifeless horde with fierce, irresistible power. Hundreds of the white-eyed monsters had fallen, but ever were there more. Too many to count, too many shambling inevitably toward the outnumbered living. Even with the deadly efficiency of their two allies, the legion of death had faltered. They might still have won, Felix thought, but then the worst thing of all happened.

The leader, the thing that had shaken the Senator, emerged. It seemed impossible, for the lifeless had no minds, but it roared and they were heartened in their dark dreary way. The heartless one at the front stood there, its large body seeming to inspire the undead behind it. Looking like Hannibal himself, it roared a challenge at the Roman forces. Four Praetorians charged, and it ripped them apart with shocking brute strength. Even without a lower jawbone, it took huge bites from their dismembered bodies.

Five more Romans, two of them charioteers advanced upon him. They locked their shields and held blades ready. The huge lifeless heaved a torso at them. It battered their shields, halting their advance. Moving not quickly, but more so than the other lifeless, the leader of the lifeless lumbered into them. Its hands closed around one of the charioteers heads and it ripped it off with a wrenching snap.

The others cut at their monstrous foe. Though their blades sliced its flesh, it did not even notice. With cruel power, it bit, chewed, and tore them into shreds. It took only moments. Felix swallowed. He was the closest living thing, and he would confront it, and he would die.

A flash of red and suddenly the man named Iullianus was there. His blade was almost faster than the eye could follow, and he knew not to stab anywhere but the head. Still, he was outsized and out-strengthened, and his attack quickly turned to a desperate defense. It snarled, mouth full of broken, pointy teeth. The Hannibal monster grabbed Iullianus by the throat, lifted him into the air. His blade dropped to the ground as he grabbed at the hand choking his life away. Even from where he stood, Felix could see the red-haired man's face turn red as he shook and struggled against the creature's awesome strength.

The big man swung his hand behind his head, drawing a blade from behind his back. Felix blinked. It was not a blade at all—it was a shovel! What madness was this? Swinging with all the power he could summon, Iullianus drove the edge of his metal shovel into the neck of his powerful foe. It was a strike with divine power.

The lifeless leader's head was sundered from its body and it went rolling to the ground. Its face was a mask of pure hate as it fell. Iullianus fell, dark hands still clasping at his throat. He stood, turned to the Roman forces, and bowed.

Felix joined the ragged cheer when at last the black lifeless had been sent back to the grave, but it had been short-lived. There were still far too many enemies clawing, gnashing, and rending, for any to have had hearts lifted.

Step by bloody step, the Romans had pushed the lifeless back. They were too few, however, far too few. They fought in single file, stretched across the road and into the fields. Else, the monsters would flank them and all would fall, but their battle lines were so thin, and one man falling meant danger to those on either side of him.

Felix cursed again the muddy terrain. He and the other charioteers were not meant to fight hand-to-hand. Already many of his *aurigae* friends had died, and the chariots sat untouched in their wagons. What difference weather could make!

He stabbed again at the chest of an undead monster. The creature's brittle ribs cracked and the scent of death choked him.

Bile filled his mouth. The lifeless grabbed at his wrist with an immensely strong grip. A chill filled his arm and the sword fell from   his   hand. Felix jumped back, but the thing did not let go and he nearly lost his balance. With inevitable joy, the corpse moved its ravenously grey mouth toward his hand.

"No," Felix cried. He punched it in the head with his other hand as hard as he could. The thing did not relent much, but it was enough that Felix was able to jerk his hand back. It felt dead, numb.

The snarling thing came for him. Felix dropped his left hand to his belt and he stabbed upward with his falx. It went into the corpse's eye, splattering pus and juices on his hand. He didn't even have time to be disgusted, as the lifeless fell, three more moved toward him.

A red rage filled Felix. This was not the cold, instinctive fury that had won for him so many matches at the Hippodrome. This was white-hot rage, the kind that overrode all other thoughts.

He was dimly aware of charging the lifeless, of stabbing, cutting, and swinging a gladius—where had that come from?—and of cutting down white-eyed foes until he panted with exhaustion. Swaths of disembodied and disemboweled lifeless surrounded him.

Something sailed over his head, and there was an explosion of thunder. "Warfire!" Felix cried. Finally something good was happening, and it felt enormously satisfying to have a weapon the lifeless did not. He turned and saw Hyacinthus and four *aurigae* holding the deadly *tzykalia*. Together, they lofted more of the deadly missiles into the ranks of the undead.

Thunder rolled through the thick air, and the sizzling smell of burning flesh filled his nose. The men were far enough, away, however, that the warfire did not deafen them. The lifeless lit up like dry kindling as the fire jumped through their ranks. Masses of burned bodies and ash fell to the ground.

Felix leaned on his sword, too weary for celebrating. His long hair hung in sweaty clumps and he brushed his fringe from his face. Hundreds of the approaching monsters were walking into the wall of flame, and hundreds more had already melted from the intense heat. He did not know if it would be enough. He narrowed his eyes and scanned through the haze of the fire. It was hard to see, but it seemed like thousands of corpses still awaited.

"This fire of yours is a boon from the gods," a voice said behind him.

Iullianus stood next to him. He was breathing heavily and his hair was plastered to his skull with sweat, but he seemed unharmed.

"I saw what you did, with that toy knife of yours. You fought well, lad."

Felix swallowed the words, judging that no insult was meant. He did look young, and he was much smaller than this brute of a man.

"You, too, Legatus. You and your woman. I've never seen someone fight with a shovel before."

"I have had too many blades break, and this shovel was my only friend for many long years," Iullianus said. He laughed, belying the craziness of his word. Felix could smell the musky sweat on the other man, though it mingled with the scent of blood and ash from the fire. "Though we have seen this many only once before, when they killed my entire legion in Dacia."

"You had said something earlier. I thought you exaggerated."
"No. Fewer than ten of us survived."

Felix could not hide his shock. "So few? What happened?"

"Much like this—we were entrenched in camp. We held off attacks for weeks, until there were finally too many of them. None of us should have survived." As the big man talked, a blur of movement near the canyon caught Felix's eye. He dismissed his initial thoughts and listened again to the big man. "We were saved by only one thing."

"What was that?" Felix asked. He glanced again to the horizon, to the edge of the horde, and this time he knew.

"Elephants," said Iullianus. "I had a force of well-trained war elephants. They managed to turn the tide of the battle enough that some of us survived. Though in truth, it took aid from a small army of Dacians as well."

Felix could feel the bitterness in his smile. It was too extraordinary not to believe. He laughed harshly. "You are in luck then, Legatus."

"I do not understand."

The charioteer pointed toward the legions of the lifeless. They were parting, allowing for great gaps. Behind them came the lumbering beasts, shimmery behind the curtain of flame. Iullianus squinted, mouth frowning in concentration.

Even at that distance, there could be no doubt.

"For Mithra's sake!" Iullianus swore angrily. "What are we supposed to do against that?" He gestured toward the mountains that moved toward them. They had once been his, presumably.

Now they were undead monsters, war elephants that could not die.

***

"It might be too late," the Senator said. "There just aren't enough of you."

"Senator," Felix said, "please."

Rufus cocked his head, studying the battle. The Legion of Death was holding—just barely—against the seething hordes that battered them. Iullianus was leading them now, and he had inspired the men to acts that surpassed mere bravery. They had dug in and with a wall of fire and a shield wall behind that were nearly intractable. Yet, the elephants had not reached them. Could they withstand those raging, disintegrating beasts? Felix doubted it. "That might be the last thing you say to me. To anybody."

Felix laughed. "You know I fear not death. The fires have dried out the ground. We have the chariots we've carted with us this entire time, and I still have a score of men who will ride out with me. With our speed, we can fight even those great elephants. Perhaps save the others."

Rufus waved his hand in assent. It was not an admission of Felix's arguments so much as an unwillingness to continue his side of the conversation. Their war was taking a toll on everyone, but the Senator was perhaps suffering the most. The effort of leading was suffocating even this practiced leader of men.

Felix nodded his thanks and jumped away, motioning to the group of charioteers who were standing nearby. As he told the Senator, the warfires had dried out the wet earth. He knew they had close to the camp, and he hoped they had further away. It would still be muddy in places, but it was the best chance for the chariots since they'd left Rome.

In moments, the smaller *bigae* were unloaded and attached to horses. Though they were the same chariots used in the hippodrome, they'd been fitted with blades on the wheels and outside. They were deadlier than any chariot had ever been made to be. Would that be enough? Felix thought about bringing amphorae of warfire—there was room on the platform—but the stuff was too flammable, too unpredictable. It wasn't worth the risk.

The charioteers were looking at him and he realized they were scared. All were veterans of countless races, but this was a storm, a deluge of a ferocity that none had encountered before. He was the eldest, the leader. It was up to him to inspire them, to give them words of confidence and fill their hearts with bravery.

"Well," Felix said, "let's go kill some things."

They got off to a bad start. The ground had dried on the surface but was muddy deeper below. Much of their maneuverability would be sacrificed, and it took sheer effort just to move forward in some of the more mired places.

But advance they did, and soon Felix's chariot was charging forward. His falx was strapped to his waist and he held a gladius with both his hands—with the momentum of the chariot, he could behead numerous of the shamblers with little effort on his own part. The spikes on his wheels were even more ferociously deadly—they ripped the lifeless into pieces. This did not always kill them, but it made them easier to slay for the now advancing foot soldiers.

Felix felt uneasy. As many as they killed, there were far more. Even if they never tired, it would take days to kill all their foes, and there were still the elephants, drawing ever closer. Much slower and ungainly than their living brethren, they nonetheless managed to stamp and stomp their way toward their living opponents.

He pulled his chariot to a stop, taking advantage of a brief lull in the battle. Those elephants would be hard to stop, but he had an idea. It was one that was likely to get him killed, but perhaps he could take a few of the beasts with him. He raced back to the camp for some supplies.

CHAPTER XXX

Italy: 89 CE, Early Spring

"Fall back," he cried. He was speaking to perhaps seventy men, covered in sweat and smeared with smoke and ash. Iullianus shook his head slightly as he surveyed the survivors. This couldn't be happening again. What cruel fate led him to lead so many disastrous campaigns?

The fires had stopped the horde. The Greek and his assistants had created a shimmering buffer that disintegrated the oncoming masses, but the elephants lumbered through, pushing their bulk through the fiery wall. The flames had caught them, clung to them, and they'd become pyrotechnic weapons. There was no fighting these beasts of inferno that the men had routed from the burning undead.

The boy, Felix, had led the charioteers directly into battle against the burning creatures. Iullianus shook his head with impressed memory. *So close.* Had the ground been dryer, or had there been more than the scant handful of charioteers, the battle could have been won. Some of the charioteers had used ropes to tangle up the legs of the giant beasts, knocking them down and leaving them immobile. The fires leaped from enemy to ally, and some of the slow elephants were quick enough to strike with tusk or trunk and kill the advancing charioteers. The pressing crush of human undead cut the margin of error down further, and eventually, only Felix and six others had escaped.

They'd regrouped at the camp, and shields were locked and *pila* were readied. The Senator was ashen-faced and much of his personal guard had joined the survivors. Those that didn't, began to pack up the camp. Though they had many wagons, they were leaving the weapons and armor. All that mattered was enough food to get them to Rome, and the wagon that Hyacinthus was personally re-loading. It sat a distance away from the sleeping tents and cook fires, Iullianus noted. That was for the better.

The lifeless were massing again. The only thing stopping their surge was their hunger, and they were feasting on the fallen soldiers. Iullianus could not hear their screams, but some men had merely been wounded, unable to flee, and now they were eaten alive. He shuddered. It was far better to die in battle.

It had taken far too long, but many of the elephants had eventually burned to death. The burning scent of long-dead elephant made him gag, but there was no time to focus on it. But as the burning elephants had pushed the men back, the warfires had died down. The last three undead war elephants had made it through with the fire only scoring their legs. Unlike their living kin, these had a taste for human flesh. They ran down fleeing soldiers or batted them to unconsciousness with their trunks.

Iullianus wanted to speak with the Senator, but the man was busy. He found instead, the charioteer, and the lad seemed surprisingly capable.

"How far back is Rome?" he asked.

"Five days, maybe," the boy said slowly. "We did not come as quickly as we could have."

"That is too long," Iullianus said. "We need to flee."

"We are faster than the lifeless," Felix said.

"Yes, while we are awake, but we need to stop. We need to piss, to eat, to sleep. Those things behind us, they will stop for nothing. If we flee, we must do so as relentlessly as they will follow."

Felix briefly closed his eyes and sighed. "Again, your words ring with wisdom, but—" He never finished the sentence. A war-elephant, covered with flickering fire, was running straight for them. Though not as fast as an elephant that yet lived, the lifeless animal was far quicker than a man was.

Iullianus and Felix scattered. The big man ran to his left, into the burnt thickets on the side of the road. Felix ran the opposite direction, into flat farmland. The elephant pursued neither of them. It thundered past with a headless Praetorian clasped in its trunk. Specks of meat and flesh clung to its teeth.

A man screamed in fear as it ran into the camp. A big German man stood before the beast and with great precision, lofted his *pilum* at it. It sunk into the dead flesh but the beast did not hesitate. The German turned to run away but it was too late. The trunk slammed down and the body of his fellow soldier knocked him aside. Iullianus watched in horror as the elephant careened to a stop. Releasing the soldier it had held, it scooped up the fallen German. Moving the man's head to its mouth and with as much effort as a man would make with a grape, bit the German's head off.

Iullianus scanned the road behind him. The horde was moving again, shuffling forward with a ravenous purpose that defied logic and reason. He glanced towards Felix to see if he had seen it yet. The boy was staring with horrified panic, but he was looking the other way, into the camp.

"Felix," Iullianus said.

"Oh, Jupiter no," Felix said softly.

The war elephant was charging again, but this time, its targets were the *aurigae* who were loading up the wagon. The wagon that was filled with warfire. If the elephant charged into that, it would kill not only itself, but also every living being that opposed it. Iullianus fought the urge to run. If the elephant struck that wagon, the difference a few seconds of distance would make, was negligible. He supposed the inferno that would consume them all would at least be preferable to death by lifeless.

The flaming beast, still clasping the headless German's body in its trunk, drew closer to the wagon. The *aurigae* had scattered, fleeing for their lives as their doom bore down upon them. Now the horses screamed and fled away, across the smoky plain. Only one man stood there; a fat man holding a jar in each of his hands.

He shouted at the beast, and then turned and ran. For a big man, he could move quickly, and he ran away from the wagon, into the burnt farmland. The beast changed course slightly and rumbled after him. Relatively fleet as he was, Hyacinthus was no match for the beast's speed.

He knew it too, it seemed. He turned and flung a jar at the lumbering elephant. He had not dared stop, and it was a poor throw. It hit the ground several paces from the intended target and plumes of smoke and a thunderous crack resulted almost immediately. The resulting explosion did nothing to distract the beast. Some of the fire caught the shaft of the *pilum* and it began to burn.

Iullianus later supposed it was there that Hyacinthus realized what he must do. His actions required a kind of bravery that not one man in a thousand possessed. He doubted his own ability to have made such a choice, but the rotund Greek was more hero than Iullianus would ever have guessed.

Hyacinthus stopped running. He held the warfire to his chest with both hands in an almost motherly gesture. The elephant lumbered up to him. It was still burning, but just slightly, so that it had an otherworldly glow.

A twitch alerted him to Felix's movement and Iullianus dropped his shovel. The lad sprang away, toward the confrontation. What good he thought he'd do was never revealed, as Iullianus grasped him from behind. He held on tight with both hands as Felix fought back with surprising strength.

"Let me go. I'm warning you," Felix said harshly.

"You'll do nothing but join him in his grave," Iullianus said sadly. He pinned the lad's arms to his sides and held on with fatigued arms.

The elephant grasped Hyacinthus in its trunk. It opened its mouth and pulled the man toward it. Hyacinthus wriggled and pulled his hands free. He must have been less than a man's height away when he threw the *tzykalia* full of wildfire into the thing's mouth. Felix struggled against his hold, but Iullianus clasped with all his strength and the young man could not break free.

The resulting explosion boomed with the raw, divine power of the Gods. The war elephant's mouth melted away instantaneously. It flung the Greek man down with horrible strength as its face continued to melt away. Smoke poured from its mouth, from its floppy ears, and from its trunk.

It stepped forward once, twice, and then fell. Even after all the bad luck they'd suffered, Iullianus was not expecting the burning, disintegrating beast to fall upon the Greek man.

It landed mostly on the ground, but its leg fell with crushing force upon the Greek. Hyacinthus lay prone and unmoving beneath the burning beast as its flesh sizzled and bubbled from the great heat.

The wagon full of warfire was uncomfortably close, but as yet, had not caught fire. They'd have to move that wagon, and quickly, though the horses would not welcome crossing that field of flame. Felix struggled against him again, and he realized that he still held the young man in his arms.

Iullianus at last released his grip, and both of them ran to the fallen man. His torso was crushed but his head and hands were free. Together, the two of them dragged him out from under the crushing leg of the monster.

There was little recognizable in the man who had been a gentle flower. His ribs were crushed and his neck had been broken. Parts of his flesh had been burned and had blackened. When he spoke, it was in a hoarse whisper.

"Ah, Felix. The gods make fools of us all."

"Hyacinthus!" Felix cried. "You are my oldest friend. You are like a father to me," he stopped talking, as his voice choked with tears. Iullianus was no stranger to death, but his insides ached. He glanced over to the wagon, feeling nervous about its very existence. It was still not burning, and seemed to be safe. Three of the *aurigae* had reappeared and were loading up the last of the containers into the back of the wagon.

"You can't die," Felix said at last. Iullianus turned back to the scene before him.

"Do you remember, a long time ago that I told you it was better to spend your coin on long odds?" Hyacinthus asked, his voice a strained whisper.

"The day at the circuses. The day before my first race. It has been in the back of my mind ever since. I remember it well," Felix said.

"I might," Hyacinthus said, and the strain in his voice was more apparent than ever. "I might have been wrong." He took one more gasping breath and then his body relaxed with horrible finality into the muddy field.

"Now," Felix said to the red-haired man. "Help me pick him up. We will burn him. Burn him in the fire he created."

CHAPTER XXXI

Italy: 89 CE, Spring

It was a toilsome, grim, and oft times unreal retreat as the survivors marched back to Rome. Though it was spring, they walked through a land of blackened ash. No flowers budded, no birds chirped, and no trees blossomed in the land of death they moved through. It was a death march, not only because they moved through lands they themselves had scorched, nor because they rode past the limp bodies of people they themselves had killed. It was a death march because all who wearied and slept, fell behind, and that meant death.

They had left all wagons behind, save for the one filled with warfire. With the horses scattered, the men took turns hauling it. It was a fearsome task and there had been no time to pack the *tzykalia* correctly, and every bump on the road threatened to extinguish them all. Rufus blinked, realized he was beginning to sleep as he walked. Exhaustion haunted all of their steps, and the line between sleep and wakefulness had never been more thinly drawn. It was hard on them all, but they were all soldiers. He was a Senator, and should have been above such things as walking. Some of his fellow Senators would have given up, or been unable to exert the effort needed, but he still wanted to live. There was too much to do in life to accept death. The Empire depended upon him.

For the first time in a long time, since perhaps his exile, he did not know what to do. All his plans, all his schemes, seemed utterly pointless in the face of this damned reality. He felt as though he were a child, playing in his bath with toy ships whilst outside his home, real war waged. He had left Rome feeling confident with two hundred men. Now he wondered if two thousand would have made a difference. The tide of undead was unceasing, and there weren't enough legions in Rome to match the legions of the lifeless.

They stopped for a short break. The company sat on a small brown hill. Behind them stretched long stretches of road, but it had been flat. It was better to walk in daylight, and all feared resting in the dark. In the light, they could see the creatures coming. At night, they were entirely too vulnerable. They'd walked through the entire night the last two nights, stopping only to rest at dawn.

Ahead of them, they climbed hills large enough give pause to tired men. This stop would be no more than an hour, and scouts watched in all directions. Some men grasped what sleep they could, others sat and stared blankly. Rufus envied those who rested, but he was far too exhausted for sleep. He pondered instead, and built more of the useless toy ships to sail uselessly in useless circles.

He scanned the area, watching the dreary men who yet lived. Both the big Celt and barbarian woman were still with them. It was unusual for him to deal with a woman that he didn't want to bed, and she was nothing to look at, a crude tribeswoman nearly past her child-bearing lives. He had seen her fight, and her savagery was something to behold. The Legatus was clearly a man of leadership and action, and with thought of that man, Rufus knew there was one small thing he could do, one broken toy ship he could still repair.

He fought the heaviness of his eyes and stared at the hills that awaited them. There was no way they'd get their wagon up there. Nor was he willing to abandon the warfire. That left an obvious, and unpopular course of action. First, though, he summoned the two men who were foremost in his thoughts.

Felix appeared before him first. Iullianus joined him a moment later. He stood there, moving his head back and forth until there was an audible pop.

"That's better," he said. "I am getting old."

Felix did not acknowledge him. Rufus inhaled deeply, and released his breath. There was no reason to pussyfoot around this.

"Hyacinthus died four days ago," Rufus said, watching Felix's expression. It did not change. "He and more than a hundred other good men."

"Senator," Felix acknowledged, knowing the greater point was yet to be made.

"In the days following, I've noticed you have not spoken to Iullianus. Not once."

"Senator, he did something I can never forgive," Felix said. "He kept me from saving a friend."

"I saved your life is what I did," Iullianus said. He sounded vaguely amused.

Felix wheeled on him. "I could have helped! I could have done something. He didn't have to die."

"He did have to die, Felix," Rufus said, interjecting. An older part of him wondered at this, in that he was explaining himself and consoling a *servus*. The world had indeed changed. "You would have joined him in death."

"And is that so bad?" Felix asked, his voice choked with emotion. "Is death so bad, when the alternative is this?" He gestured at the blackened landscape. "There is no honor now, not when I use my life to end so many others."

"You do what I say. There is no greater honor for a *servus* than to conform to his master's wishes."

"I know you are helping me, Senator, but that's strange notion of honor, even for a Roman," Iullianus said.

Rufus fought a surge of anger, knowing his irritability to be a product of exhaustion and lack of sleep.

"And are you not a Roman?" Felix asked.

"It is a matter increasingly up for debate lately," Iullianus said, "but, no, I was born outside the Empire."

"Mare's shit. You're a Legatus, a political animal."

The big man sighed. "It's a long story, lad, and one I have no stomach to recount now. I was captured from my family when I was fourteen. Before the man who had taken us could sell me, we were attacked. I saved his life, incredible though that sounds."

"What man was this?" Rufus interjected.

"Legatus Larcius Lepidus, Senator," the big man said.

The name sounded familiar, but Rufus did not know the man. "When was this?"

"A long time ago. More than twenty years. Did you know him?"

"I did not. I was exiled during that time."

Iullianus turned to the lad. "Iullianus isn't even my name, though I've used it for most of my life. I'm willing to bet that your parents didn't call you Felix either."

Rufus saw the pain and surprise that briefly shone on the lad's face. "That's right. My name, a lifetime ago, was Jotham. At least I think so, though that boy named is not me."

The big man nodded. "I know," he said.

"You still had no right to hold me back," Felix said. His eyes brimmed with wet emotion.

Iullianus drew his blade. It happened so quickly that he had it pressed against Felix's throat before Rufus could even blink.

Felix's hand dropped to his waist, but before it could move further, Iullianus pressed the edge of his sword against the man's throat.

"Don't fucking move," he said.

"Stand down, Legatus," Rufus said, standing up. He used his Senatorial voice, the one packed with the most authority he could summon. It did him little good.

"Apologies, Senator, but if this boy continues to mope that I saved his life, I will end it here. It seems to me a fair solution to the issue."

His eyes turned to the charioteer.

"Do you think you're the first to see a friend die? To see him fall before you? Others have walked this walk, and done so with considerably more grace."

Felix seemed unable to look away from the blade. His features flared with determination and hate. There was silence for far too long.

At last, the boy spoke. "All right, Legatus, Senator. I concede the point," his voice was weary. "I have been an ungrateful wretch, and I have no excuse."

The sword was sheathed again in an instant. Iullianus smiled at Felix, his expression sphinx-like. "You have many excuses. I barely knew the man and his death saddened me, but never let excuses dictate your action—that is the realm of reason, and reason alone. Senator," this last was accompanied by a farewell nod to Rufus.

That had not gone as planned, but it seemed to have achieved the desired result. Rufus was just congratulating himself when Felix moved. He had a blade in his hand and he took one big step and then leapt at the big man.

Iullianus must have sensed something, for he whirled around. His reflexes were not fast enough, however, and Felix crashed into him. They fell and the commotion alerted others to the conflict. Iullianus grabbed at the lad's legs, but they had been hardened by a thousand races and he could not gain purchase against them.

Felix had his blade at Iullianus' throat. "You spoke truly," he hissed. "I was ungrateful, and you were correct in reminding me." He spat, to the side, and his spittle landed in a clump of phlegm not far from Rufus. "But if you ever draw a blade on me—ever—you had better kill me. Or I will kill you. Understand?"

Iullianus began laughing.

"By Mithras, you've got balls after all," he said. "You keep up this spirit, and you will not have to worry."

A chagrined smile later, Felix stood up. "I mean it, Legatus."

"I know you did, *aurigae*," Iullianus said, clasping his hand, "I know you did."

Rufus watched them walk away, feeling ever less connected to reality. The dead walking was hard enough to accept, but slaves' acting as equals to freemen was stretching the realm of credibility. He wondered if the nicely drawn lines of social structure always blurred in crises, then realized there had never been a crisis like this one to compare it with.

He called for the men to gather and the sleeping men were quickly woken. "Listen," Rufus said, "we have come a long, dusty way, and Rome is close." In truth, he was not entirely sure how close it was, but he estimated they would see it late tomorrow, if they were lucky. "But we are slowed by the wagon."

"Hear, hear," one of the Praetorians said.

"You all know how dangerous the warfire is. Drop it, or even shake it overmuch and you'll burn to death instantaneously. A fast death, but a painful one. Worse, you will kill all of us as well. So hold onto caution with the amphorae."

"This is nothing new," Iullianus said. "The men who carry the wagon tread as lightly as possible. My back still aches from my stint yesterday."

There were murmurs of agreement. "We're leaving the wagon," Rufus said. "And our shields. Each man is to carry one pot of fire. We will burn the rest."

In the end, there were only three pots left. Rufus had decided to leave them unburned, in the hopes that the lifeless would somehow trigger them. And so laden, the survivors of the Legion of Death marched on.

It was the next day, after they had marched through the night, slept at dawn, and resumed marching until the sun was high overhead that they saw Rome. It was still far away, at the edge of the horizon. Rufus nearly dropped his *tzykalia* as the shock somehow penetrated his weary exhaustion. A look at the others showed him a similar defeated numbness. Another look and he screamed in frustration, willing it not to be true. His body wilted as his once indomitable spirit seemingly left him at last. They could all see it from where they stood.

Rome was burning.

CHAPTER XXXII

Italy: 89 CE, Spring

Felix swung his sword with a weary sigh. It connected with an undead neck, but did not pierce it and his blade stuck. He had seen Iullianus swing with enough strength to behead the lifeless, but the Legatus was not only freakishly strong, he used a heavier gladius. Felix kicked at the creature until it fell down. As it struggled to rise, he wrenched the sword free and drove it into the back of the thing's head. That was the last of this wave and Felix sighed wearily.

"Is there no end to this?" Felix said. "How long can we hold the will to fight?"

Rowanna nodded grimly and Iullianus said nothing at all. They were saving their energy for the relentless struggle. They were caught in a deadly trap and now, Felix realized, the survivors were merely in extended death throws. He was tired that events were rapidly outpacing his capability to process them, but even through the tired haze of shock, he could taste his astonishment.

They had reached Rome to find it a smoking, burning heap. Flames still licked and sparked as smoke poured into the heavens, and they dared not enter the dangerous remnants. The obvious fact troubled Felix far more than he would be able to express. The Eternal City was no more. The very heart of Italy, of the Empire, had rotted, burned, and now ceased to beat altogether.

There were no survivors, and more correctly, no *living* survivors. The area outside the city was full of crawling, twitching citizens of the former city. There were surprisingly few of the creatures, however. Thousands certainly, but not the hundreds of thousands that one might expect. What had happened in that doomed city? He guessed that the fires had burned most of the citizens to death.

With a horde close behind them, and the damned of Rome before them, the small troop stopped. The sheer exhaustion from forced marches and lack of sleep was an anchor that dragged upon them all. Upon discovery of the ruined city, however, there had been no time to rest. Felix had joined Iullianus and they had dug a small trench around themselves, filling it with warfire. Others, the few who did not fall to the ground and sleep immediately, began assembling ruined carts, stones, and long sticks as a sort of barricade. This was set the length of two men back from the trench, to keep it safe from the flames.

The first of the lifeless had reached them soon after. If not for the warfire, they would have been lost. Thousands of walking dead—people who had been Senators, slaves, bakers, guards, whores, cloth-dyers, brick makers, sculptors, teachers, and more— perished in those hot fires. More strange yet, were the animals— woodland creatures, dogs, cats, bears, and even exotic lions and rhinos, refugees from a gladiatorial pit somewhere. It was eerie to see them march thoughtlessly through the flames, flesh melting, sizzling, and bones blackening as their bodies disintegrated.

It had begun raining, but not even the tears of the gods could quench this inferno. Felix watched it dreamily. It roared and crackled with a ferocity no ordinary fire could hope to match, and even so far back he could feel the heat of it. How many times had Hyacinthus saved their lives with his creation? Moreover, what could they do with that gift except prolong the inevitable? In some ways, he envied his old friend, envied all who no longer had to battle for existence.

"There are too many of them out there," a voice said.

His eyes snapped open and he realized he'd been sleeping on his feet.

The Senator stood before him. He was smiling wearily and he held a muddy stick in his hand. Felix barely recognized him as the man he'd left Rome with. "If I could do it all over again," he said, "I wouldn't have been so fucking eager to get off my island. I'm sorry I got you into this; got everyone into this. We should have left Rome on the first ship after that gladiator fight." He sighed. "As Seneca said, fire tests gold, suffering tests brave men, but he couldn't have comprehended this."

"You did not create these monsters, Senator," Felix said. He was unsure of how to deal with this version of the man before him. Had he likewise changed? Would he know? Did things like personality and character matter at all anymore?

The Senator laughed. When Felix looked at him, he no longer saw a man imbued with the imperial power of Rome. He saw a tired old man, shaking slightly from exhaustion.

"There's no better way to say this than to just say it: You're a *servus* no longer," Rufus said. "My will said otherwise, of course, but it's been burnt to ashes by now."
"Senator? But I am too young," Felix said, taken aback.

"True. You are only half-free until you reach the age of thirty. Admittedly which," he said, looking out at the encroaching fields of walking death, "doesn't look too possible now."

The slap was unexpected. Old man though he might be, Rufus was not weak and his hand hit Felix hard across the face. Anger boiled in Felix but the Senator was smiling.

"Your last punishment," he said. "There is no magistrate here, so I will do this bit by myself." He touched the end of his muddy twig to Felix's forehead. "You are free."

Just when he had caught up with reality, it went and did something like this. He wanted to jump for joy, or dance, or take a woman to bed, but the cold and numbness inside him was too strong. "I will continue to fight for you, Senator," he said stiffly.

"Well, of course you will. I wouldn't have freed you if I'd thought you would flee. Not that it will matter much." He gestured at the crawling chaos that advanced upon them. "They come," he said.

Felix grasped his sword and spat disgustedly. "There are too many, but we will die fighting them."

****

Rowanna screamed as the lifeless sank its teeth into Iullianus' neck.

The red-haired man grimaced in pain and punched back, across his face, until the thing let go. He spun and clubbed with his shovel. The creature fell, grey brains leaking out of a collapsed face.

She turned from him, then, stabbing with her spear as she was overwhelmed by lifeless. A thing that had once been a Senator shuffled toward her, its white eyes glowing with hunger.

Her arms ached dully and she was so far past exhaustion that she stabbed mechanically. Her spear blade jabbed the thing in the eye and its body crumpled.

They needed more fire. They needed more men, more sleep, and more weapons. Most of all, they needed more fire. There had been a wall, a shield of warfire for two days, allowing them to catch what sleep they could while the fire burned the undead creatures. There were always more, though. She recognized some of the lifeless as men that they'd traveled with, men who had grown too tired to march on.

She stabbed and stabbed until the latest wave of undead were twitching on the bloody ground.

Iullianus scowled, rubbing at the back of his neck. There weren't many lifeless immediately about, but they still had control of the circle though the fading fires barely reached knee level. She slipped behind him and looked at the wound.

"Zalmoxis," she swore softly. The creature had bit deeply into him, and blood flowed out and there was a shallow crater in his flesh. She knew she was over-tired, but the wound seemed to throb.

"Is it bad?" he asked. "I feel strange. Dark dreams return to me and they are a welcome friend." His voice was soft as a spider web.

"What are you saying?" she asked.

"I don't know," he said, his voice returned to normal. "I was dreaming while I stood here."

She could wait no longer. "This isn't the first time you've been bitten," she said.

"What do you mean?" he asked.

"Twice before—once in Dacia, and again in Brundisium. I used potions to cure you."

"Impossible. I would have remembered such a thing." He stopped speaking and groaned from the pain of the bite. "Ah, I am holding the wolf by the ears, but cannot withstand for long."

It was then that Senator Rufus came to them. The old man was a shell of himself and his authority and dignity had melted away to nothing over the last week.

"My eyes are not what they once were," he said. "Tell me, what do you see?"

The wan morning light, weak though it was, made her feel better. She looked to the north and saw what he meant.

"There is a group there," she said slowly, "and I cannot tell if they live, but they are fighting the lifeless." There were several hundred men, and many of them were armed with bows. They moved with a coordination that bespoke some practice, and they dispatched of the lifeless with cold efficiency.

"This is hope unlooked for," she cried.

"Indeed it is," Rufus said. He stood beside her, looking across the fields of undead. "Survivors from Rome, or an army returned. They must have seen our smoke."

"We may live after all," Rowanna said.

She grabbed Iullianus' arm; he was trembling. His pleading eyes looked to her in askance and then closed shut.

"What is wrong with the Legatus?" Rufus asked.

She dared not answer. She dared not breathe. His body sagged and his sword fell from his hand.

"Is he dead?" Rufus asked. There was panic in his voice.

"I hope so," she said, though she knew otherwise.

Iullianus' eyes snapped open and only white stared at them.

He lurched at them both.

Rowanna was quicker, and she threw herself back. The Senator had not been as ready, and the creature that had been Iullianus knocked him down.

The red-haired lifeless clawed at his face and gnashed at his skull. "Ah," the Senator said. "I can hear the sea."

Her mouth filled with bile and she readied her spear. The hesitation could not have lasted more than a heartbeat, but it was enough. As she stood, poised to charge the pair and drive the point of her weapon into his brain, hands clasped at her.

She whirled and gasped. There were seven, eight, or a hundred creatures behind her. Their burning legs showed how they had reached her. Perhaps their legs would burn off, but they would certainly be able to kill her first. Her spear hung limply in her hand, and she could perhaps stab one of them before the rest reached her.

She didn't even look at the Senator again before she turned and ran. She ran around them, out of their camp. The fire was before her and she cleared it with a good jump.

She was running to find the newcomers, but there were so many undead before her. She was faster than they were, but already breathing heavily. Dodging their clumsy embraces, Rowanna weaved through the masses. She was halfway to the new group when something grabbed at her foot. She fell down to the ground hard, just managing to get her hands up to break her fall.

She looked back. A dead creature no older than ten, her blonde hair still in braids, had grabbed at her leg and tripped her. Rowanna kicked out of her grip with fevered intensity. She was up again, but the creatures surrounded her. There was nowhere to run.

A tall lifeless stood before her, his once noble toga now battered and bloody. Worms wriggled out of the cave in its chest. The creature stood before her, its hands on her shoulders. It pulled her toward it with relentless force.

"No," she cried, fighting against it. There were creatures all around her, teeth and mouths and hands. "No!"

She could see its blackened and bloody teeth in the foul pit that had once been a mouth. The smell of rotting carnage hit her with enough force to make her swoon.

"NO!" she screamed a third time, struggling to break free. It was no use. The lifeless warrior groaned in anticipation and lowered its mouth toward her face. She closed her eyes, thinking of a happy day in the morning sunlight, many months ago.

The creature's iron grip was suddenly gone. Daring to open her eyes, she saw that an arrow had taken it in the back of the head. Around her, more and more lifeless were dropping with arrows in their skulls. She did not hesitate, and ducked through two of the still-standing creatures as she fled.

The forces of men were quite close to her. In the midst of them was a man that made her heart skip a beat. There was no mistaking that beard: Natopurus had returned, and he was alive. She fought the urge to flee, but she couldn't face the Dacian after what had happened.

Then she looked again.

It was not, in fact, Natopurus. It was Zuste. His beard had grown and he had lost weight, but there was something about his bumbling manner she would recognize anywhere.

She started laughing in relief and surprise. She ran to him, wrapping him in an embrace.

"If I had known I could expect that welcome," he said, "I would have come more quickly."

"I thought you were dead!" she said.

"It came close, a few times, but it takes more than a few walking corpses to defeat the mighty Zuste, the alchemist!"

There were hundreds of men with him. Many were warriors and soldiers, and he must have half a legion. "Converting? All these men were lifeless?"

He smiled. "Half, maybe. The others were volunteers. I suspect I'd have more, but I ran out of elixir, oh, some eight days ago. We've gone from saving lifeless to executing them, but even that has grown difficult as we drew closer to Rome."

As he spoke, the men with him moved with precise brutality. Scores of lifeless fell to their blades and quarrels. Two of them stayed at his side, and it made her happy to think that he had earned a bodyguard.

"You are out of elixir?" she asked. Hope withered and died even as it bloomed.

"I still have one more for an emergency," he said. "I have had to use it on myself once, and I hope not to again. Still, it's best to be prepared." He motioned toward the city. "Truth be told, I was hoping for some solace in the city. I certainly wasn't expecting smoking ruins. What happened? How did you get out?"

"We never made it," she said. "We arrived after it fell, and saw this just as you have."

"I have noticed since I left Sarmizegetusa that the lifeless seem to have been drifting toward the city. Almost as if they were led by some will, but enough of this. Where is Natopurus? Where is Iullianus? Did Decabalus come with you?"

The smile wilted from her lips. "Dead. They're all dead."

Zuste lowered his head in a moment of silence. He gnawed nervously at the worn nails on his left hand. "All my fault," he muttered. "Rowanna, I never told you that I created this. I wanted to, but I had taken so much from you. I was a coward."

"I know what you did. I hate you, partially, but you are not responsible for this," she said.

Zuste wasn't listening to her. He was staring, aghast, at the creature that had almost eaten her.

"What's wrong?" she asked.

"That's him," he said. He moved toward the body, knelt on the ground and looked closely. The arrow had come out through its nose, but its face was largely undamaged.

"It's who?" Rowanna asked, kneeling beside him.

"This is the man who gave me the recipe for the plague. The man who said I could help him doom Rome forever, and grow rich from doing it."

"Why would a Roman plot to kill Rome?"

"He said he wasn't Roman. He was Etruscan."

Rowanna did not know what that meant. She glanced at the battle. There weren't many of the monsters left, now. She found herself smiling, as a relief she had forgotten was possible filled her. Then she spied the big red haired lifeless in the horde and her spirits fell. Even from the distance, she could see the bloody mask his face wore.

"We have to go," she said. "There is one we can save."

Zuste was not listening. He kicked at the Etruscan's body, kicked it hard in the ribs. The creature was dead and did not react, but Zuste kicked it again. She could hear bones snapping. The centurions moved to flank him, but they made no move to stop him.

She watched the advancing mob of lifeless. There weren't many left, and their efforts were at last bearing fruit. With Zuste's men, they could maybe win the war against death.

"Zuste," she said, "your last elixir. We can save Iullianus."

He had moved up to the things head, and he stomped on its face before looking up. "Iullianus? He lives?"

"He is undead. He moves toward us now."

Zuste paused. "Do you love him?" he asked.

"No!" she said, too quickly. She searched inside herself, but there was only a tangled mass of confusion. "We have been through much, and it wouldn't be the first time."

He nodded. "Don't kill that red-haired one," he said to two of the soldiers beside. "In fact, bring him here."

They moved and quickly they'd brought the snarling, vacant-eyed creature before them. There were pulpy bits of pink smeared around his lips and blood drenched him from mouth to chest. He struggled against the grasp of the two who held him, but they were too strong.

"You sure about this?" Zuste asked. "I can make more, but does the world need more of him?"

"He is a man of war, it is true," Rowanna said, "but even in peace, we need such, and it will be long before this war is ultimately over." She squinted at the fields outside the city. There were living men everywhere she could see, and the pockets of lifeless smaller and fewer than ever.

Toward the city, she saw a familiar figure. Felix was covered in ash and was visibly weary, but he lived. She waved him over and turned to Zuste.

"I would not ask," she said, "but he has sacrificed much."

"He's not the only one, Rowanna, but I owe you that much, at least," Zuste said. "And far more, in truth." He handed the bottle to her.

It was so small and filled with a clear liquid. She moved forward and unplugged the bottle. A pleasant, herbal scent reached her. It smelled more like tea than she would have guessed an elixir of life would.

Iullianus groaned as she approached and she took the opportunity to pour it down his throat. Almost instantly, he stopped struggling. The centurions struggled to support his now limp body.

"You might want to move back," she said. "When they change back, it can get messy."

"We know," said one of the guards.

"We were the first to be changed back," the other said. "It was a rough few moments."

Iullianus groaned. His eyes were still closed and it was impossible to tell if he was alive or not.

She turned to Zuste. He was watching the affair with the solemnity of a judge. A small movement caught her attention and she gasped.

"Zuste!" she screamed. "Your foot! Move it now!" she screamed, too panicked to be coherent.

If he had been a warrior or an athlete, instinct might have saved him. Instead, the alchemist looked down in time to see the Etruscan move his head and bite down hard on Zuste's leg.

"Zalmoxis!" he screamed in pain and rage. Then he started laughing. "That blasted fucker got the last laugh on me. Oh, what a jest this life is."

The lifeless smiled, and then, most horrible of all, it spoke.

"You blasted fools." Its voice was chopped granite. "You bleed for the Romans. You bleed for your masters like good sheep."

One of the guards moved to the thing and raised his sword.

"Wait," Zuste called, "wait, I will hear this thing."

"Look at you two," the creature said, rising to a half-prone position. "Dacians, yes? Rome was invading you, killing you. I know I am right. They erased us, their greatest rivals, from history. Why do you help them?"

An icy hand slapped Rowanna across the face. Each decision along the way had felt correct, but this creature spoke truly. Zuste had an answer.

"I hate the Romans," he wheezed. His skin was losing color. "But even more do I hate your idea of revenge. Look what you've done to the world!"

The thing choked in laughter. "I've only done to them what they do to all they meet. A mirror is the cruelest of gifts, to the cruel. Slay me, slay this horde, but do not forget the true enemy. Do not forget what the Romans would do to your sons and daughters."

Zuste tried to speak, but instead, coughed violently and collapsed to the ground. Rowanna motioned to the guard. With no ceremony, he chopped the head from the prone lifeless being.

"Zuste," she cried, "I can save you. Is there more elixir?"

He slowly turned his head toward her. His pupils were fading, his mouth lolling as the functions in his brain ceased. "My home…Sarmizegetusa … more elixir," he hissed. He growled at her as his face twisted into a rictus of death.

Without thinking about it, she pushed him away. His changing body fell to the ground and she turned. She could save him, though she knew not how to travel to Dacia with him. Perhaps she could restrain him, go to retrieve the cure, and come back.

The long-bearded creature that had once been Zuste rose. He came at her again, his long beard jerking from his twitching steps.

"Rowanna!" she heard a cry. "Look out." Felix, fleet of foot, ran to her and he stabbed Zuste in the head. The bearded man fell to the ground instantly, the blade sticking out from the back of his skull.

A haze of rage filled Rowanna. As if she were another person, she watched herself grip her spear, set her feet, and pull the spear back.

She saw herself jerk with the weapon, driving through his leather armor and into his soft flesh. It only took an instant, an instant that she immediately needed to have again, to undo what she had done.

Felix fell, and she screamed.

She dropped down and grabbed his body, wrenching the spear out from just above his chest. The leather armor had kept most of it from penetrating, and she'd hit the left side of his body. She had likely punctured no organs. He might live.

She rolled him over and suddenly stopped. Tears filled her eyes and she fell to the ground, her body wracked by gasping sobs.

For a moment, for a lifetime, she'd looked at his face and only seen Dapyx. She'd seen her son lying there before her, dead from a wound his mother had given. She could barely see, but she stood. Slowly, her eyes unfocused and her body sobbing, she lifted the spear. It was held in both hands, and she brought it down over her knee and snapped the shaft. Her husband's spear, the tool of her survival, fell to the muddy, bloody earth.

There were creatures around her, but she fell to the ground, awaiting oblivion or whatever doom was owed to her. She knew only one thing.

She would fight no more.

When she opened her eyes, the grave face of Iullianus was regarding her. The two centurions stood stock still. The big man pulled free from their grasp and looked down. He took in Zuste's dead body and Felix's barely breathing one. His regretful visage was more eloquent than any speech could have been.

"We have to leave, Rowanna. This Empire of the Undead is no place for the living."

She rose and nodded dumbly, too drained to form words.

Epilogue

Britannia: 89 CE, Summer

The cool blue sea surrounded them and Rowanna fought the need to purge her breakfast over the edge. This ship, on the open sea, was far worse than what she had endured before. Even the weather had grown worse—no one had told her that this land was perpetually covered in clouds and rain. Iullianus stood next to her with a knowing smile.

"I would hate to see you when there was bad weather," he said.

"Me too. Good weather, bad weather," she said, "I still hate the sea."

"Give it time," he said, "and don't get too attached to the idea of good weather. It is more a myth than a reality where we are headed."

Rowanna sighed and stared back into the sea. None of it felt real. After they had found that Felix lived, they had dragged his body off the battlefield, left Rome forever. The Etruscan lifeless had spoken too well, and Rowanna would never be comfortable with her role if the Empire survived. There was as yet, no sign of that, but Senator Rufus had died believing that Domitian yet lived. *Anyone that paranoid,* he'd said, *can't be killed by a mere infestation of bone-chomping ghouls.*

It had taken some time, but Iullianus had acquired skinny, terrified horses, and they had ridden north through Italy and then Gaul. There had been no lifeless and very few living either. In some ways it was idyllic. The entire world was emptied and left for them. Food had come from abandoned inns and houses. They had arrived at the coast two days ago and found a boat just this morning. In no time at all, she realized, they would land and she would be in his homeland. Or closer to it, as he had repeatedly disavowed relation with the southern dwellers of Britannia.

"Look," Iullianus said. There were dolphins swimming along with the boat. "*Oceanus* smiles on us," he said. "*Festina lente.*"

" *Festina lente*?" she echoed, watching one of the smaller dolphins leap free from the waves.

"Make haste slowly," he translated. "I think it particularly apt. It's what we've been doing since we met. Before, in my case."

"I have never seen such creatures," she said, unable to look away from the aquatic animals. "They are a marvel. I wonder if he's seen them." She turned from the edge of the ship, reluctant to look away for even a brief moment.

She called to him. "Come out. Come out and see this." The dolphins were splashing as they began to catch fish.

The young man walked out of the small cabin, blinking as he joined them. His bandage was bloody but not infected, he was healing. He smiled and the sun shone on his white teeth. "Dolphins," he said. "The symbol of my profession, and witness to my success in the hippodrome. It is good to see them now. Good luck to see them now."

"More than you know. They are a boon for my people as well, Felix," Iullianus said.

"My name," the other said, scratching at the bandages on his chest, "is Jotham."

Behind him, the blue sea silently rippled.

THE END